BY SARA NOVIĆ

Girl at War
America Is Immigrants
True Biz

true biz

true biz

A Novel

sara nović

Random House
New York

Published in the United States by Random House, an imprint and division of Penguin Random House LLC, New York.

RANDOM HOUSE and the HOUSE colophon are registered trademarks of Penguin Random House LLC.

An earlier version of Eliot's story was published as "Conversion" in *Guernica,* February 17, 2014.

LIBRARY OF CONGRESS CATALOGING-IN-PUBLICATION DATA
Names: Nović, Sara, author.
Title: True biz : a novel / Sara Nović.
Description: First Edition. | New York : Random House, [2022]
Identifiers: LCCN 2021024265 (print) | LCCN 2021024266 (ebook) |
ISBN 9780593241509 (hardcover) | ISBN 9780593241516 (ebook)
Classification: LCC PS3614.O929 T78 2022 (print) |
LCC PS3614.O929 (ebook) | DDC 813/.6—dc23
LC record available at https://lccn.loc.gov/2021024265
LC ebook record available at https://lccn.loc.gov/2021024266

PRINTED IN THE UNITED STATES OF AMERICA ON ACID-FREE PAPER

Illustrations by Brittany Castle

randomhousebooks.com

2 4 6 8 9 7 5 3 1

First Edition

Book design by Elizabeth Rendfleisch

For the students at Rocky Mountain Deaf School,

Pennsylvania School for the Deaf,

Florida School for the Deaf and the Blind, and

St. Rita School for the Deaf,

and for deaf people everywhere.

Those who are born deaf all become senseless and incapable of reason.

—*Aristotle, 384–322 BCE*

Those who believe as I do, that the production of a defective race of human beings would be a great calamity to the world, will examine carefully the causes that lead to the intermarriages of the deaf with the object of applying a remedy.

—*Alexander Graham Bell, 1883*

A manufacturer of amazing medical devices known as cochlear implants, which restore hearing to the deaf, sold defective implants to young children and adults for years—even after learning that a significant number of the devices had failed.

—*NBC News, March 14, 2014*

true biz

february Waters was nine years old when she—in the middle of math class, in front of everyone—stabbed herself in the ear with a number two Ticonderoga. Their teacher had been chalking the twelve times tables up on the board, providing February a window in which to sharpen the pencil, the grinding drawing her classmates up from their daydreams, their eyes following her across the room toward the teacher's corner. February stepped unsteadily on the felted swivel chair, then planted herself in a wide stance on the desk and jammed the pencil deep into her left ear.

The class let out a collective gasp, breaking their teacher from her blackboard reverie. She hoisted February, who was bleeding more than she'd expected, from the desk in a fireman's carry; February dripped a delicate trail of crimson all the way to the infirmary.

After the nurse removed the graphite and determined the damage was superficial, she gauzed up the bleeding and took February across the hall to the principal's office, where the secretary produced a suspension form for "violent and disorderly conduct unbecoming of a student." Then, once it was determined how, exactly, to contact her parents, she was sent home for the week.

Back in 4-B, February's classmates hailed her as a hero, having sacrificed her very blood to buy them twenty-five minutes of unsupervised bliss. The school, on the other hand, deemed the incident a cry for help, given what the principal had taken to calling February's "family circumstances." Really, February explained to her father when he came to get her, she wasn't upset at all, just tired of listening to the times tables, the buzz of the broken light above her desk, the screech of metal chairs against the floor. He didn't know what it was like, having to *hear* things all the time, she told him. And with that he couldn't argue.

What had pushed February over the edge specifically was Danny Brown calling singsong from the row behind her, "February's very hairy, and she eats the yellow snow." Only deaf people would name their daughter February, she'd thought then. Certain months were acceptable for use as girls' names—April, May, June—and her name was undoubtedly the result of some miscommunication of these guidelines. But February's parents had always preferred winter, the silent splendor of snow clinging to the chinquapin oaks, and in the Deaf world of her childhood beauty was taken in earnest. Her parents' friends weren't concerned with looking corny, and February had never seen any of them say something sarcastic. It was a world she disliked leaving, especially for such hostile territory as the fourth grade.

> *You can be Deaf on the inside,*
> her mother said that night
> when she tucked her in. *But*
> *you can never do that again.*

Of course, things are different now, February thinks as she looks out over the quad at the River Valley School for the Deaf, squinting against the early sun. The internet has been world-opening for deaf people, and Deaf culture has evolved to accommodate plenty of mainstream snark and slang. Plus, hearing people are naming their kids all sorts of weird things now—fruits and animals and cardinal directions.

The Deaf world is no longer her safe haven but her place of employment, and at the moment she is screwed. As headmistress, she is supposed to have her finger on the pulse of the school. Instead, she has done the worst thing possible—she has lost other people's children. Two boys, Austin Workman and Eliot Quinn, a sophomore and a junior, roommates.

In front of Clerc Hall, police have parked a mobile surveillance unit from which they access Homeland Security cameras in Cincinnati and Columbus. They try to tap into the boys' GPS location, but this only leads them back to the dorms, where three phones are found in a neat stack beneath a common room table. The third phone prompts another round of bed checks, but everyone is accounted for. Eliot's and Austin's parents arrive, yelling in a mix of languages at February, at the police, at one another. Superintendent Swall arrives, also yelling, demanding her office keys so he can go inside and write a statement. An emergency alert will be blasted out to every mobile phone in the tri-county. And February will have to speak to the morning news.

She ducks into a lower school bathroom, pins back her hair, and applies lipstick before a very short sink. She wonders if this shirt is okay, then admonishes herself for thinking about her outfit at a time like this.

She returns to the quad and lingers near the police camper. She can already tell it's going to be an unseasonably warm day for her namesake month—no snow in sight, sunlight refracting off dewy grass. It's such a nice lawn, meticulously kept Eagleton bluegrass that looks vibrant though it's not yet spring, a hardy species she chose personally because it would take the picnics and Red Rover games in stride. She has always done her best to make things as pleasant for the students as she can.

She tries to steel herself for the press, to choose words that might tamp down the frenzy, or at least not add any fuel. "Lost" is wrong; she shouldn't say that—she hasn't misplaced them. They escaped, more like it, though that makes the school sound like prison. "Runaways" is charged with a certain angst, suggests abuse. Eventually she settles on "gone missing," the passive obscuring responsibility.

Superintendent Swall emerges and hands February the statement, eight-by-tens of Eliot's and Austin's school photos, and a large mug. She stares at the pictures as she downs the coffee—both boys in button-ups looking neat and agreeable, if not exactly smiling. Austin's eyes are the famous Workman green, a light, almost spearmint color. Eliot's are so dark they're almost black, and she tries to meet his gaze instead of letting her own eyes drift down to the scars on his cheek. For a moment she is overwhelmed by the feeling that the boys are staring back, blinks hard to push the thought away. Then she hands her mug to Swall and steps up to the makeshift podium.

When they go live, February holds up the photos first, then puts them down so she can sign and speak her statement simultaneously—a short physical description of each boy, followed by the superintendent's message: The River Valley School for the Deaf is working round the clock with the Colson County Sheriff's Office and doing everything we can to bring our students back safely and as quickly as possible. If you see these children, please call the tip number on your screen. As she says the final line, her phone vibrates in her pocket. Distracted, she pauses for just a hair too long. The reporters leap in with their barrage of questions, largely unintelligible except for the one closest to her, who says,

Do you have any worries about the welfare of the boys, given the nature of their handicap?

February bristles. Not the time for grandstanding, she knows, but she has to say something.

I'm concerned for the students' welfare, she says. As I would be for any missing teenager.

But if they can't hear—

The students are intellectual equals to their hearing peers.

Are they implanted?

February is taken aback by the unabashed way he demands this information, but tries not to show it.

I'm not authorized to divulge a minor's medical history on television, sir, she says.

The reporter reddens, but isn't ready to surrender the limelight:

Any evidence of foul play? Do you anticipate charges of a criminal nature?

He pushes the microphone against her chin and gives her a sympathetic look that rings false around the eyes.

If you'll excuse me, I have to go speak with the police, she says.

She steps away from the podium, but the reporter's face will not leave her. He's right—Eliot and Austin are not as safe as they would be if they were hearing, though not in the way the man had meant it. What if a patrolman finds them and shouts for them to stop, but they keep running? Or if they *do* need help but have no way to call the police? What if everything ends well and they return unscathed, but Child Protective Services uses the incident as an in to throw their weight around in the cochlear implant debate? She's read about it happening in other states. February has to bite her lip to cut the panic short—she's getting ahead of herself again. She checks her phone. The text was from Mel: u ok? She doesn't know how to respond. She shoves the phone back in her pocket, and looks up to find another parent, Charlie Serrano's father, leaning against the police RV.

Dr. Waters? he says, his voice much smaller than his frame suggests.

Not now! she wants to scream. Yours is a mess for another day. But she holds it together, says instead:

Mr. Serrano, we're in a bit of a situation. The campus is closed today, so you can take Charlie on home.

He blanches.

You mean, she's not here?

No—is everything okay?

It's just, it looks like she snuck out last night, and she's not with my ex, so I thought, maybe—

He sweeps his eyes across the quad.

Holy shit, she says under her breath. Three cellphones.

What? says Charlie's father.

He shifts his bulk against the vehicle, wrings his hands.

I'm just going to—February points to the police insignia plastered above them—give them a quick update.

Wait—

Just a moment, sir, really, she says. Then she rounds the camper and vomits her coffee onto its front tire.

six months earlier

*t*he summer before her sophomore year, as her parents' divorce limped to a close, Charlie's father won the custody battle and signed her up for Deaf school.

Colson, Ohio, in August was so muggy and laden with gnats it felt almost tropical, and they all broke a sweat on the short walk from the parking lot into family court, her father peeling off his suit jacket in the atrium, her mother dabbing at her brow with a paisley handkerchief. In the courtroom, the judge delivered his ruling, but Charlie could hear only the industrial-grade box fan propped on the windowsill beside them. It pulled flyaways from her ponytail, and eventually she gave up trying to smooth them and settled for counting the boards in the wood paneling.

When the judge finished speaking, it took everything in her not to shout WHAT HAPPENED? Instead she followed her parents outside, where, it turned out, she didn't have to ask. Both her mother's and her father's eyes were glassy with tears, but her father was smiling.

His and Hers teams of expensive lawyers had been evenly matched, and in the end, Charlie figured it was her lousy report card—another semester squeaked by on social promotion—that convinced the judge more than anything. There was also a ream of behavior infractions from her elementary school days, though on paper they looked long resolved. In reality they weren't, not exactly, but most grown-ups cared little about the real world, except when they were threatening teenagers about their impending expulsion out into it. Whatever pushed the judge to his decision, she was just happy to get out. At Jefferson High, even a small misstep could get you bullied for years. As far as she could tell they were still teasing some kid for a lethal fart he'd let fly back in sixth-grade gym class, so whatever you imagine a deaf-voiced cyborg girl caught, it was worse. The things that happened to girls always were.

It'll be different now, her father said on their way back to his apartment.

Of course, the ruling came with stipulations. Charlie would still have to wear her implant during instruction hours, even though it gave her a headache, even though its uselessness was half the reason her parents were getting divorced in the first place, though they'd never admit it. It's No One's Fault: the mantra in their house. But no one believed it.

When she was younger, Charlie's father once listened to a series of cochlear implant simulations on YouTube. Charlie stood beside him as he clicked through video after video, but the sound through the computer speakers was indistinct.

It's terrifying, he said. Everything sounds like the demons in *The Exorcist*.

It's not scary to her, her mother said. She doesn't know any better. She was right, to a point. What scared Charlie more was her mother talking about her like she wasn't there at all.

Charlie's mother was a pageant coach and a musician who'd never had her *Mr. Holland's Opus* moment, though that would've been bad in a different way. Charlie's father was a software engineer, whose constant proximity to technology was probably the reason why he was more willing to accept its shortcomings. He'd also grown up with a deaf cousin who had what Charlie considered the good fortune of being been born in the seventies, and to a family of seasonal farm workers. Antonio's parents, new to the country and still learning English themselves, weren't consumed with fears of what would happen if he couldn't pass, or how bilingualism might do him harm. His family learned a few of the signs he brought home from school; he graduated and learned a trade, soldering or something, and one-upped his parents, ears be damned, American Dream style.

Charlie wondered whether her parents had reached out to Antonio when they found out she was deaf, asked him what he thought about implants and deaf education, or if those first years were ruled autocratically by her mother's fear. Either way, the window for such a conversation had long passed—Antonio died in a car wreck when Charlie was four, and his memory was invoked almost exclusively by Charlie's mother, when she wanted to curse her husband's genes. Charlie hadn't met another deaf person since. Isolation was a requirement of the implant, her doctor cautioned; she needed to be one hundred percent dependent on it to learn how to listen. The device could only bring sound to her brain—it couldn't decipher it, or even do much to sift through what was important and what was just noise. Still, sign language had always been off the table—that would've been a cheat code, a crutch. If she had learned sign and could communicate her needs and understand others, what would motivate her to learn English?

Countless experts confirmed that the best way to ensure she reached maximum implant potential was to practice, and a mainstream setting was where she'd practice the most, albeit in a sink-or-swim kind of way. This combined with the therapy appointments would equip her with the tools to parse the meaning hidden within the sound.

Charlie had been implanted at age three—not ideal, but still plenty of time left to build new neural pathways. By all measurable standards, her implantation was a success, and though no one ever said it to her face, she knew this meant the fact that she couldn't hack it was a personal deficiency. Maybe she just hadn't tried hard enough.

The educational term for her was "oral failure" (imagine the fun her classmates would have if they got wind of that), which from what Charlie could tell, basically meant she sounded stupid when she talked. Charlie wasn't stupid. She'd just had to learn everything herself, and in an environment not at all conducive to learning: the public school classroom—endless tumult of squeaking furniture, student chatter, teachers spewing lessons with their backs to the class as they wrote on the board. Really, she thought, the fact that she could work out about sixty percent of what was going on with the robo-ear, maybe more with some good lipreading, was impressive. But in school, sixty percent was still a D.

She wished she could be rid of the implant, even as she knew the requirement that she keep wearing it was her mother's consolation prize, a sliver of hope Charlie might one day wake up able to make sense of the relentless static it pumped into her head. But being under her dad's governance was undeniably a victory. She'd enroll at River Valley as a residential student, and the two of them would attend community sign language classes the school offered after-hours. Things might finally take a turn for the better.

Her mother didn't appeal the ruling, a surrender Charlie found both a relief and a little upsetting. Mothers on TV always fought to win their kids back; it was their reason for living, all that. Then again, the three of them were pretty tired of going to court.

Now Charlie was packing, shifting most of her stuff to the apartment where her father had lived for nearly a year—new construction on the riverfront with big windows and an open kitchen, right out of the dictionary for "bachelor pad," which as a bonus made her mother, French country devotee, crazy. From there, Charlie would bring an even smaller subset of belongings to the dorm.

Two weeks before the semester began, she and her parents went to a meeting at her new school. The headmistress was a tall, shapely woman with short black hair tied back close against her head. Charlie found her somewhat formidable even after they all sat down and the distance between their heights diminished. She signed and spoke simultaneously, her arms and hands moving with the grace and speed of a much more compact person. To sign and talk at the same time was an imperfect operation, the headmistress warned, and one Charlie wouldn't see much of at River Valley after today. Charlie longed to find meaning in the arc of the woman's hands, but that meant looking away from her lips, something she couldn't afford to do. Not yet.

Headmistress pulled a series of papers from the tray of her printer and laid out Charlie's academic program. She would retake algebra and be enrolled in remedial English. She would still have to go to speech therapy.

But how will she learn sign language? Charlie's mother said.

We're signed up for community classes, said her father.

Great, said the headmistress. She looked back to Charlie. The _____ here at school will be key, she said. As with any language.

The what? said Charlie.

The headmistress removed a notepad from beneath a pile of paperwork.

IMMERSION she wrote.

Charlie shrugged.

To be surrounded, said the headmistress. The sign will come, if you put some work into it.

Charlie read the doubt on her mother's face—fair enough, considering Charlie's scholastic record. And hadn't the doctors said the same thing about English? Just one more lesson or therapy or specialist could be the thing to tip the scale. The headmistress, though, also registered the skepticism.

It's different with sign, she said. You're programmed for visual language.

She smiled, and Charlie knew she was trying to be reassuring, but the word "programmed" just made her think of the audiologist. Charlie watched her mother dig through her purse for her Chap-Stick, a signal she knew to mean the discussion was over.

Are you okay? the headmistress said.

At first, Charlie didn't understand why she was asking, then realized she had been rubbing the scar behind her ear again, the incision site of her implant. It had been feeling tender lately; Charlie had even made her mother check the spot, parts of which she couldn't see well in the mirror. But everything had looked normal.

Implant's on the fritz, said her mother with a forced brightness, and mumbled something about an upcoming appointment.

For about twelve years, said Charlie, and the headmistress tried to swallow her smile.

*a*fter the Serrano meeting, February's mood soured. The girl was intelligent, unmistakably so, but who could say where she was academically? Her transcripts even had her failing some courses, a rarity in the mainstream these days, where teachers routinely passed difficult and underprepared students just to be rid of them, sending them forth to wreak havoc on somebody else's state test scores.

Charlie's behavior record was relatively clean. February found this surprising for someone so clearly bound up in frustration, but she was relieved for her faculty. There was a theory among linguists that the brain's capacity for language learning—language as a concept, a modality for thought—is finite. Scientists called the period from ages zero to five the "critical window," within which a child had to gain fluency in at least one language, any language, or risk permanent cognitive damage. Once the window shut, learning anything became difficult, even impossible—without a language, how does one think, or even feel?

The critical window remained "theoretical," mostly because intentionally depriving children of language was deemed by ethicists too cruel an experiment to conduct. And yet, February saw the results of such trials every day—children whose parents had feared sign language would mark them, but who ended up marked by its absence. These children had never seen language as it really was, outside the speech therapist's office, alive and rollicking, had never been privy to the chatter of the playground or around the dinner table.

Often the Deaf community levied their anger at implants, though in truth language deprivation had been prescribed by professionals long before that technology existed. For February, the appeal of implants was clear, but the false binary they created was the real danger.

There was no reason assistive technology and sign language should be an either-or affair; time and again some of her strongest students proved that, when it came to language, more is more. Often when she found herself in pedagogical arguments with fellow administrators across the district, she put it this way: imagine telling someone that learning French would ruin their kid's English, hurt their brain. Usually people scoffed at her and February would nod. It *did* sound ridiculous. And yet, though fear of bilingualism in two spoken languages had been dismissed as xenophobic nonsense, though it was now desirable for hearing children to speak two languages, medicine held fast to its condemnation of ASL.

Perhaps it didn't matter much. February supposed parents would dig up a reason to avoid sign language whether or not their doctors handed them the pseudoscience to back it up. Your basic shame, or fear of change or failure. Whatever it was, over the years, River Valley had received many children who couldn't have a conversation with their own families.

So it was no surprise that students coming from language-poor environments often arrived with explosive tempers. Some were so far gone that even learning ASL was beyond them, though whether it had been their brains' language centers or the desire for human contact that had atrophied, it was hard to say.

Charlie was far from the worst she'd seen. She had language. She'd just had to work way too hard for it. Still, as February filled out the paperwork to complete Charlie's transfer, she felt herself seething on the girl's behalf—all those years of energy poured into achieving the aesthetic of being educated rather than actually having learned anything.

At the end of the day, February waded through the afternoon heat toward home, to what was affectionately referred to by staff as "New Quarters." Nowadays, only a handful of overnight dorm-keepers and security detail were necessary, but when RVSD was established at the turn of the twentieth century, nearly all of the school's faculty lived on campus alongside their students. The headmaster lived in the studio apartment atop his office—that is, until Head-master Arbegast and his wife had two sets of twins in rapid succession. As a result, the school had purchased seven acres of land adjacent to campus and built New Quarters, a craftsman cottage, at the far end of the plot.

In the seventies, when RVSD was feeling the recession squeeze, they parceled out most of the land to developers, who built a tract of houses two streets wide backed up against the campus gates. But New Quarters had remained the school's, its severe, sloped roof easy to spot from the center of campus even with the block of ranch-style homes that stood between them. February loved the old house and was grateful for the few minutes' distance the neighborhood afforded her from her work, the walk home a chance to clear her head. Some-times, though, it was just more time she spent stewing. Today was that kind of day.

By the time she got home she was full-on peevish, even though Mel's car was already in the driveway, a sight that would normally delight her.

It is so damn depressing, February said as she pushed through the side door. That the biggest dream some people can muster up for their child is "look normal."

Here comes my sparkling personality! said Mel.

Sorry, it's just—

—a bad one? Aren't they always?

February plopped her bag on the kitchen chair.

You're home early, she said.

Mel had swapped her suit for a tank top, basketball shorts, and an oven mitt, and was stirring instant mashed potatoes in a saucepan. A rotisserie chicken sat providentially in its Kroger bag beside a pile of Mel's depositions.

You're late, said Mel. Especially considering there are no children in your school.

There was one today! February protested. She looked around. How's Mom?

Seems like a good day, said Mel. She's out on the porch.

Reading? Oh, that is good.

Her mother's condition had been wobbly of late—it was to be expected, the doctors had all said so—but February was still finding it difficult to adapt, if adapting to constant change was even possible. The best she could do was find respite in the good days, and try not to think too much about how many of them were left. February pressed herself up against Mel's back, wrapped her arms around her waist.

You, said Mel, turning to meet February's lips, are making me sweaty. Go get changed—dinner's ready.

Thanks for picking it up. I know it's my turn.

Only you could outwork a lawyer.

Hey, I have that class to teach, too. It's been a long time since I've made a syllabus. How *did* you get in before me?

I came home after court let out. Figured I could read the deps here.

Aha! You're still working! said February.

So are you, Mel said, tapping a finger to February's temple. Go change.

February pulled on shorts and a T-shirt and found her mother curled up on the porch swing reading a paperback thriller, something Mel had bought in an airport. She stomped her foot to get her mom's attention. Her mother dog-eared her page and looked up, wherever the book had taken her clearing from her irises as she offered February a wide grin.

You hungry?

Hi, sweetie. How's school? All set up?

Getting there.

How was the meeting?

Man, when she was with it, she was really with it. February didn't remember having mentioned the Serranos to her mother, and she regretted it now. Her mom's grasp of cochlear implants was tenuous, she being of the generation for which hearing aid technology was still a transistor strapped onto one's chest. February didn't want to upset her mother—the doctors had stressed the importance of maintaining a calm, stable home environment—and the plight of yet another deaf kid deprived of language by her own parents was a surefire way to blow that up. February took a deep breath.

Fine, she said.

The girl struggled in mainstream school. No surprise there.

I'm sure you'll fix her right up.

We will. Come eat.

February helped her mother to the kitchen and spent the rest of dinner asking rapid-fire questions about the novel, the weather, Mel's caseload, anything to avoid having to say more about her own day. Finally, when they'd washed up and February's mom had gone to her room to watch TV, February and Mel sat on the couch, paperwork in each of their laps and bag of barbecue-flavored Grippo's between them. February reopened her Serrano file, raked her hands over her face.

So, what is it? Mel said.

It's just so frustrating! She's implanted, but it obviously didn't take, she's spent her whole life chasing conversational English, she's failing almost everything up at Jefferson, and her mother still seems more concerned about the way it all looks!

The magic of narcissism, said Mel.

If we can't do enough for her in the next three years, she's fucked. I have to get her mother to see the stakes here.

Not gonna happen, babe.

You don't think—

I know there's no lecture in the world that'll convince a mother she doesn't want her kid to be just like her. And nobody ever got anywhere leading with "I know better than you."

But—

Look, they're your people, I get it. But that's not how the mother sees it.

February knew Mel was right. And though it was beside the point, this sort of situation always picked at the scab of her own lifelong fear that her existence had robbed her parents of some quintessential human experience. What if they, too, had wanted a child just like them? She sighed, glancing at their photo on the mantel.

Oh, don't even go there, said Mel.

It was a neurosis she found tedious at best.

I didn't say anything.

You've got more Deaf pride and better ASL grammar than half your Deaf staff, and the new girl is through your doors now, so she's going to be fine.

Mel kissed February lightly and went into the kitchen, returning with a pair of napkins to wipe the chip grease from their fingers.

Her parents are divorced, said February, gesturing to Mel's paperwork.

Of course they are, Mel said.

*C*harlie and her father were late to their first ASL class. They had quite literally missed the memo directing them to use the "after-hours" entrance at the side gate and spent five minutes idling at the main gatehouse instead, her father leaning out the car window to press the buzzer. Then, when he checked his phone to reread the registration email, another five minutes driving round the campus perimeter, searching for said side gate, which was, of course, on the side opposite from the direction he'd chosen to go first. The wrought-iron fence looked foreboding in the waning daylight, but between the spires the grass looked lush, the freestone façades familiar. The tawny rock of the East Ohio hills where her father's father had been a quarryman was everywhere—the Roebling Suspension Bridge, the courthouse, even the walls at Jefferson.

But the similarities between her old high school and River Valley ended at their shared stone, and even that seemed different here. Where Jefferson was cold and utilitarian, RVSD seemed warm, well-worn in a way that looked loved rather than deleterious. From the outside, everything she'd heard about River Valley had been negative: its students were low-achieving, it was a last resort for those who couldn't make it at the regular school. But now, in the reddish evening light, the place took on an almost magical cast, like the grounds of a castle. Charlie wanted to stay and drink in the landscape, to marvel as the sun slipped behind that big building where they'd met the headmistress—what was that one called? Clerc? But it would have to wait. Her father was holding the crumpled map they'd been given at her intake meeting far out in front of him, like a magnet that might pull them to the correct classroom if he gave it enough leeway, and she had to jog to catch up with him.

Finally, they came to Cannon Hall and were relieved to find the door unlocked. Inside, though, their map was no longer helpful, and they peered into one empty classroom after another.

Can't you hear anything?

Her father shook his head. They found the class through the last door on the left. Inside, the other students were already there, an odd mix of adults who looked out of place in a classroom, some visibly uncomfortable squeezed into their tablet-armchair desks. Though Charlie could identify no discernible teacher, the students had begun practicing something, hands already in motion and buoyed by varying degrees of confidence. It was quiet.

The desks were arranged in a semicircle so everyone could see one another—it made sense, but walking into the crescent felt like she was imposing on some kind of group therapy. A man who looked not unlike a clean-shaven Santa, complete with red-tipped nose and potbelly, arrived soon after and launched immediately into some kind of story, though Charlie could grasp only its most iconic bits: *person checking watch, running, breathing heavily, cup, spill down the front of a shirt.* If the teacher could hear or speak, he let evidence of neither slip.

Their class was supposed to be for beginners, but it was clear everyone there was ahead of Charlie. She knew the alphabet, but that was only thanks to an internet cram session in the hours before class, and one that turned out to be less useful than she'd imagined. The alphabet was a shortcut back to English, and Charlie watched her fellow students lean on it, tortuously spelling and redoubling strings of words to one another. But the teacher never spelled anything, not even when students looked at him in wide-eyed terror, like Charlie and her father were doing now. If blank stares became the majority, he reversed course and performed a deft pantomime of whatever he'd said: there he was, getting on a bus, giving his seat up to an old man with a cane, standing the rest of the way, hanging on to the strap handle for dear life when the bus took a sharp turn. The atmosphere lightened. Maybe she could figure this out after all.

The teacher turned to the chalkboard and wrote, How are you?

He tapped the "how" with his chalk, then signed:

How.

A twisting motion, like taking something apart to see how it works on the inside.

He tapped the "you."

You.

Easy enough—point at the person.

He tapped the question mark, then pointed to his eyebrows, which he'd raised.

How + you + eyebrows

When it came time to respond, Charlie just gave a thumbs-up.

The teacher repeated the process, writing What's your name? and demonstrating corresponding signs, though this time they were out of order:

You.

Name, one set of pointer and
middle fingers tapped twice on
top of the other set.

What, almost like the gesture,
hands up and out like a shrug.

Eyebrows again, down this
time.

You + name + what—eyebrows

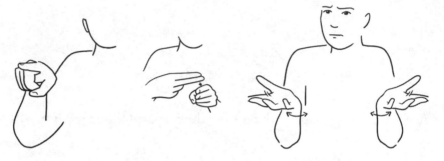

Here the alphabet did come in handy, and Charlie was grateful that
she could at least spell her own name.

Me name C-h-a-x-l-i-e, she
said.

The teacher shook his head, pointed to his own hand.

          C.

He pointed to Charlie.

  C.

          H.

  H.

          A.

  A.

          R.

Dammit.

  R, she copied.

He gave her a thumbs-up.

          Again, he said.

Everyone waited, watching her.

> *Me name C–h–a–r–l–i–e.*

The teacher nodded and continued around the circle. Once everyone had a turn, he returned to the board and wrote, Deaf, Hearing, Son, Daughter, Brother, Sister, then pointed to each and signed its equivalent:

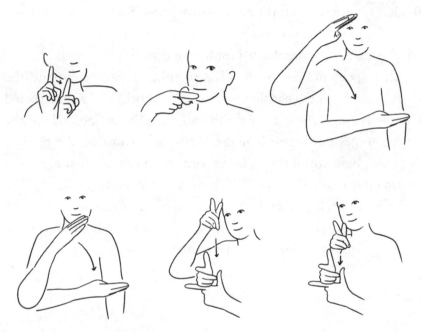

Her fellow students introduced themselves. Most of them were parents or relatives of younger River Valley kids:

> *Me hearing. My son deaf.*

Some seemed either accepting of or resigned to their child's deafness, while others were openly enduring a crisis, though they were all leagues ahead of her parents, or at least her mom, in the grieving process—that is, they were all in the room. There was one girl who looked like she might be in high school:

> *Me hearing. My sister deaf—*

but from what she could tell, Charlie was the only actual River Valley student there. Because, when you thought about it, it was kind of ridiculous—a deaf kid at a Deaf school who didn't know sign language.

Me deaf, she said when it came
her turn.

The teacher winked. Her father said his piece, eyeing Charlie as he practiced the amalgam of root words *girl* + *baby* that meant *daughter,* and she was pleased and embarrassed by the tenderness with which he produced the sign. But as Charlie watched the other students, she found something about the phrases unsettling. Something was missing. Where was the verb "to be"? How *are* you? What *is* your name? Maybe it was too complicated for beginners.

They spent the rest of the class pointing at objects around the room and learning what they were called, but this only exacerbated Charlie's curiosity—what might the noun for "being" be, and did the answer to her missing verb lie there? She wanted to ask the teacher, but didn't have any of the words to form the question. That night she stayed up searching online ASL dictionaries, endless scrolls of GIFs and line-drawn bald men frozen in sign. She looked for the sign for "to be" and found several sites confirming that it did not in fact exist, but no satisfying explanation for its absence.

*f*ebruary had been born on the edge of East Colson in her family's blue clapboard house, in the back bedroom that would later become her own. Once the contractions were six minutes apart, her mother had sent her husband into the city to retrieve her sister Mae while she paced the kitchen and tried to swab the amniotic fluid from the linoleum with a dish towel under her foot. TTYs, clunky electromechanical typewriters wired up to landlines, had made an early form of text messaging possible since the sixties, but they were still expensive. At the time, February's mother had deemed the splurge unnecessary when most of their family lived just a few minutes farther into town. Those moments laboring alone in the late August swelter must have made an impression, though—one of February's earliest memories was playing at the keyboard of the family's TTY.

February's mother was slight and asthmatic and would have certainly benefited from some medical oversight during labor, but she had long made up her mind to have the baby at home. It would be much scarier, even dangerous, to give birth in a place where no one knew sign language. The Deaf community was replete with hospital horror stories, particularly of the labor and delivery variety. Her mother's friend Lu had been wheeled into the OR without anyone telling her that she was about to have a cesarean; a woman down in

Lexington had died from a blood clot after nursing staff ignored the complaints of pain she'd scrawled on a napkin. The Americans with Disabilities Act, which would mandate that hospitals provide accommodations to deaf patients, was still more than a decade away. So February's mother wasn't taking any chances—if she couldn't have an epidural, at least she would know what the hell was going on.

There is a misconception in the hearing world that deaf people are quiet. If the Waterses' neighbors hadn't realized the inaccuracy of the stereotype before, they were certainly disenchanted of the notion on February's birthday, when her mother screamed so loudly Mr. Callhorn came running across the street and straight through the front door, sure that someone was being murdered.

Her mother always got a kick out of telling this story on Feb's birthday, complete with her transformation into Mr. Callhorn in the way that only ASL allowed, the assumption of his bulk and posture as he stalked into the bedroom, and the look of horror on his face when he realized what was happening.

> *For him, seeing all that was*
> *probably worse than murder!*

She said this every year, too, and though February had now grown wary of repetition as a sign of her mother's worsening condition, she was grateful for this particular story.

February had taken the afternoon off to have lunch with her mother, a birthday tradition that felt almost urgent to her this year. As she drove them down into Colson, she glanced sidelong at her mother, who in turn looked out the window, watching the city pass. Lately February had found herself wanting to know everything about her parents' childhoods, their courtship, her own early years, before it was consumed by the dementia. What had Colson been like when they'd moved there? Was the North-South trolley, which February had only heard spoken of like a fairy tale, running then?

Colson had changed so much even in February's lifetime, things shifting in the jagged, undulant way of the Rust Belt. Once flanked by industry—GE on the west end and Goodyear in the east—the city had spent the last several decades shrinking, burning, rising from those ashes.

Today, GE's plant was still limping along against someone's better fiduciary judgment. People at headquarters over in Cincinnati probably felt a southern Ohio allegiance, February thought. That same solidarity had sent Colson up in flames in 2001, when Cincinnati police murdered nineteen-year-old Timothy Thomas over some traffic tickets. February had been a doctoral student in Cincy, and had marched peacefully that afternoon. But when Cincy's protests turned violent, so did Colson's—she had returned to her apartment after a night class and switched on the TV to find East Colson on fire.

Amid the ruin, Goodyear found the excuse they'd been looking for to cease operations. The unrest lasted only four days, but the plant never reopened. The higher-ups went back to Akron, the contracts to Brazil, and Colson's laborers languished in the aftermath. The city cried bankruptcy when it came time to rebuild, and while it was true Colson's tax revenue would take a hit without the tire giant, February knew better than to think the reticence wasn't tethered to East Colson's working-class demographic. Next time, she thought, they should hold the protest downtown, see if the city had money to rebuild then.

There had been a round of white flight, and afterward city officials promptly defunded all they could. So the neighborhood's potholes went unmended and the streetlamps' dead bulbs unchanged. The public middle school was shuttered, the building sold to a charter who'd folded after four years. Anyone who could moved in toward the city center, or out to the burbs. But her parents had stayed in the little blue house, and even after February had grown and moved out, East Colson remained her heart's home. She loved it with the kind of territorial ferocity characteristic of overzealous sports fans.

Twenty years on, some pharmaceutical offshoot occupied a wing of the old tire building, and a few artisanal ventures were cropping up on the fringes, but much of East Colson remained hollowed out. When the Southeastern Ohio Regional Transportation Authority cut the trolley's Goodyear and Vine Street stops, the joke was that public transport was simply living up to its acronym—does it run through East Colson? SORTA! The neighborhood earned the nickname "the No Fly Zone," one February found both unoriginal and problematic, though she didn't really have any grounds for judgment—she hadn't been there in months either, not since her mother had moved in with her.

But on the inner edge of East Colson, just as the neighborhood gave way to downtown, was February's favorite lunch spot: the Chipped Cup. It was an unfussy luncheonette where the mugs were mismatched, the coffee was strong, and servers were armed with copious refills. More than that, it had what February considered to be the most important indicator of good food—a 3:00 P.M. closing time. If they could make their living off only breakfast and sandwiches, safe bet it was going to be a good sandwich.

February fed the meter and helped her mother from the car, got her situated in a booth by the front window. Mel liked to sit farther back, but February and her mother liked to people-watch. The inside of the Chipped Cup was vintage, all vinyl and Formica, but not in a way that was trying to be cute. More like the owners just couldn't be bothered to change it. While her mother perused the menu, a waitress came by and poured coffee automatically, as if no customer had ever declined. Her mother lifted her mug and they clinked.

Cheers! she said. *And don't forget, I'm buying.*

No way. My treat.

It's your birthday.

But you did all the work.

Her mother laughed, a deep-gullet sound totally uninfluenced by what the world decided laughter should be.

I guess that's true.
Tell me again about how you and
Dad met, said February after a
while.

And her mother put down her mug and told her the story.

*C*harlie was aware from a tender age that she was not the daughter her mother wanted. It wasn't, she was starting to realize, the fact of her deafness (though that wasn't helping her case). It was an ordinary clash of personalities, and that made it all the worse.

When she was younger, it was easy to be angry about their relationship and all the ways her mother misunderstood her. But recently Charlie had been finding herself seized by moments of empathy for her mother. In flashes, she'd see herself as her mother must have— a tomboy stamping through her mother's beauty queen aspirations, torn jeans and grass stains and pockets full of rocks that clogged the dryer vent, fighting her on wearing a dress to her grandparents' house until one of them cried. Her mother was slender, fine-featured, perky whether or not she was actually happy. She had been the kind of girl that was popular at Jefferson, the kind of girl that would pick on Charlie. It occurred to Charlie that before she'd come along, no one had challenged her mother on anything in quite a long time.

One thing they did share was a tendency toward repression, and this was usually the defining feature of their interactions, but it had all come to a head in a good old-fashioned mother-daughter blow-out last year, in the mall no less. It was around Christmastime and Charlie couldn't remember what they'd been bickering about, but the body odor and department store perfume and cinnamon pretzels and the screams radiating out of Santa's photo station had all served as accelerants, and her mother had blurted out:

You don't know what it's like to have made a human who hates you!

Then, when she realized her shouting had drawn attention from other shoppers, she ran across the food court and into the bathroom.

Charlie had been stunned. Her mother never left the house without a thick lacquer of Debutante—hair and teeth brushed and bleached, French manicure, a bag that matched her shoes. Even through years of her parents' shouting matches, Charlie had never seen her mother lose it in public. Charlie had gone into the bathroom and stood in front of the stall under which she spied her mother's sensible loafers.

I don't hate you, she'd said to the door.

But she had no idea what to do after that. They hadn't been to the mall since.

So when her mother messaged and asked if she wanted to go school shopping, Charlie wished she could say no. She wanted to stay at her father's and finish sorting her stuff, not trek out to the suburbs to fight with her mother about whether they should enter through the Old Navy or the HomeSense. But now that they no longer lived together Charlie felt guilty—was she even *allowed* to decline? And also, RVSD had just emailed a list of school and dorm supplies she did not currently own. This was how she found herself standing beside her mother outside a behemoth H&M, her mother sporting obviously false excitement about Charlie's new school and going on about first impressions. Her mother's bathroom outburst hadn't been all wrong: it was difficult to imagine that the two of them had ever been a single entity.

You could reinvent yourself! said her mother.

Charlie considered telling her mother that she had not yet invented herself a first time. She *had* co-opted a certain style at Jefferson, some amalgam of punk and mod that meant she got to wear a lot of dark clothes and scowl as part of her aesthetic. Her commitment was lukewarm (gone completely if she overslept), but the look did offer a certain visual armor. It was a nod of solidarity to the other rejects, and suggested to the popular kids that perhaps she wasn't a total weirdo, just into art, or something else they didn't understand. As a perk it pissed off her mother, rankling her school-days nostalgia for white sneakers and pleated skirts.

Charlie had low hopes for the outing as they ventured into the mall's main pass, but after a while they struck a rare harmony with one another. At Boscov's they bought extralong sheets and a laundry bag, a caddy for toiletries, a pair of towels. And while their fashion senses were irreconcilable, her mother was a seasoned professional in the search for jeans that wouldn't gap at the waist. They even shared a laugh at some point—something about the audacity required to wear a button fly.

Finally fatigued by their looping course and each other's company, they found themselves at the food court.

Should we get some frozen yogurt? said her mother.

O-k.

Her mother was still for a moment, and Charlie worried she'd angered her. She hadn't meant to do it. Every night since that first sign class, she'd sat in front of the computer looking up new signs before bed; during the day she wandered around her father's apartment, fingerspelling the names of random household objects to practice her alphabet. Now, though part of her was proud that she'd successfully encoded these two letters into her muscle memory, she folded her hands tight in her lap.

Show me, said her mother softly.

Charlie modeled the letters, then took her mother's hand and helped her shape the k.

They got two cones of orange swirl and sat at a table. Charlie's scar was feeling sore again but she didn't want to bring it up. Her mother's face, too, looked pained, like she was trying to work a math problem out in her head.

So, her mother said after a while. Do you just have to spell every-thing?

No, said Charlie, careful to keep her expression neutral, nonjudg-mental. It wasn't like she had known any better just days before. You really don't spell much at all.

Then whole words are—

Words and concepts have their own signs. They're not related to English.

Her mother nodded, looked down at her cone with regret. Charlie realized it would be quite a splurge from her mother's normally strict diet.

You know, Charlie said after a moment. You can come to ASL class, too, if you want.

Maybe, said her mother, in the way that meant no.

Now Charlie's cone was growing soggy, and she watched the orange cream drip onto the table. There was something buzzing, horsefly-like in her head, more a feeling than a sound, and she didn't know if it was her implant or an unkind thought.

spelling doesn't count

THE ASL MANUAL ALPHABET: FINGERSPELLING DO'S AND DON'TS

⊘ Use fingerspelling for proper nouns, like people, places, and brand names borrowed from English or other languages. Many people and places have sign names, too—introduce these words by spelling first, then signing. The signed name can be used thereafter.

⊘ Use your dominant hand and try not to bounce. While reading fingerspelling, learn to look at the overall shape of the word instead of individual letters.

ⓧ Don't conflate knowledge of the manual alphabet with fluency in ASL. Spelling is a very small part of any ASL interaction, and is used mainly for vocabulary borrowed from elsewhere.

ⓧ Don't use fingerspelling as a shortcut back to English syntax or vocabulary. Try thinking of a synonym instead.

💡 **DID YOU KNOW?** Sign languages aren't universal. They weren't "invented" by any one person—instead they grew organically out of Deaf communities. They're grammatically unrelated to spoken language, so countries that have the same spoken language may have different signed ones. For example, American Sign Language (ASL) and British Sign Language (BSL) are very different—they even use different manual alphabets! ASL's closest linguistic relative is French Sign Language (LSF) because of Deaf teacher and Frenchman Laurent Clerc's role in founding the American School for the Deaf.

*t*hough it always arrived before she was ready, February relished the first day of school. It was an unpopular sentiment, she was reminded when she attended the districtwide meeting. Not at her school—she made sure of that as best she could, though the job was largely self-selecting. Most of her teachers were Deaf and propelled, if not by a love of children, then at least by a devotion to the community. From an administrative standpoint she was lucky; fewer things were more motivating than a fear of one's own extinction, and Deaf people were already on the verge. It was the loss of a culture war some members of her faculty simply referred to as "The End."

Nine out of ten deaf kids had hearing parents, and those parents held Deaf fate in their hands—the fate of their own children, of course, and the future of the Deaf community at large. Problem being, most parents understood deafness only as explained to them by medical professionals: as a treachery of their genes, something to be drilled out.

Like her faculty, February dreaded the day scientists would perfect some stem cell transplant or in-utero tweak that would rid the world of deaf people and render her native language obsolete, when there'd be no students waiting at the foot of the hill for her to unlock the campus gates. More than a few times she'd even prayed, selfishly, for The End to hold off until after she was dead and buried, so that she might be spared the pain of bearing witness to it.

For now, though, River Valley had lived to see another year. To tell the truth, the school was better positioned for survival than most Deaf schools, though that had more to do with the disadvantages of the surrounding population than with successes on RVSD's part. Colson County struggled with both rural and urban varieties of hardship, and high poverty rates translated to fewer implants and less cash for private speech therapy, a narrower achievement gap between RVSD and the underperforming mainstream schools, and parents desperate enough for food and childcare that they'd send a kid to board at a "special" school without concerns about how doing so might look to their neighbors. For some, three meals a day and individual attention from teachers was more than their other children might get.

Geography, too, was on their side—Kentucky was just a bridge away, the West Virginia line only fifty minutes out. The next closest Deaf school was St. Rita in Cincinnati, but that was small, Catholic. With the Ohio and Kentucky state institutions each a three-hour drive from the river border towns, it was easy for parents to petition that their kids attend River Valley. The result was that February ran a monopoly of sorts, with her school at the center of a wide pool of people who really needed it. While the decline of the Deaf population might well be inevitable, for RVSD at least, it was stalled.

Now a motorcade of minivans was cresting the front drive, brimming with things the students didn't need, more often than not missing things they did. Younger siblings carried bedrolls bigger than themselves because they wanted to glimpse this magical intersection between school and sleepaway camp to which they could not belong. Some parents in tears, some heartbreakingly indifferent in the face of their children's departures.

February kept an eye out for those students, ones whose parents had chosen boarding as a matter not of necessity but of convenience, an alternative to the pressures of learning to communicate. Of course, in a situation like that, language deprivation was all but guaranteed, so February and the parents were in agreement—the dorm *was* the best place for the child. But that didn't stop her from feeling sorry for them. Your mother is your mother, and that didn't change, no matter where the kid slept.

She forced her eyes back to her computer. Moments earlier, Dr. Swall had sent through the projected district budget, packed with plenty for her to worry about. Beside her, on a legal pad pilfered from Mel's stash, February had a list of improvements she'd been planning. Now she would have to cross most of them out. No new computers for the digital lab (but perhaps they could update Windows?). Graphing calculators would be on the parents. New football helmets they'd need regardless—God forbid someone cracked his head open on her watch.

Updated history texts would have to wait another year, along with replacements for the cadre of wonky desks held steady by wedges of cardboard and sugar packets. The carpet in the boys' lower dorm *had* to go; she left that on the list, along with the new Spanish curriculum, designed, finally, without a listening component.

She sighed. Swall would try to weasel his way out of paying the teachers if he thought he could get away with it. And up and up the chain it went—austerity measures handed down from city council, the state senate, the DOE. Among other things, it meant that February herself was headed back to the classroom for the first time in almost a decade, to cover Diane Clark's maternity leave. It had quickly proven impossible to find a long-term history sub fluent in ASL, and hiring a hearing one with a team of interpreters would've decimated her emergency reserves. So she'd jerry-rigged a plan: she'd given the middle school teacher a double overload for two of Diane's courses, foisted a third on the English teacher, and took on the remedial course herself. She'd pored over the curriculum, made and remade her syllabus, fretted about whether she could handle both teaching and administrative duties. The weight of it all made her wish, momentarily, that summer would last a bit longer after all.

She would sleep on the school grounds tonight, in the Old Quarters above her office. The space had long served as storage—what her assistant headmaster, Phil, jokingly called "the archives," though it was just a collection of collapsible file boxes (also courtesy of Mel's firm), much too disorderly to be deserving of the title. Mel thought it was silly of Feb to sleep there, and said so every year. Their own home was a stone's throw away, February could be summoned instantly by videophone should she be needed, and anyway, nothing bad ever happened when it was expected. But February was a sucker for tradition, and so she stayed in her office, peering out onto the drive at the parental procession now in reverse, until she saw Walt lock the gate for the night.

She lugged her laptop and duffel bag up the spiral stairs, navigating around the boxes to her bed, a twin with an old iron hospital frame. It had been made up with fresh sheets, and she smiled at the thoughtfulness of the dormkeepers. Good kids. On the kitchenette counter, they'd left her some Campbell's, and jars of milk and coffee from the cafeteria. She opened a can of tomato soup and warmed it on the hotplate as the eyes of headmasters past peered down at her from their frames. Gazing up at the record of unfortunate facial hairstyles, she had an idea for how she might help the Serrano girl.

Even though February had technically settled on her course materials, she had wanted to do something different, and now, standing before the wall of her intellectual ancestors, she knew exactly what it should be. Charlie was untethered; she had no understanding of the culture to which she belonged or the history that belonged to her. Few of the remedial students did—most were late arrivals to River Valley, those who enrolled after having failed in the mainstream. So February would write her own curriculum, a series on Deaf culture. It was more than they would have learned with a random sub, she reasoned, and anyway, how could anyone be expected to learn history when they didn't know the first thing about themselves?

As for Charlie, assuming her language loss could be rectified, the ASL would come from interacting with classmates more than any structured tutorials. But what if she was shy? What if the students shunned her for not knowing how to sign? It had been known to happen—the Deaf world was certainly not immune to pettiness, often succumbing to a caste-like system of who had the "purest" ASL. Charlie was not the only new student to arrive this year, but she was the only high schooler. Tipping her bowl to catch the last drops of soup, February decided she would call in a ringer, one who would guarantee Charlie language immersion—she would assign Austin Workman to be her mentor.

The night had finally cooled, as if the students' presence at school had spurred the weather into feeling autumnal, and February pushed open the dormer windows. The breeze was restorative, but the moths descended upon the room immediately, so she switched off the over-head light in favor of a bedside lamp. She texted her mother good night, called Mel, who didn't pick up, made a note in her calendar to talk to Austin in the morning. Then, in the spirit of the antique room, she abandoned her phone for the novel she'd thrown into her duffel at the last minute.

The book was about a French voyage of exploration and its subsequent shipwrecks, and though she had anticipated an anxious night—the unfamiliar bed and a big day before her—she felt the rhythm of the ocean in its pages, and soon fell into an easy sleep.

*f*or Austin Workman-Bayard, Deafness was a family heirloom. The story of his great-great-grandparents had been passed down through the community with a reverence similar to the way hearing people spoke of war hero gallantry: on a rainy night in October 1886, Herbert Workman and Clara Hamill breached the perimeter of the Michigan Asylum for the Deaf, Dumb, Blind and Insane under cover of darkness and fog. All manner of terrible things had happened to them there—they had had their hands tied down to keep them from communicating; they had been deprived of food and water as punishment for signing anyway; they had been beaten with sticks and belts for each botched attempt at stealing food or sneaking out; a teacher had once tried to put his hand down Herbert's pants. And they had gotten off easy. They left only when their friend Bucky had warned them about the operations.

Bucky wasn't deaf—he was one of the insane ones. They had a joke about it: Herbert and Clara were locked up because they couldn't hear voices, and Bucky was locked up because he heard too many. But he'd also heard the screaming. Six people in his wing had been sterilized, he wrote across Herbert's wide palm at dinner, and who knew if it might cross over to the deaf wing. Bucky was older than they were, and said it had happened before.

Clara and Herbert mulled the warning over in their secret spot beneath the janitor's stairs. On the one hand, Bucky was supposed to be nuts. On the other, they were institutionalized, too, and he'd never done anything weird to them. In the end, high on young love and the Industrial Revolution, they hoarded four days' food and fled south across the Ohio border, where they walked until they hit Columbus. They slept on the steps of a church and begged for money and work until the foreman of a textile mill decided he liked the idea of employees who couldn't back-talk him.

Clara trained to work a loom while Herbert shoveled coal for the boiler. They rented a room on top of a pub for cheap because the noise from the bar fights didn't bother them. And they worked their way up in the world.

They moved to Cincinnati for the GE jobs, and had two boys—Jack and John—who cleared middle school before being released into the Queen City to work the line. The brothers bought row houses beside one another, took pay cuts in the Depression but proved their worth, even helped the war effort working weekend hours in the post office, searching for enemy microfiche concealed beneath the stamps.

Jack stayed a bachelor, serial ruffler of feathers at Cincy Deaf Club socials; John married and had a son, Willis, who grew up running between the two houses, equally at home in both. Willis finished high school before he joined the rest of the family at the factory. He had a fling with a redhead who did shorthand work for the foreman, but that could only last so long—he wanted, he was somewhat surprised to find, someone he could talk to. So, though it pained him to do it, he asked his mother and aunt to put out the call at the Society of Deaf Women's Christmas party.

Enter Lorna Levine. Lorna had gone to college and taught history at River Valley, which was considerably less asylum and more actual school. She spoke well, or at least hearing people understood her when they went out to restaurants. She was smarter than Willis, and that scared him a little, but also made him want to cling to her. His mother offered him her own engagement ring, but he saved up and bought a diamond on installment.

Their wedding was the talk of the club—by now the Workmans were iconic—a boozy all-nighter with a discount band. Not a year later they had a daughter, Beth. Lorna was strict about her schooling, scrimping to put her through Gallaudet. School came easy to Beth, and she was the student-government representative for the cognitive science department by the time she was a sophomore. And it was there, at an SGA meeting, at a university for deaf students, that Austin's mother fell in love with a hearing man.

Henry Bayard was a grad student, an interpreter fluent in ASL, and overenthusiastic about Deaf culture the way assimilates are, but this was all cold comfort to Beth Workman's very Deaf family.

They'd come around at the birth of their grandson, Austin—fifth-generation Deaf in the Workman line, a fact they cherished just like anyone takes pride in a newborn's resemblance to his family. Austin had a charmed childhood surrounded by sign language and people who loved him fiercely, and grew into the kind of bubbly, self-assured boy one can be only if he feels wholly understood, the prized child of the tri-county Deaf community.

Now whenever Austin struggled in school or was scolded for being moody, his lineage was served up to him like a fable, his relatives shining beacons of patience and fortitude in a world designed against them. And the moral of each story was this: Austin was very lucky.

He knew it was true. He caught it at school, too, from the teachers, the other kids. A lot of his friends did have it rough—solitary confinement in their own houses, their mothers crying over having birthed broken babies, constant prodding by surgeons and therapists. All this while Austin's own mother had, on more than one occasion, told him he was perfect.

She'd found him less angelic this most recent summer, his tendency to irritate her growing in direct correlation to her abdomen

and the morning sickness that came with her expansion. "An acci
dent baby," she'd called it once, though she'd told him not to repeat
that. Of course they wanted the child, it was just that everything
with the roof had made money a little tight right now, nothing for
him to worry about, though. Then she'd cried. His father had found
him distraught in the backyard and placated him with talk of hormones, but Austin still felt bad about the burden his insatiable ap-
petite undoubtedly added to the family grocery bill.

Now it was late August in southern Ohio, and Austin's mother
was eight months pregnant and very hot. She sweated while she
cooked, or shuffled from car to side door, or when she lay absolutely
still on the couch in the front room, her hair matted down flat against
her head like the skin of an onion. Even his father's T-shirts clung
tight across her stomach, a sweat ring around her protruding belly
button.

It all made Austin nervous. He found himself eager for school
and its distractions, his move back into the dorm. His family's house
was only a half hour from campus, but his mother had lived in the
dorm at her school, and so had her parents—all four generations
back if you counted the asylum—and every family had its traditions.
His parents told him living with Deaf peers was important for his
social skills. His teachers told him he was a linguistic role model for
the kids who weren't blessed with the lifelong exposure he was so
very fortunate to have. Austin had always thought it was kind of silly
to board when he lived so close and had such a good home life, but
now he was glad for the arrangement.

He started packing two weeks out, something he'd never done
before and, as it turned out, was an imprudent thing to do now. He'd
quickly run out of clothes, especially with him and his father on
laundry duty, and wound up digging through his suitcase each morning in search of boxers, another T-shirt, everything an indistinguishable rumple until eventually he'd dumped the contents of the case
back out on the floor.

His father found him pantless amid this pile the morning they

were supposed to move him in at school. He took a paternal surveying posture, as if deciding whether or not he was going to scold his
son. Then he bent and fished a pair of shorts from the far side of the
mound, threw them over.

Thanks.

> *Leaving in half hour. I'm going*
> *to put your bedding in the truck.*

Austin pulled on the shorts, righted his suitcase, and began to shovel
his clothes back inside. It was only when he got out to the car that he
remembered the trouble that might be waiting for him at school. He
was so eager to be sprung from the tension of his household he had
forgotten all about the love he'd professed, and the drama that had
followed.

> *You coming?*

Austin opened the door for his mom up front, then climbed into the
backseat.

Sorry about the messy room.

> *Don't worry, you have nothing*
> *else to do this weekend!*

For a moment Austin thought his father had looked right inside his
head and was teasing him about the breakup, but Austin couldn't
recall mentioning it to either of his parents. If his father had learned
about the relationship through the River Valley grapevine, he didn't
say anything more, just twisted the key in the ignition. His other
hand flicked a *h-a-h-a*, the visual accompaniment to laughter in the
habit of most signers, and Austin wondered, not for the first time,
what such a thing might sound like.

triple duty—nouns, verbs, and adverbs in asl

💡 **DID YOU KNOW?** The number or quality of repeated movements within a sign can mean the difference between a noun, verb, or adverb, or provide multiple kinds of information simultaneously. This grammatical feature means ASL is often more economical than spoken language.

NOUN: Repeat the sign's movement twice using a small range of motion. For example, the pointer and middle fingers are tapped against each other to make the sign **"chair."**

VERB: The sign's movement is made only once, using a larger range of motion. Sometimes this movement is altered to more closely mirror the real-life action (**see: "cup"** → **"drink"**). Here the pointer and middle fingers of one hand are set on the other to make the verb **"to sit."** Greater force and a stern facial expression can form the command **"sit down."**

ADVERB: Some signs can be imbued with descriptive information by tweaking or adding movement. For example, to add the information **for a long period of time,** a sign can be adjusted to incorporate a slow, circular motion (**see: working, sitting**).

NOW YOU TRY! Using the base sign **study,** tell a partner about a time when you had to study hard or for a long time.

*C*harlie remembered the earliest years of her education with a certain fondness—less unsupervised time and therefore less bullying, snack breaks, and coloring and scissor skills she could ace alongside her peers. But the language acquisition the doctors had promised post-implant had been slow to materialize. For a while she made progress in a little white room, where she sat at a table across from a well-intentioned blond lady who dealt largely in spit. Charlie had spent hours with that woman, learning about mouth shapes and airflow by blowing out candles, or holding her nose, or pressing an upside-down spoon on her tongue. But outside the confines of the therapist's office, so many sounds were still inscrutable. Her classrooms were noisy, and she couldn't find the words they'd practiced out there, amid the din.

It started to show. The students began learning to read, spell, even add via call-and-response, a mire of sounds through which Charlie waded with trepidation. Her teachers scolded her when she was slow or off-task, raised concerns at parent conferences about whether she had "additional disabilities." Charlie did not know how to explain that she couldn't possibly find the answers when she didn't know the questions.

She became prone to what her mother called "spells." Her teachers called them "behaviors," as if any action from a child beyond total compliance was implicitly bad. Charlie, of course, called them nothing at all, which was part of the problem.

She didn't remember much about the outbursts now, just flashes: her teacher trying to peel her from the tile floor while Charlie thrashed in her grip, the heat of her tears and phlegm midtantrum, and most of all that burning feeling that ran from her forehead straight to the pit of her stomach, when the word you need is on the tip of your tongue but you can't quite wrangle it. Except for Charlie it was all the words. And this was how she'd come to do a stint in special ed.

In the special ed room, Charlie spent most of her time alone. She was given a desk, workbooks, pretzels, and water in a spill-proof cup with a spout that looked like it was for someone much younger. Perhaps they originally had other plans for her, but day in and day out the teacher and aides were consumed by the room's myriad emergencies—feeding and washing and toilet training, the constant sidelong minding of a boy who was prone to banging his front teeth against the cinder-block wall when he was upset.

One of her new classmates had a flip-book wallet full of little pictures that she wore hooked to her belt loop—cartoon images of a toilet, various foods and drinks, classroom toys. Charlie liked the bright, bold pictures and wondered if someone might make such a book for her, but they never did. Some afternoons the girl would appear at Charlie's side and show her a picture of Lego, and the two would retreat to the circle time carpet and build a tower. Besides her, Charlie didn't interact much with the other students, save for one kid who'd scratched her when she'd unwittingly taken his favorite seat at the craft table. The teacher had sent Charlie down to the nurse with a note pinned to her shirt requesting antiseptic, harsh stuff that chapped her cheek.

At first Charlie's own "behaviors" continued, too, meltdowns in the face of unfathomable phonics workbooks. The special ed program was equipped for these moments; Charlie was placed in the Quiet Room—an empty closet lined with blue gymnasium mats. Charlie hated the Quiet Room. Quiet was not hard for her to come by and more of it certainly didn't calm her. The closet door had a small window, but it was too high for Charlie to see out of, and she worried that her teachers would be distracted by some crisis and forget her in there. She knew the only way to keep from being trapped forever was to stop the spells, so bit by bit she learned to swallow them, curl her toes inside her sneakers and clamp her back teeth down hard when she was angry. Her visits to the room became fewer and fewer, but with little instructional time and no friends, her academic progress was still bleak. Some days, the speech therapist was the only person she talked to at all.

In a surprising twist, it was her mother's preoccupation with appearances that eventually saved her. People talked in Colson, and a neighbor had seen Charlie at the bus stop in her special ed–issued orange safety vest. The looks, the gossip, the prying questions about the state of Charlie's mind—it was too much for her mother, and eventually she stormed the school to have it all reversed. She was met with little resistance—the special ed teachers themselves had been against the placement from the start—and soon Charlie was returned to the mainstream classroom. But her record bore the mark of her time away, and both students and teachers took note. Her classmates focused their attention on her in ways she would rather they didn't, and the teachers did the opposite. In a public school strapped for resources, extra tutoring and empathy had to be rationed, and they could not risk wasting it on her. They resigned themselves to passing her on to the next grade until she was gone.

How might her life have been different if she had always gone to River Valley? Charlie thought as she and her father joined the move-in queue. Alight with activity, the campus looked different than it had when they'd come at night. The main drive was crowded, the surrounding lawns busy with smaller children and nervous parents sitting close together in the grass, older kids playing soccer or passing cellphones back and forth. And everywhere there was the flurry of hands and arms in flight, telling tales of the summer, no doubt, though Charlie wouldn't have been able to understand them at that speed even if she was close enough. The enchantment cast by those large stone buildings the night of their first sign class was diluted somewhat by the activities around them, but in the multitude of signs, Charlie saw a different kind of magic.

She and her father collected her ID card and a folder containing her room assignment, class schedule, and another campus map, then made it to the loading zone in front of the girls' dorm, where a dorm-keeper pushed a canvas laundry cart their way. Charlie stood beside the trunk of the car trying to look useful as her father unloaded her two suitcases, backpack stuffed with school supplies, the trio of clear plastic bags containing her new sheets, duvet, and pillows, a shower caddy, laundry bag containing towels, hair dryer, and new galoshes, and the unopened box that held the laptop her parents had bought her as a "going away present."

Inside, the dorm was darker than she'd imagined, sallow with the green cast of fluorescent lights, and she tried not to let this disappoint her. There was a small foyer with a security desk—the gate was propped open for move-in, but Charlie could see the machine at which she would be expected to swipe her ID in the future. For some reason, this made her nervous. She'd never carried a house key before; her mother had always left the side door unlocked for her. Charlie gave the paper with her room assignment to the guard, and he pointed down the long center hallway. With her father behind her pushing the cart, she followed the wall plaques down to room 116. KAYLA and CHARLOTTE were taped in construction paper letters to the door.

Gross, she said aloud.

She hated the long form of her name. She swiped her ID in the lock. Nothing. It took three more tries.

Charlie considered herself a pretty light packer; even though she would be home on weekends it wasn't *that* much stuff if you thought about it in the context of an entire year. But when she finally got the door open and pulled her cart inside, she found her roommate already there, sitting cross-legged on a bare mattress, with no other belongings in sight. The girl was wiry with dark skin and jet-black hair gathered in twists across her head. Charlie could tell her roommate was much taller than she was, even though she was sitting down.

Hi, the roommate said. *Me name K-a-y-l-a.*

Thank god her name had been pasted on the door—the girl spelled so fast she never would have caught it.

C-h-a-r-l-i-e.

Sign name?

They'd discussed sign names in ASL class—only another Deaf person could give you one. Charlie shook her head.

K-on-cheek, Kayla said, twisting the letter in the space on her cheek where a dimple would be.

Nice meeting you, said Charlie.

Same, said Kayla, though she didn't look that enthused.

Do you want help with this? said her dad, gesturing to the cart.

No thanks, said Charlie.

O-k, said her father.

He looked down at his shoes.

So I guess I'll just—

Yeah, okay. Thanks, Dad.

They hugged, and Charlie could feel his heart beating too fast.

Text if you need anything.

O-k.

Love you.

Love you too, she said.

For a moment she stood frozen, resisting the urge to go after him. She'd spent the night away from home only a handful of times—she didn't have good enough friends for many sleepovers. Maybe she should have stuck it out at Jefferson.

You o-k?

Charlie nodded.

The door?

She closed it, looked around. The room had a wardrobe and bed on each side, one desk by the door and the other by the window, the setup symmetrical except for a small television screen on the left wall. No wonder her roommate had chosen that side. But where was all of Kayla's stuff? Maybe her belongings were coming along later, Charlie thought, though she could see a pant leg sticking out from one of the drawers, and Kayla's backpack hung from its straps on the back of the desk chair she'd claimed.

You _____?

What?

_____?

What?

Charlie could feel herself starting to panic.

I don't understand, she said aloud. Do you read lips?

Kayla sighed.

R-i-c-h, she spelled. *Rich.*

She pointed to Charlie's cart and drew a heaping pile in the air between them.

Rich, Charlie copied. *Me? No.*

Kayla didn't say anything else and Charlie didn't know how to, so she heaved her suitcases from the cart and laid them on her bed.

Overhead, a light flashed. Charlie jumped, thinking it was the fire alarm, but Kayla got up and opened the door, revealing a dormkeeper with an armful of linens. The woman was fresh-faced and bubbly, her look and demeanor not unlike those of the pageant girls Charlie's mother usually worked with, though her mother's beauty queen world felt light-years away. Kayla flung herself at the woman, who returned the hug with her free arm, and the two had a quick and frenetic exchange of which Charlie could not understand a word. Then the dormkeeper handed Kayla a set of sheets stamped with PROPERTY RVSD in faded blue.

The dormkeeper looked to Charlie and said something. A smile and a wave seemed to be a fine enough answer, because she turned to go.

Wait, said Kayla, then another thing Charlie couldn't catch.

The woman nodded and pulled a length of masking tape from a roll she was wearing around her arm like a bangle, handed it to Kayla.

Thanks.

She gave them a thumbs-up and left. Charlie watched as Kayla pulled something from her pocket and unfolded it gingerly—it was a pair of photos of a woman in a bright yellow basketball jersey, torn from a magazine. Kayla ripped the masking tape into eight pieces and taped the pages to the wall. She began to make her bed, then stopped.

What?

Nothing, Charlie said, realizing she'd been staring. *Sorry.*

Kayla shrugged and Charlie began to make her bed. She was still hanging clothes in her wardrobe when Kayla flicked the light switch to get her attention.

Food-night?

Right, dinner! Charlie wasn't hungry, but she knew the cafeteria served food for a limited amount of time, and also she had no idea where it was, so she dug her ID from beneath the pile of clothes and followed her roommate down the hall and out onto the quad.

Charlie had assumed that the majority of students would be boarders, but the cafeteria was only half full when they arrived, with probably about seventy-five students altogether. There were a few tables of younger students with their dormkeepers; the smallest were still puffy-eyed from crying, but the rest of the kids seemed to know one another and were falling back into their old rhythms. Charlie wondered what she would have been like at their age—would she have cried as her parents drove away, or been glad she was in a place where she could understand everything? She scanned the faces of the older elementary students; no tears there. A school week would feel a lot shorter to them than a little kid, and anyway, they'd probably gotten used to goodbyes. Or perhaps, for them, the meaning of "home" had transformed and their families' houses were just "home" on a technicality.

Across the room was a table of middle schoolers, most of them gathered tight around a girl playing a video on her phone, elbowing one another to get in for a closer look. And then there were her classmates—a few coupled off and holding hands, some just chatting in pairs, but all clustered around a boy she could see only from the back, constellations within his gravitational pull.

The headmistress had recommended that Charlie stay at school to facilitate her language development, but from what Charlie could tell, most of the kids there signed quickly and fluidly, and she wondered why they'd chosen to board. She resolved to ask Kayla about it when they got back to the room, but after dinner her roommate went out into the common area to watch Netflix on one of the other girls' computers. Charlie stood in the doorway, seeing the group greet each other after a summer apart with hugs and emphatic signs, but when one of them made eye contact with her, she got flustered and slammed the door. Being alone in the room just made Charlie feel worse, claustrophobic, but she didn't dare go out there. She could barely understand her roommate one-on-one, never mind a whole group of girls going at top speed. Now they probably thought she was an asshole, but at least they didn't think she was stupid. That was tomorrow's problem.

From deep in her backpack, she retrieved a baggie containing the last of the weed gummies Kyle, a boy from Jefferson she sometimes hooked up with, had given her the last time they'd been together. She wondered what he was doing now, considered texting him, but stopped herself. Her mother had been right in one regard—coming to River Valley was her chance for a clean break. She popped the little yellow bear into her mouth, put on her pajamas, and waited for the abatement of her anxiety or for sleep, whichever came first.

*b*oth of Austin's parents came to drop-off, his mom picking at the pilling upholstery on the couch out in the common room while he and his dad unloaded his gear. He was on a different floor than last year, but the room looked the same. Austin always arrived early and chose the side of the room where the videophone was installed. He used it more than his roommates anyway; most kids were from hearing families and didn't call home much. His parents kissed him on the forehead and made to leave, but he walked with them back to their car.

> *Swear you'll call when the baby is*
> *coming?*

They promised, and he stood on the curb and watched them pull away, then returned to the dorm, missing them fiercely. The fact that he had done this many times before mitigated the length of the homesickness, but not its intensity. When he was in elementary school, he'd cried each time his parents left; as a first grader he'd been damn near inconsolable for two days. If he thought about it long enough, he could still transport himself back there and relive the gnawing anxiety that he'd felt in the moment, though he pushed away the urge to do so now. Instead he tried to remember his classmates in their first hours at school. Had they, too, been upset, or had the fact that he'd had more to lose made it harder on him? In his mind's eye, he conjured up his first breakfast in the cafeteria, tried to scan the faces of his peers, but they were all a blur.

Back in the dorm, he opened his door to a blast of humid air and the smell of cigarette smoke. Across the room, Eliot Quinn had arrived, removed their screen, and was leaning out the open window, tapping ash into the grass.

When Headmistress Waters had approached him at the end of last school year about having Eliot as his roommate, he was happy to oblige. He didn't know Eliot well—he was a grade above Austin, but over the years, Austin had learned that it was much better to be cordial with your roommate than to be best friends. It lessened the chance you'd really get on each other's nerves. Austin had heard the rumors about what happened to Eliot, and nodded along with the rest of his friends when they discussed how fucked up it was, but now he worried that the problems of the boy sleeping in the bed five feet away from him were about to become his problems, too.

What are you doing?

Eliot looked at him like he was an alien.

Smoking? You mind?

Austin considered how to answer without coming off prudish. Did he want to get in trouble, or catch some secondhand lung pustule? Not particularly, though that wasn't the real question. What Eliot was really asking was whether he was a snitch.

You're gonna get caught.

He motioned with his head at the alarm above their door.

Am not, Eliot said, and turned back toward the window to exhale.

Austin studied the rutted skin running down from Eliot's ear. On his cheek, a strip of stubble had been permanently razed away, and an ugly splay of vesicles disappeared beneath the neck of his T-shirt. But so what? Even if the stories were true, that didn't give him free rein to be a dick.

Whatever. I'm going to dinner.

> *Heard she's already looking for*
> *you.*

　　What? From who?

Eliot laughed, a bit too heartily for Austin's liking.

> *I'm messing with you. I haven't*
> *talked to anyone yet. Should've*
> *seen your face though.*

He dropped the cigarette butt into an old Gatorade bottle, and Austin kept his eye on it until he was sure it had burned out completely.

*t*he morning of the first day of school, Charlie brushed her teeth twice. A neurotic tic of hers, too much time spent staring at people's mouths. She was late because of it, which was particularly annoying given that she had barely slept at all, had finally drifted off just before dawn only to be woken a couple hours later by her bed shaker, an older model than the one she had at home, with a more aggressive vibration pattern that scared her awake. She hadn't given herself a buffer for the bathroom line—there were four sinks for twelve girls, and some had doubled up but Charlie didn't know how to ask. Then, even after all that she'd still gone back for a final, extra brush. Now she bolted down the path to the upper school building. That was simple at least—the girls' and boys' upper dorms sat on opposite sides of Cannon, the building where her ASL class was held. She found her homeroom with merciful ease, but when she went inside the other students were already in their seats.

She approached the teacher, who signed something so quick and smooth that any of the ASL Charlie knew from night class drained right out her feet.

Sorry, what? she said, but it was the teacher's turn to look bemused.

Oh god, Charlie thought—she's deaf, too. Shit. The teacher signed the thing again, slower, the equivalent of the patronizing voice in which hearing teachers had spoken to her at Jefferson. Charlie was sure she'd seen one of the signs before—had the dormkeeper said it?—but could not dredge up the meaning.

Shit, she said aloud.

The teacher launched herself, via rolling chair, toward the chalkboard.

Introduce yourself, she wrote.

Me name C-h-a-r-l-i-e, she said.

But obviously I'm a girl, so . . . she said.

A few kids, the lipreaders, snickered. The teacher made the *introduction* sign again, and Charlie was puzzled—had she done it wrong? But then the teacher smiled and wrote,

Welcome, Charlie, beneath her first line.

She pointed to the "welcome" with her chalk and made the sign again. Funny, Charlie thought, that the sign meant these two things. In hearing school, they'd always seemed like opposites.

By lunchtime Charlie was practically cross-eyed from all the signing. It was one thing to feel comfortable in a semicircle of adults painstakingly explaining what they'd eaten for breakfast, but this was another realm completely, and Charlie wanted nothing more than to stare at a blank wall for a few moments. At Jefferson, she'd also disliked lunch—all that chatter so thoroughly garbled—until she learned to switch off her implant and drift in the quiet. But she didn't have the option of turning off her eyes, or at least she didn't think she could close them and still feed herself.

You're fine, she said to herself aloud in the hall to feel her voice in her chest.

As with dinner the night before, she ordered by pointing—this was not a language issue, the food was just beyond recognition—and chose an empty table in the corner. She traced her finger along graffiti etched into the tabletop, smiled despite herself:

SILENCE IS GOLDEN, it said.

Then she turned her concentration to the task of cutting the gravy-slathered meat product before her—hardened by age and chemicals and industrial ovens, her plastic silverware no match. When she surrendered, she looked up to find a boy flipping through her binder.

Yo, she said, though of course nothing happened.

She reached over and smacked the cover closed. He looked up, startled, as if she were the one violating his personal space. His eyes were green like AstroTurf, so bright she might've thought they were fake had the rest of his appearance suggested he was the type to put effort into something like that. She stared.

He pulled a pen from behind his ear and wrote on a napkin: Charlie, right?

She nodded.

I was looking for you this morning, he wrote.

Me? I . . . L-a-t-e.

Late.

Late, she copied.

He turned the napkin over.

Headmistress wants me to show you around.

She nodded again, unsure of what to say.

Can't today. Tour tomorrow?

O-k.

Tour.

Tour, she copied.

O-k.

He flipped the napkin back to where he'd first written her name.

Me . . .

He made a C shape with his hand and tapped it on his chin, then pointed back to her name on the napkin. Charlie felt her heartbeat quicken. Was it possible he was naming her?

Me?

He nodded.

She took his pen, another napkin: What does it mean?

He wrote: You talk too much.

She tried not to look disappointed. Of course her name sign would reference her dependence on speech. What else was there to say about her?

I don't, she said.

But the boy put a finger to his lips and she felt something electric run through her, different from the usual static in her head.

Charlie, she said, trying out the new sign.

He smiled, his teeth large and white, with a gap between the front two large enough to mean he hadn't had braces. Not a smile tortured into submission like hers.

> *Charlie,* he signed again, then made the mafia *I'm watching you* signal as he got up from the bench.

When he'd gone, she sat unmoving for a few moments, thrilled and unnerved by the encounter. At Jefferson she'd learned not to trust the preppy ones, though this boy—shit, she hadn't even asked his name—was more fresh out of the shower than purposefully coiffed. Maybe things were different here. Plus, those eyes.

She comprehended basically nothing for the rest of the day, anxious to return to her night sign class, where things moved slowly and precisely.

So? her dad said after class, as he walked her back to her dorm.

What?

How was the first day?

It was hard, she meant to tell him. Hard and strange and exciting. But she had spoken only a few sentences all day long, and her throat felt closed off and warm. She shrugged.

That night in bed, Kayla already asleep across from her, Charlie went back to trolling an ASL dictionary online, not looking for anything in particular, just opening the videos in alphabetical order and signing back at the monitor through the dark like a weirdo, hoping something would stick. She dozed off sitting there, snapping back at 1:00 A.M., confused and with a sore neck, in between languages, waking, and sleep.

*i*t was one of those nights she could tell they were going to argue, a drop in atmospheric pressure trailing Mel into the house after work. February had made it a point to get home early, set her mom up with a word search in the living room, and start on dinner, thinking that modeling some domestic bliss might allay the tension, but Mel wasn't having it—nitpicking as February cooked, sulking at the table as she slurped her zucchini bisque without a word of thanks.

Something had been simmering between them all week, ever since the night February had slept at the school. She had been holding out hope that it would pass without confrontation, but when Mel left the table in a huff without even bothering to clear her bowl, February's pacifism began to wane. Still, she scrubbed their dishes clean and left the pot to soak, helped her mom to her room for the night. When she returned to the living room and pulled out her laptop, Mel made a sigh so hyperbolic it might've been comical had it not been so goddamn annoying. February batted the computer closed.

What's your problem? said Mel.

My problem? You're the one huffing and puffing like a goddamn asthmatic.

Does seem like a girl may have to die around here to get some attention.

I just cooked you dinner.

You only talked to your mom the whole time.

You could've said something. Takes two, you know.

Says the woman who sleeps wherever her heart desires.

Babe, said February. It's a hundred-and-twenty-three-year-old tradition. For one night.

And?

And nothing! I ate soup! I read a book and passed out.

In reality it had felt more escapist, romantic even, but February didn't dare say that. Mel looked down at her hands in her lap.

I thought you said she was moving away, she said, her voice low. So there it was. February had been hoping it wasn't this. A year ago, the advanced science teacher at the upper school had retired, and February had replaced him with Mrs. Wanda Sybeck. Wanda and February had been colleagues years ago at the institute up in Columbus, back when February was still a teacher herself. When February hired Wanda at RVSD, she relayed happily to Mel that she had employed an old co-worker whom she knew to be a dedicated teacher. She thought it neither prudent nor necessary to note that Wanda had maintained all the shapeliness she'd had in 2007, her skin untouched by age and marked only by twin patches of freckles on the apples of her cheeks. Nor did she mention their four-month fling of that same year, a hot and heavy affair that had had them behaving like the teenagers they taught, even reduced them once to a quickie in the science supply closet during Wanda's planning period. Mel had always erred on the side of jealous, and anyway it was a long time ago. Wanda was married now. To a man.

February had been a little nervous about the two crossing paths at the staff holiday party, but Mel had been in good spirits and by the time dinner was served, February relaxed. Wanda was Deaf, so the depth of hers and Mel's interaction was cursory—most of the signs Mel knew from being with February's mom were of little use in a social setting. For her part, Wanda smiled at Mel a lot, and during dessert Mel had even leaned over and whispered to February that her friend seemed sweet.

There had been wine, and then eggnog, and Mel humored February as she and Wanda danced with their cheeks almost touching—they were old friends, after all—but in the end it had been Dennis, Wanda's oaf of a husband, who'd leaked the story. Wanda had apparently given him the explicit details of hers and February's time together as fantasy fodder and he'd made some offhand comment, on this part February had never been clear—had he made a joke about their wives' past lives to Mel, or had she simply overheard? All February remembered was looking up from the dance floor to see Mel storming from the cafeteria.

A multiday blowout had followed, Mel oscillating between silent treatment and tirades, first that February was a no-good liar, and also that Mel had even *liked* the woman—this seemed to be the biggest betrayal. February could not reason the anger away. Though she technically hadn't done anything wrong, her duplicitousness had opened a small patch of mind perfect for a growing doubt, and Mel was a talented horticulturalist. If February's motives were pure, why hadn't she been up-front about the relationship? It was a question for which there was no satisfactory answer, and February had slept a night or two in Old Quarters because of it.

I thought they were, February said. But Dennis's job offer fell through.

And?

And I can't fire her just because you don't like her!

Oh she's fine, Mel said as she stalked up the stairs. It's *you* I don't like!

She gave the bedroom door a triumphant slam. Even after all these years with a hearing partner, February could not bring herself to yell across the house. She followed Mel and jiggled the handle, but it was locked.

She's practically straight now, for fuck's sake! February yelled at the door.

She could hear Mel scoff on the other side.

February went back downstairs to work, but couldn't concentrate.

She shoved her laptop back in its case. When it was clear Mel wasn't going to come down for round two, she went to her mother's room. It was risky to disturb her this late in the evening, when she often mistook February for her favorite sister, Phyllis. If her mother didn't recognize her, she'd just feel worse. But February heard the muffled *Family Feud* theme song seeping through the door and decided to take her chances.

Does Mama need us?

February sighed.

> *No Mama, I'm your daughter,*
> *February.*

Her mother removed her glasses, as if her vision was the problem, rubbed the bridge of her nose. When she put them back on, she smiled.

Right. February. Sorry!

> *Sorry to disturb. I just needed to*
> *grab a book.*

February walked over to the bookshelf on the far side of the room and selected something at random, which turned out to be *If You Don't Feed the Teachers, They Eat the Students!* a gift from Mel when February was officially named headmistress. Before they'd moved her mother in, this had been their home office. They'd had a pair of desks and had often worked late into the night without saying a word to one another, but it'd felt nice to be side by side.

February held up the book halfheartedly. Her mother patted the bed for February to come sit beside her.

I just love this show.

> *I thought* Wheel of Fortune
> *was your favorite.*

Nah, too much English. Was your
father who had the hots for V-a-
n-n-a.

The mention of her father in the past tense filled February with relief. Her mother was back, at least for a few minutes.

Where's my Mel?

She's up in the bedroom. She's a little angry with me.

Your father used to have a temper.

I remember, February said, though at the moment she could not think of a time she'd made her father truly mad.

He mellowed out when you came around. Can we still go to the farmers market this weekend?

Sure, if you want. Saturday morning?

Oh good. Mel, too, of course.

If I can win her over.

She signed it big and sweeping, like she was kidding, but then that was the thing about jokes.

Morning is smarter than night, said her mother.

It was just like her mother to offer up the exact opposite advice everyone else did. What about "never go to bed angry"? Then again, her parents almost never had the kind of big argument she and Mel were prone to. February pulled up a chair beside her mother's bed and turned her attention to the TV, where the next *Feud* rerun was about to start.

*i*f there had been such a thing as homecoming at River Valley, Austin Workman and Gabriella Valenti would've been king and queen. He didn't feel conceited when this thought occurred to him. Some things were just true.

Gabriella was widely agreed to be pretty—strawberry blond hair with a delicate spray of freckles across the bridge of her nose—and Austin was good-looking, at least good-looking enough that Gabriella would have him. They had played opposite each other as Curly and Laurey in last year's run of *Oklahoma!* despite an unspoken rule that leads were reserved for upperclassmen. But the real source of their popularity, he knew, had little to do with looks or talent; it was embedded in each of their last names. The Valentis were no Workman clan, but Gabriella and her little sister were second-generation Deaf, and the privilege of signing parents heaped on yet more privileges—Austin and Gabriella were strong students because their parents had read to them when they were small; they were solid performers because they had grown up attending Deaf theater exhibitions; their fluid, confident signing only made them more admired by their peers.

So everyone knew Austin and Gabriella, and everyone knew they were supposed to be together. Technically they *had* been together since preschool, when Austin had proposed at the top of the slide one afternoon. The fact that he had no memory of the occasion did little to unstick it from its place in the Ohioan Deaf gossip archives, and even though they had not actually dated in the decade between their engagement and Austin's suggestion last year that they go out for ice cream, their togetherness had been considered a foregone conclusion. Which was why it had come as a shock to everyone, Austin included, when he found himself in the middle of a very public breakup at the community pool on Freshman Day.

This part he felt bad about—he hadn't wanted to ruin the end-of-year celebration they had both been looking forward to. And he'd certainly never meant to embarrass her, never mind in front of their entire class. But the other thing about Gabriella was, she wasn't very nice. More often than not she was angry with Austin—she considered each moment he wasn't actively doting on her a slight. She was also deeply vain, which had certain benefits: she was always dressed to impress, had an Instagram-ready body, and allowed him frequent access to its pleasures. But her obsession with looks extended beyond the bounds of her own person, and disparaging others was a go-to pastime Austin found both in bad taste and very boring. He was routinely taken aback by her willingness to slice right through someone they'd known their whole lives, the casual way insults glided off her fingers. For his part, Austin couldn't care less who was wearing what, or who had received an unfortunate haircut, or who—as had been the victims that day—looked lumpy in their bathing suits.

He and Gabriella had been in the pool, leaning against the wall in the shallow end, Austin enduring her gleeful tabulation of unsightly thigh dimples and feeling the back of his neck begin to sunburn when, finally, he blurted:

Oh my god would you shut up!

Here was his regret: he should have requested that they go somewhere private to talk. Instead, they'd stayed out in the open and the number of eyes on them grew as Austin told her he didn't think this was working anymore. Gabriella redirected all the energy she normally spent on berating their peers toward him—he was inattentive, withholding, had bad breath. He had taken her virginity and cast her aside like used goods. Austin stood stunned through most of the tirade, but the last accusation shamed him into action, and he tried to reach for her hands to stop her, or at least get her to sign smaller, and she slid from his grasp and let out a scream that scared the lifeguard. The guard, only a few years older than they were, and already on edge about a pool full of deaf kids, came running and threw the rescue can toward Gabriella, cracking Austin in the back of the head instead. Then it was Austin's turn to shout, and another lifeguard appeared. As he and Gabriella were dragged up onto the concrete, he felt he should say something, but the only thing that came to mind was

You were a virgin?

School had let out two days later; the pool incident was the last time they'd spoken. Part of Austin believed she was biding her time to execute an elaborate revenge plot, but when they'd seen one another at dinner the first night back, she'd only sat down at the far side of their table and stared.

Then Headmistress had asked him to show the new girl around. It was no big deal at first. He went over and introduced himself without much fanfare, but found that for the rest of the day he could not stop thinking about Charlie, her eyes, in particular—the furtive way she cast them about the cafeteria, the warm hickory color that enveloped him when she finally looked up at him.

When he saw her again the next day, he slipped her a note about where and when to meet for a tour, but stopped short of any further interaction—he couldn't invite her over to their lunch table, not yet. He felt cowardly when she ended up at the far end of the room with the Pokémon nerds, but his table was packed and he just wasn't ready to deal with the wrath of Gabriella. Anyway, the jury was still out on Charlie. Usually a high school student transferred only if their family was new to the area, or if they'd been expelled from somewhere else. Who knew what kinds of issues she might have?

Most of Austin's peers had learned to sign here at school—for them, River Valley was synonymous with safety, a place where they could understand and be understood. But he knew the consequences of living without a safe harbor, had heard all the stories of completely out-of-control kids who'd come in from mainstream school: a few years ago, a fourth grader had slapped his teacher during a math test, and last year, a middle schooler set fire to the dorm carpet.

The tantrums he'd seen up close had always been more mournful than violent, though. The clearest memory was of a morning in second grade, when a boy had stood in the center of the classroom howling, inconsolable, for nearly an hour. The rest of them had been instructed to choose a game and take it to the circle time rug while the teacher and her aide tried to sort out what was wrong. Austin watched, churning Play-Doh through a press while his classmate wailed and pointed at his stomach. The teachers removed and checked the boy's implant, then gave him an early snack of animal crackers and apple juice, which he promptly vomited in a pinkish puddle on the floor, splashback on the teacher's pants. The aide took him to the nurse.

At the time, Austin was incredulous that parents could have forgotten to teach their child basic signs about feeling sick, ones he was sure he'd always known. It wasn't until later he learned that ASL had likely been withheld intentionally, an attempt to motivate speech. Sign language had been so thoroughly stigmatized that in trying to avoid it parents had unknowingly opted for a modern version of institutionalization, locking their children away in their own minds. To Austin this sounded cruel enough to be against the law, but there were a lot of things about the hearing world that made no sense.

The notion of being friends with someone like Charlie both intrigued him and made him nervous. He had been at RVSD his whole life, knew everyone there and almost no one anywhere else. Besides his dad's side of the family, whom they saw only once or twice a year, Charlie was the closest thing to a hearing person he might socialize with in any meaningful way. But if she didn't know sign, how meaningful could it be?

It was true that deafness was rarely an all-or-nothing affair—they all felt vibrations, and most heard loud sounds. Some could hear speech, and hearing aids and implants made the range of what was possible even broader. But while most of the other kids used their voices at home, or when they went down into Colson, Austin had no hearing aids and was fully voice off. He knew that this was part of the reason Headmistress had assigned him to be Charlie's guide. He wouldn't be able to revert to speaking, and neither would she.

What's up? he said when they met out front after school.
She shrugged, shifted her weight between her feet. They both stared at her shoes, a pair of red Converse high-tops. Besides the sneakers she wore all black, with a trio of spiked cuffs on one arm. From this angle, he couldn't see her implant, though out of curiosity he had tried to look. Her hair was a glossy sheath so dark it nearly matched her shirt. He found her completely striking, but the starkness of her outfit made it difficult for him to come up with a compliment that didn't sound creepy.

You ready? he said instead.
She nodded. He began to walk, and she followed close at his elbow. Too close. Man, she really was a beginner. He drifted toward the middle of the path so there was more space between them. Had she looked disappointed by this, or was that his imagination? Either way she seemed to realize it made it easier to see one another, and kept to her side as they walked.

The campus was divided in halves, with the athletic fields and the administrative building, Clerc Hall, serving as a massive spacer between the upper and lower schools. Lower school students weren't allowed on the upper school side, but upper school students generally had freedom to roam the breadth of the campus, often going down to the lower school for after-school jobs or tutoring gigs. So Austin led them that way first, dipping down the gulley into the soccer fields. Initially unsure of what a tour should be, he just pointed to different buildings—*dorm, classrooms, gym*—but any map could've told her that. To what, exactly, was Headmistress hoping he'd guide her? He led them to the outermost path, a sidewalk that ringed campus just inside the fence, and headed back toward the upper school. The sun was warm and mild. He began to relax and settled into sharing whatever popped into his mind:

*That dorm is named for first
Deaf pro baseball player. Here
students had solidarity demon-
strations with Gallaudet protesters in the eighties. Here I broke
my foot on a pogo stick when I
was nine.*

He stopped in front of his dorm.

This is mine.

Her face changed then, as if a film cleared from her eyes. She hadn't understood anything he'd said, had she?

Yours?

Well just the last thing, then.

Lived on campus since I was six.

Charlie nodded solemnly, but the gleam of her eyes was receding again. He took out his phone.

we live in colson but it's kind of tradition, he wrote. my mom boarded @ her school too.

Wait. Your parents—deaf?

*My mom. And her parents. My
dad's an interpreter.*

u understand? he typed. u look surprised.

Charlie started typing a few different messages, then deleted each of them, all the while her mouth coiling tighter. He slid his palm over the screen.

What? he said.

I—

She sighed, finished typing.

i was just remembering something. how i thought I'd grow up to be hearing b/c i never met a deaf grown-up.

Austin laughed. He wasn't trying to hurt her feelings or anything, but it was all so evil.

happens more than u think, he wrote. Lots of kids show up here thinking same.

Do you ever talk?

What?

Sorry, she said, blushing again.
I mean—

had speech therapy for a while

But?

i'm not very good, he wrote. do u . . . care about that?

No.

i think it's great, she wrote.
She looked at him shyly, and now it was his turn to be embarrassed. It was rare that he was flustered by a compliment, if you could call this one. Charlie seemed to notice that she'd caught him off-guard. She flipped her hair over one shoulder.

O-k, he said. *Cool.*

Candy, she said.

No, c-o-o-l. Cool.

He reached for her hand, bent her finger into the "x" handshape, and guided it back up to her face. Her cheek was tan and silken and he let his hand linger there longer than he meant to, enchanted by the warmth radiating off her skin and across his fingertips.

Cool, she said.

You got a thing for that girl?
Eliot said when Austin
returned.

Eliot pulled his eyes almost reluctantly away from the window, as if Austin had been the one to initiate the conversation.

No. Which one?

The new one. With the spiky bracelets.

Headmistress made me give her a tour, that's all.

"*Made you.*"

Eliot laughed.

She did!

She's cute. You should make a move.

I don't even know her.

Before someone beats you to it. Everyone loves a foreign exchange student.

Why, you gonna make a move?

Eliot rolled his eyes and took a long drag, gestured to the gnarled skin of his face. Here was the problem with an ASL conversation—it required eye contact and afforded little opportunity to hide one's true feelings.

Sorry.

Whatever.

Eliot turned away and exhaled out onto the quad.

What makes you think I like her?

Eliot smirked.

Deaf, not blind, he said.

visual syntax and the art of storytelling

When forming phrases or narratives in ASL, ask yourself: What order makes the most sense visually? If you were to draw the scene on paper, what would you set up first?

Consider translating the sentence "The cup is on the table." First establish your noun, then describe placement or action:

First, the table:

Then, the cup:

Then the placement of the two together in space:

There is some flexibility to word order. For example, some signers might introduce both nouns, "cup" and "table," first, then describe them after.

TEST YOURSELF: When thinking about visual grammar, why does it make sense to share information about the table before the cup?

NOW YOU TRY! Tell your partner about your childhood bedroom.

*t*hings were touch and go in the weeks after the Wandapocalypse, especially when, seventy-two hours post-blowup, February had referred to it as such aloud.

Now see, don't do that, Mel said.

What? she said, trying to look innocent.

Put it on me like I'm crazy.

And it was easy to relapse from there. That was the thing about fights—it only took one big one to deplete the downy layer of goodwill they'd been building for months. They'd had their irksome moments, of course, but nothing that would call into question the underpinnings of their relationship, and with the cushion in place, they could quickly rebound out of a foul mood, or give one another the benefit of the doubt.

But now there was nothing to break their fall. Each little slight—the wrong lilt in a voice, a careless mistake with the laundry—could send them spiraling back to the depths, where Wanda was always waiting. February had posed the question to Mel—what would she have her do? It wasn't as if there were a gaggle of qualified, certified high school science teachers fluent in ASL just lounging around the tri-state, waiting for her call, not to mention that Wanda hadn't even done anything wrong. Mel knew this, but logic had gone the way of goodwill.

So February had moved on to the current tactic—ignoring the problem. She tried throwing herself into work, but as rocky as her home life was, River Valley was running so smoothly even she was surprised. Besides a few tantrums in the lower school and a report that the upper school boys' dorm sometimes smelled of cigarettes, there'd been no infractions. They would catch the smoker soon enough, she wasn't worried. In fact, she was grateful—without him, the semester's calm would be downright suspicious.

She spent afternoons at school writing her new lesson plans, using the course as an excuse to stay late when she normally would have done the work at home. And though she was stoic in the face of Mel's arsenal of jabs (all crafted with a litigator's precision), February began to feel like the recipient of a slow-acting poison, each dose compounding the effects of the last. Still, she ignored it, and she ignored being ignored, until finally one night, after asking Mel what she wanted for dinner and receiving only a glowering look, she broke.

This is so ridiculous! she yelled. Then she laughed the way she was prone to when a situation was so frustrating she could not muster any other response—a wide-eyed cackle that made her look a bit unhinged, though Mel was on record as finding it endearing. That wasn't why February was doing it; she didn't have the acting chops to force herself into a fit for pity points, but Mel looked up from her paper stack, and, eventually, a light welled up in her irises and brimmed over until she was smiling too, albeit with less frenzy.

Come here, said Mel.

February, now with a wheeze and a cramp in her gut, went and put her head in Mel's lap. Mel ran her fingers over February's forehead until she quieted.

Jesus, February said after a while. And to think all I had to do to get you to love me again was have a complete mental breakdown.

I always love you, Feb. It doesn't have an off switch. That's the problem.

I know, she said.

For a while they sat without speaking, something they often did after a big fight, waiting to feel less awkward in the knowledge that they had bared their ugliest, most childish parts to one another.

How's work? February ventured.

Then, the floodgates. They'd been so busy fighting, they'd had little time to talk, and they had a lot to catch up on. Mel detailed her latest cases as they'd played out in family court, each more harrowing than the next. Some were clear-cut instances of child or spousal abuse, but the ones that haunted February were always murkier—stories that left her questioning whether the court's interventions into people's private lives were actually making things worse. When it came to their work, Mel's skin had thickened in a way February's never had, and February was always equal parts surprised and jealous of the nonchalance with which Mel could speak of her cases.

What about you? said Mel. How's your new course coming?

Good, I think. It's nice being back in the classroom.

And the Serrano kid?

Too early to tell, said February.

ear vs. eye: deaf mythology

EYETH—GET IT?

In the Deaf storytelling tradition, utopia is called *Eyeth* because it's a society that centers the eye, not the ear, like here on *Earth*.

In the Deaf world, there's a famous story of a utopian planet where everyone signs and everything is designed for easy visual access. In some tellings, hearing people are the minority and learn to conform to the majority sign language, in others the planet is completely Deaf. Have any of you seen an Eyeth story?

Eyeth may be a pun, but it's not a joke—it's a myth.

MYTH (N):

1. a traditional story that reveals part of the worldview of a people, or embodies the ideals and institutions of a society
2. parable; short fictitious story that illustrates a moral attitude or principle

The importance of Eyeth in Deaf culture is twofold. First, it highlights the things we value: sign language, communication, accessibility, community. It expresses our dreams: equality, a special place to call our own free from the demands of hearing society, recognition of our culture.

Eyeth is also important because it reinforces Deaf culture *as* a culture. Storytelling and myths are an important part of what makes us human and a common thread across all kinds of ethnic groups.

⚲ DID YOU KNOW?

- Deaf scholars have proven that Deafness meets the requirements to be considered an ethnicity.
- Historically this was the common view before oral education nearly eradicated sign languages.

- Even Alexander Graham Bell, who wanted to rid society of deafness, spoke of "a race of Deaf people."

DIY

Work with a partner to design what Eyeth means to you:

1. What Deaf-friendly architecture, technology, or other design elements would you include?

2. How would you manage accessibility for a hearing visitor on Eyeth?

*f*ebruary had run out of dusk by the time she finished stuffing the last of the day's paperwork into her briefcase—a pipe had burst in the lower boys' dorm and the afternoon had gotten away from her. She hoped she would still beat Mel home. She didn't want to do anything that might disturb the new peace they'd established.

Besides the pipe, though, the day had been a good one. She was finally getting back into the swing of teaching (and no longer bungling basic Smartboard commands), and her students had done a good job of imagining Eyeth as a world of clear sight lines: glass buildings with balconies, automatic doors, and wide hallways where two pairs of signing people could pass each other without having to break conversation to squeeze by. Hearing visitors, they'd decided, would be issued glasses that would caption ambient sign in English for them, but for in-depth interaction, they'd have to request an interpreter. Earplugs should also be available for visitors. On Eyeth, they'd said, they would yell when they felt like it, and no one would be embarrassed by their accents or tell them to pipe down. February had laughed at this declaration, and smiled again when she thought of it now. River Valley was already loud, and she tried to imagine what it might be like if none of her students had to spend their nights and weekends tiptoeing around their parents.

February heard her cellphone ring, but it was muffled, and she realized with dismay the sound was coming from the bottom of her freshly packed case. She cursed and thrust an arm into it but no dice. She had to remove most of the papers to free her phone, only to find a number she didn't recognize. Normally she didn't answer unknown callers, but now, having worked so hard to dig the phone out, she figured she might as well.

Hello? she said.

February, said a man on the other end.

The voice was familiar, but she couldn't quite place it.

Yes?

It's Edwin Swall. Sorry, did I call your cell?

You did, sir.

I meant to call the office and leave a message.

No problem, sir.

Anyway, listen, I want us to get something on the calendar.

Yes, sir. Regarding?

Swall cleared his throat.

Some restructuring for next year. Budgetary, et cetera.

Of course, sir.

What's better for you? Tomorrow, or next week?

February glanced at her wall calendar. Monday was clearer, but she didn't want to wait the weekend to find out what was happening. She had heard the word "restructuring" a few times in her career, and it never meant anything good.

I'm free at lunch tomorrow, she said.

Perfect, I'll meet you at the Panera on Oakley. Twelve thirty.

Great, she said.

But there was nothing great about it, not the suddenness of the meeting, nor its vaguely menacing subject matter, and definitely not Panera—that was a real pet peeve of hers. She tried not to let her mind spiral as she walked home in the dark.

You okay? Mel said.

February had gotten home before her, but not by enough to scrub the worry from her face.

Yeah, I'm fine. Just a weird conversation with Swall. He wants to have lunch tomorrow.

Swall, the superintendent?

That's the one.

Did he say why?

Nope.

Well, free lunch at least.

I wouldn't bet on it, February thought.

Speaking of, feel like a pizza? I had those pork chops I wanted to do, but I'm beat.

Sure. You call it in, I'll pick it up, said February, and went to check on her mother.

February? Are you with me?

February blinked, hard.

Of course, sir, she said.

February was finding it difficult to pay attention to anything besides the lumpy drip of New England clam chowder at the center of the superintendent's tie.

You do agree to keep this in confidence? Swall said. It really is of utmost importance.

So far Swall had only made vague intimations of "districtwide shifts," and she was finding it hard to track his through line. She didn't think she could repeat any of what he was saying even if she tried.

Of course, she said.

Good, because I really think you're owed the information early. Due to the nature of your living situation.

What? she said, finally drawing her eyes up from the stain.

Though he'd never done anything to suggest it, February found herself fearful that Swall was about to say something homophobic.

My situation?

Well, you live there, he said.

Where?

On campus.

Technically we're off campus, sir.

Yes, but.

Dr. Swall sighed, leaned in close over his soup. He was going to have to retire that tie.

Look, February. You know I admire your work with those kids. I need you to understand this is not personal.

Sir?

Effective July 1, the district will no longer be able to support River Valley.

February felt what little she'd managed to consume of the baguette turn leaden in her stomach.

I don't understand.

To be honest, the district will be taking a big hit just to finish out the academic year, but we want to prioritize continuity.

February slammed her mug down, coffee sloshing over the sides as Swall hurried to steady their table.

Are you firing me in a Panera right now?

What? Swall looked around, as if to confirm that they were, in fact, still there. He leaned in. I'm not firing you, he whispered. And I'm gonna need you to lower your voice.

What about the kids?

I'm telling you this as a courtesy because of your housing situation. But all further details about the transition will really have to wait until the administrative conference.

You can't do this. There has to be another way.

You know River Valley is by far the most expensive school in the district. The dorms alone—

We could convert to a day school.

—all the rehabilitative programming . . . the teacher-student ratio is smaller than even some of the other special needs classrooms.

You think it's going to be cheaper to mainstream them? The number of interpreters you'll need is going to blow my teachers' salaries out of the water.

We'll be able to return some of the students to their home districts to help defray those costs.

Sure, just ship them back to Kentucky and pretend like it's not your responsibility.

Frankly, February, the out-of-state students *aren't* my responsibility.

Oh my god, February growled. And you call yourself an educator?

I'm trying to do what's best for the entire district here.

You have a responsibility to your most vulnerable students. What about the DeafBlind kids? The ones with other disabilities? This is going to be a disaster.

Again, this really needs to wait until the conference—

February gave Swall a look so dark it halted him midthought. She held his gaze. If he wanted out of the stare, he was the one who'd have to look away. Eventually he did, feigning a cough.

I can't believe you're doing this, she said.

That's not fair. My hands are tied here.

You're right. It's not fair at all.

February, I'm really sorry.

It's Dr. Waters, she said.

She stood and pushed her chair in, hard. It thwacked against the table, sending another slosh of soup at his tie. Leaving Swall to bus her dirty bowl, she stomped out of the restaurant, across the strip mall parking lot, and back to her car, where she turned the radio up and sobbed.

She'd white-knuckled it through the afternoon, most of which she spent listing and crossing out ways she could appeal River Valley's death sentence—maybe she could apply for a grant?—things she knew wouldn't work even as she wrote them down. Then she walked home, and sat beside her mother on the porch as she worked on her knitting, a "scarf" she was making for Mel that February guessed was now about twenty feet long. February waited until she was sure her mother wasn't watching, was looking down to count her stitches, and said aloud:

It's finally happening, Ma. They're closing River Valley.

There, steeped in her mother's silence, she felt a sense of solace, at least for a few minutes. Her mother, satisfied by the count, began a new row.

The night darkened, and February chopped a heap of bell peppers with meticulous fervor. How to tell Mel that she was being laid off, that they would lose their home? How to explain that, for her, the eviction didn't feel like the worst part of the news? She needed time—a few more days to ensure there was absolutely nothing she could do, a little more distance from her and Mel's last blowout to be sure they were on solid ground. Most of all, her mother could not find out. Mel arrived home in high spirits to find February swishing a wok of stir-fry and lavished praise on her for cooking.

Hey, what did Swall want?

February willed herself not to do anything weird with her face.

Oh, you know, she said. Budgetary crap.

Her mother looked up, wanting to be filled in on the conversation.

Meeting with S-w-a-l-l today.

Budget stuff.

Well, if anyone could squeeze soup from a stone it's you, said Mel.

What?

February smiled weakly. Mel turned to her mother.

I think she's Superwoman, said
Mel.

Me too, said her mother.

Mel had drawn an S on her chest like the comic book emblem—the correct sign for "super"—and February wondered whether she had learned it somewhere or had intuited it. Either way, it was the furthest thing from the truth, and she vowed not to let herself wait too long to tell Mel what had really happened, lest she'd have to add "liar" to her ever-growing list of personal failures.

2:34 A.M.—starburst explosion at the foot of the bed. Disoriented, Austin lunged toward his alarm clock before he realized the light was the flasher on their videophone. He fumbled with the remote. A roll of tube socks soared from across the room, pegging him square between the shoulder blades. He spun toward the origin of the projectile, where Eliot was holding one arm in the air signing on a loop: *W-T-F.*

The phone! Austin said.

Though of course, the call would only be for him. When he answered, it was his father in his undershirt, hair askew. Behind him, his mother was sitting in a kitchen chair, breathing heavily and trying to pull on her shoes.

Baby time!

Now? What do I do?

It could be a while. I can pick you up in the morning once the baby's here? Nothing to do in the hospital anyway.

But—

Gotta get Mom in the car before the next contraction. Call you with news!

His father hung up, leaving a screen of dark static.

Sorry. My mom's having the
baby.

Eliot said nothing, and Austin couldn't tell whether he was still awake. He returned to his bed, but he knew there was no chance of sleep. He wanted to be there. He could probably get Walt to take him to the hospital. Walt had been head of security at RVSD for Austin's whole life—he knew Austin's parents, played dominoes with the remains of the Deaf club down in Lexington. Austin pulled on his jeans, crawled beneath his desk to retrieve his sneakers, slipped his wallet and phone in the pouch of his hoodie, and ran down the stairs to the security desk.

Can you call Walt for me? Austin
said.

The guard, a new guy, looked up from his laptop. Then, to Austin's horror, the man began to speak. Shit. Did he seriously not know sign? Austin groaned and reached across the partition for a sticky note.

I need Walt, he wrote. I need to go to hospital.

Are you sick? the guard wrote back.

My mom's having a baby.

That's not an emergency. For <u>you</u>, he wrote.

Just call him! said Austin finally with his voice, a slurry, untamed thing, and loud. He had never progressed beyond lesson one of volume modulation—on or off—and now that came in handy. Startled, the guard pulled the walkie-talkie from his belt and called for backup. Walt pulled up in his golf cart moments later, disheveled, having obviously been asleep in the front tower. Austin ran to meet him at the door.

Mom's having the baby!

Want to go?

Yes! Thank you!

Hop in. We'll take the squad car.

Austin managed a scathing look at the desk guard as they left.

They jumped in the car—a retired cruiser purchased from the

county with the RVSD crest stuck overtop the Colson PD logo. The
sky was navy blue and the roads were empty. Walt was a faster driver
than Austin would have pegged him for. The radio was loud, and he
could feel the beat of the music in the seat leather. Austin's parents
had decided not to find out the baby's sex, but now, staring out the
window, he remembered a scene from an autumn long ago, when he'd
arrived home covered in mud and with a sole torn from his brand-
new sneaker. As his mother fretted, Grandma Lorna patted her
shoulder, laughing and saying, *Thank god I had a girl!* He sent a wish
for a sister into the fading night; his mom deserved a break for once.

When they pulled up to the hospital, Austin saw the unmistakable
outline of his father, his crooked gait loping across the parking lot.

 My dad, he said.

He pointed to the figure and hopped from the car.

 Thank you!

Walt gave him a thumbs-up and Austin took off after his father,
waving his arms, though unwilling to unleash his voice again. He
caught up to him in the vestibule and grabbed his wrist from behind.

How did you—

His father hugged him, a wraparound affair, and Austin was struck
by how much smaller than his dad he still was, despite having grown
too tall for his jeans over the summer. He felt little again, protected,
until his father pulled back and began to jog away.

Tell me later. I gotta go find your
mom!

Austin followed him down the corridor toward the maternity wing,
where his father instructed him to wait. So he sat, his dad running
backward down the hall pointing at him and yelling at the receptionist, He's deaf he's deaf, just so you know. The receptionist seemed
uninterested in the news.

Love you! he said, and disappeared.

Austin settled into the waiting area, empty except for one very liver-spotted man, an expectant grandfather, maybe. They were all the same, these rooms: TV in the corner flashing out a cooking show, floor overwaxed as if to offer up proof of cleanliness, the saucerlike reflections of the lights in the tiles. He had seen many waiting rooms over the years—audiologist appointments, mostly, the casting and recasting of ear molds for the hearing aids inserted into his rapidly growing head until all hope of capturing residual hearing had finally been lost.

He sifted through a stack of magazines, the kind that exist only in doctors' offices. All of them were either adult in the worst way—*Health Today, Gentleman's Golf*—or too childish. It was the problem with everything these days. Books, clothes, television shows, he was between them all. He still took comfort in the cartoons he'd grown up watching, though he never mentioned them to anyone, ashamed that his preferences had not automatically matured upon his matriculation to the upper school. But it was the middle of the night, and beside the old man there was no one else in the room. He picked up the *Highlights*. What's Wrong with This Picture? What's Wrong with This Picture? After a while, all the pictures started to look ridiculous. *What* is *wrong with having different-size buttons on your coat,* Austin thought, and put the magazine back down. He fell asleep sideways in an extrawide chair and awoke to his father standing over him.

Baby's here! Want to come see?

Boy or girl, which? Austin said, groggy.

Surprise, his father said. Austin followed and found his mother sitting up in bed holding a bundle of pink, and he felt light-headed—a girl! The fates had gone easy on his mother after all.

Want? his mother said with her free hand, pointing to the baby.

His excitement was quickly replaced by apprehension. He had never seen so new a baby up close.

Sure, Austin felt himself sign.

He wasn't sure. What if he broke her? He sat down in the chair beside his mother's bed while his father transferred the baby into the crook of his arm.

Support her head, his mother
said.

So red and wrinkly, and smelling of soap. So, so small. Austin felt something inside him open, a fullness in his heart beyond the pride of a good grade or leading role, more satisfying even than lying naked beneath Gabriella's sheets at her parents' Memorial Day cookout. He would protect this tiny person squinting back at him. His sister.

Her name what? Austin asked
after a while, when he could
bring himself to look away
from the baby.

*S–k–y–l–a–r. You'll see when she
wakes, her eyes—so big and blue.*

Skylar. Austin knew no one else with the name; it was a word he'd never spelled before. He tested it out, feeling the way the letters rolled across his hand like an ocean wave. He'd learned in science class once that babies' eyes could change color as they got older, but the name felt sweet on his fingers so he said nothing.

Hi S–k–y, he said to the baby,
though she slept. *Welcome.*

Eventually his mother fell asleep and Austin gave the baby back to his father.

Pretty amazing, right?

So small. Doesn't seem real.

*She's a good size for two weeks
early. You weren't much bigger.*

Austin tried to imagine his own first hours, his parents a decade and a half younger and having their first child. Had he been born in this hospital? He assumed so, though he'd never asked.

Skylar woke and cried; his father woke his mother to feed her; a nurse appeared and had a terse conversation with his father that Austin couldn't follow.

What'd she say?

What'd she say?

Austin and his mother both looked to his father as the nurse scooped up the baby and took her down the hall. His father sighed.

What? said his mother. *Don't make me nervous.*

She wanted to know how you would hear the baby cry.

Oh for fuck's sake.

His mother smiled, relieved—Austin, too, had been expecting something worse.

She's just taking her for her standard screenings.

I don't understand how nurses can be so ignorant after all that school!

What'd you tell her?

That we have more flashing alarms in our house than a fire station. That deaf people have been raising children for thousands of years.

And she should mind her own damn business?

I can tack that on when she comes back if you want.

They laughed, and Austin found all his anxiety about the new baby melt away. They turned on the television and watched the morning

news—morning! He had completely lost track of time. He was supposed to be in math class.

> Don't worry. I'll write you a
> note.

Hopefully Walt remembers to tell
the office.

> Here. His father pulled out his
> wallet. Go find the vending ma-
> chine. Breakfast Cheetos?

No Cheetos! It's 8:00 A.M.

> Or hot fries!

Austin took the money and bounded down the hall with a goofy
smile on his face. He bought Cheetos and pork rinds, and returned
to find Skylar back in his mother's arms. The nurse had said something his father was on the tail end of interpreting, and whatever it
was left his mother blanched and his father flushed—his body vi-
brating with an energy Austin didn't recognize. The nurse brushed by
Austin and left.

Everything o-k?

> Yup, his father said. Nurse was
> explaining test results.

All good?

> Perfect.

Austin thumbs-upped the news but could tell something was wrong.
His mother's brow was furrowed, her lips drawn inward.

He raised an *And?* eyebrow.

> Well—

Baby's hearing, said his mother.

Oh.

There was a saying in the Deaf community: passing the hearing
screening was called "flunking the deaf test," a joke to counter all
those times parents had been apologized to, told that their infants
were already failures. But at first it didn't seem like such a big deal to
Austin. His father was hearing, he loved his father, he signed all the

time, and there was no question the baby would too. Plenty of hearing CODAs—children of deaf adults—were fluent, native signers, like Headmistress Waters. Then, surveying his dad again, his ruddy complexion, the smile he was trying so unsuccessfully to conceal even now, Austin understood.

Wait—that's *why you're so happy?*

What?

Austin pointed an accusatory finger at him.

"Perfect," right?

I didn't mean it like that.

How did you mean it?

But Austin allowed only a moment of false-start responses before he pulled a move he hadn't since he was a small child—he stomped out of the room, slid down to the hallway floor with his back to the wall, knees pulled to his chest, and squeezed his eyes shut, blocking out the foot traffic, the horrible fluorescent lights, his father's secret hopes and dreams laid bare, and his flawless baby sister, who had, in a few short hours of life, already taken down more than a century of family tradition.

a month and a half in, Charlie had hit a wall, and not just in the figurative sense. Things had been going well for a while—between night classes and the 24/7 exposure, her conversational ASL had made great strides, and she'd even gotten a B+ on an algebra test. But on Wednesday night, as they were getting into bed, Kayla said something Charlie didn't understand, and when Charlie asked her to repeat it, she rolled her eyes and said the phrase that was the bane of Charlie's existence: *forget it.*

In English, it was usually "never mind," but the message and the feeling were the same: you are not worth the trouble. By morning Kayla was her regular self and had forgotten the forget it, but Charlie could not—not when she again sat alone at lunch, or when Headmistress Waters handed back their first essay assignment and Charlie saw that she'd earned a D on that paper, and especially not when, moments later, Headmistress called on her to answer a question she hadn't even seen asked.

I don't know, she said, motioning to the essay on her desk that
had been holding her attention.
But Headmistress wouldn't let it go, waved her up to the board. Charlie stood, hesitated.

Hurry it up.

I'm going, she said.

You don't have to be a bitch about it.

Excuse me?

Shit. Had she said that aloud? She had forgotten Headmistress Waters could hear.

Nothing?

Out.

And Charlie got out, except that she was so mad she just stood outside the classroom and kicked the wall until her big toe went numb and Headmistress poked her head into the hall and pointed toward the vestibule.

My office. Now!

Charlie walked down to Clerc and paced the waiting area of the main office, despite the headmistress's secretary's repeated attempts to get her to sit down.

She's teaching right now, said
the secretary.

I know, said Charlie.

I fucking know.

If the secretary heard her, she made no acknowledgment. Charlie didn't care. She would've said it to someone's face. She was jittery, charged up—it was special ed all over again.

After a while, Headmistress appeared and motioned her into the back office. Charlie stood before the behemoth oak desk, shuffling from foot to foot, head as low as she could hang it without obscuring her vision.

What was that? said Headmistress.

Nothing.

You didn't call me a bitch?

Charlie shook her head halfheartedly.

Please sit down.

Charlie sat.

To be honest, said Headmistress, I've been expecting this.

You have?

Well, not this exact thing, but . . . Look.

Headmistress scrawled two lines on a legal pad and turned it around so Charlie could see: Language deprivation.

> *Language deprivation,* she
> signed. *Heard of it?*

Charlie shook her head. Headmistress went back to the pad, wrote more: Humans learn their first language by around age five. If not, it can cause problems.

She put down her pen and tapped her temple.

Up here, she said.

Great, said Charlie.

> *It's rare to be in your position
> and have zero behavioral*
>
> ————.

What?

> *S-y-m-p-t-o-m-s.*

You think I'm language deprived?

> *Do you?*

Charlie thought about her spells, about the Quiet Room, the anger Kayla's brush-off had reignited.

I don't know.

> *I don't know, either. But I know
> you've had to work too hard to
> communicate.*

No kidding, Charlie thought.

> *You need to be patient with your-
> self,* she said. *Language doesn't
> just happen.*

What if it's too late?

I've seen too late. You're not it.

Even though it was probably just a thing teachers were supposed to say, something about the swiftness with which the Headmistress had answered made Charlie believe her.

> BUT. *That doesn't mean you can flip out at your teachers.*

Charlie nodded.

Guidance counselor next three Wednesdays, 3:00 P.M., she wrote on the pad.

> *Understood?*

Yes.

> *And. One other thing.*

Charlie bit her tongue.

> *I want you in an after-school activity. Drama Club.*

Charlie shook her head.

> *Winter play. They're doing P-e-t-e-r P-a-n.*

A play? No way.

Not a suggestion, Headmistress said.

I'm no actress, said Charlie.

> *You can be _____ _____.*

What?

> *S-t-a-g-e c-r-e-w. Stage crew.*

Stage crew?

> *Work backstage.*

But what if I mess it up?

> *You can't mess up stage crew.*

I guess.

> *Again, not optional.*

Right. O-k.

The end of day bell flashed above Headmistress's desk.

And I never want to see that kind of name-calling again. Not in any language.

O-k.

Headmistress gestured with her head to the bell.

Go on then.

Charlie thanked her and stood, began her walk back toward the upper school—she'd left her books on her desk in the history classroom. She was embarrassed, but it could've been worse. The headmistress had gone easy on her, and she hoped most of the other students hadn't caught what she'd said. And though she'd been resistant, the idea of the drama club did intrigue Charlie. Being part of a club of any kind at Jefferson, especially theater, would've been impossible. But here it was different. Maybe one day she could even be *on* the stage—what might her mother think of that?

She walked up the path toward her dorm, still mulling over an alternate life in which she and her mother shared an interest in performing, a daydream so absorbing that she passed right by her actual mother, the white Volvo parked in the loading zone.

Charlie!

Her mother had thrust her upper body out the car window and was now waving frenetically.

What are you doing here?

Nice to see you, too.

Sorry, Charlie signed.

What?

SORRY! she yelled.

Charlie, relax.

Sorry. Hi.

Get in, we're going to be late.

Late?

Your implant checkup? It took me a while to get past that security guard! I mean, you'd think it was Fort Knox.

Isn't it good for a school to have security?

Of course. Her mother sighed. Will you just get in the car? Charlie got in, and her mother drove them back toward the main gates.

We're doing a winter play, said Charlie, trying to fill the silence as they waited for the guard to check her mother's ID. I'm going to be stage crew.

She decided not to mention that the activity was compulsory.

A play, said her mother. That'll be something.

Something?

Her mother looked up at the pair of old oaks that shaded the security booth.

It's very pretty here, she said.

It is, said Charlie, and tried to hide the uncertainty on her face.

Colson Children's Hospital was a colossus, but a familiar one, and Charlie knew where everything was without even looking at the signs. She and her mother checked in at the Implant Center, and Charlie leaned in close to the receptionist's window.

CAN I REQUEST THE INTERPRETER ON CALL, PLEASE?

What's with the megaphone voice? her mother said.

Charlie shrugged, but realized that at school no one had told her to be quiet in weeks.

I'll see if he's still here, the receptionist said.

What do you want an interpreter for? said her mother.

So I can understand the doctor.

The receptionist picked up the phone.

The interpreter sat in a folding chair in the center of the exam room, and as the doctor and her mother exchanged pleasantries, Charlie felt almost gleeful; she was slowly becoming accustomed to signing with other deaf people, but she had never had an interpreter before. Now she could focus all her attention on this one man in his rumpled blue shirt—no guessing or ping-ponging between mouths. This, she thought, much more than the filament in her head, must be what it was like to hear.

Charlie introduced herself to the interpreter, showed him her sign name with pride. He dabbed at a milky stain on his tie, apologized, said he had a new baby at home. The doctor shuffled through her chart and Charlie's mother sat with her hands in her lap, looking stricken.

When the doctor began to speak, the interpreter's demeanor shifted abruptly. He sat straighter, cleared his face of the small degree of familiarity they'd cultivated in their initial conversation. It was uncanny how he could empty himself, create space to be inhabited by another.

S-o Charlie, tell me what's been going on?

The doctor did a double take as the interpreter signed his question.

I feel something, b-u-z-z, inside my head, said Charlie.

She watched her words on the interpreter's lips. Her voice cradled inside this man's voice.

I get headaches.

Is the sound different than before?

I think worse.

Worse how?

Like, blurry.

The interpreter shifted in his chair, pinched his lips together.

Like, underwater? her mother's question, brusque on the interpreter's fingertips.

I don't know. I've never heard underwater.

Nobody said anything for a second after that.

All right, let's run some tests.

The doctor said something into his intercom; his assistant appeared and Charlie was ushered into the sound booth for the standard panel. She raised her hand in response to a series of beeps, repeated words back out into the room—"Baseball. Airplane."—shrugged when they got too muddled to tell apart. It was perhaps the most asinine medical exercise in which Charlie had ever participated (and that was saying something). What did it matter whether she could hear a beep funneled directly into her head in a soundproof room? Or discern among the same ten words they'd been using on her since she was toilet-trained? It was nothing like real listening, and the results were predictably useless.

> _____ is the same. Speech
> _____ is slightly below your
> regular levels.

Speech what? Charlie said, and looked to the doctor.
DIS-SCRIM-IN-ATION, he mouthed dramatically.

> So, it's working? said her
> mother.

It never worked!

> Probably normal "w–e–a–r and
> t–e–a–r." This wire here looks a
> little frayed. We can order a new
> _____. Should take maybe
> three weeks.
> Weeks? Don't they make them at
> that place right down the road?

No rush, said Charlie. I don't
need it.

> I can see that.

The interpreter signed it straight, without a hint of condescension, but Charlie wondered. Her mother glared.

What do you want from me, it's broken! Charlie said aloud.

> You can keep wearing this one
> while you wait. _____ will
> book your follow-up, but it should
> be a quickie. I'll _____ in your
> most recent M–A–P and we can
> tweak from there.

Charlie made the interpreter spell out then repeat the signs she didn't know, just as Headmistress Waters had done.

Receptionist. Program.

She copied them on a loop, logging them into her memory. The doctor handed back her processor and she reattached it to her head, watched her mother and him exchange thank-yous (no, thank you!). The interpreter winked on the way out.

Charlie felt the absence of sign as a hollow inside her as soon as they left the exam room. That was probably the most she'd understood a multiperson exchange ever, in any language. By the time they'd booked her next appointment, exasperation had grown in the empty space and, forgetting she should take charge of the route back to the parking garage, she followed her mother, whose woeful sense of direction brought them to the wrong elevator bay. They landed in the hospital's decorative vestibule, each enlarged photo of a smiling miracle child salt in her wound. Out on the sidewalk she got her bearings, reset their course back toward the car.

Hey, slow down a sec, said her mother. Do you wanna get some, uh, coffee or something?

She gestured to the Starbucks across the street. When Charlie was a kid, her mother had purchased her cooperation at these appointments with the promise of ice cream, and now Charlie wanted to reject this offer of consolation coffee on principle, but her mother looked genuinely upset, so Charlie nodded and they jaywalked over.

She considered the strip of shops before her that made up Northeast Colson—fast-food joints, cellphone stores, a dollar store, and a kitchen supply shop. It was a part of the city they usually bypassed, launching straight from the garage back to the highway. Charlie had often fantasized about moving to a big city, someplace with a view and a body of water grander than the sluggish brown Ohio River. Mainly, she wanted somewhere she might blend in. Here, people on the street sometimes did a double take at the hardware on her head, which embarrassed her almost as much as it did her mother. But no one in a place like New York would give a fuck about the wire protruding from her hair, or her wonky voice, not with actually interesting people—artists, models, celebrities, naked cowboys, and creepy off-brand Sesame Street characters—to look at. Anonymity was what she craved most, she thought, as they entered the Starbucks.

Though it appealed to her conceptually, she still didn't like the taste of coffee, so she ordered a Frappuccino, hoping that the ice and sugar would sufficiently mask the bitter undercurrent, then stood at the counter absently fingerspelling the drink list while they waited.

You're getting good at that—she lifted her hand—stuff, Charlie's mother said as they claimed a small table by the window. Her mother had a knack for the backhanded compliment. Charlie had watched her level acquaintances at WASP parties like Serena at Wimbledon.

Sign language, Charlie said.

Yes, well.

ASL.

Look, I understand why you're frustrated.

Gee, thanks.

But you have to be reasonable. It could've gone a different way.

Meaning? Charlie stabbed at the icy chunks in her cup.

It's not like we got you implanted to torture you. It was supposed to be a good thing. It could have worked.

Charlie nodded, now chewing her straw with vigor. It was a time-worn conversation. And somewhere in her depths, Charlie did know her mother's intentions were good. But as it happened, it hadn't been a good thing, not by any of their standards; it had been one tiny disaster after another. And now she'd have to start again—new processor, old tedium of calibration and the accompanying headache—all because her mother couldn't let it go. There was no point fighting it. She was her parents' possession for another two years, a voodoo doll on which to exorcise their sorrows. She pushed back from the table and stamped outside. She was only headed back to the car, but she needed to put some distance between herself and her mother.

The doctor said those wires fray all the time, said her mother as they got back in the car. Maybe a new processor will make a difference.

Charlie said nothing, looked out the window as they drove out of Colson, hurtling past Edge Bionics as they went. The plant made all kinds of prosthetics, including CI components—perhaps her next processor was being forged in there right this second. She wondered if her mother ever thought of the factory's proximity to their home as an omen the way she sometimes did, if her mother gleaned serendipity from what Charlie had always read as inescapable menace. Edge had painted their name in blocky navy blue, but beneath it, she could still make out the faded outline where Goodyear's logo had been, where the brick was bright red and clean from years of having been shielded by those big, cursive sheet metal letters. What other little cities had seen a fate like this, Edge fleshing out the skeletons of old warehouses and industrial towns, wielding the shiny hope of a new future?

She glanced at her mother, who was staring resolutely at the road in front of them. They returned to the highway, the cityscape quickly dissolving into townhomes, subdivisions.

Don't forget to take me back to school, said Charlie.

I know.

It's Exit Three.

I know.

It's on the left.

Please, Charlie. I know how to drive.

Her mother pushed up her sunglasses and rubbed the bridge of her nose. Charlie picked at a hangnail and thought about how unfair it was that she could be deaf and still bothered by awkward silences.

I thought you'd be happy about the play, she said after a while.

What makes you think I'm unhappy? said her mother.

*a*ustin spent the weekend at home vacillating between love for his sister and a growing disillusionment with his father, whom he watched curate playlists of children's songs on his phone, shush and whisper things as he rocked Skylar to sleep. Austin fumed and cranked up the TV's volume as far as it would go. Sky cried.

His mother, who'd managed to circumvent the subject of Skylar's hearing in the initial videophone conversation with her parents, was now exhibiting her own brand of frenzy in the face of their imminent arrival—trying to cook though she definitely should have been resting.

If you keep opening the oven that bird will never cook, his father said.

Great, dinner canceled! she said.

Please go sit down. Austin will take care of it.

His father gestured to the green beans cans on the counter. Austin twisted the opener around a can, thinking about whether one day Skylar might explain to him what kind of noise the puncturing of metal made. He wondered if his mom had a plan for how to break it to his grandparents. He wondered if she had regrets. But for all the intimacy of ASL, and the emotional umbilical that Austin still often felt between them—mother and son bonded in silence—he could not bring himself to ask her. Instead he dumped the beans in a pot and took the cans out to the bin in the garage.

He saw his grandparents pull in the driveway and considered whether he should just blurt it out and be done with it, but they emerged from the car so happy to see him—their bright dentured grins, the suffocating hug from Grandpa Willis, and a cloying, perfumed one from Grandma Lorna—cowardice quickly won out. Surely his mother was better equipped to handle it.

As it turned out, Skylar would break the news herself. Austin, tasked with retrieving the gifts his grandparents had bought for Skyler from their car, let the screen door slam and Skylar winced and began to cry. Grandma Lorna noticed right away. Having come from a hearing family, she had cared for her siblings as babies, all the while carrying a piece of them within her, a genetic time bomb she knew was bound to surface eventually. Austin had been her great reprieve, and for fifteen years, her daughter had not tempted fate or Punnett squares to reveal another variation on the family DNA. Now, though, Lorna was giving Austin and his mother a knowing look, and neither of them could dodge it.

Grandpa Willis, on the other hand, had never studied a hearing infant for any length of time and didn't catch on, though after a minute even he could tell something was off with everyone else.

What's wrong?

Hearing, Grandma Lorna said,

and pointed at Sky.

True biz?

Austin's mother nodded. Austin braced himself. But Grandpa Willis only leaned in close over the bassinet.

Congratulations, S-k-y, he said.

You won the easy life.

Then he went outside and smoked two cigarettes, one right after the other, and none of them mentioned it for the rest of the evening.

That night, when Austin got into bed, he finally opened a text from the new girl asking what he was up to. Just a few days ago he would have found this thrilling, but now he couldn't bring himself to answer, or even just apologize for not answering, though the message had come through the day before. What could he say by way of explanation? That he'd thought his life was perfect but now that he had a hearing sister it suddenly wasn't? He thought of Gabriella, started writing to her, but stopped halfway through. Even if she would understand the value of their intergenerational deafness, it wasn't her he wanted to talk to. In the end he wrote to neither girl, stuck his phone on the charger, took out his chemistry textbook, and fell asleep doing Sybeck's homework.

His father dropped him off at school Monday and Austin pushed through the morning. He hadn't ended up writing back to Charlie, but he had been looking forward to seeing her, and so he was disappointed when she didn't turn up at lunch.

He couldn't bring himself to tell his friends about Skylar's hearing, though he wasn't quite sure what he was afraid of. It was no secret that his family history was what made him popular or, at the very least, why everyone on campus knew who he was, but did he really think they liked him *only* for this reason? He zoned out through the afternoon, was inordinately angry to find that he'd left his homework for Sybeck on his bed at home, though he knew his father would probably be on campus for a job at some point this week, and would bring it if he asked. What a waste of a day. He returned to his room after last period, letting the door swing wide and smack against the back of Eliot's desk chair. Though Austin had rushed out of the upper school building, Eliot had still beat him home and was lounging on his bed messing around on his phone.

Hey. Eliot waved without looking up.

Austin plopped down on his bed but couldn't relax. He stared across the room at the bare wall, at the pack of cigarettes on top of Eliot's dresser. His roommate wasn't even bothering to hide them, which was annoying—if there were dorm checks they'd both get in trouble. Of course, dorm checks *were* at the same time every night, it wasn't exactly rocket science. Austin got up and examined the pack, pulled a cigarette from it.

Can I have this? he said.

Before Eliot could say anything, he tucked it behind his ear like he'd seen in movies.

Sure?

Thanks.

Where you going?

Out.

O-k, badass.

Shut up, said Austin.

He pushed open their window and stepped out into the hedgerow.

*f*ebruary was crossing the quad after a meeting with the secondary school teachers when she came upon her semester's great mystery—the smoker! She heard him first, a hacking from behind the boys' dorm. This was always how the kids got caught—sounds they didn't think to stifle. Catching them that way felt like cheating sometimes, until she remembered she was in charge.

Around the back of the building, she was shocked to find Austin Workman doubled over coughing, a cigarette heavy with ash perched precariously between two fingers. When he saw her shadow, he jerked upright and she put her hands in a "surrender" position, as one might move toward a scared animal. She was thick around the gut and approaching middle age, no match for this lanky boy if he took off. Then she'd have to summon security, file a report, call his parents, all things she wanted to avoid almost as much as he did.

February fancied herself somewhat of an administrative progressive, at least for Colson. Teenagers got a bad rap, she thought, because people didn't understand why they were so volatile. The problem, February had decided, was a simple lack of language. The vocabulary and logic that had served them in childhood were inadequate in the face of new and much more complex challenges and emotions. The teen years were, in effect, a second-wave terrible twos.

To combat these high-grade tantrums, February had instated the

True Biz policy as a way to get the students to talk to her when they were up to no good. The implication was that she'd soften their consequences if they told her about *why* they'd done whatever they had; she'd probably dole out the same punishments either way, but they didn't need to know that. Besides, she'd almost never had a chance to test it—kids always wanted to explain themselves.

In the moments it'd taken for February to approach, Austin had regained composure and crushed the cigarette beneath his sneaker.

What are you doing here so late?

Being the boss knows no limits.

When she was younger, February had considered "boss" and "champion" ASL rhymes, because of their matching handshapes; these days the similarities between "boss" and "burden" were much more apparent.

Real question is what are you
doing?

True biz?

He said it like an informant who'd agreed to go "off the record" and wanted to confirm his deal was still in place. She nodded.

Go ahead.

My mom had the baby. A girl.
S–k–y–l–a–r.

Heard from Walt. All healthy
and good?

Yeah, healthy.

Congratulations!

Austin said nothing.

And this inspired you to suck poi-
son into your lungs . . . why?

He looked at his feet.

You know, it tends to be cigars
men smoke when a baby is born.

She's hearing, the baby.

February tried her best to remain expressionless at this news. It was an almost comical reversal from the hearing parents who often appeared in her office, despairing about having a deaf child. But the Workman clan was somewhat mythical in the Deaf community, the playing out of a great sociolinguistic isolationist fantasy. And now—

> *My dad. He talks to her. Sings and everything.*

The baby will be bilingual, like you.

> *I never learned lipreading. I'm the worst in the whole class!*

You read and write English, though. And S-k-y-l-a-r will sign.

> *I can't understand when he talks.*

February was torn between hugging Austin and reminding him that this was how nearly all his peers felt at home. She decided to do both. Austin didn't try to shrug her off like some other kids might. He was attentive as she reminded him that his whole family was still fluent in ASL, that CODAs still counted as "big D" Deaf, and whether or not Skylar could hear didn't change anything. Of course, whether he believed her was another thing entirely. She wasn't even sure she believed herself.

At some point, it occurred to her that Austin was probably not the smoker she'd been seeking. His had been the dry, urgent cough of an amateur. The snitch code at any residential school was ironclad, never mind the additional wagon circling of the Deaf world. There was no way he'd tell her who the real culprit was. But what kind of headmistress would she be if she didn't try?

Two weeks cafeteria cleanup. One if you tell me who's been smoking in the dorm.

> *Bummed this from a guy at the mall,* he said without missing a beat.

It's a fire hazard.

> *Sorry, don't know.*

So his roommate, February thought, sighed. She did not want to have to punish the Quinn boy, not after everything he'd been through. And she'd specifically paired the two as roommates because she'd pegged Austin as most impervious to influence when Eliot's rebellion inevitably appeared. But perhaps that wasn't fair of her. She had set him up, in a way.

O-k. Two weeks then.

> *You won't call my parents?*

Not this time, she said. *This is your warning.*

Austin thanked her, but stayed standing, unsure what to do next.

Go on then, she said, then gestured toward the cigarette under his foot. *And throw that out.*

She watched him go, then pulled out her cell. What would a boy like Austin do next year at a school like Jefferson, or Covington High? Would the Workmans send him over to St. Rita, or to live with relatives so he could board up north or out-of-state? Either way, his world was going to be shattered, there was no way around it. She was relieved on baby Skylar's behalf, though she felt guilty even as the thought was forming. But what was she supposed to do—pretend like hearing kids' lives *weren't* easier than deaf ones'?

Which reminded her, she still had to deal with Serrano. February had been gentle with her, too, but she had no illusions that a stint in Drama Club would have magic rehabilitative properties. And anyway, whether or not the girl went around calling her a "bitch" was the least of her worries—Charlie wasn't the first and she wouldn't be the last. There was still the matter of her academics. February would have to put in a call to Victor Serrano. They would have to formulate a plan.

figuratively speaking

💡 **DID YOU KNOW?** Like any language, ASL has idioms that, in context, can mean something different from the denotations of the signs and handshapes of which they are constructed.

SIGN	ASL-ENGLISH GLOSS	MEANING
	train go sorry	missed the boat
	many question marks	your guess is as good as mine no idea
	closed small c or x handshape	cool
	lump in throat	embarrassing cringeworthy

	innocent plus	old-fashioned
		uptight
		square
	finish touch	been there
		went
		have visited
	swallow fish	gullible
	true biz/true business	seriously
		literally
		deadass
		no kidding
		real talk

*C*harlie was eager to put the rocky week behind her. At Jeff she'd always looked forward to the weekend, a break from school and its sounds, but by Thursday afternoon, she noticed some of the others were organizing to meet downtown for ice cream, or forging signatures on permission slips to stay at one another's houses, and found herself wanting more time with her classmates.

Want to meet up this weekend?
she asked Kayla that night.

Can't. We're going down to KY.
My cousin's wedding.

O-k, cool.
Charlie could feel her face burning pink—she was not one to put herself out there. Kayla undoubtedly noticed, too, because after a minute she said:

Maybe another time?
Yeah, definitely, Charlie said.
Emboldened by the exchange, she woke Friday morning determined to tag along to wherever Austin might be headed to that weekend, but he wasn't at lunch, and when she finally caved and texted, he didn't answer. Afterward, she felt embarrassed that she had messaged him at all. It wasn't like they were friends; he was literally assigned to

be nice to her. As she sat alone on the couch in her father's apartment, her thoughts returned to Kyle.

Kyle was tall, gangly, nondescript, and when it came down to it, she knew little else about him—he'd been a supersenior when she was a freshman, and they'd had no mutual friends or classes together, had crossed paths only in study hall. Part of her knew she was too young to be with him, and knew that *he* knew this, but another part of her didn't care, and study hall had offered some plausible deniability. It was unusual for a freshman to be in study hall at all—Charlie was an exception, since it alternated with her speech therapy and reading tutor appointments—so maybe Kyle just assumed she was an upperclassman.

For Charlie's part, people rarely noticed her, and never in a positive way. Strictly speaking, Kyle wasn't her first. She had exchanged rations of her self-worth for protection, or to be left alone, mainly on her knees in darkened classrooms and custodians' closets. Though none of the encounters were pleasant, there had also been moments in which she'd felt powerful, to have something someone else wanted so intensely.

With Kyle it was different. She'd been ecstatic when he first started paying attention to her. Their exchanges had been genuinely friendly, then flirty—him holding her arm tenderly as he markered silly stick figure doodles on her skin. The more time they spent together—mostly hooking up and getting stoned on the couch in his basement—the clearer it'd become that they had almost nothing in common, and that her excitement about being with him would've probably been the same whoever it was, as long as he was nice to her. And Kyle was nice enough, despite his proclivity for referring to them as "fuck buddies." They'd met up from time to time throughout the year until, she presumed, he graduated. She'd messaged him once or twice over the summer, but never heard back.

She knew she shouldn't text him now, tried to convince herself that River Valley was her chance to leave Jefferson and all it stood for behind. She spent Saturday night in an Instagram rabbit hole, scrolling through the feeds of old classmates, friending new River Valley ones. At certain points their feeds were indistinguishable— peace-sign-wielding girls posing for selfies in crop tops, football games and cheer squads and smoothies—and then every once in a while she was jarred from the mindlessness of the exercise when an RVSD student posted a video, their signing bright and sloppy and still largely much too fast for her to understand. She passed out around midnight and woke early, dead phone still in hand. She plugged it in and watched its revival—still nothing from Austin— then shuffled out of her room and into the kitchen.

Morning, said her father.

The kitchen smelled sweet from her dad's famous French toast. Charlie sat down and let her father pile three slices onto a plate in front of her, which made her feel little again, and also a little spoiled. She wondered what Kayla's house looked like.

Let's go for lunch later?

Yeah, great, she said.

But her father, a workaholic, returned to his desk and stayed hunkered down long past lunchtime. He'd told her more than once that he always wrote his best code on the weekends, when no one else was around to interrupt his flow with questions. So she left him to it, made herself a peanut butter sandwich, and pulled up Kyle's number. Maybe she could at least get more weed.

hey, she said.

C! glad u messaged. just about to ditch this phone. how u been? how's jeff?

dunno. transferred.

U move?

No, going to deaf school.

right on. I'm in east colson now.

wanna meet up?

have a show tonite . . . u should come tho!

A show, Charlie thought. She couldn't remember Kyle having played an instrument. Then again, she hadn't asked.

the gas can at 7. it's on vine.

ok, she said.

She flicked on the television, half-watching as she weighed her options. She eventually settled on a classic tactic from the Divorced Parents Playbook: she told her dad she was going to visit her mother and would go straight from there to school the next morning.

You're staying at your mom's . . . on purpose? he said.

Charlie shrugged.

I'm helping with Junior Miss Ohio costumes, she said.

Have you been eating those laundry detergent tablets? I saw that on the news.

Charlie rolled her eyes and told him she would take the bus—this part was true, technically—then took the SORTA over to East Colson.

She disembarked in the parking lot of a casino, nauseous from the bus's sway and heavy brake. It was already dark out, and though she didn't want to admit it, Charlie was afraid. It wasn't that she'd been fed a diet of six o'clock news horror stories by her high-strung mother—well, it wasn't *only* that—what felt scarier was all the empty bits, where there was no one around at all. The stretch of Vine between the shops in Colson Center and the Gas Can was an expansive ruin. Even though she knew that just two streets over, hipsters were lining up for BBQ and microbrews, here was block after block of buildings boarded, sealed, and posted with neon No Trespassing edicts. The plywood was painted with candy-colored windows and doors and flower boxes, like a defunct gingerbread village—someone's well-intentioned attempt at manufacturing cheer had quickly devolved into a metaphor for the city's failures: surface-level disguise for decaying foundations.

Charlie had not been alive for the riots, but she knew about them, or of them; all through her childhood, East Colson would routinely make the list of Ohio's most dangerous neighborhoods, and talking heads would appear on TV to point fingers. There were always re-newal projects—tax abatements that enticed the breweries, the bion-ics plant, and that casino testing the waters. There were even rumors that an apartment complex not unlike her father's was in develop-ment. Though most of the night's more illicit activities had now been pressed out against the city's seams, the disquiet remained in this boneyard of row homes.

When she got to the Gas Can it looked closed, with only a few teenagers and their smoke cloud out front, but the door opened when she pulled it, and inside there were a few promising signs suggesting a concert: a bar with stools and hanging lamps and booths around the perimeter, a shuttered window with COAT CHECK spray-painted opposite, and a plastic table with a pair of cardboard boxes, off which someone had ripped a flap and written T-SHIRTS $15. Charlie walked by the bar and through a set of black doors, which led to a large room with a stage at its front, also empty. A black sheet hung across the back wall, THE ROBESPIERRES! scrawled in uneven white paint across it.

She looked at her phone—it was 7:06. Two boys appeared—one with shaggy hair, the other with a mohawk—together heaving a huge black amplifier across the stage. Surely she was in the wrong place if the stage wasn't even set. She turned to leave, but she could see the shaggy boy had spotted her. He shielded his eyes against the spotlight and called:

Hey! You know seven means eight, right?

The mohawked boy snickered.

I was, uh, looking for Kyle?

The boys shared a glance, then busted out laughing.

Oh shit! said the shaggy one.

Is he here?

The boy jumped down from the stage.

Did you say "Kyle"?

She nodded.

Oh SHIT!

The mohawked boy, still onstage, was now doubled over with his hands on his knees. The boy beside Charlie turned and said something to him she couldn't see. Dicks, she thought, and shuffled back toward the swinging doors. He gripped her shoulder.

No no, he said. He's waiting for you.

Slash! The boy shouted toward the wings and devolved into laughter again as he pulled Charlie up the steps to a greenroom off the side of the stage.

Inside, the room was dim and hazy with smoke. A girl with short blue hair looked Charlie up and down with a gaze so searing Charlie felt preemptively embarrassed for the uncool things she was bound to do that night.

Your jailbait's here, the girl said.

The boy who had been Kyle looked up from a tangle of wires and smiled. He was recognizable around the eyes, but little else about him was as she remembered. He was much skinnier, but his clothes were also tighter, his hair longer and greasier. At Jeff his style had been nondescript, borderline preppy—a boy in a polo shirt among a sea of other boys in polos. Now he wore a black shirt with the sleeves cut off, revealing slightly crooked black and red flag tattoos, one on each deltoid, that she knew were definitely not there last year. The starkness of his transformation was bemusing—what could have changed him so quickly and so thoroughly? She wondered whether it had been a mistake to come.

C! he said. Long time.

He stood and threw his arm around Charlie, offered her his cigarette. She shook her head. He shrugged.

Save yourself for _____ anyway. Everyone, this is Charlie.

Kyle pointed to the shaggy one, the mohawked one, the girl.

Greg, Sid, Lem, he said.

Lem? said Charlie? Like . . . lemon?

Yeah, said Kyle, just as the girl shook her head vigorously. Yes, that's what it sounds like, ignore her.

Why did they have a fit when I called you "Kyle"? she said.

He reddened.

Long story. But it's Slash now.

The silliness of this nickname was a relief, in a way, and Charlie felt the urge to roll her eyes, but when the light hit right, she noticed a sheen of scar tissue running diagonal across his forehead to the bridge of his nose, a bald spot in his eyebrow in its wake.

I'm not jailbait, said Charlie, though in truth she didn't know exactly how old Kyle-Slash was—nineteen? Twenty? *Was* that illegal?

Still an infant, Lem said looking up from a pile of makeup she'd dumped on the floor. That was the problem with hearing people— you never could tell when they were paying attention.

Doesn't look like an infant, said Sid.

Kyle-Slash laughed. The girl jumped up and whacked the front spike of Sid's mohawk, leaving it hanging limp to one side.

Goddammit, he shouted, torn between lunging back at Lem and repairing his hair.

And you—she pointed a finger at Kyle-Slash. Just because you won't go to jail for fucking her doesn't mean you should _____ drugs.

Chill your hormones, it's just a little _____, he said. He turned to Charlie: Plus, you're staying over, right?

Charlie felt herself blush.

Yeah maybe, she said, though she had already made up her mind.

Although, he said, elbowing her in the ribs. Isn't it a school night?

I'm off tomorrow, Charlie said.

Oh yeah? What for?

Fuck School Day.

My favorite, he said.

Kyle-Slash kissed her on the mouth, more an overflow of hatred for school than passion for her, but pleasant nonetheless. Then he dug into his pocket and pulled out a baggie of translucent crystals, which he poured onto the seat of a stool and deftly crushed with his library card.

You've done molly before, yeah? he said to Charlie, dividing the powder into five small peaks.

She hadn't.

Sure, she said.

Kyle-Slash squinted as he looked around the room. He found a half-empty bottle of Gatorade and sprinkled one of the mounds into it.

Order up, he said.

The others gathered around the stool, pinched their doses, and dropped them beneath their tongues. He shook the Gatorade bottle, handed it to Charlie.

Here. It's better this way for newbs.

Charlie looked with uncertainty at the bottle, then took a swig. Beside her, Greg was fiddling with a sheet of paper dotted with what looked like miniature stickers of Donald Duck. Charlie craned her neck to see better, but Kyle-Slash batted the paper from Greg's hand and stuffed it into the front pocket of his bass case.

No candy flipping before the show!

It won't kick in that fast, Greg whined.

Don't be a fucking baby, Lem said. You can have your candy back after.

Charlie stood there, unsure of exactly what had happened, but soon Kyle-Slash's face was light again, and his attention returned to her.

Almost forgot, he said, jamming his hands back in his pockets. Brought you something.

You need a fanny pack, Charlie said, and she saw Lem snort.

He pulled out what Charlie thought was an unwrapped condom, and she grimaced when he held it out to her.

Jesus, ya perv! It's a balloon! he said.

Charlie took the thing between her thumb and forefinger, still holding it away from herself.

Thanks? she said.

I saw it in a documentary. About the punk scene in _____, where they rented out a Deaf club for shows. You blow it up and you can feel vibrations through it.

Concerts at a Deaf club? she said.

He shrugged.

That deaf people went to?

Sure. It was their club.

She took the balloon and shoved it in her back pocket.

Thanks.

You get that you have to blow it up, right?

I'm not going to stand out there with a fucking balloon.

It's not Jeff. They're not gonna make fun of you.

You can stay backstage anyway, said Lem. If you want.

Whatever, said Kyle-Slash. You're not gonna give a fuck in about twenty minutes.

He tapped the Gatorade bottle in her hand, grabbed his bass, and motioned his bandmates toward the stage. Charlie chugged the rest of the drink and searched for a way out of the greenroom and back to the audience.

What she didn't tell Kyle-Slash was that she knew all about the way sound traveled through balloons. Speech therapists at Colson Children's had invented myriad ways to use them against her: blow up the balloon; suck the air back out; hold it to feel loud and soft, high and low. Those appointments had always left her feeling sad for the therapists, who insisted on calling their sessions "games." She wondered whether those sweet-smiling women were really so easily amused.

Generally, Charlie understood music as an extension of her mother, the grace of it in dance and in the orchestra, the gentle ballads she coached her pageant girls in singing. For her part, Charlie could hear the sounds that made up music, but she always had the sense she was doing it wrong—music for her was flat where it should've swelled and dipped, sounded far away when it should've been intimate.

This wasn't like that. When she returned to the floor, the music razored through her, a thousand scrapes of knives across plates. Quickly she removed her processor, relieving the pressure in her head, but even without sound the room was overwhelming—she lingered at the back watching with no small horror as the audience collided in a circular crush, boys hurling their bodies at one another with abandon, centrifugal tumult. The room had already taken on an acrid, beery smell—sweat and yeast and weed—and the floor was coated in spills in various states of drying, slippery in some spots and tacky in others, booze and soda gumming up the soles of her Chucks.

She considered leaving, but when the crowd came for her it was easier not to fight it. The sensation was even enjoyable (except when she took an elbow to the chest), to be carried along by an energy that wasn't her own. This is what the ocean must feel like, she thought, or those churches where people fainted, the arm of a spiral galaxy sweeping her inward.

Eventually the maelstrom thrust her forward and she scraped the lip of the stage while the musicians thrashed before her—Slash sweating and nodding the bass line, Lem's blue hair and purple guitar a blur as she passed.

Charlie's vision was growing streaky, as if she'd stepped into someone's night photography art project—she could see the aura of the stage lights, the jump trail of Slash's and his bandmates' every movement. She could feel the music on her skin, but it wasn't until she reached the front corner, the speaker stack hulking over her, that she felt it *in* her, a ripple in her stomach, a strike in the back of her throat, pulse quickening to keep time with Slash's rhythm. It was both enthralling and a little nauseating. She pulled herself from the current and pressed against the speaker's mesh face. Music banging hard inside her rib cage, music like a heart attack. She closed her eyes, felt the strobe against her lids and the music on her skin, and stayed there until the lights came up.

The next thing she knew the crowd had dispersed, she had slid down to the floor to sit with her back against the mains, and Slash was standing in front of her, kicking the toe of her sneaker.

Jesus, you're like the only person in the world who's ever nodded off while rolling, he said.

I wasn't asleep, she said.

Slash held out his hand and she took it—he was stronger than she'd anticipated and she wound up pressed fully against him. Slowly, she raised her eyes to his. He slung his arm low around her hips, and she felt a tingle run the length of her torso, as if some of the music was still trapped inside her. She slipped a finger through his belt loop, their bodies melding together without them trying—without her trying, anyway—thighs and stomachs a single surface as his lips brushed hers. But when Charlie raised herself on tiptoe to kiss him harder, he lurched backward and yelled something over her shoulder. He paused, then threw his arms up in exasperation.

Right fucking there! In the pocket!

Charlie turned around to see Greg clamoring through Slash's bass bag.

If you're too fucked up to find it, I don't think you need a tab, said Slash. I'm not carrying you home again.

Greg just smiled, ripped one of the Donald Duck squares from the sheet, and dropped the paper in his mouth.

You're the worst, said Lem, snatching the rest of the sheet from him.

Charlie's heart was racing now, sweat prickling at her hairline, but somehow it felt thrilling, more amusement park than anxiety attack. Her field of vision was wider, the front of her mind broad like her forehead had hinged open. She reattached her processor and the sound gathered again at the top of her head in a warm tidepool.

Are we going or not? said Lem.

Of the group, she was the only one who seemed impervious to the high.

Where? said Charlie.

Waste of a flip if we didn't go dancing! said Slash, pulling Charlie close to him again.

Outside, Vine Street had transformed before her eyes—its empti-

ness full of possibility, the Day-Glo plywood now celebratory. Each
traffic light had a tail like a kite, each headlight a shooting star.

Do you see the comets? said Charlie absently.

Lightweight, said Lem.

They walked in the street, Slash and Charlie with hands clasped,
swinging their arms. Charlie could no longer follow the group's conversation, but she also no longer cared, taking pleasure in the soupy
mix of their voices and the sounds of the city.

They stopped at a strip of warehouses, each adorned with signs
warning of security cameras and fines. The sign on the last building
in the row declared it condemned. But Charlie could feel things
buzzing on the other side of the wall, and when Slash hopped onto
the loading dock and tugged open a set of metal doors, an electronica
throb spilled out as if from a vacuum seal. Inside, a woman drew Xs
on their hands in Sharpie, then gave them each a Jell-O shot. Lem
sucked hers down and hung the plastic cup on one of Sid's spikes;
Slash and Charlie followed suit. Greg hung back, leaning against the
wall, staring intently his hands.

Sid waved his hand to show they should leave Greg be, then
shook his head to launch the cups from his hair; they fell to the floor
with dozens of others. Charlie liked the sharp crunch underfoot—it
reminded her of the handful of times they'd had decent snow in Colson, and she imagined crushing icicles while Slash pulled her toward
the center of the warehouse. Beneath a pulsing strobe, about a hundred people were already dancing.

This place is awesome, Charlie said.

What?

Best illegal activity ever!

I can't understand you! said Slash.

I can't understand you! she parroted.

He pulled her hips to his and kissed her fiercely. She allowed herself
to follow his sway, in time with the rhythm of the room, and rubbed
against him until she could feel him growing hard. Eventually they
stopped kissing, but kept dancing braced tight against one another,

Slash gently parting Charlie's knees with one of his so she could slide along his thigh. The pressure made her woozy—her body was alight, her skin hot and prickly at the slightest touch, as if every sensory receptor had floated to the surface. Charlie thought again of her mother's dancers, wondered if they ever also felt this weightless when they moved, but the thought didn't stay long. She was rolling hard enough now that not even her mother could infringe on her high.

Lem and Sid appeared beside them, and she and Slash split apart and blended into the rest of the crowd, most of whom were now jumping with a hand in the air screaming song lyrics—like a cousin of the mosh pit, raw and sweaty, all moving as one.

Charlie lost Slash for a while, had a fleeting feeling of nervousness that was quickly subsumed by another tide of euphoria, and she kept jumping. When he returned, he offered her another Jell-O shot, and showed her his forearm, on which he'd written in Sharpie:

Wanna get out of here?

She downed the shot and pulled him out of the warehouse.

BODY LANGUAGE

flirt

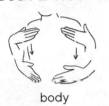

body

naked

wet

strip

make love

dirty

rough

breasts

vagina

penis

erection

blow job

go down on

69

fuck

*C*harlie woke naked atop the blankets the next morning, harsh winter sunlight slicing through Slash's broken blinds. She scanned the surrounding area for a condom wrapper, spotted one, and let out all the breath she didn't realize she'd been holding. As her panic abated, she took in the room: Slash's bed was a mattress on the floor and there was no other furniture, only stacks of books lining the remaining perimeter. She felt a hand on her shoulder and rolled over to find Slash looking at her with concern, no doubt from the weight of her sigh.

You okay?
She felt like she'd swallowed sand. She tried clearing her throat a few times, then just smiled and nodded instead.

Get in here, said Slash, holding up the blanket and beckoning her back toward him.
She slid closer, but he moved toward the wall. She tried not to look disappointed. She knew he had done it for her benefit; he wanted to talk and wanted her to be able to see. He had always been good about that, even when she was just meeting him for a hookup, like it was intuitive to him, like they were a team in figuring out how to make a conversation work. She wondered if things would've been different if more people at Jeff had seen it the same way.

So—he said, reaching over to brush her hair from her face—did you have fun last night?

I did, she said.

He ran his hand up her neck and the back of her head, to the place where the magnet sat beneath her skin. The scar had always interested him and she let him trace it.

What about you? she said, touching the bald spot in his eyebrow, the shiny tissue at the bridge of his nose.

Oh, it was nothing.

What happened?

Bottle to the face. At a protest.

Charlie winced.

Eh, it wasn't anything, he said. Face skin just scars easily. The beating I took from the cops after was a lot worse.

The cops beat you up? Why?

Comes with the territory.

The band? said Charlie.

Among other things.

What things?

Oh you know, he said nonchalantly. The revolution.

Slash flicked his eyebrows up as if he was teasing, but she could tell he wasn't. He was different, and it wasn't just the scar, or the new clothes, or the tattoos. At Jeff, he'd had been the goofy kind of stoner, playing pranks on the aides who oversaw study hall, then laughing too loudly afterward. Now his appearance was brash but he was quieter, and in that quiet there was a depth that made Charlie feel a little nervous.

What *happened* to you this summer? she said.

Just started paying attention, is all, he said.

In their time together, Slash had never said anything political that she could remember. No one she knew at Jeff talked much about politics—not in a way that felt actionable beyond slogan T-shirts or stickers on notebooks. For her part, survival had kept Charlie too busy to care much about the bigger picture. But now the word "revolution" pinged something in her. She thought of the banner with the band's name on it from the night before; she felt certain it meant something important, but whatever wisps of it she might have captured at school she couldn't dredge up now.

Teach me your band's name?

He looked confused at first, but when she placed a hand on his neck diagonally so it grazed his Adam's apple he understood.

Robe-spee-air, he said.

She copied his sounds.

You got it. Not too hard, as French goes.

Why them? she ventured.

Who?

Robe-spee-airs, she said.

She could see he was thinking about laughing at this before he realized she was serious.

No, Robespierre. He was a dude, like, the inventor of the French Revolution. He stormed prisons, killed a bunch of rich fucks. Very radical shit.

A hazy memory of last year's history class was surfacing, a Power-Point about some kind of riots, and—

Wait, she said. Is this the guy with the—

What was that word? She tried to picture it on the slide, but even if she could, she wouldn't have known how to say it aloud.

You know, the head chopper thing?

So you do know!

But he killed a lot of people!

Sometimes violence is necessary for change, Slash said calmly. You don't think so?

I don't know, she said. What about, like, MLK?

Slash rolled his eyes.

Martin Luther King wasn't some hippie, he said. That's just how white people _____ after they murdered him.

How white people what? said Charlie.

Trussed him up. T-r-u-s-s. It's like, how you tie up a turkey's legs.

I don't get it.

Charlie was losing the thread. She didn't know what a turkey had to do with anything, and besides that, she was bemused by the way Slash talked about white people as if he himself were not paler even than her mother, nearly translucent, so that his veins ran bright green beneath his skin. She shrugged.

Look, he said. Say you've got cancer. A huge tumor! You're not just going to leave it in there. So, what do you do?

Get surgery? she said.

Exactly. Cut out the bad stuff. Surely there's something in your life you'd be better off without?

Probably a few things, Charlie thought—her implant, math class, maybe even her mom—though whether she was willing to cut any of it out to the degree Slash was suggesting, something so permanent, she wasn't sure.

I guess, she said.

That's all the guillotine was.

Guillotine! She reached her hand out to touch his neck again, made him repeat himself, trying to reconcile Slash's Robespierre with the considerably more criminal one projected on the cinder-block wall of Mr. Brewer's classroom.

You know, Robespierre also helped _____ slavery, pushed back against church corruption—

He helped slavery?

No he helped ab-o-lish it. It means get rid of. Probably wouldn't have learned that at Jeff, though, even if you could hear.

Charlie traced the outline of his tattoo and felt a sudden rush of affection for him, a sugary burn at the base of her throat. Though she still didn't understand exactly what had inspired his transformation, it was undeniably intriguing. She leaned over the side of the bed and dug through her pants in search of her phone, handed it to him. He seemed confused.

You said you were getting a new phone number?

He looked at her outstretched arm, suddenly sheepish.

Sorry, C. I can't.

Right, she said.

It's not you.

She slid from the bed and scooped up her clothes, but standing made her light-headed, and she had to sit again to flip her jeans right side in. Slash looked like he wanted to say something more, but she turned away; though she had inherited her father's complexion, she still blushed bright red when she was upset, and especially when she was embarrassed. Why did she always manage to put herself on the back foot? If he had wanted to see her again, he would have asked. She wondered if there was something to her mother's ideas about dating and demureness after all.

Seriously, he said, stepping in front of her so she could see him again. I'm going off the grid for a while.

Whatever. I'm not trying to get with you or anything.

Slash looked over her shoulder at his rumpled sheets.

I mean, I don't date hearing guys.

Not anymore, she said.

Slash looked down at her hands. Charlie could tell she had thrown him.

Oh. Fair enough, then.

Her belongings—wallet, keys, phone, processor—were strewn on the floor and she struggled to gather them. It seemed impossible that she'd gotten it all here in the pockets of her jeans.

Wanna get breakfast? he said.

The mention of food reminded her how hungover she was, flipped her stomach.

I'm good. I better head out.

She reattached her CI to give herself one less thing to carry and was jolted when the wail of a passing siren drilled through the center of her head. Without the drugs, sound was once again her enemy, neither velvety nor exhilarating. Slash pulled on his boxers, placed a row of kisses along her collarbone that made her knees go to gelatin.

Well, I'll come let you out at least, he said. The _____ kind of heavy.

The what? she said.

Slash didn't answer, but as they emerged into the front room, she saw the house had been stripped to its subflooring, and its windows were boarded up from the outside. A thick orange extension cord ran the length of the room, powering its sole light source: a lamp perched on a cardboard box.

On the couch, an unsightly brown corduroy affair, Greg was passed out, head hanging off the cushion over a bucket. The room reeked of vomit, but Slash didn't seem to notice.

Does the whole band live here?

Slash nodded, surveyed Greg.

Glad someone dragged his ass back home, he said.

Then Slash opened the front door, revealing a piece of plywood he slid to one side and ducked beneath. Outside on the stoop it was too bright, but cool enough to shock a break in her nausea. She watched gooseflesh spread across Slash's chest.

Go inside, said Charlie.

Come back to the Gas Can sometime?

Maybe, she said.

He tried to kiss her goodbye, but she only offered him her cheek. Then she left. Slash watched her to the end of the street, arms crossed against the morning cold, and she saw him slip back behind the board as she rounded the corner. She was clammy, her mouth putrid and dry. She stopped in a Circle K and bought a bottle of water, then walked in the direction of Colson Center until she found a bus stop.

Though she'd probably only miss first period, she couldn't bring herself to go back to school, so she went to her father's and stood in the shower for a very long time.

Afterward she plugged in her phone and was immediately greeted by a series of increasingly frantic texts from her mother, most of them a variation of "where are u?"

school? Charlie tried.

yeah right some robot just called & said ur absent.

A robot called u?

WHERE RU

Still at dad's. I feel sick.

jesus christ

Sry. Didn't mean to scare u.

Have your father call u out then.

ok, said Charlie. She texted her dad, threw herself across her bed, googled "Robespierre," then cried into her shirtsleeve until she fell asleep.

Maximilien Robespierre

From Wikipedia, the free encyclopedia

"Robespierre" redirects here. For other uses, see Robespierre (disambiguation)

Maximilien François Marie Isidore de Robespierre (6 May 1758 –28 July 1794) was a lawyer and influential leader of the French Revolution. He spoke on behalf of citizens he considered "voiceless"—typically those without property, education, or other resources—and advocated for their right to bear arms, be in the military, and hold public office. He also campaigned for universal suffrage among men, the abolition of slavery, and to remove the celibacy requirement for clergy.

In part because of his work, the French Monarchy fell on August 10, 1792, and a National Convention was summoned. There Robespierre called for an end to feudal practices, equality before the law, and direct democracy, though he was later accused of trying to establish a dictatorship.

By 1793, Robespierre's idea for a *sans-culotte* army (literally meaning "without breeches," the army was made up of common people rather than officers of the former ruling class) was realized, in order to enforce the new laws of the land. In July 1793, Robespierre was appointed to the Committee of Public Safety; in October, the Committee declared itself the acting revolutionary government.

While Robespierre was distrustful of the Catholic church's power, he was not an atheist, and so established a form of deism, The Cult of the Supreme Being, in order to serve as France's new state religion, seeing belief in a "higher moral code" as an essential tenet of a just republic.

While experts differ on a definitive start date for France's Reign of Terror, most agree that its height was between the summers of 1793 and '94, during which 16,594 death sentences were assigned, and an additional 10,000 prisoners died while incarcerated. Executions were usually public and completed by guillotine, and targeted the wealthy, clergymen, and those under suspicion of being counter-revolutionary.

. . .

Though Robespierre was technically an equal member of the Committee, his influence far outpaced any other single man in France at the time. It is because of the impact of his foundational beliefs, as well as his forceful propagation of The Cult of the Supreme Being, that so much responsibility for the Reign of Terror is attributed to him.

Eventually, Robespierre's desire for ideological purity within the republic turned the people against him, and he and his allies were arrested and removed from Paris's town hall. Robespierre and approximately 90 others were executed, effectively bringing the Terror to an end.

Robespierre was beheaded and buried in a common grave in <u>Errancis Cemetery</u>. His legacy, and the chasm between his ideals on paper and practices in actuality, remains a matter of historical controversy today.

*f*ebruary had received her share of 4:00 A.M. phone calls, but that never made them easier—the desolate ring cutting through sleep, the feeling of having gulped down her heart, of not recognizing her own extremities. The night her grandmother died she'd answered a call like this, another a few years later when her uncle was crushed between a tree and a drunk driver's Land Rover. Back then it'd been down the stairs to the kitchen, linoleum cold on her bare feet while she spoke hoarsely into the receiver. She had been a child both times, but the calls had been meant for her, or at least her as a conduit through which information flowed to her mother and father.

Now her phone was a thin rectangle glowing through the blue-black of her bedroom, the caller ID flashing "RVSD Security." She broke a sweat before she could even answer. Beside her in bed, Mel swatted at her own phone, then rolled over to glare at February when she realized it was much too dark for her alarm.

Sorry, February said, and jabbed at the accept button.

Ms. Waters? came the harried voice of her head of security. We got a problem over here.

Who is it? Mel hissed.

February gave Mel a "hang on" index finger.

What's wrong, Walt? she said into the phone. Everyone okay?

Kids are fine. It's your mother.

What? What do you need her for? What time is it?

No no, Walt said. She's here. On campus.

What?

February leapt from the bed, but the sheet ensnared her ankle. She lurched backward and caught her toe on the bed frame.

Fuck! February said.

Mel groaned.

Ma'am? said Walt.

Sorry, not you. I mean yes, you too. Just—

She ran to the edge of the stairs and looked down to find their front door wide open.

I'll be right there.

Ms. Waters?

Yeah.

Maybe bring a bathrobe.

Walt hung up and February limped to the bathroom, threw her phone on a pile of dirty towels, and swaddled her bleeding toe in tissue, then pulled yesterday's clothes from the top of the hamper.

What's going on? Mel said.

My mother. She's on campus.

What?

Walt has her. I'm taking your robe.

What can I do?

I don't know, February said, and hurried down the stairs and into the night.

February found her mother in Walt's office, wrapped in his rain slicker.

Thank god you're here! He won't read me my rights! Tell him I want a lawyer.

Sorry about the— Walt gestured to the slicker. She's missing some pants.

You're not under arrest. This is
Walt, remember? From RVSD?

February watched her mother survey Walt, and for a moment she
thought she saw a glimmer of recognition.

My sister is going to post my bail
and sue this whole department.

February sighed, mouthed Sorry to Walt. He nodded.

Let's go home, February said to her mother, holding out the robe.
Walt left the office and February removed his jacket. Wearing only
February's father's old Cavaliers T-shirt, her mother looked very
small. February wrapped her in Mel's robe and took her elbow.

Thank you again, Walt, she said on the way out. I'll call you later.

Good night, ma'am.

We need to talk, said Mel a few nights later, after dinner was cleared
and February's mother tucked safely into bed.

February had been working from home in the days since the incident, calling in to meetings via videophone, answering emails, and
then forcing her mother to accompany her to Holden's Hardware,
where she purchased a pair of dead bolts and installed them on the
front and side doors, just out of her mother's reach.

I know, February said. I'm thinking we need a security system—
and maybe something to put on the stove knob covers. Those baby-
proofing things?

Feb.

They make systems with webcams and everything, said February.
We could keep an eye on the feed from work—

You know that's not going to cut it, said Mel. This could have
been so much worse. What if she had walked out into traffic?

But—

You can't just lock her in the house all day.

February tucked her feet up under her, willing the couch to swallow
her whole. In her life's biggest decisions, she had always consulted

her mother, who had unfailingly given good advice. She had given February tips for navigating high school bullies, had helped her realize she wanted to be a teacher, had encouraged her to go back to school for administration. She had been good-natured as February dragged her through Cincy's cluster of jewelry stores trying to find the perfect ring for Mel, offering opinions and serving as hand model. February was drawn to the larger jewels—it was, after all, supposed to be a kind of grand gesture. But it was her mother who first selected a smaller setting with a yellow diamond.

I don't know. You're sure it's . . .
fancy enough?

She has to wear it every day for the rest of her life—you don't want to weigh her down, her mother said.

February had asked the saleswoman to take the ring out of the case for her, turned it over and over between her fingers.

Anyway, she'll love whatever you get because it came from you.

I know.

But get the platinum band, she never wears gold.

How hadn't February noticed that? It seemed so obvious once her mother said it.

Thank god you're here, February had said.

I'll take it, she said to the saleswoman.

Her mother had been right; Mel loved the ring. But that had been years ago. Now, even if her mom was lucid, what was February supposed to say—*mind if we ship you off to the home?*

I think you should call what's-her-name's daughter, said Mel.

Gonna need another hint.

Your mom's best friend, from when they were kids.

Lu?

I think so?

No way, said February. They put her in Spring Towers.

It's a new facility. It'll be clean, all the best doctors nearby.

It's all the way in Cincy!

But wouldn't it be good for her to be with a friend? Someone Deaf?

Not only good, it would be essential. Without ASL, her mother would be totally isolated, which would exacerbate the dementia, which—

Maybe they could room together, said Mel.

Her tone suggested that she'd been repeating herself.

Sorry, said February.

I know it's a lot.

I'm not ready. She's been doing so well.

How about this? said Mel. I'll call Spring Towers tomorrow, just to see. Ask a few questions.

I don't know.

Just a little research, okay? said Mel.

Okay, February said.

*a*s payback for her truancy, Charlie had received a red-faced diatribe from her father (*You're really gonna blow this? After all I've done for you?*), a follow-up lecture in ASL and Post-it notes from Headmistress Waters upon her return to campus, and another week's detention tacked on to her previous sentence, with a special exemption for the Drama Club.

Now she trekked up to the auditorium and through the stage door, waved meekly at the rest of the crew kids giddily organizing the prop table; they were clearly not here as a punishment. They were all wearing camping headlamps so they could sign to one another backstage, and somebody handed her one when she reached them. One of the girls showed her how to work the curtain pulley and what tape marked which set pieces, which props she'd manage and costume changes she'd facilitate.

Do you want this? she said, brandishing a plastic sword. *Austin's.*

Sure? said Charlie, thrown by the girl's knowing look.

I thought since you two seem—

Seem what?

Little school, big eyes, she said.

Charlie took the sword and laid it on her prop shelf.

We're just friends.

Whatever. Just be careful.

What do you mean?

He's a good guy. He's just like _____ here.

Like what?

R-o-y-a-l-t-y. He's used to getting what he wants.

. . . O-k.

She wasn't sure she even wanted to know what this meant, but it didn't matter. She didn't have the words to ask more.

Charlie, right?

Yeah.

I'm friends with your roommate. I'm A-l-i-s-h-a.

She showed Charlie her sign name, and Charlie copied it.

Kayla's cool, she said timidly.

She meant it—Kayla *was* cool, and their relationship had been growing closer in the past few weeks. But Kayla signed so quick that Charlie still got lost often, and she did not want to ruin the budding camaraderie by constantly saying so.

Yeah she's the best. I keep saying she should try out for the plays, but she's too sporty.

Do you ever act?

Me? No way. I prefer it back here.

Me too, said Charlie, and when she saw it on her hands, she knew it to be true.

Welcome to the dark side, said Alisha.

a s the weeks passed, Austin found himself uncharacteristically apprehensive about play practices and what they would mean for dealing with Gabriella. Casting had gone as he'd expected—he'd landed the role of Peter, and initially he'd been pleased about it, until he realized what it likely meant for the female lead. He ran back to the bulletin board outside Fickman's room only to find his fears confirmed: Gabriella would be Wendy.

These days, he couldn't even bring himself to look at her across the cafeteria table, and spent most of his last periods crafting mental pep talks about the valuable experience of acting alongside one's ex—surely professional actors had to do it all the time. Occasionally, though, another self would pop in and suggest he drop out of the play completely to avoid the real-life drama. But each day after the last bell flashed he dutifully walked to the auditorium, and now he was standing in the wings staring at Gabriella, who was already in costume and center stage, holding court with the boys who would play John and Michael. Up in the catwalk, the tech crew fiddled with the gels, casting her in spots of different hues—first a ghostly blue wash over her nightgown, then a red that gave her hair a crimson halo.

She really was beautiful, and it bothered him that he still felt a bit of longing when he saw her. The accusation that he'd used her for sex niggled at him, even though he hoped she'd only said it to get under his skin. Gabriella had been *his* first, and there were rumors that she'd hooked up with a now-graduated swim team captain when they were still in the eighth grade. He rubbed his eyes, as if he could wipe away his attraction, then turned from the stage. It didn't matter how hot she was; they were simply no good for one another. In the wings, he watched as the crew sorted through old props, pulling out ones that might be of use in a Peter Pan world. That's where he noticed Charlie.

She had her back to him, but it was definitely her—her hair pulled up into a messy ponytail, revealing the tiny green, glowing indicator light of her processor. He went to her and took her wrist; she wheeled around and shouted what even Austin and his shoddy lipreading skills could tell was definitely "Fuck."

Sorry.

You scared me.

Sorry, he said again, now to
both her and Alisha—he could
see he'd interrupted them.

Alisha waved them off as if to say *go ahead,* and he led Charlie into the back wing, where a floor lamp with a naked bulb was glowing orb-like. They were alone.

*Wanted to say sorry for not an-
swering you this weekend. Family drama.*

Her expression, which had been flat, almost businesslike, softened under the apology.

All good.

S-o, you're in the play?

Not really. Stage crew.

*Did you do theater at your old
school?*

At this she laughed.

*No way. True biz? Headmistress
Waters is making me.*

Like, as punishment?

         What?

P–u–n–i–s–h–m–e–n–t.

         Yeah. I called her a bitch in class
         the other day.

What?

Austin tried to imagine a scenario in which he might curse at Headmistress Waters, but couldn't. He didn't think he'd ever seen anyone do it, even another teacher, or in the off-hours at one of his parents' parties.

         It was an accident, she said.

She looked down at the floor. Austin took a step closer, fiddled with the zipper toggle on her hoodie. He was pretty sure he'd never seen Gabriella wear a sweatshirt. He wondered what it would be like to kiss Charlie; he wondered whether there was something wrong with him, his desire flitting from girl to girl in just a few seconds, as if it was completely outside his control. He wondered whether kissing her would be worth the inevitable social aftershocks.

In any case, Charlie didn't give him the chance to find out—though she had leaned in ever so slightly as he toyed with her sweatshirt, he was nearly a head taller than her, and she was still looking down at her feet. And it was in this position—gazing absently over Charlie's head onto the stage, the zip of her hoodie still between his fingers—that he locked eyes with Gabriella.

He hadn't done it on purpose, but he knew Gabriella would see it as a challenge. Maybe, deep down, part of him did, too. As she marched toward them, he tried to warn Charlie, but she didn't understand the sign for *watch out,* and soon Gabriella took hold of her ponytail and pulled.

         What the fuck?

Charlie spun around, wrenching her hair from Gabriella's grip.

         Hope you know who you're fuck-
         ing with, Gabriella said.

         A bitch in PJs? said Charlie.

Austin couldn't help but smile at this. She was quick.

        You don't belong here.

                What are you gonna do about it?

        I'm warning you. Leave us alone.

She'd said "us," but she was looking at Austin.

    Hey—

        You stay out of this, Gabriella

        said to Austin.

She turned back to Charlie.

        Watch your back. Freak.

Gabriella stalked out of the wings, and Austin looked to Charlie, mortified.

        Your e-x?

Yeah.

        She seems fun.

    I'm really sorry.

        What was the last thing she said?

Austin shrugged, feigning forgetfulness, but Charlie made an approximation of the sign. He sighed.

    F-r-e-a-k, he said.

Charlie said something with her mouth. She looked more pissed than wounded, but he couldn't shake the feeling of wanting to comfort her. Even if she didn't need his protection, he liked the way she needed *him*—sure, at the moment it was mostly as a walking ASL decoder ring, but wasn't need close to desire?

    Come with me? he said.

She nodded and Austin took her hand and led her to the emergency exit.

*b*ackstage was cavernous, bigger than she'd realized, and Charlie followed Austin deeper into the darkness until they came to an emergency exit. ALARM WILL SOUND was stamped on the door in orange and white but Austin opened it without flinching, laughed at her wide-eyed look.

Half of them don't work, he said.
She followed him out, feeling foolish and a little impressed. It was one of the things Charlie was coming to like best about Austin—watching the comfort with which he moved around campus. He was perfectly attuned to the space, the way Charlie knew the loose floorboards and crooked hinges of the house she grew up in. He could show her each quirk and secret passageway River Valley had to offer.

This particular exit, though, released them only onto a concrete loading dock. They sat down on the edge of the platform and swung their legs over the lip. Beneath them was a ramp and a pair of parking spots, but beyond that there was only an open field, browning in that late October way. Fall in Colson was a wild, capricious thing—the weather shifted from muggy to cool without notice, and squalls often pushed in from the river. Charlie was struck by how much colder it was than it had been just that morning. Fat gray clouds hung above them now, and she pulled up the hood of her sweatshirt.

Sorry about her, he said.

Not your f-a-u-l-t.

Your fault, he said, demonstrating. *Still, she shouldn't have done that.*

Charlie nodded and looked back out across the field, allowed Austin to put his arm around her. They didn't say anything else for a long time.

She rested her head on his shoulder, again gripped by the feeling she'd had that first moment they met: an attraction not only to him but to the kind of person he was, the life that might have been hers if she had his stride and sureness and a hundred years of sign language coded right into her bones. When she nestled up closer against him, she undeniably felt desire—to be with him, sure, but also to sop up his knowledge, the confidence propelling his every sign, to absorb his good fortune and the flash in his eyes, swallow him whole.

time passes

Grammar note: In English, verb endings are conjugated to reflect tense. In ASL, markers of time are added as separate signs.

past   future

finish

Past tense = *Finish,* both hands flicked outward at the wrist.

English: I went to school.

ASL: *Finish go school.*

past   now   future

finish   will

Future tense = *Will,* a hand thrust forward from the side of the head.

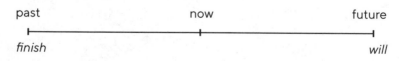

English: I'm going to school tomorrow.

ASL: *Go school tomorrow will.*

NOW YOU TRY! Tell your partner about a past or future dentist trip.

*f*ebruary had repressed her anxiety in the lead-up to her mother's move by maintaining a workload so large she had little time to worry about anything else. True to her word, she'd said nothing about River Valley's impending closure, not even to Mel, though she wasn't proud of it. At first, she told herself she was holding off until after the midterms—perhaps she could reverse the decision with some good old-fashioned civic action. For weeks she spent each spare moment drafting pleading letters to the state legislature, even phone banked for some progressive-leaning PAC. But the first week of November came and went, and the statehouse had only gotten redder.

It wasn't as if she'd ever doubted Ohio could end up here—she knew fear to be a potent motivator, had witnessed how easily it could sway a person. As a child, she'd seen her parents' presences rouse insults in the mouths of impatient bank tellers and clerks, which February always heard, always carried with her, even when she wasn't yet tall enough to see over the counters. By the time she was in college, she had seen the body of a man killed on the stoop of a liquor store, and the city burned, and reconstruction delayed again and again until its smolder was internalized. Even here in the bluer slice of the county, someone had twice planted a God Hates Fags sign in Mel's herb garden. So, while the conservative doubling down wasn't necessarily surprising, it was still a disappointment.

In education, like everything in America, money ruled the day, and Deaf education had been hyperstratified by the rise of the cochlear implant. Wealthier kids whose parents could pay out-of-pocket for surgery and rehabilitative therapies often found success in the mainstream; kids whose families couldn't pay stayed deaf. But even as a shift in Medicaid coverage meant access to the device itself increased, access to the therapies and educational resources didn't. The hearing world was shocked to find that the working-class kid of a single mom who couldn't stay home and funnel practice sounds into his head, or drive him to countless therapy appointments all day, was not "cured" as the implant sales reps had promised. Those kids often wound up back at Deaf schools, only now with vast cognitive deficits. The more vulnerable her student body was, the less politicians cared, or even pretended to care, about their fate. She wrote to the new legislators anyway, but seldom heard back.

At the same time, she was drafting backup plans—mini deaf programs that could operate in microcosm within the public schools. She wanted to have them ready, to be able to make her demands and implement a transition team. The move needed to be as seamless as possible for the kids, especially the youngest ones, who were still learning to read. How would they communicate with hearing teachers and peers without English as a fallback? Surely she could guilt Swall into procuring them an empty classroom where her teachers and students could hole up for a few periods.

But the details were difficult to nail down when she couldn't collaborate with anyone, and anyway, her attention was so often usurped by the urgent matters of the day—grading and PowerPoints for her own class, Serrano and Quinn to keep an eye on, and a dozen other crises in miniature that crossed her desk each week: the third-grade boys who'd made a pact that had ended in them flushing their hearing aids down the toilet; a two-day phone call shouting match with the textbook people, who'd sent audio recordings instead of braille copies of the midterm materials for her DeafBlind kids.

Then there was the ream of paperwork for her mother's admission to Spring Towers—questions about her needs and preferences so granular February was both heartened that they'd thought to ask and distressed that it had fallen to her to dictate her very opinionated mother's answers. She had avoided that latent role reversal embedded in every parent-child relationship with her father—he was gone so suddenly—and despite her mother's diagnosis she was unprepared for it now.

She tried once to discuss the forms with her mother, but her mother had only grown agitated by the onslaught of questions. February could see she was scared that she could no longer find answers to inquiries about the basics of her own daily routines, things she had done for years, things she should know. February didn't ask again, and was left to fill in her best guesses about what her mother might like to eat or watch on TV for the foreseeable future.

She continued this way for a few weeks, using the collapse of her school to distract herself from her mother's departure, and her mother's departure as an excuse for not talking to Mel about school. When her mom was all settled in and safe, and she and Mel were alone together again, then she would tell her. There was over a month before the district administrative meeting. She still had time.

Mel was prone to carsickness, so she would drive them into Cincy; that was a given. But when it came time to leave, February couldn't stand the idea of putting her mom in the backseat alongside her suitcase and comforter, like she was headed off to summer camp, so February situated her mother in the passenger seat, then squeezed herself in beside the luggage. Her mother said little on the ride there, and Mel's alternative rock station was in the middle of an acoustic hour so melancholy February almost asked her to turn it off, but she was afraid silence would feel worse.

They drove along Colson's periphery, passing the graying Goodyear-turned–Edge Bionics plant and some desolate streets before the last of the city finally melted into pastures, fire and brimstone billboards looming large over soy plants and plastered to sides of barns. It was flat and brown like this for a while. Her mother asked twice where they were going, but February was grateful that when they reminded her about Spring Towers, she seemed to know what they meant.

Then up from the fields grew the exurbs, subdivisions, and warehouses that signaled they were approaching Cincy's city limits. As Mel guided the car off the highway, February felt her mind pick up speed, and she worried she might enter a full-on panic attack, but instead she plucked one of the thoughts from the stream and tried to anchor herself to it: once she lost her job, she could get her mother back, and stay home to care for her. The idea briefly stayed her, but it left her with a bitter aftertaste.

Inside, Spring Towers was pristine—light walls, fresh-scrubbed tile, and chrome elevator bays. February wheeled a pair of her mother's suitcases as they followed an aide up to the third floor to a room near the end of the hallway, where a tiny woman was hunched in a recliner watching television. The aide flicked the light switch to get Lu's attention. Lu looked up, and the aide approached a large whiteboard on the side wall.

Guess who's here? she wrote in large print.
Lu looked up at them with delight. Relief swelled in February at the interaction—they knew how to care for deaf people here. Her mom would be okay.

Who is that? her mother said, bursting through February's moment of calm.

It's your friend, L-u.

L-u?

From high school.
Lu rose from her chair and shuffled toward them, then pulled February's mother into an embrace.

I'm happy you're here, she said.

Me too, said February's mother.

Mel returned to the car to retrieve the last of the bags while February helped her mother unpack, placing stacks of clothes neatly in her dresser, hanging her robe and blouses in the wardrobe. While her mother and Lu chatted about Spring Towers's amenities, February stacked and restacked a selection of word searches and paperbacks on the bedside table. Then Mel returned, and the aide returned and walked February through a clipboard full of final forms.

The dining room is open for lunch, said the aide. It'd be good for her to go down and get acquainted with everything.

February knew this was their not-so-subtle cue to leave, and that the distraction of food and meeting new people would make an easier transition for her mother. She nodded, went to her mother, now sitting in a recliner opposite Lu's, and knelt down in front of her.

*Mel and I are gonna go so you
can have lunch,* she said. *But I'll
be back to get you as soon as I can.
And you can come home.*

Her mother just nodded and said okay.

I love you so much.

Love you too!

February stood and kissed her mother on the forehead. Her mother smiled brightly and February was a little hurt that she was taking it all so well.

Drive safe!

Mel gave her mom a thumbs-up, then took February's hand and led her from the room. February pressed her tongue hard against the roof of her mouth to keep from crying. She thought of the day she left for graduate school, her parents standing at the end of the driveway, waving fervently, her mother's eyes welling up, tears magnified behind her thick glasses. How thrilled February had been that day, to leave her parents' house and Colson behind, even if she wasn't going very far. What kind of child had she been, to practically delight in abandoning them?

At the front desk, the receptionist handed February a family welcome folder with a pamphlet listing special dates and events, and an index card with her mother's room information and videophone number on it. February hugged the folder tight to her chest and kept it there the whole ride home.

You okay?

Yeah, said February. I think. I don't know. I just feel guilty.

I know, babe, but it's the safest place for her.

February nodded.

Hey, what did you say to her before we left?

That I loved her?

Oh, okay.

What?

I thought you said something about coming back to get her, said Mel.

February's neck hairs prickled. Mel's ASL had really improved in the months her mother had been with them.

Yeah. I did.

Here was where she should have told her wife everything. It was the perfect in—Mel might even take pity on her in this state instead of berating her for having kept it a secret.

For Thanksgiving, I mean, February said instead.

Coward. She began to pick at her cuticles, peeling a thin line of skin away from one finger until Mel reached across the armrest and took her hand.

Don't do that, she said.

Listen, said February.

Yeah?

I, uh—

She couldn't bring the words up into her mouth.

Thank you, she said. Really, thanks for all you did to organize this. You know how much she means to me.

I know, babe, Mel said.

She patted February's arm tenderly, not unlike her mother might have done, then returned her hand to the wheel to merge onto the highway toward Colson.

*W*ord about Sky's hearing—like all Deaf gossip—had spread quickly through the community. Austin sometimes thought that if hearing people ever studied the power and speed of the Deaf rumor mill, they might think twice about classifying deafness as a "communication disorder."

Most of his friends still didn't know, though, since most of their parents weren't Deaf. So while he wasn't trying to hide it, exactly, he saw no reason to bring it up. Anyway, most teenagers weren't that into talking about babies, beyond the terror of accidentally making one, and how best to avoid it. Then the news trickled down through the Valenti parents to their daughters.

Gabriella had appeared beside his locker one afternoon, and Austin remembered a time when seeing her there would have delighted him, but now his heart's skipped beat was dread-induced.

Heard your mom had the baby.

He nodded.

Congratulations.

Thanks.

Gabriella smiled, but her eyes narrowed, a tell Austin knew meant she was about to strike. He waited for a moment, then gave in.

What?

I heard someone failed her deaf test.

And?

Nothing. Just fun to see the mighty topple is all.

What are you talking about?

Come on—the poster family for Deafhood has a hearing kid? You have to admit it's kind of funny.

What does that even mean?

Of course Austin knew there was clout embedded into his family's Deafness, but he wasn't sure about "poster family." It wasn't as if he walked around policing people the way Gabriella sometimes did, making snide comments about someone who used English word order, or mouthed English words as they signed. Most days—at least before Charlie and Sky—he'd rarely thought about an "ideal" version of deafness at all. He was hardly marching around like some reverse Alexander Graham Bell. Then again, maybe standing for something wasn't always a choice.

Hello? Gabriella was cackling now. *Anybody home?*

I—

Whatever, say hi to the baby for me.

She batted her eyes, looking demure.

I mean, if you can.

Oh, fuck off, he said.

She only laughed harder. He slammed his locker door and went to lunch, directly to the corner of the cafeteria where he knew he'd find Charlie.

You can sit with us, if you want,
he said.

*N*ow Charlie's language was burgeoning. During the school day, she sat on the edge of her chair, eyes tracking wildly between her teachers' hands and whatever clues she could glean from the whiteboard or PowerPoint. The night classes were still useful, chugging along with their methodical repetition, she and her father working as partners and slowly recounting to one another the day's events. Then, in the cafeteria, the other ASL.

Charlie had always been fond of curse words. In hearing school, kids would teach her strings of vile things to say and she'd parrot them back as best she could to make them laugh. She was willing to be the butt of this kind of joke if it diverted their attention from other ways to hurt her.

Here, too, curse words were an easy bridge. Since the incident with his ex, nothing more had happened between her and Austin, or her and Gabriella. But after a while he had invited Charlie to sit with him at lunch. On the far end of the table, Gabriella and another blonde spent a lot of time staring pointedly and then laughing at Charlie, but the rest of Austin's tablemates—a pair of brawny football players, two gangly boys who looked like they'd never played a sport of any kind, plus Alisha and another girl from Drama—had quickly descended upon the language gap and offered up their favorites: "shit," "fuck," "slut," "bitch," "asshole," and several variations on the theme of "motherfucker."

She saw English, rigid and brittle, crack before her eyes—concepts that took up whole spoken phrases encapsulated in a single sign. Other signs were untranslatable even with multiple words: a sign that sometimes meant *I see* and sometimes *I understand* or *that's interesting*, or an affirmation that you were paying attention; another that seemed to be a more emphatic version of "real talk," and which was transliterated for her alternately as *true business* and *true biz*.

There were sign names for every social media and internet abbreviation, emoticons enfolded into signed puns and, along with them, she learned about an array of technology she hadn't even known existed. In the past, her phone had felt mostly useless, good only for exchanging text messages with her parents or playing arcade games when she was bored. But now there was a way to co-opt nearly every platform—ASL on any app that could handle video, or even GIFs.

Kevin, one of the gangly boys, commandeered her phone and downloaded things for her—one app that flashed a light to alert her to loud sounds, another to send video messages without clogging up phone memory, and several that translated speech to text with accuracy ranging from passable to hilarious. Charlie thought about how these things would've come in handy at Jefferson, but of course there had been no one there to show them to her.

There were, too, a series of secret signs among the girls that happened behind backs and below tables. The first time Charlie found one directed at her, it had come from Kayla, who'd crossed the cafeteria with such a purposeful stride Charlie was convinced she'd unknowingly done something terrible to her roommate. But when Kayla got close enough, her demeanor shifted, and she produced a few furtive signs below the rest of the table's sight line.

What? Charlie said, *I don't understand.*

After the third try, Kayla gave up and said the same series of signs to

Alisha. Charlie watched their covert exchange from the corner of her eye and realized she'd been asking for a tampon.

Sorry, she said, as Kayla turned to go.

No worries.

Part of Charlie remained on the defensive, expecting that at any second her River Valley classmates might level her hopes for friendship, turn hostile at her invasion of their territory, or be fatigued by her shoddy ASL and rally behind Gabriella to make her life miserable. In the beginning, people had snickered at her when she said something clunky in class, and a girl once popped her implant magnet off in the bathroom and giggled. As the girl walked away, Charlie had noticed that she, too, had an implant—she saw a fair amount of them around campus—but she knew the hardware itself wasn't the target on her back. The other implanted kids were all fluent signers, or at least fluent compared to Charlie. It was annoying that people would make fun of her about this, as if it had been her choice not to learn. But after a few days of sitting beside Austin in the cafeteria, most of the teasing subsided. Now they were patient with her, an unflappability uncharacteristic of other teenagers she'd known, herself included.

Slowly she was becoming aware of how much she had believed the hearing world, the thousand little hatreds that had leeched into her being. It disgusted her now—when she looked across the table at Austin, or whenever someone was nice to her, really—the unworthiness that still washed over her, and the memories of how she'd behaved at Jeff to chase down the sensation of belonging. But with each successful social interaction, Charlie accrued new slivers of self-confidence. After a while she even got up the nerve (and the receptive skills) to ask her lunchmates about the verb "to be."

What that? she signed, pointing to one boy's lunch tray.

Pizza, someone said.

What i-s that? she said. She fingerspelled emphatically, question-marked her eyebrows. Austin understood first. With a flash of recognition, he scrunched up his face and gave her a scolding finger wag.

I-s. Finger wag, he said.

Charlie was disappointed—so "is," and "am" and "are" just . . . weren't? How could a language exist without so fundamental a concept? Perhaps, she thought grudgingly, her mother and doctors were right about the limitations of signing. Could you have a real language without the notion of being?

But Austin just pointed to Charlie's hand, then made his own gesture, sweeping up from his stomach out into an arc across the room. Charlie copied the sign, but that didn't seem to be what he wanted. She stared.

Me, said Austin, pointing to himself.

He patted his chest, then his arms, then held out his hands, flexed his fingers before her.

You, he said.

He took her by the wrists and held her own hands out before her. She looked down at her palms and understood—her being was implied, her potential thoughts and feelings coursing through her body, the names of everything she knew and those she didn't yet, all in perpetual existence in her fingertips.

As the weeks passed, Charlie faded from the conversation's focus to regular conversant—she had learned all the curse words there were to know, and was getting better at following along wherever the discussion went. Her shoulders relaxed, she allowed herself to smile.

When one of the football players made an English-ASL pun—a person standing upside down for *understand*—she laughed and Austin raised an eyebrow at her.

You got that?

Yeah.

Not bad, hearer.

It wasn't until he said it that she realized she couldn't hear anything at all, not even the normal static; it was like she'd taken off her CI for the night. She detached the processor and examined it, but the battery was good, or at least the indicator light still glowed "on." She reattached it to her head and felt something unfamiliar flutter through her as the sound returned. It gave her the chills, but it didn't hurt, exactly, and she'd forgotten about it by the time she got to play practice.

martha's vineyard: case study of a real-life eyeth

In 1694, deaf carpenter Jonathan Lambert and his wife, Elizabeth, arrived on Martha's Vineyard, part of a group of Massachusetts Bay colonists who moved to the island. The shared ancestry of many of the colonists tracing back to Kent in south England, in conjunction with the difficulty of travel between the Vineyard and the mainland, meant very little genetic diversity was introduced into the community for nearly a century. The result? A high incidence of hereditary deafness on the island.

THE NUMBERS

- Martha's Vineyard's deaf population peaked in the 1850s.
- At the time, **1** in approx. **5,700** Americans was deaf.

BUT

- On the Vineyard, it was **1** in **155**.
- In town of Chilmark, it was **1** in **25**.

THE NUMBERS (CONT'D)

- **1** in **25** is 4% of the town's population.
- **1** in **155** is only 0.6% of the Vineyard's population, but compared to the nation's average at the time—0.018%—it made a big difference.

What do you think happened next?

LIFE ON REAL-LIFE EYETH

- Deaf islanders developed their own language, "Chilmark Sign," now called Martha's Vineyard Sign Language (MVSL).
- Deaf and hearing islanders all signed.
- Deaf and hearing people worked and socialized together without barriers.

- Hearing people sometimes even signed without deaf people around!

Does MVSL still exist? Not exactly. In 1817, the American School for the Deaf opened in Connecticut, and many children from Martha's Vineyard attended. They brought MVSL with them, and it mixed with French Sign Language (LSF) and other home signs to create the ASL we speak today.

Deaf people began staying on the mainland after graduation, and this, combined with easier transportation to and from the island, meant less genetic isolation and the decline of the deaf population. By 1952, MVSL was considered extinct.

ASK YOURSELF:

In a community where everyone knows sign language and things like employment discrimination aren't a problem, is deafness a disability? Why or why not?

*W*raparound headache—pain slicing from ear to temple, across her vision, and down her neck. Pressure, as if someone had applied a tourniquet to her brain while she slept.

Charlie lay back down, squeezed her eyes shut, opened them again, but the do-over won her no relief.

Dad! she yelled, hoping she'd been loud enough for the sound to carry through her door. When he didn't come, she felt around for her phone and tried to text him, but the letters melted before her eyes. Even worse, she realized through her squint, she wasn't home at all. She rolled over to face Kayla's bed. Mercifully her roommate was still there, pulling on her socks.

You're gonna be late.

Then, when she actually looked at her:

You o-k?

Charlie could only point to her head. To her surprise, Kayla came to her side, felt her forehead.

No fever. That's good.

She winced. She was grateful Kayla was here, but also wished she hadn't touched her—the pain now pooled in the spot where her hand had been, as if magnetic.

I'll go get the dormkeeper.

Thanks, Charlie managed.

First school sick sucks. You'll be all
right.

Charlie did not feel all right, and though it didn't really occur to her until Kayla said so, being ill away from her parents *did* add a layer of terror to the experience. Their dormkeeper, Michelle, escorted her to the infirmary, Charlie with her hands out in front of her like a sleep-walker, afraid to fully open her eyes in the morning sun.

With a decade's worth of school nurse interactions under her belt, she wasn't expecting much. Charlie remembered a running joke from middle school: if a kid turned up carrying his own arm, Nurse O'Leary's first course of action would still be to offer him a Tums. Once she got to Jeff, the protocol was to accuse students of drug habits—no matter the ailment, the nurse would demand a list of illicit substances ingested, as if there was no other possible way for a teenager to fall ill. So Charlie was expecting Tylenol if she was lucky, and that had done jack shit the last time. But when they arrived at the infirmary, she was momentarily stunned out of cynicism when the nurse stood from her swivel chair and said:

Can I help you?

Except for via interpreter at her last visit to Colson Children's, Charlie had never been able to understand a medical professional. She flashed back to all the notes pinned to her shirt in elementary school, all the appointments at which a doctor and her mother had talked right over her head.

Hello? The nurse waved.

Headache, she said. *A strong*
one.

The nurse opened a large white cabinet overhead filled with generic bulk medicines. She took down a bottle, then stopped midtwist of the cap, and placed it on her desk.

Have you taken anything in the
last 48 hours?

Despite the gouging pain, Charlie smiled a little. Some things were the same everywhere.

No.

The nurse motioned for her to come, sheathed a thermometer in plastic, and took her temperature.

Perfect—98.6.

I run cold, Charlie said.

But the nurse just poured two pills into Charlie's hand and told her she could rest until they kicked in.

Thanks.

Charlie peeled back the curtain that cordoned off three cots wrapped in exam table paper. She lay down, but the room's fluorescent light cut through her eyelids.

Hello? she called to the nurse, hoping she might be able to turn off the light.

No response. She would have to get back up. Maybe, she thought, if she moved as fast as possible, her body wouldn't have time to register that it was happening. And so Charlie hurled herself at the curtain, and immediately vomited the remains of last night's chicken salad onto the gray tiled floor. When she opened her eyes again, the nurse was standing there, trying not to look peeved about having to clean up puke so early in the morning.

I'll call your parents, she said.

At home her father helped her into bed and told her to sit tight.

Dad? she said as he turned to go.

The words felt unlikely in her mouth even before they were fully formed:

Can you call Mom?

He returned a few minutes later with water and pills and a bag of frozen spinach. He helped lift her head and put the icy bag at the base of her neck.

I talked to your mother, he said. She said she used to get migraines when she was your age. Something about hormones.

It was hard to decide what felt most improbable: Charlie's mother having been a teenager, the two of them having this visceral thing in common, or how very much Charlie wanted her here now, how the pain bore a mother-shaped hole her father's tenderness did not fill. But the pain was also exhausting, and soon—despite the chill of the ice pack and the fact that she never slept on her back—Charlie felt herself sliding out of consciousness.

She woke later, startled by something she'd dreamt. She had a feeling she was supposed to be somewhere. What time was it? She tried to reach for her phone, but her arm was heavy, torpid. She dipped into sleep again, waking some time later, clammy, her father's hand on her shoulder and her pillowcase mottled with spinach melt.

How you feeling, sweetie?

She considered. Her vision was gauzy but the pain was no longer viselike. It was broader, but as it spread it had also thinned.

Better.

Do you want me to call you out tomorrow?

Charlie shook her head, said she wanted to make sure she had all her assignments for over the break, but really she just wanted to be back with her classmates. She thought of the people she was slowly coming to count as her friends—Austin, Kayla, and even the stage crew kids—and hoped she hadn't missed anything interesting.

That night, she opened her phone to find an unfamiliar icon in the notification bar. When she clicked it, a small video of Austin appeared.

You o-k? Missed you today.

She set her phone upright on her bureau, smoothed down her hair.

Sent home sick, but I'm o-k.

Good enough for pizza Tuesday?

For sure.

Charlie sent the message, then stood there staring at her phone screen until it went black and the reflection of her own goofy grin snapped her out of it. She wondered whether the invite for pizza counted as a date, though even if it didn't, it had to mean something that he'd checked in on her. What exactly, she wasn't sure. She wasn't even sure what she wanted it to mean. Still, the exchange warmed her, and she went to sleep buoyed by the hope of what tomorrow could be.

and you're sure they're treating you well. You swear?
February sat on the couch, rolling and unrolling her shirtsleeve as her mother gave her all the latest Spring Towers news via videophone. Her mother was thriving, constantly busy with a daily spread of activities, and February once again felt conflicted—mostly pleased, of course, but not without a pang of jealousy, too. It was infantile, she knew, to want her mother to miss her the way she missed her mother. Selfish. But if she couldn't help feeling it, at least she could quash it quickly.

We're having a great time! said her mother. *It's so nice to be with Lu again.*

I tried calling yesterday.

I saw that, but you know, in the morning we were playing shuffleboard, and then for half the day we couldn't find the remote to check the message. And do you know where it was? In my slipper!

At the sound of her mother's laugh February could feel her own smile shift, no longer forced.

I'm glad you're having fun.

> *I feel young again!*

Excited to see you next week,
February said.

> *Me too! Can't wait for Mel's pie.*

You and me both.

> *So you'll pick me up Thursday*
> *morning?*

I will. I was thinking around 10.

> *Perfect. Now will you go get your*
> *father for me? I need to ask him*
> *something.*

Dad? said February, stalling.

She couldn't tell her, not again. She'd broken this news dozens of times, and each time her mother was stunned and wounded, just as she had been the night he died. What a cruel disease, she thought, to steal from a person all their best moments, and make them relive the worst ones nightly. To force their loved ones to deliver these blows of memory until they, too, were subsumed by the echoing grief.

He's resting.

February heard the jangle of Mel's keys as she came in the side door and plopped them on the kitchen counter.

Hey, babe, Mel called. Do you want me to do something to this lasagna?

> *He ate too much pie?* said her
> mother.

February nodded.

> *He always does that!*

Her mother smiled again, and so did February. He had always done that.

> *Well, I should go down to dinner*
> *now. Can't wait to see you!*

Me too. Love you.

February hung up and padded into the kitchen, still unable to have a conversation across rooms after all these years. Mel sighed.

The whole point of me calling to you is that you don't have to get up, Mel said.

But this is nicer, right?—February hooked a finger in Mel's belt loop, pulling her closer—face-to-face?

No argument here. Hey, you all right?
But February did not want to talk about dementia or her dead dad. So instead of answering, she kissed Mel, and was relieved when she kissed her back. She let her body relax into Mel's, clinging to the small of her back to bring her closer, until there was no space between them at all. Mel ran a hand up February's thigh.

The lasagna needs forty-five minutes, said February, and led her toward the bedroom.

classifier trip

ASL Classifier (CL): A handshape that functions as a specialized pronoun. A signer will first say a specific sign, then introduce a classifier as a stand-in through which the signer can more seamlessly elaborate on the size, shape, manner, location, and action. For example, a signer might say "teacher," then use the classifier for "person" to show how the teacher walked across her classroom. Unlike pronouns in spoken languages, classifiers aren't just static stand-ins for a word, they can move through space to create a three-dimensional narrative.

COMMON CLASSIFIERS INCLUDE

Person i. old, hunched ii. large, fat	
Multiple People i. pair ii. threesome iii. large group iv. horde	
Animal i. small animal ii. large animal/ head details	
Vehicle i. land and water ii. flying	

Thin Items i. line, wire ii. rope			
Flat Items			
Squat Objects/ Buildings			
Containers			
Light			

NOW YOU TRY!

English: The red car speeds down the street headed right.

ASL: *car+ red + (CL: vehicle move fast toward right)*

English: The boy walks to the school down the street.

ASL: *school + (CL: squat building) + boy + (CL: person shows walking path)*

*a*fter play practice on Tuesday, plans for a trip into Colson materialized—this had been the pizza Austin was referencing, and Charlie tried to gauge whether she was disappointed or relieved. Together, a small group left the theater and crossed the quad.

Shit. Need to get my wallet.

Part of her expected them to leave without her, but instead, the group followed her back to the girls' upper dorm without discussion, and stood out front to wait for her, which was sweet and a little embarrassing—she was still the new girl, running behind. In their room, Kayla was sitting with a book in her lap, but staring listlessly at the wall. Her hearing aids—a bulky brown analog set—were beside her on the bed, and she'd dedicated one hand to fiddling with the old-fashioned on-off toggle.

You o-k?

Yeah, fine.

*Some of the theater kids are going
into Colson for pizza. Fickman
signed off. We can add you to the
list.*

No thanks.

It'll be fun, maybe.

Kayla pointed to her book.

Big test tomorrow.

Still gotta eat dinner . . .

Kayla sighed.

I can eat here for free.

You sure you're o-k?

I'm fine! she said, too forcefully.

Charlie raised her hands to show that she was letting it go.

Just, not really looking forward to Thanksgiving.

Sorry, Charlie said, though she wasn't quite sure what she was apologizing for.

Not your fault. Anyway, could be worse. My mom's boyfriend is garbage. But I've got a deaf aunt at least.

I had a deaf uncle, I think.

You think?

Never met him. Does your mom sign?

So-so.

Mine doesn't.

I assumed.

Well, my dad's been trying.

Now that you're grown.

You sure you don't want to come? I can buy.

O-hhhhh R-i-c-h-i-e Rich, said Kayla, though not unkindly.

Charlie dug through her desk drawer and pulled her wallet from the mire.

So you got the hots for King Austin, huh?

What? No.

Not what Alisha says.

Charlie tried not to resent the way everyone at River Valley seemed to know more about her than she did herself.

I don't know. We're just friends.

Look, he's just kind of—

Kayla started to sign something, then stopped and spelled it instead.

E–n–t–i–t–l–e–d. You know?

That's what Alisha says.

*Great minds. Really though—
you have to think all that golden
boy stuff has gone to his head.*

He's been nice to me.

Of course he has.

What's that supposed to mean?

I'm just looking out for you.

*Show me the sign. E–n–t–i–t–l–
e–d.*

She did.

So you'll come? said Charlie.

Thought you drowned in there,
said Austin, when Charlie and
Kayla turned up.

O–k if I join? said Kayla.

A few people nodded, Alisha with vigor, glad to see her friend. With Kayla they were eight: Austin, Tinker Bell, and two Lost Boys, plus Alisha and a pimply boy named Tim who did lighting. Gabriella, Charlie noticed, was conspicuously absent.

You should bring your roommate!

Kayla said.

She was looking at Austin, but elbowed Alisha in the ribs so swiftly afterward it almost became part of the sentence.

He . . . doesn't get out much.

Hot and older, Kayla explained
to Charlie.

Damaged goods, though, said
one of the Lost Boys.

You say, "damaged," I say "bad
boy."

Charlie was intrigued, but she could see Alisha was mortified and
trying to edge her way to the periphery of the conversation, so she let
the subject drop. Soon enough, Kayla had turned her attention back
to Austin.

Do I need to sign something? The
list?

Austin nodded, pulled Fickman's attendance sheet from his back
pocket and a pen from behind his ear.

The group walked down the drive together, and Charlie watched
as the others broke into little pods to chat. Austin, unpaired, led the
pack and handed the form to Walt. Charlie noticed the easy way
Austin approached the guard station, the fact that Walt didn't question their exodus at all, opened the exit gate without hesitation. Perhaps Kayla's distaste for Austin was jealousy, but that didn't mean
what she and Alisha had said about him was untrue. And if Austin
was the king of River Valley, what *did* he want with her, besides the
obvious? This was something that Charlie had recently found herself
turning over in her mind in those moments before sleep, her dorm
wall slipping in and out of focus as the time between blinks length-
ened. At Jefferson, her standing was clear—she hadn't fit in, and it
had been deafness, great and glaring, that made it so. Now at River
Valley, where deafness was the baseline and plenty of kids had implants, her identity had been hollowed out—who was she now that
she wasn't the deaf girl?

They tramped down the hill to the SORTA stop, and when the
bus arrived, swiped passes and dumped loose change into payment
receptacles while the driver looked on in dismay, though whether he
was annoyed by the appearance of a group of students, or by a group

of *these* students in particular, it wasn't clear. Charlie spent the ride marveling at her classmates' abilities to surf the lurching bus to keep their hands free for conversation. A few held on and signed in quick and incomprehensible (to Charlie, at least) one-handed bursts, or had one arm hooked around a pole for stability, but most could balance without it, their feet planted in wide stances, knees bent to absorb the pothole jumps. It was hypnotic, and as the bus turned down Colson's main drag, Charlie rubbed her eyes, dry from staring too long.

They poured from the bus into the center. Now, from her place in the middle of a pack, she saw Colson afresh. The city was sun drenched, warm enough for just a windbreaker even in late November, State Street's brick façades awash in magic hour orange. Her classmates were rowdy, bumping into one another, jumping and running ahead and then back again, joining different pockets of conversation.

Some of the stores were pure kitsch, all lawn ornaments and wind socks, but there was also a quaintness about the city's core businesses—the Chipped Cup's vintage aluminum sign, and the Moorlyn Theater's marquee; even Starbucks and Skyline Chili had gone with muted versions of their corporate colors to fit in on the block. If she were here with her parents, she would have found this disingenuous, but now she felt a sudden flash of pride in her city. She was glad to live here.

But if Charlie was seeing Colson anew, it returned its gaze differently, too. At first, she almost liked the feeling of strangers' eyes on them. Sure, they weren't like other kids, but look, there was a bunch of them, there was power in that. And she was in on the secret. Unfortunately, Steele's Candy wasn't a fan of their collective power, and swiftly ejected them from the store. Out on the corner, they regrouped. A shoulder tap. Charlie turned to find Austin chewing on a thick rope of licorice. He held out a piece to her.

Hey.

Hey.

> *Missed you yesterday. How you feeling?*

Better, thanks, she said.

She accepted the candy, sticking one end in her mouth.

> *What's new with you?*

Austin shrugged, then reached to brush a stray hair from her eyes. Something about the tenderness of the gesture made her throat feel tight. It seemed like a thing a thoughtful person would do, not a spoiled one.

> *I want to know about you. True biz, I have a very important question for you.*

The knot in her throat swelled. Whatever it was, she hoped he signed it small.

> *What's your favorite pizza?*

Charlie laughed.

> *Super important.*

> *It's not funny! It's c–r–i–t–i–c–a–l knowledge.*

That's easy. Pepperoni.

> *You like the classics.*

Why mess with the best?

> *Have you tried bacon?*

On pizza? Gross, no.

> *They're both pork!*

You're not one of those people who thinks p–i–n–e–a–p–p–l–e goes on pizza, are you?

> *What's wrong with pineapple?*

Charlie made a face and a playful push at his shoulder, but he was more solid than she'd been expecting, and she let her hand linger there. He brought his hand up to meet hers, ran his fingers along her wrist. She let herself be drawn into the greenwater wells of his eyes. Maybe it'd been a mistake to dodge his kiss when she'd had the opportunity, out on the loading dock all those weeks ago. In fact, she would've liked nothing more than for him to lean in right this moment and—

> *Did he just say he puts pineapple*
> *on his pizza?* said Kayla, evi-
> dently unmindful of said mo
> ment. *What'd I tell you about*
> *him?*

Charlie smiled, but she could see a flicker of concern across Austin's eyes.

> > *What did she tell you about me?*
> *None of your business. Roommate*
> *talk.*

> > *Fine—what's your pizza?*
> *B-b-q* _____, said Kayla.

What?

> *C-h-i-c-k-e-n. Chicken.*

Charlie started to copy Kayla's sign, but Austin held up a hand to stop her.

> > *Sign it like this,* he said.

The signs were quite different—Kayla's had been two-handed, a pinching of the pointer and middle fingers and thumbs, like a pair of beaks pecking downward, while Austin's was one-handed, the pointer finger and thumb creating a slender beak beside his nose. Charlie raised a hand to her own face skeptically, copying Austin's sign.

> *Chicken, chicken. Same differ-*
> *ence.*

> > *Your sign looks like,* _____
> Austin said to Kayla. Then,
> turning to Charlie: *d-i-a-p-e-r.*

Tinker Bell, who had been drawn to the growing heat of the conversation, stifled a laugh at this, and Charlie had to admit, Kayla's sign for chicken looked nearly indistinguishable from the one Austin had just done.

Fuck you and your diaper, said
Kayla, and stormed off.

*You're not the only one who's got
Deaf family, you know!* Alisha
said to Austin.

Then she looked to Charlie.

It's Black ASL, her sign.

There's . . . Black ASL? said
Charlie.

*Of course. Deaf schools were
also _____.*

What?

*S-e-g-r-e-g-a-t-e-d. Language
developed differently.*

But, wasn't that a long time ago?

It's cultural, said Alisha, then
looked back to Austin. *And
you're being racist.*

Charlie didn't know the sign for "racist" but Alisha had mouthed the
English word with such vigor there was no mistaking it. For his part,
Austin's whole body had gone rigid, and Charlie could see he was
about to protest, but instead let his hands drop. Alisha kept walking
until she'd caught up with the rest of the group, motioning for Charlie to come with her. Charlie felt herself hesitate, but when she found
her feet again, Alisha pretended not to have noticed.

Charlie tried to take in the conversation between Alisha and one
of the Lost Boys, but she couldn't concentrate. She knew it was un-
realistic, but she'd so wanted River Valley to be different than the rest
of the world. They had been mostly welcoming to her, and she'd assumed that was the benefit of a school full of rejects. But the realization that segregation and racism pervaded here, too, meant the Deaf
world was just as fraught as everywhere else.

She looked over her shoulder for Austin, but he was no longer behind them—at some point he'd circled round and caught up with Kayla. The two were having a fast and emphatic conversation Charlie doubted she would understand even if she were close enough. At the pizza place, Charlie ended up on the opposite end of the table from both of them, stuck beside Tinker Bell, who wanted to talk exclusively about Broadway shows Charlie had never seen. The waiter arrived looking peeved and threw a spread of menus down in the middle of the table, a pile of napkins atop that, leaving them mostly to fend for themselves.

By the time the pizza arrived, Tinker Bell had given up trying to make conversation with her, and Charlie was content to gaze out the storefront window. It was twilight, and the foot traffic was already clearing. Then, into the center of the frame stepped Gabriella, staring directly at her with a grin she didn't like. She pointed at Charlie.

Me? she said.

Gabriella nodded, then signed Austin's name, eyebrows raised in request. Charlie waved across the table to get his attention—asking someone to tap or flag down a friend was common practice in a world where calling one by name was pretty much useless—but regretted it as soon as he looked up. The fact that her body had chosen this particular moment to fully integrate this cultural norm into her muscle memory was annoying; she certainly did not want to help Gabriella. Plus, now everyone was staring at her.

Your girlfriend . . . e-x girlfriend, wants you . . .

A few people giggled, but Austin just looked bewildered.

I mean, she's outside. Standing in the window.

Austin blanched, then got up and walked toward Charlie's side of the table. When Gabriella saw him, she waved, and he gave a reluctant hello nod. Then she pulled a sandy-haired, muscular boy—he looked too old to be a River Valley student—into view and thrust her tongue into his mouth. Austin blushed and made a beeline for the bathroom.

Somebody's having a rough day,
Alisha said.

And while Austin had deserved the trouble he'd caught that afternoon, Charlie also found herself relieved that he would not hear his classmates now erupting into laughter.

*K*ayla could see that Austin had done it automatically, not like he was actively trying to be a dick. But did it matter? The hurt had come automatically, too.

And so had the sign. Usually, Kayla was careful to switch to blander, more standard versions of signs in mixed company to avoid the inevitable white people meltdown—not to appease them or anything, just because she just didn't feel like *dealing* with them. At least on this side of the Ohio. When her family had done a stint in Texas, things were slippier. More BASL users meant less shock and awe when a Black person happened to use a different sign.

But that was the problem with the North in general—things were still racist, they were just coy about it, all holier than thou because they happened to be living on the "right" side of some invisible line.

Anyway, Kayla decided to go easy on Austin this time. She could've gotten him in trouble if she wanted. She could have gone in and talked to Sybeck, or even Headmistress Waters—she knew neither of them played when it came to that kind of thing. But Austin had already doled out the harshest punishment to himself, acting a fool in front of Charlie like that, her looking at him like someone had ripped the stars right out of her eyes.

That didn't mean Kayla wasn't going to leverage his clout, though, and Austin was agreeable in the way guilty-feeling people are. So she had brought him on her TikTok and slapped him. The video went like this:

Kayla signs "chicken" and Austin makes his correction; Kayla slaps him and Austin spins round dramatically and falls to the floor, where Kayla zooms in and lays a caption over his eyes that says, BASL WITH THE KO. Austin rouses briefly to sign a groggy "Respect BASL" before passing out again.

It wasn't her best work, but it was something. And it already had four thousand views.

She had plans for a follow-up series—the history of BASL, or something about how in some cases segregation wound up giving Black kids better language access, because when oralism took over white Deaf schools, Deaf teachers were sent to Black Deaf schools, since no one cared whether Black kids learned to talk. She was still working on the angle, though. Most people swiped right by a video unless it was funny. Then again, a system so hateful that it ended up depriving white kids of language and accidentally giving it to Black kids was kind of funny, in a way.

Kayla loved the internet. TikTok, Instagram, YouTube, Twitch—she consumed it all. It reminded her that there were other people out there, beyond the claustrophobic walls and iron gates of River Valley. Sometimes she dreamt of going viral, the kind of viral that made you money, the kind of money that could free her mom and aunt from a life of cleaning other people's houses or clearing other people's plates. She would pay someone to clean their house and take them out to restaurants; she would buy her own damn sheets for her dorm bed; she would hire a personal interpreter who followed her around to every event, and she would sign *chicken* any way she pleased.

Even if TikTok didn't save her, in two years, she would be out of this place. She would graduate and collect her diploma and take her straight A's to Gallaudet, or RIT, or hell, even Ohio State or Wilberforce. Her goodbye to this place, to all of Colson, would be unsentimental, as unremarkable as the city itself. She would learn as much as she could and do whatever she could to dismantle all that she knew to be broken, brick by brick, by hand if she had to. She would keep the bricks, though. She would use them to build something new.

*f*ebruary found the emptying of the dorms before holiday breaks to be one of her more difficult tasks as headmistress. It was a chaotic affair, frenetic energy of students and parents eager to leave, their begrudging the security sign-out measures that slowed them down. Privately, February agreed with their frustration—she knew all her families by name—but the protocol had come straight from Swall, districtwide operating procedure post-Columbine–Virginia Tech–Sandy Hook–Parkland. Even the oldest of today's students wouldn't remember a time before.

Not everyone was in a hurry to leave RVSD, though. There were the good-naturedly late families—those with too much on their plates in the way of work or children, or Deaf clans like the Workmans, who ran on what the community called Deaf Standard Time, a reliable forty-five minutes late for almost any occasion. February scanned the crowd and saw no sign of the Workmans. Austin was probably still in his room, knowing better than to come out and stand waiting on the curb.

On regular weekends it was easier—kids who couldn't or didn't want to return home could get standing permission to go to a friend's instead. But for a holiday, those permission slips were null, meaning students who hadn't established a bus route with their districts had to be retrieved by their parents. No surprise that these children were also usually the school's most vulnerable. Here were the screaming kindergarteners and first graders who had found language in the classroom and tantrumed ostentatiously at the thought of going home. February felt both protective of these children and an acerbic mix of pity and anger toward the parents, who looked at her forlorn, as if this was fate and there was nothing they could possibly do to change it. You could *try*! she wanted to shout, though she knew it was judgmental of her to assume they weren't, in their way. The most she ever did was remind them of the school's free friends and family ASL classes. But usually she said nothing, did her best to keep her head down and attend to logistics: directing traffic, dispatching deep-cleaning crews, or fondling her walkie-talkie in a performance of security.

Here were the foster children whose erratic placements meant no bus would come, waiting for some harried social worker to turn up. And then there were the "Malloys"—those who neglected or sometimes downright refused to retrieve their children. It had been years since she had seen the actual Malloys, but they had been the first such people February had encountered in her career, and the name had become her personal umbrella term for the kind of parent who would rather not have their kid. The original Malloys had a lovely, wide-eyed boy named Jamie, whose black hair stood on end—as if he needed another attribute to distinguish him from his fair and freckled family. The first couple of pickups, she'd thought it was an accident. It was not yet in her nature to assume that a parent did not have a child's best interests in mind. But by the end of Jamie's first year, when the Malloys had failed to materialize to collect their son and his belongings for summer break, February realized they were doing it on purpose. She'd called and called the numbers on his emergency contact card, waited until 5:00 P.M., long after everyone else had gone—it had been a half day. Then she called the police.

The deputy sheriff had turned up to take Jamie to the station, where the Malloys, she'd later heard, had been threatened with Child

Protective Services before he was released into their custody for the summer. The next Thanksgiving it happened again. February watched helplessly while Jamie was foisted off on various relatives before finally applying to emancipate himself. She learned via the Deaf world's gossip trellis that he now lived in Rochester and had become an electrician. By all accounts, he was happy. By all accounts, this was exceptional.

This year's Malloys were the Schneiders, their daughter Emily pacing the length of the curb with increasing speed as the crowd waned, obviously nervous that she would be the last one standing, again.

Like the Malloys, the Schneiders had another kid, a hearing one, which made things worse for the contrast it provided. While Jamie had swirled through the foster system, his siblings stayed in the home. For her part, Emily was nearly always dressed in her older brother's enormous clothes, which was no crime, of course, but it added insult to injury when combined with other persistent parental efforts to forget her. By 5:00 P.M., February was in a dark place, mulling over how the Schneiders' propensity for neglect was particularly irrational given that Emily spoke well and was one of the most successful CI users at the school. As if these things were value-addeds. As if a child who could be made "hearing" enough was more worthy of love.

She pulled her cell from her back pocket and made the call to the sheriff, admonished the part of her brain that would even entertain the ranking of children. But whether or not she banished the thoughts from her own head did little to help Emily, or any of the kids whose parents' affections were distributed on a sliding scale tethered to how well said kid could perform normalcy. By the time she hung up, her rage had cooled and soured into despair at the thought of what might happen to Emily, and all the others like her, next year, when her parents were forced to care for her full-time.

Come on, February said after a
while. *We can wait in my office.*
I've got cookies.

She heard sirens in the distance as she walked the girl inside. Though
she had called the nonemergency line, she assumed it was the sheriff
heading their way. Must be a slow day in Colson County.

i said, how was school? If I'm signing you can't i-g-n-o-r-e me!

Charlie was a little shocked by how adept her father was becoming at sign language. His vocabulary was limited, but conceptually it seemed to come easy to him, and he got by on fingerspelling or talking around a word just fine. In their night class, he'd already surpassed a couple of the other parents who'd been at it longer, moms for whom the effort of learning a new language was obviously challenging. So Charlie was glad that her father was making progress, but also angry that he hadn't tried to learn sooner. She wondered what he'd been afraid of—failure? his wife?—and what her childhood might have looked like if she'd had a bastion of language, however small, to which she could have run when she needed it.

Sorry, was thinking.

Daydreaming, you mean.

More like drowning in a pool of her own mortification, Charlie thought, the pizza outing's events still replaying in her head. She'd been too cowardly to say anything much to Kayla about what had happened between her roommate and Austin, beyond apologizing for her own dearth of knowledge about Black ASL. Kayla had brushed her off, saying, *Girl, you don't know ASL either,* and they'd both laughed a little, but that had been it. Charlie felt contrite on Austin's behalf—after all, she'd been the one to cajole Kayla into coming along in the first place.

Still, when Charlie pulled her own phone from her pocket, she found herself disappointed, then repulsed at that disappointment, to see none of the four new messages on the screen were from Austin.

Comingover.to drop smtng of okay?

*off

Aare u hokme?

*home!

Shit, Charlie said to her father.

Mom's coming over.

Now?

She wants to drop something off,

she says.

What?

No idea.

Her mother was parked out front, leaning on her car and poking at her phone with one long acrylic nail. She seemed flustered by their arrival, as if Charlie and her father had shown up at her house instead of the other way around.

Sorry, I figured you'd be—she glanced again at her phone—home by now. Anyway, just wanted to drop this off.

Charlie didn't know what her mother was talking about, but she could see her father remove his glasses and rub at his eyes, a tic she'd come to know was his attempt at disguising exasperation. Her mother began rooting through the contents of her purse, finally drawing out a small white box, the shape of which Charlie recognized right away.

Popped down to the clinic to grab this. So you have it for school and stuff.

Dad just picked me up for Thanksgiving break. We don't have class.

Oh, well. Anyway, she said. Here it is.

Charlie tried to maintain a neutral expression, but she could feel her own frustration surfacing. Her mother had to have known she'd be out on break; she just wanted Charlie to show up to Thanksgiving dinner with her implant on. Why couldn't her mother ever say what she was really thinking? Were they really still playing this fucking game after all these years?

Once, at the clinic, Charlie had seen a boy with a cochlear implant talking on the phone. At first, she entertained conspiracy theories. Maybe he was an actor hired by Edge, and this was a rehearsed conversation. Maybe there wasn't anyone on the other end at all. It didn't feel so far-fetched, given the chasm between the task this boy seemed to be enjoying and the subpar work the thing in her own head was doing. Given what she knew of implant sales reps.

In that same hospital, she'd also come upon two women with name tags and pencil skirts plucking their eyebrows before the bathroom vanity, one bragging to the other how much product she'd sold, that she was going to Biloxi for the weekend and drinks were on her. At the time, Charlie didn't understand much beyond a gut-level aversion to the woman's smarm, but thinking back on it later, she realized that someone must have earned a commission on her own mother's worst nightmare.

So it was hard to watch her mother now, gingerly removing from its case the processor she'd driven out of her way to retrieve. She handled it like a family heirloom, but for Charlie it felt more like watching an alcoholic have just one beer.

They preset your last MAPping on here, her mother said. But I made an appointment for an adjustment if we need it.

We don't need it, thought Charlie, though she said nothing aloud. Instead she took the processor, hung it over her ear, swept her hair back, and attached the magnet.

How does it feel?

Charlie was used to being asked questions about her deafness, but the one that really irked her was "What does hearing with an implant sound like?" It wasn't the all-time dumbest inquiry—someone at Jefferson had once asked her if her ears got cold in winter—but it was the one she most hated, perhaps because it bothered her that she would never know the answer. How could she know what it was like when she had nothing to compare it to? But now, the three of them standing there looking at one another, Charlie cocking her head in discomfort, her mother all hope like a helium balloon, she felt more sad than annoyed.

Feels good, I think, said Charlie. Might take a while to tell.

Of course, said her mother. Have to get used to it.

Charlie nodded, shifted her weight between her feet. She wondered whether other people felt so awkward in front of their mothers.

Well, I better go. Ms. Sweet Potato Pie costumes wait for no woman.

In a different mood, Charlie might've had a good joke about pageants named after starches.

I'll be over Wednesday night then, said Charlie.

Her mother made the one-armed reach that Charlie understood was her version of a hug, then returned to her car, where she backed out of her parking spot a little too fast, as if she were being released from captivity.

Your mom's just trying to help.

Doing a shitty job.

Her father sighed.

The goal of your implant was always—

To make her life easier?

To make your *life easier.*

This *makes my life easier.*

Charlie held her hands outstretched toward her father.

Yeah, she guessed wrong, he said. But her heart was in the right place. She has her regrets.

Regrets? I've got a chunk of
metal inside my head!

And what if you never had it? Never learned to speak at all?
Plenty of people don't talk at all,
she said, though really Austin
was the only one she knew for
sure. *And they've had more nor-*
mal lives than me.
Normal? he said. Isn't that what you're always raging against?
Why are you defending her?
I'm only saying she loves you. Tough love, maybe—
Was that what it was with you
two? "Tough love?"
Oh no, she hated me, he said.
Charlie groaned.
But she doesn't hate you. Despite both your best efforts.
I have homework, Charlie said.

                              Now?

Charlie rolled her eyes and retreated to her room. Previously, she'd believed her relationship with her mother to be a great injustice, but lately she'd been thinking that the truly unfair thing was the expectation that a mother should completely understand another human just because she'd given birth to them. Charlie was constantly letting her father off the hook for being clueless. Why wasn't a mom allowed to be wrong? Maybe *Peter Pan* was messing with her head somehow, all the talk of lost and imported mothers. Either way, Charlie had not turned the processor on and her mom had not been able to tell, and for now, she thought, that was just fine.

the cure for you

Since ancient times, hearing people have been trying to "cure" deafness, with some tactics more successful (or harmful) than others. Throughout history, swindlers and medicine men have frequently been charged with fraud for their false claims to have cured hearing loss.

ANCIENT TIMES

- An Egyptian recipe from 1550 BCE says to inject olive oil, red lead, bat wings, ant eggs, and goat urine into the "ear that hears badly."
- This is the earliest written mention of deafness.

ANCIENT TIMES–EARLY CE

- The New Testament contains the story of Jesus healing a deaf man using saliva.
- "Faith healings" remain popular throughout the Christian fundamentalist tradition.
- Healing rituals are also common in other religions.

EARLY CE–17TH CENTURY

- Herbal and spiritual methods persist.
- This period is considered the heyday of manual (signed) education, so less historical emphasis is based on cure-finding.
- Use of ear trumpets begins.

18TH CENTURY

- Ear trumpets gain popularity.
- Acoustic throne: hidden amplification device attached to a hollow chair.
- Trumpet variants include double-sided acoustic horn and acoustic headband.

19TH CENTURY

- Harsh chemicals like mercury, silver nitrate
- Catheterization—trying to reach ear "blockages" through the nose
- Electricity, UV light, and vibration applied to different parts of the ear
- Artificial eardrums placed in ear canal
- Increased desire for "hidden" aids

20TH CENTURY

- Airplane rides, particularly upside down, to "correct" ear pressure
- Electromagnetic head cap
- Hypnosis
- Hearing aids: analog body, behind the ear, in the ear, and bone-anchored aids with digital aids increasing programming specificity
- First cochlear implants introduced

21ST CENTURY

Rise of cochlear implants:
- internal and external device components
- bypasses inner ear to stimulate auditory nerve rather than amplify sound
- earlier models destroy residual hearing
- success varies widely

In development:
- rehabilitative stem cell therapies
- gene and genome editing

While hearing people have attempted to cure deafness for centuries, it's important to note a difference in technological power, age of application, and permanence for 21st-century cures, raising questions of ethics and consent.

Deaf children are already non-consensually implanted with CIs, but what happens when an infant is injected with stem cells and made hearing, or a fetus is "edited" in utero?

DISCUSSION QUESTIONS:

1. What are the medical community's ethical obligations when it comes to preserving human diversity?

2. At what line does the practice of "designer babies" become un-ethical, and who gets to decide?

*a*ustin spent the rest of Tuesday evening and all of their truncated Wednesday schedule awash with humiliation, playing The Incident on a loop in his head—how pigheaded he'd been, how thoughtless, how extremely *white*. He felt terrible about it, and that had been the impetus for his apology, though even as he'd talked with Kayla there was the nagging thought of Charlie having witnessed it all. Would Kayla tell Charlie he'd tried to make it right? That he'd met with her after school to do her TikTok, and had also promised expressly not to be a dick?

He hadn't talked to Charlie since. He'd given her an anxious hug that night as they parted on the walkway between dorms, but Austin had felt her hesitation, a hairline fracture blooming between them in the dusk.

Then there was the matter of his family. Something was off. Austin hadn't talked to his parents much—really talked—since Sky was born. He'd spent his weekends splayed on the couch half-watching reruns of old medical dramas and Spider-Man movies, or sequestered in his room doing homework; he'd even gone over to Cole's house to play video games, though he'd never had the taste for them—anything to avoid prolonged interaction with his father. His mom was exhausted and consumed with tending to Sky, but things between her and Austin had basically returned to normal. With his father, though, it still felt hard.

Returning to school each Monday was a relief. He and his parents had a long-standing text thread just to check in, where they asked him about school and scheduled times to video chat. But besides the occasional baby picture dropped in without comment—Sky in a Buckeyes onesie, or footie pajamas, or looking lopsided in tummy time—the chat had grown quiet over recent weeks. When his father finally did call, it had been to tell Austin to take the SORTA home. He'd been hoping they would pick him up so he could make a dent in his laundry, but he didn't mention it. They were busy with a newborn, after all.

Now he arrived home to find the house empty. He tucked his duffel bag in his room and beelined for the kitchen, where he crammed himself with leftover pot roast, cold and straight from the Tupperware, eating around the bits of congealed fat. His parents found him this way, carrying with them a groundswell of tension that ran through the kitchen like a cold snap. His mother didn't even chide him for eating standing up—a pet peeve of hers—and instead clutched him in a tighter than usual hug. Over her shoulder, Austin thought he saw his father roll his eyes.

Welcome home, said his mother.
Still in the car seat on the floor, Skylar began to fuss. Austin surveyed his father, anticipating a lullaby or a coo, but he said nothing with his mouth, just retrieved the baby from her seat and nestled her in the crook of one arm, signed to her about warming a bottle.

How were midterms? said his
father as he stuck the bottle
beneath hot water.
*Pretty easy. Trig was my only
test. The others were papers. And
Sybeck always forgets to deduct
points for Deaf grammar.*

Great, his father said.

Everything o-k?

Fine, said his mother.

Where were you guys?

Doctor.

His father motioned with his head to Sky.

She's fine.

Any shots? Is she still tall for her age?

70th percentile!

Wow!

He reached for Sky and carefully positioned her the same way his father had held her, then congratulated her on how she could become the first ever Workman to be good at basketball.

Wanna feed her? said his mother. *Test it on your wrist.*

He took the bottle and watched Sky drink fervently. He could feel his parents saying something in his periphery, their signs growing forceful behind him, but he was spellbound by Skylar's wide eyes— still blue—and the concentration she devoted to eating. When he finally looked up, it was because his father had stomped on the floor. He'd done it to get his mother's attention, but the vibrations ran through Austin and Sky just the same, and they both turned to him.

You tell him.

His father stalked off toward the den.

Tell me what?

Your father's just upset. He doesn't like change.

What's wrong?

We weren't at the pediatrician. We were at the audiologist.

With Sky? I thought—

*Your father noticed her respond-
ing less to voices, sounds. I figured
she's an infant, how can you tell?
But they tested, and her threshold
has dropped to around 40 d-B.*

She's . . . hard of hearing?

*Seems like it. But with today's
hearing aids they can amplify so
much. That's where we were just
now—earmold fitting.*

And Dad's upset?

Burp her, his mother said,
handing him a cloth.

Austin threw it over his shoulder and hoisted Sky up, tapped her on
the back.

More.

He clapped her harder; a wet burp rattled through them both.

She burps like an old man! he
said, and they laughed.

*Don't be too tough on your father.
When you were born, I was
happy I had someone to share
Deaf culture with. He felt the
same about Sky.*

Hearing culture?

*You know, podcasts, being im-
pressed by rhymes, hatred of sub-
titles?*

His mother winked.

*At least Dad doesn't hate subti-
tles.*

*Dad works hard making sure ev-
erything's accessible for us.*

I know, Austin said.

> *He just needs time to process.*

Austin returned Skylar to the dregs of her bottle.

What about you?

> *I loved Skylar before and I love her now. I do worry things will be harder for her, same as I did for you. But . . .*

Austin raised his eyebrows.

> *It's tradition,* she said.

His mother flashed a small, impish smile. The bottle emptied, Skylar began to cry and Austin returned the baby to his mother.

> *Remember, gentle on your dad.*

He nodded and went into the den. A series of spreadsheets were open on the monitor, but his father was playing with a Slinky.

Hey, Austin said with his mouth.

> *You talk with your mom?*

Yeah.

> *You have a little Workman cele-bration?*

What? No.

> *Sorry. That was outta line.*

Mom said you're upset.

> *No excuse.*

Austin looked at his feet.

> *Of course it doesn't matter, deaf, hearing. But when the nurse came in that first day, I started thinking of songs my mom sang to me when I was a kid. Things I couldn't give to you.*

Mom said you sang to me.

His father smiled.

> *I did.*

*Mom said she'll hear well with
the aids.*

> *She will.*

She'll be o-k.

His father motioned for him to come around to his side of the desk, hugged him one-armed. A feeling of pride swelled in Austin, that he could comfort his father for once.

> *You know something?*

What?

> *That pot roast you were eating
> was really old.*

Great.

> *Like, REALLY old.*

Austin groaned and shrugged off his father's arm.

> *Think we can convince Mom to
> go for burgers? She's usually game
> for takeout before a big cooking
> holiday.*

*If we both give her sad puppy
eyes at once?*

> *Wait till we can teach Sky, too.*
> *Poor woman will be defenseless
> against three of us!*

Austin and his father returned to the kitchen in good spirits, and his mother brightened at the sight of them together. Skylar was craning her neck to get a look at everyone, and in the wake of her tiny, crooked grin, he even stopped pining for Charlie, at least for a while.

*C*harlie was always ambivalent about the holidays. On one hand, she took more than a little pleasure in seeing her mother frazzled at the prospect of her own mother's arrival. On the other, this meant she, too, had to be in the presence of her grandmother.

Charlie's mother's mother was, unsurprisingly, overbearing in concentrate. Her scent was sickly, almost funereal, lilies in lieu of her mother's lighter, citrusy smell. Her hair, also bleached and bobbed, was teased higher at the crown, her shoes (fuchsia, kitten heel) less practical than her mother's favored loafers. And then there was her personality.

Charlotte! her grandmother twanged when Charlie answered the door.

She clutched Charlie's face, insisting on a pair of French-style cheek kisses, knocking Charlie's processor from her ear and sending it skidding across the foyer floor.

What'd you do to your hair?

Nothing? Charlie said.

Her grandma tugged at a faded turquoise strand at the base of her neck, a summer experiment Charlie had forgotten was there. The woman was good.

Oh, that.

Charlie twirled the dull blue strip around her finger, tucked it back

beneath the rest of her hair. Her grandmother had already lost interest and was clacking her way into the kitchen. Charlie hung her
grandmother's coat—a burgundy fur she really hoped was fake—on
the hat rack and followed her in.

Smells good, said her grandmother as she ran her hand along a
sill, then inspected her fingers.

Mother, please. It's a little early for the crime scene investigation.
Her grandmother tucked her hands behind her back.

I haven't said a word.

I cleaned the house.

Of course, dear. Is Wyatt here?

Charlie's mother nodded her head in the direction of the living room,
where her boyfriend of nearly a year was standing too close to the
television, watching football. Wyatt, Charlie had decided upon careful inspection, was a schmuck. Technically there was nothing wrong
with him, besides his being attracted to her mother, though of course,
her father had been, too. But Wyatt was doughy, pale in both complexion and temperament, and she had once seen him watch an entire evening's worth of March Madness while still wearing his tie all
the way up, tight around his neck. Still, he might come in handy, if
only as a warm body to deflect some of her grandmother's attention.
Across the island, Charlie could see her mother having a similar
thought, albeit with different bait:

What time's your father coming? she said.

Not sure. I can text him.

Charlie pulled her phone from her back pocket, sent her dad an SOS.

Need help? Charlie said to her mother afterward.

Potatoes?

Sure.

Charlie took the peeler from the side drawer and watched her grandmother interrogate Wyatt about something she couldn't understand.
She peeled the whole bag's worth, quartered the potatoes, and put them
in a pot of salted water, then moved on to set the table. Her mother's
grateful eyes caught hers as she slipped the linen napkins through their

rings. This was the thing Charlie liked most about her grandmother's visits—she and her mother were a united front, at least momentarily.

It was only a matter of time before her grandmother turned her inquisition to Charlie. Her father showed up right as they were sitting down to dinner, and attracted surprisingly little attention beyond the signature sweep of her eyes, designed to decimate any remaining ounce of one's confidence, and the question, though trussed in Southern politeness, of why he was still hanging around.

Charlie lives with me.

Well that's very admirable. To be honest I always assumed you were _____ on Lynnette.

Umm, no? said her father. No ya _ing.

Mother—

What? Y-a-r-n-i-n-g? Charlie said.

Y-a-r-d-i-n-g, her father said.

Cheating . . . I think?

Charlie hadn't meant to do it. She had been planning to avoid the topic of her new school entirely. Her mother wouldn't have mentioned it—that would mean admitting defeat—and her father wouldn't have spoken about anything at all if he could've gotten away with it. That had left Wyatt, oblivious to controversy, as the only person who could have spilled the beans.

But Charlie had gone and blown her own cover. How quickly she'd become accustomed to understanding what was happening around her, where for years, she'd been resigned to drift in a low-tide quiet, letting conversation wash over her. She knew it was a change for the better, she just wished she could have let this *particular* exchange go. She steeled herself for the inevitable barrage.

Charlotte? said her grandmother, raising her own hands slightly. Where on earth did you learn that?

The internet? Charlie said.

But both her parents gave her a look.

And—at my new school. River Valley.

Private school? said her grandma.

Well, said Charlie's mother.

School for the Deaf, Charlie said finally.

Her grandmother froze, her wine halfway between the table and her lips, then reversed course and set the glass back down.

Really? she said.

Charlie nodded. Her mother nodded. Wyatt, who at some point had swapped his own silverware with the serving spoon Charlie had laid out, was shoveling large scoops of stuffing into his mouth without looking up. Her grandmother stood.

Well, Charlotte, I think that's wonderful! How do you say "wonderful" in your language?

Charlie blinked hard to clear away the shock.

Wonderful, she said.

Her grandmother copied her motion, then pulled Charlie into a sideways hug. Charlie raised her eyebrows at her parents over her grandmother's shoulder.

It's about time, her grandmother said. Why are you all looking at me like a hair in your biscuit?

I'm not, said her mother. I'm just surprised by your reaction.

Well come now, Lynnette. It's not as if she was fooling anyone.

Mother!

That's more like it, said Charlie's dad.

And how do you feel, Charlotte? At the new school?

It's great, she said through a mouthful of green beans. I'm learning a lot.

Don't talk with your mouth full, Charlotte, goodness, she said, smiling and thwacking another serving of mashed potatoes onto her daughter's best china.

They'd plowed through dessert by six and were standing on the front step wishing her grandmother farewell within the hour.

Can I go with you? Charlie asked her father as he pulled his shoes back on.

Thanksgiving's your mom's, he said.

What? said her mother, lurching back into the foyer.

Nothing, said Charlie.

Good night, her father said.

He kissed her on the cheek and Charlie closed the door behind him, trying not to let her face betray her disappointment as she turned back in to the house. But her mother was apparently too intoxicated to keep up appearances, and gave Charlie a sour look. She was listing, as if one leg was longer than the other.

You, she said.

What?

Why would you do that?

I didn't mean to. It just came out.

Her mother scoffed.

You really do live to embarrass me, don't you?

Charlie was so used to fighting with her mother it was almost second nature. But something about the earnest drunken nature of the question gave it a unique sting.

No, she said softly.

She watched her mother lurch back into the kitchen and snag her toe on the island barstool, shout something she couldn't see, but assumed was a swear. Her mother never cursed, and she was almost sorry to have missed it.

Whatever her mother had said was bad enough to rouse Wyatt from the couch; he poured a glass of water and took her hand.

Let's get you upstairs, he said.

Her mother didn't argue, but managed to glare at Charlie dramatically as Wyatt led her back through the foyer to the front staircase. Charlie stood in her wake, just staring at the front door for a while, wondering what to do.

*f*or February, intuition was a kind of intelligence, and her instincts were perhaps all she considered exceptional about herself. She'd been prone to anxious dreams since childhood, inscrutable images laid out before her in a code she hadn't yet cracked. One night when she was seven, she dreamt the family dog was abducted by aliens, and woke to find him dead on the kitchen floor, tongue lolling from his open mouth. She'd thought that when she got older, her dreams would become proper premonitions, narratives from which she could extract useful information. When her father died, though, she'd felt nothing ahead of time, leaving her bewildered. Why hadn't her subconscious warned her? She took comfort in the fact that the doctors had said her father hadn't felt much of anything, either—the coronary was so massive, death would have been instantaneous—but still the events threw the instincts February was so proud of into doubt.

This time there was no excuse. She woke at dawn Thanksgiving morning, though that wasn't special—she'd long ago lost the capacity to sleep in. Mel, who was functionally useless without a full eight hours, rolled herself into the warm space February left in their bed.

February showered, dressed, pinned up her hair, emailed Swall to demand he meet with her and Assistant Headmaster Phil next week, to bring him up to speed. She needed help to draw up plans for the students' future programming. When a vacation autoreply bounced back, she forced herself to close her laptop. Today she would finally follow through on the oft-made promise (to herself, to Mel) of a work-free twenty-four hours.

In the kitchen, she hefted the turkey from its perch in the refrigerator and onto the counter. The smell of raw meat usually flipped her stomach, but Mel had given the bird a dry rub that was salty and aromatic, the garlic and thyme masking the metallic tang of blood. She wrested the bag of giblets free and emptied it into a frying pan to sear before starting the gravy—no escaping the smell there, and February had to childishly pull her T-shirt up over her nose to keep from gagging.

Neither she nor Mel was much for stuffing, but their parents—Mel's father and February's mother—had both taken a liking to it in recent years. Softer on the dentures. She spooned some dressing Mel had made the day before into the bird's vacant inner cavity. Was she supposed to tie it up now—trussing, was it? She tried to remember what she'd seen Mel do in years past, but they had no string in the junk drawer and anyway the bird was nearly too big for the pan as it was; she doubted anything would be able to shift around. She stretched strips of bacon in a crosshatch across the turkey's back and preheated the oven.

Now for the good stuff. February wondered how the whole turkey tradition had stuck. She'd never met anyone who actually liked to eat it, except maybe in a sub. But the sides, those she could get behind. Sweet potato pie, cornbread, mac and cheese. She jiggled the pan of giblets, browning now, to keep them from sticking.

Mel appeared in the doorway, bangs askew, and surveyed February's work with a look she'd come to know as gratitude, though Mel rarely said such things aloud, and pretty much never spoke at all in the first fifteen minutes of being awake. She'd like sign language, February often thought.

Morning, hon.

Mel nodded and pulled two mugs down from the cabinet, fixed their coffee. She handed one to February, who placed it absently on the counter.

Thanks, she said, and returned to the stove.

What's wrong? said Mel.

Nothing. Why?

Mel gestured to the mug.

No coffee?

I just want to get this going.

You'd mainline coffee if they'd let you.

I was thinking I could use a detox.

And you think Thanksgiving is the day to start a dietary cleanse?

It did sound ridiculous once she heard it aloud.

I suppose not, she said.

She retrieved her mug and took a sip. It always tasted better when Mel made it.

That's my girl, Mel said.

She clinked cups with February and kissed her on the corner of her mouth, then disappeared into the next room. February heard the television hum on, then the sounds of the parade in New York.

You're not gonna help me in here?

Feb, it's eight thirty. Damn, that float is creepy. Come see this!

I wanna be done before I leave to get Mom. Do you think we need another vegetable? Salad?

Did you not hear what I said about the cleansing? Nobody's coming to Thanksgiving dinner for the salad.

What time did you tell your dad?

Three.

Should we invite the people across the street?

Oh look, Snoopy!

Mel!

I'm sure the neighbors have plans.

We have, like, twenty pounds of turkey.

Tell you what, said Mel. If you can tell me their name, then yes, we should invite them.

The, uh— Not fair, you know I'm terrible with names—

Or anything about them at all—

They've got a red minivan.

Are you looking out the window right now?

He works for Amazon. Down in Hebron.

I suppose that counts.

The Jacksons! February shouted.

Bravo, said Mel.

You knew their name the whole time, didn't you?

Of course, Mel said. They're our neighbors.

February started toward the living room, but Mel met her in the doorway.

You love me and find me witty and charming, said Mel.

True, said February.

She pressed Mel into the doorframe and kissed her with an intensity that surprised them both. Then the phone rang, the landline.

They ignored it at first. No one they knew would call that number anymore. February had been meaning to cancel the service for months but kept forgetting, in part because it so seldom rang. But after a few rings, it was more difficult for her to ignore it than to pick it up, so she shuffled back into the kitchen and collected the handset from its cradle, intent on asking whatever telemarketer was on the line to remove them from their list.

Perhaps she'd had a premonition after all, in the urge to pick up that call. They would've called her cellphone eventually, but February would be glad for the extra seconds' head start while her favorite Spring Towers nurse explained that her mother had been found unresponsive during breakfast rounds, that she'd had a large stroke and had been made comfortable with a combination of pain and anti-anxiety medications, that February should come right away.

Anti-anxiety? February said as she ran to the bedroom and pulled her jeans up over her thighs. Is she awake?

The nurse cleared her throat.

It eases discomfort without slowing breathing, she said. Then, with so much care it was almost a whisper: For patients experiencing terminal agitation.

I'll be right there, February said.
She pulled on a hoodie and lapped the house looking for her purse. Had the nurse said "terminal"?

Go, said Mel. I'll clean up and be right behind you.
When February arrived at the Towers, the receptionist gave her directions to the hospice ward, where her mother had been moved, directions February immediately forgot, or more likely had never absorbed, so bloated was the word "hospice" in her mind there was no space for anything else.

Her mother was asleep when she got there. Of course she was. The nurse said it was unlikely she would wake again. But February nevertheless clutched frantically at her mother's hand, spread kisses across her forehead in hopes that she might startle her into coming to for a moment, just to know that February was beside her.

She remembered the day she'd learned about Helen Keller in elementary school, how she'd gone home full of wonder that they had discussed a deaf person in class, one who could understand sign language just by feeling it. Her mother had taken pleasure in her excitement, and they'd practiced fingerspelling words into one another's palms: *c-a-t*, *F-e-b*, *m-o-m*. Now February pressed an *I love you* into her mother's hand, and was met with a small moan.

February had not expected the sound of her mother's voice to be the thing to carve out an ache in her. Her mother had rarely spoken, only when she was angry or frightened. It was her other sounds, the laughs and grunts, that February knew she would miss. She allowed the sorrow to well up in her until its pressure throbbed behind her eyes, then climbed into the hospital bed and cried with such force that her mother's eyelids fluttered, and her lips curled subtly into a kiss that grazed February's cheek. Then, as if on strings, her mother's arms raised from the bed like the caricature of a sleepwalker, and

February felt equal parts awe and shame at the power of the instinct to comfort one's child. She guided her mother's arms back down and smoothed her hair until she was calm again.

Mel arrived with coffee and two bags of hot Cheetos, their preferred snack for stress eating. She pulled up a chair beside February, who was still in the bed watching the second hand between her mother's breaths. Neither of them said anything for a very long time.

She never fell asleep, not exactly, but somehow night came, and Mel urged her to stretch her legs. February ungracefully freed herself from the bed's rails, went to the bathroom and washed her face, bought a Coke from the vending machine. Her arm was numb, her neck stiff from craning to look at the clock. She'd been tired in her mother's dim room, but now beneath the violent hall lights, she was jittery and short of breath. She tried walking around the ward, but the sharp smell of antiseptic made her claustrophobia worse, so she took the stairs down to the main lobby and went outside, stood there on the sidewalk and let the cold nip at her cheeks, the automatic doors gnashing open and shut behind her. She waited until her toes went numb—the chill took just a few minutes to get through her sneakers—then turned back to the vestibule, the doors opening again to beckon her inside.

All right, I'm going, she said aloud.

She claimed Mel's chair while her wife went for takeout, but about a half hour into Mel's absence, February's mother began to emit a terrible sound, a wet crackle every time she drew breath. February poked her head into the hall to summon a nurse.

I think she's choking, she said.

The nurse shook her head but followed her into the room anyway, drew a stethoscope from her scrub pocket.

Like you need a fucking stethoscope to hear that! February shouted. Sorry, that was—I'm just—

The nurse put a hand on February's shoulder.

It's normal, she said.

February wanted to say that it was most certainly not normal, that

Mel was usually the hothead and that she herself rarely cursed, and also there was no way the alien sound bubbling up in her mother's chest could ever be misconstrued as ordinary, but instead she swallowed all of it and nodded when the nurse assured her that her mother wasn't in any pain. February knelt beside her mother's bed and prayed until Mel returned with a bag of Wendy's that smelled sweet and oily and made her feel a little ill.

You better get off your knees if you wanna walk tomorrow, sweets, said Mel, and offered a hand.

Who says I want to?

Why don't you get back in bed?

It's so hard for her to breathe. I don't want to crowd her.

She'd want you to crowd her.

So February climbed as gingerly as possible beside her mother. She took her mother's palm, and spelled *M-e-l* into it.

What'd you tell her? Mel said.

That you're here. You know she liked you best.

Mel smiled.

As if. You're the biggest mama's girl this side of the Ohio.

Mel bent in over the railing and took her mother's palm, pressed more letters into it.

What'd *you* tell her? February said.

Just that it's okay.

It's not okay.

Of course not. But I don't want her to worry about you. I've got you.

O-k, February said. *O-k.*

February lay there for hours with the bed rail sunk deep into the flesh of her hip, watching as her mother's breath became shallower and sparser, until she could tell she was still there only by watching her pulse jump in her neck. At around midnight, the nurse listened to her lungs once more, said goodbye for the night, told February to

press the call button if they needed anything. Mel, who'd commandeered a second chair for her feet, finally fell asleep, and though her
presence was still a comfort, on some level February knew that this
was what her mother had been waiting for—a quiet moment alone.
In the end there was only an exhale, a low hiss that contained more
air than she had seen her mother take in all night, so that February
wondered where it had been hidden and whether it might have been
breath her mother had carried for a very long time. Then it was gone,
commingled with the dry and acrid hospital air, no longer special,
and her mother was gone, and February had no idea what to do.
She'd had her parents for more years than most, and they'd lived
good lives; this was bound to make certain aspects of her coming
anguish easier. For now, though, the pain was not abated by adulthood, or prayers, or last goodbyes, or even Mel's reassurances. It was
a wound, a stone fruit ripped in two, red and bruised and sweet-
tinged with rot, a yawning void where the pit should have been. And
she would stay that way, emptied and splayed open in the putrefac-
tion of grief, for weeks. It was 4:04 A.M. on Black Friday, and February nearly laughed when the nurse wrote it down for the record—as
if it was something she could possibly forget.

*C*harlie let the bite of her mother's accusation ripple through her for a while, standing stuck in the foyer even after Wyatt came back down the stairs and gave her an odd look that made her wonder how long she'd been there. Finally, she shook herself loose and returned to the kitchen, where Wyatt neatly lined the wineglasses to dry on a strip of hand towels before retiring to the basement to do whatever he did down there. It was only 7:30, but it felt much later. She tried casting about on Wyatt's satellite for something to distract her, but everything was reruns and commercials for tomorrow's sales, and she soon turned the TV off. She wondered what Austin was doing and switched on her phone to send him a video message, but once she'd pressed record, she wasn't sure what to say. She imagined him at home, he and his family gathered around a boisterous dining table like a big Deaf Brady Bunch, so sure they were exactly who they were supposed to be. She stopped the recording, pulled up the web instead, and googled the Gas Can—"Open," their hours said. It was a Thursday, after all. Was Thanksgiving a holiday for anarchists? She was about to find out.

She had never known her mother to emerge from any substantial interaction with her grandmother without a blistering hangover, and tomorrow promised to be no exception. She slipped into her mother's bedroom and mumbled nonsense at her sleeping form until she said, "Okay Charlie, okay," and rolled over. In the morning, she'd be forced to take Charlie's word for whatever permission she claimed to have extracted. Her mother, a proper lady, would never admit how drunk she'd been.

Charlie pulled on her sneakers and boarded the bus into East Colson. Already she was feeling a little giddy at the possibility of seeing Slash, and when a lick of remorse about whether she should be feeling something toward Austin surfaced, she snuffed it back out. The real problem, she told herself, wasn't that she needed to choose Slash or Austin, but that she had positioned them to be diametrically opposed in the first place. There was no reason why she shouldn't be friends with multiple boys, neither of whom she owed a thing, so what if she did find them both attractive? She disembarked at the casino and trekked up to the Gas Can.

Inside, it was warm and nearly empty. There were a few people spread out at single tables across the room, mostly older men who looked like they'd been at it a while, but no sign of Slash or his crew. She took a stool at the end of the bar, and the bartender held out a beer like a question mark.

Thanks, she said.

Oh, you talk.

What?

Slash mentioned you were deaf the other night, so I didn't know, said the bartender.

Slash mentioned me?

He did.

I talk.

He didn't mention that.

The bartender took his own beer out from under the bar.

Cheers, he said.

They clinked bottles, and he stayed there, staring at her so intently she swiped her sleeve across her mouth, thinking there was something on her face.

What? she said.

Nothing, sorry. My cousin's deaf.

Charlie was always unsure what she was supposed to do with this kind of information. Congratulate him?

Cool, she said.

He has one of those implant things, though. He hears like everything.

Good for him.

Did you . . . ever think of getting one?

She brought the bottle to her lips, took an aggravated slug. She wasn't a stranger to this line of questioning—when her fellow students at Jefferson had deigned to engage with her, it was often in exchanges like this, to inform her that they had once had a deaf dog, or inquire why she didn't want to get cured like those babies they'd seen on YouTube hearing their mothers' voices for the first time. She'd just been hoping maybe the world outside of high school was different.

I have one.

The bartender's mouth twitched in a way that might have been imperceptible to a person less accustomed to studying mouths.

See?

She pulled the magnet from beneath her hair.

Right on, he said, and put his beer to his lips as if to silence himself.

You're surprised, she said.

No.

No what?

It's just you—he—never mind.

I what? Don't talk as good as him?

Just . . . different, he said weakly.

Right on, she said, letting the magnet snap back against her head.

Sorry, he said. That was really rude.

Yeah, well.

It was Charlie's turn to wash her words down with beer. Then she felt a hand on her thigh and turned to discover Slash on the stool beside her. She found respite in his touch, and not only from the prospect of getting her out of this conversation.

What was rude? Slash said.

I was just putting my foot in my mouth, said the bartender.

It's fine, Charlie said. My implant's shit, it's not a secret.

She began the habitual rearranging of her hair to camouflage the spot.

The fuck you say to her?

Forget it, said Charlie. Hi.

Hi, he said, and kissed her on the cheek.

Didn't know if you guys would be here tonight.

Every Thursday, he said.

Charlie couldn't tell whether he even realized it was a holiday. For a moment she pictured his mother standing on the porch of their McMansion, with her arms crossed, peering out into the windy night, and felt a little sorry for her.

Come on, he said, taking her hand. I gotta tune up.

They reconnected after the show, Charlie tearing herself away from the front left speaker.

So, do you have to get home, or . . .

Or what?

You wanna stick around for the real fun? Actually, we could use you.

Use me? said Charlie.

A project we're doing. You could lend a hand?

O-k, she said.

O-k.

Wait. You know how to fingerspell?

She wondered whether she'd taught him while rolling. Then she felt hurt, as if this were a secret he'd been keeping, though in fairness it wouldn't have come up in most of their Jefferson-era relationship—if you could call it that—*she* hadn't known sign language then.

Only what I learned in Sunday school. So, the alphabet. God Jesus Bible . . .

SIN, he signed dramatically,

baring his teeth at her.

Charlie laughed. She couldn't imagine Slash, even Slash when he was Kyle, anywhere near a church.

Let's go, she said.

Out on the street, Slash unzipped his backpack, pulled out a fistful of woolly hats, put one on his own head, and handed the others to Greg, Charlie, and Sid, who was nearly unrecognizable now that he'd combed down his mohawk into a flat crust against his scalp.

Ice skating? said Charlie drily.

Not quite, said Slash.

He pulled the fold of his hat down over his face to reveal a full ski mask. Charlie unrolled the hat in her hands and felt her stomach drop.

Where's Lem? she said.

Slash pushed the mask back up off his face.

Oh, we always leave one out in case we need bail.

What?

Extra precaution. Totally unnecessary.

No eye in the sky in the No Fly, said Greg cheerfully.

What eye? said Charlie frantically.

We'll be long gone by the time they get here.

She looked over her shoulder. Behind her, she could see the neon Gas Can glow. There was still time to back out of . . . whatever this was. She didn't need to know what was about to happen to know that it wasn't good.

And you double-checked for security? said Greg.

Triple-checked.

_____, said Sid. All that copper _____.

Oh, they've got a camera. But only by the front door. And their alarm system says _____ right on it.

So? said Greg.

That security company went out of business in 2015.

Charlie was torn between trying to parse out what the hell they were talking about and just fleeing the scene before it became a scene.

Okay, what are we doing? she said finally.

                    H-o-l-d-e-n-s, Slash said.

What?

Your friendly neighborhood kitchen and hardware supply.

Isn't it closed? she tried.

She wasn't naïve—she'd assumed they were planning to steal something, but for some reason a break-in felt different than shoplifting.

You don't want to help? said Slash.

Not really.

Come on, I thought you were Team Guillotine.

I—

Charlie had found herself mulling over Slash's postcoital tutorial in revolution in the weeks since she'd seen him, but she was unsure what to make of it. For one thing, if Slash was going "off the grid," what stake did he have in messing up the grid for others?

I don't see what knocking out a hardware store has to do with it, she said finally.

Knocking *over*, he said gently. We've got an easy job for you.

I won't be able to understand you with the masks, she said.

I'll tell you everything now. Bad form to talk on the job anyway.

You got a phone? said Greg.

Charlie nodded and pulled it from her back pocket.

Turn it off, he said.

They pulled down their masks before they got to the store. Charlie reached beneath hers to take off her implant, which crackled as it rubbed against the knit. The sign for Holden's was still lit, though the store itself was dark, except for the red glow of its emergency exit. Slash stuck his arm deep into his backpack, then punched the glass panel of the door. It cracked but didn't shatter and he hit it again and again until he busted through. He turned the lock on the inside and let them in. When they opened the door, the boys stared at each other for a beat too long and Charlie could tell they were saying something, but couldn't see what. Greg and Sid pushed past her and Slash pointed to a barrel filled with snow shovels, then the security camera, then back at Charlie.

She took a shovel from the display and hoisted it above her head to block the camera. Slash nodded and went down the aisle after the other two. Her peripheral vision was compromised by the mask, and her arms were shaking from nerves and the weight of the shovel, so she couldn't even look around much, though a few times she felt things crash to the floor. Surely they were making too much noise. Someone in the neighborhood would call the cops, wouldn't they? Should she run, or wait until the police came and play deaf and dumb?

Before she could decide, the boys were running toward, then past her, arms full of pipes and boxed kitchen gadgets. She took off after them, assuming they were headed back to the house, but they made a sharp left off Vine instead, crossed York, and pitched into the shadows of the underpass. Charlie felt her heart beat out an arrhythmic protest at the sprint, but terror kept her moving until they reached the railroad tracks. Slash, Sid, and Greg slowed, dropped their haul on the ground, and pulled off their masks.

Shithead! Greg cried. I thought you said they didn't have an alarm!

Who cares? We got out before the cops got anywhere close!

What's wrong? said Charlie.

Slight glitch, said Slash. Turns out there was a burglar alarm. No big deal though.

My ears are ringing! Sid said.

The three of them continued bickering, but Charlie was no longer paying attention, was instead watching a shadow lengthen in the corner of her vision: an old man materialized, bare-chested beneath an open winter coat, his hair Einsteinian. Charlie froze, but Slash gave the man a smile of recognition and the two exchanged a complex handshake.

Hey, guys, Robin's here! she thought she saw the man say.

At his beckoning, more people appeared at the edge of the darkness, most dressed haphazardly and pungent with dirt. A few chatted with the boys, or with one another, and Charlie could no longer keep up. Her eyes adjusted to the darkness, and an encampment took shape, corrugated metal and cardboard and blue tarps strung together like a motley block of row homes. Beneath her feet, a crush of broken glass, chicken bones, and orange syringe plungers. One by one, people ringed the pile the boys had made, selected some plumbing or a metal trinket, and receded back into the darkness along the tracks. When the pile was gone, Slash and Greg picked up the remaining haul—twin boxes that had been placed off to the side, obviously not up for grabs—and Sid motioned for her to follow.

You look like you've seen a ghost, said Slash once they'd returned to sidewalks and streetlamps.

My first robbery.

Burglary, he corrected.

Did that guy call you Robin?

Yeah, he said smiling. Robin Hood.

So you just steal stuff to bring to them?

That was . . . bonus stuff, he said.

He tapped the lid of the box beneath his arm.

This was what we went in for. But copper is a good _____

A what?

d-e-c-o-y.

Like . . . Slash thought for a moment. A distraction. Cops automatically assume junkies.

But won't those guys get in trouble? Charlie said.

Nah, said Greg. They know to cross the bridge to sell it.

What if they say something?

All three of them laughed.

They don't snitch, said Sid.

Come on, said Slash. Let's get these back to the house.

.   .   .

They're good guys, Slash said when they returned home, as if no time had passed. The guys by the tracks. Helped me out when I needed a place.

Charlie couldn't imagine Kyle sleeping beneath an overpass, but then apparently a lot had happened since he'd become Slash. Greg opened the coat closet and wedged his box atop a tetris of about ten others. On the front of each, Charlie noticed a blond woman not unlike her mother standing over a steaming roast.

You stole a crockpot? she said, incredulous.

Pressure cooker! said Slash.

Two pressure cookers, said Greg.

He glanced back at the closet.

Well, now there's ten altogether.

These can't be worth anything! said Charlie.

Depends who you ask, said Slash.

You could've just walked into Meijer and bought one for like twenty bucks.

That's where you're wrong, rookie, said Sid. We—he tugged a strand of his slumbering spikes—cannot walk into anywhere and just *buy* a pressure cooker. You, maybe. Or Lem in a wig.

And we already used Lem in a wig, said Slash.

But what are you gonna *do* with them?

You gotta get out more, Slash said, laughing, and handed her a vape pen.

She took two long hits, and he led her toward his bedroom.

U.S. anarchist movements, history of

From Wikipedia, the free encyclopedia

This timeline is part of a series. Return to main article: "Anarcho-communism."

Early 1800s: American Individualist Anarchism advocates for private possession of only what one produces by his own labor. Originally linked to transcendentalist philosophy and the abolitionist movement, it is visible through the Civil War and into "pioneering" and westward expansion.

Late 1800s/Turn of the Century: Anarcha-feminism and Free Love is the application of individual anarchism onto concepts surrounding sexual freedom. *(For the history of free love and use in other contexts, jump to "free love" series.)* An early feminist movement, anarcha-feminism engages in pushback against sex-based legislature, including marriage and birth control restrictions, that place undue burden on women.

Freethought was a related anti-religious movement.

Late 1800s/Turn of the Century: Anarcho-Communism begins as part of the late 19th century labor movement. Anarcho-communists advocate for socialism and basic rights for women, political prisoners, people of color, and the homeless, and against militarization and the draft.

An anarcho-communist demonstration turns deadly in May of 1886, when a bomb is thrown in Chicago's Haymarket Square at a workers' rights rally, killing a police officer. In the unrest that follows, 7 more officers and 4 workers are killed.

Early 20th Century: Luigi Galleani advocates for "propaganda of the deed," the use of violence to overthrow oppressive institutions. In 1901, American anarchist Leon Czolgosz assassinates president William McKinley. Galleanists go on to complete a series of assassinations and bombings, including the 1920 bombing of Wall Street.

Post–World War II Period: Groups of **anarcho-pacifists**, anarchist Christians, and early environmentalists develop and are influential in 1960s counterculture and student antiwar protests.

Late 20th Century–Present: Anarchism continues to influence twentieth and twenty-first century leftist politics, including Black civil rights and gay rights activism, the Occupy movement and anti-fascist organizing in response to a rise in far-right visibility after the 2016 election. *(Jump to "Antifa.")*

*C*harlie woke in the morning to find Slash staring at her. She jumped.

Sorry, he said. Didn't mean to scare you.

O–k.

She relaxed back into the crook of his arm, but as the adrenaline from being startled faded she found an uneasiness in her gut and a fetid taste in her mouth. She tried to remember how much she'd had to drink, but the night's memory was shadowed, only a dark feeling radiating from it. She saw a flash of them running from something across her mind's eye, but wasn't sure if she'd dreamt it.

You did good last night.

Did I?

At Holden's.

The store's name brought clarity back to the night's events, though she still didn't quite believe it. Charlie couldn't think of another time she'd broken the law, at least not in a way that affected anything outside her own body.

Guess I'm a natural, she said, trying to smile.

Slash tried, too, but his wasn't quite convincing either.

You o–k?

He nodded.

Yeah, fine. Just thinking about some stuff I gotta do today.

Charlie reached for her jeans and extracted her phone. When she turned it on, it vibrated a continuous thrum, flush with messages stuck in the ether from a night off. She didn't open any of them, but she saw "mom" pop up a few times in the run and was arrested by competing threads of concern—that she had likely worried her parents, but also that she could have inadvertently put Slash and his friends in danger. What if her mom had sobered up and called the cops when she realized Charlie was missing?

Are *you* okay?

Yeah, I just—she pointed to her phone—better head out.

Well, come back down for New Year's, he said. You don't want to miss the fireworks.

Yeah, maybe.

Big party at the warehouses. They'll probably open around ten. Slash stood and pulled on his jeans, but Charlie waved him off.

I can let myself out.

She shouldered her way through the plywood, and stood on the stoop reviewing the thread of messages from her mother, the last of which was just a string of question marks.

at dad's, Charlie tried.

try again. already.call.ed. him.

Charlie scrolled back up to see that her father had messaged, too. She broke into a jog toward the casino bus depot and began formulating a story that might be acceptable to her mother:

had brunch with a friend. on the bus home now.

Her mother loved brunch—it was a soft spot in the dietary restrictions she imposed on herself. Once, at an Easter buffet, Charlie had actually seen her mother applaud a plate of quiche. She boarded the bus; it lurched out of the parking lot. Her mother hadn't responded.

sorry to scare u, Charlie wrote.

At home Charlie arrived steeled for battle, but her mother was propped up on the couch with a blanket on her lap, looking relatively calm. Charlie noted with no small horror that she was wearing sweatpants. Her mother offered her a bag of cheddar popcorn. It smelled like feet, but Charlie took a handful anyway.

So, who is it? said her mother after a while.

Who?

The boy you were having brunch with.

What boy? No one.

Charlie imagined Slash shaking her mother's hand, pulling up the extra chair at the dining room table, her mother gaping in horror through the gauged holes in his earlobe.

Tell me or I make you have this conversation with your father.

A boy from school, she blurted. Austin.

A deaf boy?

Charlie rolled her eyes. Austin had been the least offensive person she could offer up, and even that was too much for her mother.

No, Mom, he's hearing. He just goes to Deaf school.

Don't start.

He's Peter Pan, Charlie said, thinking his theater skills might warm her mother to him. In our winter play. But really, we're just friends.

If you're just friends then why didn't you tell anyone you were going to meet him?

I *did* tell you. Last night. But I guess you were . . . tired.

Her mother stared down at her hands as if her maternal instincts might suddenly kick in and she'd be able to discern whether Charlie was lying. Fortunately, none materialized.

I'm sorry, Mom. Can we just let it go for now? I've got a headache.

Her mother brought a hand to her own temple. Charlie tried not to read into the way she seemed to brighten at the mention of her daughter's pain.

Hey, how's that new processor been?

Can we talk about that later?

Her mother pursed her lips, then stood abruptly, the fleece blanket now a static-cling skirt against her sweats. She took a few steps into the kitchen, balled the popcorn bag, made a seamless shot into the trash can, and returned to the couch.

Charlie withdrew to her bedroom and slept away the afternoon. Then she showered, scrubbing herself raw, and emerged feeling new and light, as if a breeze could pass right through her. She went downstairs and helped her mother with dinner, and didn't even think ill of Wyatt, who was sitting blearily before the television. Screw Slash. No more drugs or stealing, no more punk boys with their fears of commitment and closets full of weird, looted cookware. So what if he was attractive, and even sweet at times? It wasn't worth it. From now on, she would be Good.

That night, she curled up in the recliner reading until her mother and Wyatt went to bed, then took out her phone and was surprised and pleased to find a message from Kayla.

ready to go back?

Charlie looked around the empty living room.

yeah actually lol. how's home?

fine. mom is boring af.

same, Charlie wrote. and her bf even worse.

don't get me started.

hey . . . just wanted to say i'm really sorry about the whole austin thing. i feel bad.

not on you. anyway he apologized.

good

he let me slap him on tiktok lol

. . . good?

baby steps, said Kayla.

*i*n the days after her mother's death, February felt about as close to deaf as she ever had—a membrane of grief thick and phlegmy around her that the outside world could not penetrate. Even Mel, who had liaised with the florist and the undertaker, who shuttled paperwork to the minister for the funeral and stood beside her in the receiving line, could not fully puncture it.

February had grieved when her father died, had felt tired and angry and cried herself hollow. As her mother's condition had worsened, she sometimes tried to moor herself to the memory of that sadness in preparation for its inevitable recurrence. But as it turned out, the heartache February suffered at the loss of her father provided her with no coping mechanisms in the face of this one. Being motherless was different than being fatherless. It was primal, the archetype for human suffering, like losing the North Star. And as she stood shaking the hands of her parents' remaining friends and colleagues, her cousins in from Georgia, she wondered whether there was an age limit on orphandom, emotionally speaking. Surely the feeling of desolation one experienced as the last of one's nuclear family knew no statute of limitations.

The funeral was the easy part, the performance of mourning and all of its trappings an effective diversion. It was returning home and the bleak, ever-darkening winterward days afterward that were difficult.

Their house was bursting with turkey—casseroles and sandwich fixings and soups their friends and neighbors had salvaged from Thanksgiving leftovers. The smell made February queasy, though she ate the leftover pies. She tried to work and read and watch the backlog of movies she and Mel had been too busy to see, but she could not concentrate. Instead she lay on the couch for several days straight, watching the entire canon of *Big Brother* punctuated occasionally by *American Ninja Warrior,* piling food onto paper plates, then throwing them out untouched.

Mel was thoughtful, helpful, but her company did not fill the absence left by February's mother. At first, this didn't bother February. How could her wife possibly provide the same things her mother had? Would she even want her to? The comforts of childhood seemed diametrically opposed to all things romantic. Then one day, Wanda appeared at her door with a roast beef.

> *Thought you'd be sick of turkey,*
> she said in casual, one-handed
> sign.

February smiled, just a little, at how Wanda's ease and wit were exactly the same no matter the situation. But as Wanda handed over the platter and invited herself in, February felt something different than fondness for a friend or old flame: an anchor back to the essence of herself, a moment's peace. The film of February's sadness was peeled back by Wanda's signs, which were faster but otherwise not unlike her mother's. In that moment, February knew she would be okay.

Then, at the realization that it was Wanda who'd lifted the haze, a new disquiet. What did it mean that it hadn't been Mel? And how bad would Mel flip if she came home from work to find Wanda here?

February checked the time as she offered Wanda some coffee. She'd have to leave a big buffer to account for the Deaf Goodbye, which simply could not be completed in under a half hour. But Wanda remained oblivious to February's anxious eye on the clock, or at least she pretended as much, sipping coffee and prattling on about how Thanksgiving dinner with her husband's side of the family had ended in a politically fueled brawl that had her brother-in-law up-ending the gravy tureen. And it happened again—for a moment, Wanda's story, the world she crafted so vividly before her, pulled February from her worry and she laughed.

How's school? February said tentatively.

She hadn't thought much about River Valley at all in the past few days, and now felt ashamed for having abandoned her students both in practice and in thought.

Getting on without you all right. Phil looks a little like a deer in the headlights, but he held it all down.

I think this is the longest I've ever been gone.

It's only been four school days! Don't you ever whisk Mel away anywhere?

I do my whisking during summer vacation.

Girl, you better take next week off, too.

Wanda laughed and patted February's arm, but now that February had begun thinking about school it was difficult to stop, especially given the chaos that would crash through its gates once the closure news was out. Swall would alert the district's principals to what was coming at the December administrative meeting just two weeks from now. And if it somehow stayed secret through the holidays, all hell would certainly break loose after the all-faculty summit in the new year. She placed her hand on top of Wanda's and held it there.

Yeah, maybe, she said.

.   .   .

Later, when February had again deflated and returned to the couch, Mel arrived home from work and made a beeline for the refrigerator.

How was your day? said February.

Same old same old. You know, it's not exactly good for you to be lying there twenty-four-seven.

Of course it's not. It's grief.

Grief doesn't have to be unhealthy, said Mel. You could, like, develop a yoga compulsion or something.

Can a compulsion be healthy?

Hey, good roast.

Yeah, said February, propping herself up on her elbows so she could see into the kitchen. Wanda brought that over.

February saw Mel freeze mid-chew, then catch herself and continue.

That was nice of her, said Mel.

It was.

Why you looking at me like that?

Nothing. I'm not. I just thought—

She brought us food. Really, Feb, I'm not some kind of ogre.

Okay. Sorry.

Also it's delicious, Mel said, heaping more roast and potatoes onto her plate.

We should buy some lettuce, said February. No one ever brings salad.

No one is comforted by salad.

Mel carried her plate into the living room and sat down on the couch.

I don't know if I can go back to work, said February.

Don't be silly, of course you can.

Everything reminds me of her.

Maybe that's a good thing. A little bit of her all over campus. In all those kids.

I guess.

You could always take more time, said Mel. Lord knows you have the sick days.

I can't, said February.

I know.

That night February finally pulled her laptop from her briefcase, feeling wary as it hummed back to life. Her work account contained 176 unread emails—from her teachers, her bosses, and students. From the subject lines, she could tell some were offering condolences, but most appeared to be regular items of business, the world, swift and savage, having moved on without her.

*b*ack at school, things fell into their old rhythms. Or not quite—they were better. She and Kayla chatted easily about their breaks (though Charlie didn't mention the crockpots) and Kayla invited (insisted that) Charlie come out to the common room to watch YouTube videos with her and the rest of the girls on the floor. In class, she was following her lessons, even in history, once Headmistress finally got back from vacation. The next week at play practice, when Austin came for his sword, he kissed her hand and she felt her curiosity bloom once again. With Austin, it was different—it wasn't a hunger like she felt with Slash—*she* was different. Whatever was between them, it was something much quieter. But maybe that was good. After all, there *were* other emotions beyond lust and anger. Maybe she was hitting her stride. Then, one night as practice was winding down, Austin returned to tell her that the football team had a night game over in Masonville.

O-k?

She wasn't sure what to do with this news, but its effect was a pinhole through which the swell of affection building in her was now dissipating. Charlie had thought she and Austin had been growing close these past few weeks, at the very least as friends. That he might see her as the kind of girl who wanted to go to a football game—which was to say he pretty much didn't see her at all—dismayed her.

I mean . . . an away game. My roommate will be gone for a while? he said, threading his fingers through hers.

Oh! she said.

She felt herself giggle. She was coming off too eager for her liking, especially when the idea of a room of their own was a little frightening to Charlie. Hadn't she promised herself just days before that she was going to change? On the other hand, what if being with Austin was part of that? He offered something that Charlie had never before been attracted to, a wholesomeness without games or strings or power struggles attached.

And the other thing was, Charlie liked sex. And why shouldn't she? She strong-armed her body into countless unpleasant tasks each week: waking up when the morning was still blue, listening and lip-reading, circuit training in gym class, flossing. Shouldn't she be allowed to do something fun without being hamstrung by heirloom shame? Sex was all boys her age talked about, and no one ever bothered them about it. So when Austin asked if she wanted to come over and see his room, Charlie said okay.

Outside it was cold and bright, though the sun was noticeably lower in the sky than it had been at the same time just yesterday, all things barreling toward the equinox. They didn't say much as he led her up the drive, but it was a comfortable lull, until he stopped short a few feet in front of the entry path.

What's wrong?

Nothing. Come this way.

He glanced around, took her hand, and steered her behind the building. There was a hedge, and they had to turn sideways to slide through the space between bushes and wall.

Wait, he said.

Charlie watched him slip out the far side and run back around the way they'd come. Cold from the building's façade seeped through her jacket, and she tried to stand up straighter to avoid touching the stone.

Just as her imagination began to weave a tale of abandonment, she saw a hand emerging into the hedge. She inched her way toward it and found Austin standing in an open window, the screen removed. He took her by the forearms and pulled her inside.

His room looked the same as, or rather the reverse of, hers and Kayla's. On the wall by the foot of Austin's bed was the same television and bulbous camera atop it, only there was something wrong with his; it was emitting a series of piercing flashes. Charlie jumped back, but Austin just sighed and aimed a remote at the screen to quell the lights.

What the hell was that?

> *Probably my parents, I'll call them later.*

But what— She pointed to the screen.

> *What? The _____?*

What?

> *V–i–d–e–o. Phone. Videophone. You have one in your room, too.*

God, what an idiot. She had wondered why Kayla and friends only ever watched TV on their computers.

We don't . . . have anyone to call.

> *You can call hearing people, too. An interpreting service trans– lates.*

Really?

> *And there's a way to use your voice. The interpreter just signs the other person's responses.*

Really?

> *You can get one for free at home. All deaf people can.*

Really?

It won't be that useful if you only know one word.

Charlie laughed shyly, imagined her younger self with a phone like this, and the language to use it. Texting was easy now, but that hadn't always been the case. Before she could read and write, before kids had their own phones, she was cut off from anyone not directly in front of her. She pictured herself at age ten—same gawky, frizzy-haired girl, but confident like Austin, maybe even extroverted. She would call her dad and remind him not to be late for dinner, or her classmates and invite them for playdates. The classmates would turn into friends, maybe one of them would even grow into that mythical being she'd only witnessed from afar or on TV: a best friend, someone who would call her first.

Teasing, Austin said with a look on his face like he'd been repeating himself. *T-e-a-s-i-n-g?*

Sorry. I was thinking what it'd be like to call people.

Who would you call?

I don't know, she said after a while. *My family. My mom I guess.*

Hearing, right?

Extremely. And she's got nails— Charlie gestured the claw of her mother's pointed manicure—*she's bad at texting. Might be easier, calling her.*

You're sweet.

What?

To think about what's easier for her.

Charlie smiled, but the thing she hadn't said was that receiving an interpreted video call would probably upset her mother, which was appealing in its own way. She knew this was perverse, to find pleasure in things that might rile her mother up, and she didn't want Austin to think of her like that, but she could see him seeing her, looking through the veneer of her smile.

> *Or . . . it'd scare the shit out of*
> *her,* Charlie said.

Austin laughed.

> *Bonus,* he said.

Austin sat down on his bed and Charlie wrung her hands, watched him watching her.

> *You know who else you could call,*
> he said after a while.

> *Who?*

He reached for her wrist and pulled her closer, so their knees touched. She tried to come up with a reason why she shouldn't hook up with him. If it ruined their friendship, she might once again end up an outcast. But the thing about River Valley was it made her hopeful—and anyway she'd already been to the lowest point heaps of times. She hadn't yet been to the top.

He took her by the hips and deftly swung them both into bed, Charlie on top. He'd never said or done anything to suggest a lack of experience, but she was taken aback by his self-assurance as he ran his hands across the range of her rib cage. She let him unhook her bra—another seamless maneuver—her hips pushed forward to meet him, the seam of her jeans hitting just right, when the wall beside them shook. Both their eyes flew open at the tremor; Austin craned his neck to see around Charlie, who quickly climbed off him and drew her knees up, hunching in on herself. Standing beside the bed, his hand still on the doorknob, was a tall boy in an RVSD football jersey, with duffel, shoulder pads, and helmet in tow.

> *Close the door!*

Austin jumped out of bed to retrieve Charlie's bra, tossed it to her.

> *This is my roommate, E-l-i-o-t.*
> *Eliot.*

Hey, Eliot said.

Charlie nodded. Eliot seemed neither surprised nor embarrassed by her presence.

I thought you had a game.

> *Canceled. Gonna snow tonight.*
> *You know how they get about the*
> *roads.*

Kayla and Alisha were right—Eliot was handsome, his arm muscles rippling as he opened the window and lit a cigarette. But when he turned to tap his ash out the windowsill, she saw thick fingers of scar tissue blooming from his ear down his neck, disappearing beneath the collar of his shirt. The scar was gnarled and pink—pale and angry against his healthy skin. It was difficult to look away.

> *Sorry,* Austin said, gesturing to
> his bed. *This is Charlie.*

Eliot shrugged, tapped his ash out into the grass.

> *Sorry,* he said again, this time
> to her.

It's fine. I should go.

Austin kissed her on the cheek. He pulled on a hoodie while Charlie tied her shoes. Eliot moved aside and Austin offered his hand as she climbed back out the window.

See you, she said.

She gave him a small, close-lipped smile, trying to look as alluring as one could while standing in a hedge.

> *Maybe another time?*

She nodded, lingered for a moment, catching sight of Eliot and tracing the trajectory of his scar with her eyes, snapping out of it only when Austin moved to close the window.

I know where you live, she said.

I met Eliot today, she said to Kayla that night.

They were in their respective beds surrounded by homework. Charlie pulled her hair into a knot high on her head, a hairdo she had never dared at Jefferson because of the way it revealed her implant.

Pretty, right?

Yeah, but . . . what happened to him?

Charlie copied the outline of his scar down the side of her own face.

Well . . . Kayla leaned in. *I heard it was his mom.*

Charlie could see Kayla was trying her best to hold in whatever gossip she knew, but it was brimming in her eyes, the spark of something lurid.

His mom?

Kayla nodded.

But what would leave that kind of mark?

They say she lit him on fire! she blurted.

What? No way.

It looks like a burn though, right?

That can't be true.

I thought so, too. But then I started thinking, maybe she didn't do it on purpose.

She accidentally lit him on fire?

Well, no, but like she didn't mean to hurt him.

Charlie rubbed her temples. Either Kayla wasn't making any sense, or Charlie's ASL skills had lost the thread of this conversation.

She didn't mean to hurt him . . . when she lit him on fire?

Kayla swept her eyes over Charlie, like she was waiting for her to have some kind of epiphany, but none came.

I don't get it.

Anyway, it was just a rumor.

Either way, you were right.

He's hot.

She could see Kayla realizing something, the sheen of her eyes shifting to something like mischief.

> *Wait. Were you over in their room just now?*

Charlie could only blush.

> *O-h-h-h, damn!*

Kayla jumped from her bed and offered her a high-five.

> *Put in a good word for Alisha next time,* she said.

I'll try to squeeze that in.

Kayla clapped her hands over her mouth in mock scandal, and she and Charlie laughed all the way to dinner.

alexander graham bell, milan 1880,

AND WHY YOUR MOM DOESN'T KNOW SIGN LANGUAGE

In the late 19th century, manual language versus oral communication for deaf children was a hot topic of debate among educators, embodied by Thomas H. Gallaudet, the cofounder of the American School for the Deaf, and your friendly neighborhood eugenicist, Alexander Graham Bell.

Gallaudet, who'd learned sign language from French teacher of the deaf Laurent Clerc, had seen the success of signing Deaf schools firsthand in France, making him a strong proponent of signed languages. But Bell believed deaf people should be taught to speak, and sign language should be removed from Deaf schools.

Q: Why would a man with a deaf wife and mother want to eradicate sign language?

A: Eugenics

Eugenics (N.): The practice or advocacy of controlled selective breeding of human populations (as by sterilization) to improve the population's genetic composition

IN HIS WORDS:

"Those who believe as I do, that the production of a defective race of human beings would be a great calamity to the world, will examine carefully the causes that lead to the intermarriages of the deaf with the object of applying a remedy." —Alexander Graham Bell, 1883

Eugenics was a popular pseudoscience at this time in the U.S., and Bell was a big advocate. The belief was used to justify the forcible sterilization of disabled people, a program that Hitler admired and is said to have learned from.

Bell was against forced sterilization himself, but instead believed getting rid of sign language was the key to eradicating deafness. Without sign, deaf people would integrate into the general population rather than marry one another, thereby producing fewer deaf babies.

Besides his ethics, Bell's actual science was wrong—most deafness isn't directly hereditary—but his ideas remain prevalent in deaf education circles today.

DELEGATES AT THE MILAN CONFERENCE IN 1880:

HEARING	DEAF
163	1

In 1880, educators gathered in Milan, Italy, to discuss the state of deaf education. The delegates had been handpicked by the oralist society sponsoring the conference with the express goal of eliminating manual language from schools.

The conference passed eight resolutions, effectively banning signed language from schools for the deaf around the world for about 80 years. Some schools, including the school that would become Gallaudet University, pushed back against the resolutions, but most adopted them.

MILAN'S FIRST RESOLUTION:

The Convention, considering the incontestable superiority of articulation over signs in restoring the deaf-mute to society and giving him a fuller knowledge of language, declares that the oral method should be preferred to that of signs in education and the instruction of deaf-mutes. *(Passed 160–4)*

MILAN'S SECOND RESOLUTION:

The Convention, considering that the simultaneous use of articulation and signs has the disadvantage of injuring articulation and lip-reading and the precision of ideas, declares that the pure oral method should be preferred. *(Passed 150–16)*

Where Milan's resolutions were implemented, deaf children were forbidden from using sign language in the classroom or outside of it. As punishment, hands were tied down, rapped with rulers, or slammed in drawers. The period between 1880 and 1960 is considered the dark ages of deaf education.

In the U.S., the National Association of the Deaf, founded in 1880 in response to the conference, became the first disability rights organization, and was and is run for and by Deaf people.

Worried that ASL would become extinct, they also used brand-new film technology to document the language, making some of the earliest recordings of their kind.

MILAN'S LEGACY

1. Deaf teachers removed from schools because they cannot teach orally:

4. Deafness further stigmatized

2. Deaf students language deprived, no deaf role models

3. Fewer successful deaf professionals

In the U.S., eugenics became unpopular after it was associated with Nazism. Subsequent deaf education conferences have apologized for the harm done by the Milan resolutions. Science has since proven ASL is a fully realized language, and that its use does not inhibit the learning of speech. Nevertheless, the shadow of eugenics persists in medicine and education today. The Alexander Graham Bell Association continues to advocate for the pure oral method of educating deaf children.

ASK YOURSELF:

1. What would the world be like if ASL had gone extinct?
2. What other effects on deaf life stem from the Milan conference? Work with a partner to add another example to the cycle graphic.
3. Where else in today's society can you see the legacy of eugenics?

*f*ebruary spent her first week back at River Valley overwhelmed, and returned home each night dazed—though everything felt terribly important as it was happening, by the time the day was over she couldn't remember any of it, just that it had been hard and she was worried and had no idea how to help her students. That Friday, as she and Phil walked into the district office, she knew she would have to go home, tell Mel, and finally reckon with an uncertain future.

Swall took the podium to call the meeting to order, and she found it unbearable to look at him. Instead, she fixed her eyes on Henry Bayard, who sat beside Swall, interpreting for Phil. Henry was a good interpreter, and she'd seen him work in all manner of high-pressure and unpleasant circumstances—tense parent-teacher conferences, health crises in which students had been wheeled off campus by EMTs. She'd never seen him flinch, not even as he'd hoisted himself up into an ambulance midsentence. Now, as Swall began an extensive list of programs to be dismantled "in light of new legislative fiduciary constraints," she could see Henry's eyes narrow slightly. Most of the cuts were small, school-specific programs with which February wasn't familiar, though she had no doubt the students they served would be disenfranchised by their loss. But when Swall announced the closure of the River Valley "special needs" institute, she saw it—a quick jump in Henry's shoulder—as he announced the news that his son's school would soon cease to be.

From there, Swall launched into some faux-inspiring lecture about how they as educators should see the changes as opportunities—victories for integration and inclusion. He encouraged the administrators to begin "fact-finding" about what they might need in order to best support River Valley's students at their own campuses, but implored them to keep the information confidential at the administrative level until the all-faculty summit in February. He left little time for an open floor, no doubt to curb the number of questions he'd have to answer aloud.

"Feel free to email," he said against the swell of frustrated voices. While February and Phil had borne the brunt of the loss, the district had still been dealt enough large-scale blows for the room to be alight with anger and fear. February tried to get to Henry afterward, but he had slipped away before she could reach him.

You o-k? she said to Phil, as they returned to their cars.

Phil nodded, but didn't say anything.

> *I'd really like to keep this locked*
> *up until after break. No sense ru-*
> *ining everyone's Christmases,*
> *right?*

Another nod.

> *All right, drive safe.*

February watched Phil get into his car, and stood there leaning on her own hood until he pulled out of the parking lot. Then she got in the driver's seat and took out her phone. She had every intention of calling Mel and letting her know she was on her way home, maybe offering to pick up something for dinner, but instead she felt herself glance into her rearview before placing a video call to Wanda. Wanda answered on the second ring, as if she'd been waiting for her.

> *How's it going?* February said,
> flustered.

It usually took deaf people a while to notice the flash of the phone and pick it up; February had been expecting more time to get herself in order.

Fine, Wanda said, gesturing to a stack of papers on the table beside her. *Grading labs. Are you in your car?*

Yeah, just got out of a meeting up at the admin building.

Oh right. How'd it go?

Well—

There was a lump gathering in February's throat and she was thankful that she wouldn't have to overcome it with her voice. Still, her eyes began to fill and she swiped at them with embarrassment.

Aw, I told you you should have taken another week. It's too much.

No, she said, shaking her head. *It's not that.*

What then? What's wrong?

The color left Wanda's cheeks. February tried not to think about how it only made her freckles more prominent.

River Valley? she said.

February nodded.

Not good.

We're finished, aren't we.

She nodded again. She was full-on crying now, and dug an old napkin out of the cupholder to dab her nose.

Yeah. End of the school year.

Shit.

She waited for the fireworks, but Wanda simply dropped her hands into her lap.

You seem . . . calm.

No. I'm just not surprised, is all.

But our enrollment numbers are
actually good! Our test scores are
up from two years ago—

> *You know it's not about that.*

February usually admired Wanda for her clarity of vision, but the other woman's foresight bothered her now. She had been blindsided by the loss of River Valley, and resented that Wanda somehow wasn't. Then again, February would never truly understand what it was like to stand guard against an encroaching enemy for so long, to watch the cavalry barreling toward you and be helpless to stop it. From Wanda's position, on the precipice of extinction, she would have seen this coming on the horizon for a very long time.

I know, I know. Money talks.

> *Money, yeah. But not only that.*

February sighed. It would be much easier if it really was just about money—in a vacuum, or even in the regular ways money for education was politicized.

I just kind of thought The End
would be more high-tech.

> *This has always been their end-*
> *game. They can't get away with*
> *lining us up for mandatory sur-*
> *gery anymore—at least not in*
> *this country. They're going to*
> *fear-monger and isolate us.*
> *They'll strip us of money and*
> *power until the last of us goes*
> *willingly.*

I just wanted more time. I'm
worried about the kids.

> *Me too.*

They sat for a moment looking at one another, a stretch made awkward not because they were uncomfortable in each other's presence, but because they couldn't quite get close enough—the curse of video conversations, trying for eye contact, but finding only your own gaze.

Wait, said Wanda after a while. *You two have to move out.*

We do.

Shit.

That's the refrain.

When will you tell the faculty?

Not till after the holiday, if we can manage it.

Good idea.

Maybe even wait until the summit. Let Swall break the news.

Wanda nodded.

Thank you, said February.

For what?

I don't know.

She gestured at the passenger window, as if there was something out there, a concrete representation of their plight. But there was only an empty parking lot, unseasonably warm in the last dregs of daylight.

She and Wanda said goodbye, and February phoned Mel's favorite Chinese place, picked up their order on her way home. Mel arrived a few minutes after her, pleasantly surprised by the spread.

Thought it was my night for dinner, she said.

What, I can't spoil you once in a while?

You may, said Mel, leaning in to kiss her.

They carried the cartons to the dining table and heaped lo mein, sweet and sour pork, and scallion pancakes onto their plates.

Good batch, said Mel with a mouthful of pancake. You okay? Your eyes are red.

February nodded. Normally, the more reticent February became, the harder Mel pushed her to talk. While this sometimes led to arguments, usually it also made her feel better, so February had been expecting, almost looking forward to, this exorcism. But Mel remained gentle and accommodating, and February had neither the capacity to jump-start an emotionally difficult conversation nor the will to disturb calm waters.

The next week passed, and still she said nothing. The longer she stayed quiet, the easier it was to sink into the folds of the lie. Was it even a lie if she didn't say anything at all?

It was easy to justify: she still had plausible deniability until the summit. Was she so wrong in wanting to squeeze the last few weeks of normalcy from their home and her partner and the life they'd built? She and Mel had never lived together anywhere but here. The real reason, though, was that February needed the future to stay suspended in magical thinking just a little longer. Once Mel knew, Mel would begin to plan, and River Valley's lot would be concretized, and there would be no going back.

It's a process, Mel had said, carrying a pair of grilled cheeses to the living room Sunday evening.

What?

Grief, she'd said.

So that was it—Mel thought she was still mourning her mother. Which she was, of course. But grief aside, February had begun to feel a different kind of uneasiness. She assumed it was shame about having put Wanda before her own wife, but when she really thought about it, she wasn't sorry.

*W*anda had seen the end of the world once before. She was seven, her older brother seventeen, the night he opened their front door to put out the trash and was met with two shots to the neck. Over the years, they'd come to assume it was a case of mistaken identity—it had been early when it happened, the sun not even all the way set, an unlikely time for a burglary gone awry, and the crew her brother ran with wasn't anything. But he had bled out almost immediately, and no one else had seen anything, leaving them with only guesses and a cold case file.

Wanda hadn't been there. It was a Tuesday night and she'd been asleep in her dorm at the Deaf school an hour away. She had not felt her brother leave this world, and there had been no way to contact her.

In the morning, a note summoned her to the headmaster's office, where her mother and father were waiting. Her parents didn't know sign language—an interpreter told her that her brother was dead. She was not given a chance to ask questions. She returned home for two weeks, watched grief swallow her parents whole.

Before Eric's murder, Wanda's relationship with her parents had been neutral, the way one might regard neighbors or second cousins—an exchange of pleasantries and a little extra interest around the holidays, but no real bond. How could there be—their language was inscrutable to her, and they'd never tried to learn hers. Now, though, Wanda could read one thing plainly on their faces: they would have preferred to lose her. She saw a lot of things more clearly after that.

And even though it didn't quite make sense, Eric was the first person she thought of now, at the news of River Valley's closure. Her big brother's death was the lens through which Wanda understood all loss—cruel and inevitable and without any good reason. More than that, it underscored the ways in which Deaf school had saved her own life; she would have never survived that look in her parents' eyes without it.

If anyone could understand this, it would be Feb. But she had a lot on her plate, her own grief included, and Wanda could not show her Eric without the risk of baring the rest of her soul, including the torch she still carried for February herself. Instead, Wanda spoke pragmatically of The End. She assumed this was why February had called her—she was a friend, yes, but also a woman of science, of facts. And science was another of Wanda's unrequited loves. Attempts to eradicate the Deaf world came in waves, attacks dating back to the ancient mystics, but now their fate was firmly in the hands of doctors, researchers, engineers—cochlear implants and the latest string of therapies designed to delete them from the human genome before they technically even existed.

Still, as Wanda rehashed the centuries' long march toward her people's extinction, she hoped February might see what she was really saying: *This is not your fault; this is the way it always has been; there is nothing any of us can do; I love you so much for trying.*

*t*he atmosphere in the dorm the night before Christmas break was charged, holiday giddiness undercut by a run of tension because of what going home meant for so many River Valley students. Kayla, Charlie, and the rest of the girls on the floor spent the evening in and out of the common room, where the dormkeepers had set up stations for them to make gifts to bring to their families—origami ornaments and construction paper cards. Even Kayla seemed eager for the semester's end, but Charlie could not tap into the Christmas spirit. Another holiday to spend sitting at the table, bewildered and bored, trying to lipread her chewing mother. Until now, it hadn't occurred to her to wish for something better.

What's with you? said Kayla.

Just thinking about going home . . . and about Headmistress's class today.

She's not giving you a test on the half day, is she? That'd be fucked.

No. It's just fucked up is all, that M-i-l-a-n stuff. A-G-B-e-l-l?

Oh, Deaf *history. Is that what you guys are doing? I was won-*

*dering why Kevin was going on
about Martha's Vineyard the
other day.*

That's not what you're studying?

*I mean, I learned about that
stuff—*

For a moment, Kayla cut herself off as if embarrassed, though Charlie could see it was on her behalf.

*—when I was younger. We're
doing WWII now. But yeah,
B-e-l-l was an asshole.*

*We learned about him in hearing
school and no one ever mentioned
any of this!*

Kayla laughed.

*You think that's bad, you should
hear about the Founding Fathers.*

Right, yeah.

Charlie blushed, turned back to her duffel bag, where she was throwing clothes for the week in at random.

*That's why I want to be a
teacher,* Kayla said. *Right all
this bullshit directly with the
next generation. Maybe even
become headmistress.*

*What kind of headmistress would
you be?*

*Probably like Waters—maybe a
little tougher. She's kind of a
softie.*

"Soft" was not the adjective that came to mind when Charlie thought of Headmistress Waters, who she found intimidating, even though she technically had gone easy on Charlie for the whole calling her a bitch thing.

*And I'd build Black Deaf history
into the curriculum—not just for
one month. Maybe even a whole
BASL course.*

That'd be cool, said Charlie unsteadily.

Charlie hated how awkward she became when faced with any mention of race, or especially racism. It wasn't that she didn't know it was
wrong. She just didn't have the right words to say something meaningful. Then again, that was true of a lot of topics. In her time at
River Valley, the fact that Charlie had learned to name her own
oppressors—ableism, oralism—had been liberating. Now she had
the words to describe the things she always knew to be true. But the
more she learned, the more tangled it all became—the same struggles of race and class inside the gates as outside, and strands of power
and subjugation all twisted up like the rubber band ball she'd made
for her father last year for Christmas.

Can I ask you something?
Kayla nodded.

*Do you think River Valley is just
as racist as everywhere else?*

Of course. Why wouldn't it be?

*I don't know. I guess I just kind
of hoped it would be . . . better.*

*Yeah . . . white Deaf people al-
ways think that. It's because you
feel safe here.*

You don't?

Sometimes yes, sometimes no.

Charlie looked down at her hands, deflated and unsure. She wanted
to ask if she could help, but she had no idea how she might be able
to change anything, not concretely.

I'm sorry, she said after a while.

You know, now that you know,
you could stand to read a book
on it. Or at least a Wikipedia
article.

Charlie nodded.

Any suggestions?

Kayla gave her a pointed look like she was thinking about scolding her, but then walked over to her computer and pressed a few keys.

Emailed you.

That was fast.

I have it on standby. Call it my
white people primer.

At this Charlie couldn't help but smile.

Lesson two is next time do your
own research. I'm not on a teach-
er's salary yet.

Do you wanna go to Gallaudet,
for teaching?

Yeah, but . . . Depends on the
money.

Charlie nodded, even though she knew money would not be the thing that stopped her from going to college.

They'd be lucky to have you.

I know, said Kayla.

Kayla grabbed her jeans from her armoire and rolled them tight so she could stuff them into her already brimming backpack.

I have another bag if you want to
borrow.

That's all right. This is easier for
the bus.

She pressed down on the bag with her knee to bring the two sides of the zipper closer together.

Charlie went to her desk and retrieved her notebook, still opened to the day's history lesson. She closed the cover and threw the book in her duffel bag.

> *What do you think the world*
> *would be like? If those guys had*
> *gotten their way.*

> *Who, B-e-l-l and them?*

Charlie nodded.

> *Yeah. A world without sign.*

Kayla looked at her, surprised for the first time in the exchange.

> *Don't you already know?*

Black American Sign Language (BASL)

From Wikipedia, the free encyclopedia

Return to main article: "American Sign Language (ASL)"

Black American Sign Language (BASL) is a dialect of ASL used by Black Americans in the United States, often more heavily in the Southern states. ASL and BASL diverged as a result of race-based school segregation. Because student populations were isolated from one another, the language strands evolved separately, to include linguistic variations in phonology, syntax, and vocabulary.

BASL is often stigmatized when compared to "standard" ASL. The measurement of "standard signs" is particularly fraught, because it is based on signs used at Gallaudet University, a formerly segregated institution.

The belief that one variant of a language is superior to others is called prescriptivism, and subscribers frequently conflate nonstandard usage with error. In the United States, progressive linguists argue that prescriptivism and prestige languages are tools for preserving existing hierarchies and power structures, with ties to Eurocentrism and white supremacist ideology.

LINGUISTIC DIFFERENCES

Phonological: BASL signers are more likely to produce two-handed signs, use an overall larger signing space, and tend to produce more signs on the lower half of the face.

Syntactical: A higher incidence of syntactic repetition appears in multiple studies of BASL signers. A study documented in 2011 also showed more frequent use of constructed dialogue and constructed action among Black signers.

Lexical Variation: Some signs developed at Black Deaf schools diverge completely from standard ASL signs, mostly for everyday objects and activities discussed frequently by students. Linguists have also noticed an increase in lexical borrowing of words and idioms from African American Vernacular English (AAVE) among younger Black signers.

Due to the prevalence of the <u>oral method</u> in white deaf education after the <u>Milan Conference</u>, many white deaf children were denied access to American Sign Language, and ASL was subjugated by spoken English. However, significantly fewer resources were dedicated to Black deaf education, leaving many Black Deaf schools to pursue manual language. As such, scholars note that some variations common in BASL, like a higher incidence of two-handed signs, are actually a preservation of the linguistic qualities of early ASL. (*Jump to "ASL, origins of."*)

NOTABLE PEOPLE

<u>Platt H. Skinner</u>, <u>abolitionist</u> and founder of <u>The School for Colored Deaf Dumb and Blind Children</u>, circa 1858. (*Jump to "Directory of U.S. Black Deaf Schools."*)

<u>Carl Croneberg</u>, a Swedish-American Deaf linguist, was the first person to note differences between ASL and BASL in writing, as coauthor of the 1965 *Dictionary of American Sign Language on its Linguistic Principles* (see also: <u>William Stokoe</u>).

<u>Dr. Carolyn McCaskill</u>'s 2011 book, *The Hidden Treasure of Black ASL: Its History and Structure,* features data from a series of studies performed by McCaskill and her team, and is considered a foundational work in the field.

Further Reading: Joseph Hill, John Lewis, Melanie Metzger, Susan Mather, Andrew Foster, Ida Hampton

*C*hristmas Day, for Austin, was always tinged with bitterness, because they were obliged to celebrate it with his father's fully and hopelessly hearing side of the family. When they were younger, his cousins had picked up some sign, and that had been all they needed to put together a game of backyard football or hide-and-seek. But now the cousins were content to stay at the dinner table after the eating was finished, intermittently glancing up from their phones to chime in on what appeared to be a heated debate—Austin's father's side of the family considered political blood sport a bonding activity—while Austin and his mother looked at one another over the mountain of mashed potatoes that sat between them, lost. Normally he felt sorry for himself at these events, but today he thought of Charlie and realized this was a rare moment where he had to experience the world—or rather, not experience it—the way most of his friends did at home.

Sky began to fuss, and his mother turned to entertain her. Austin gave in and pulled his own phone from his pocket, texted Charlie to wish her a Merry Christmas, scrolled through the Instagram deluge of his classmates' pets coerced into wearing Santa hats. His father, who had started off interpreting the family argument, was now all-in on the fray, red-faced and gesticulating alongside his brothers.

Miss u, Austin wrote to Charlie and watched as the three dots signaling her reply hung there for an age.

Me too u, she wrote after a while.

Austin grinned, rejuvenated by the thought of her.

What? said his mother.

What? Nothing.

You got all red.

It's hot in here. Too much yelling.

Yeah right, she said, but he could see she was happy for him.

Austin swiped at his cheeks, as if he could remove the blush.

Invite them over sometime.

Who?

Whoever made you turn that color.

Maybe.

He stopped signing—a few of his relatives were watching them now. Why was it that they were allowed to blather on for ages, but the minute Austin and his mom started their own conversation it was as if they'd volunteered to put on a show?

It was nice to return home after the gathering and begin his traditional campout on the couch for the frigid week between Christmas and New Year's, lounging before an unending stream of B karate movies, and allowing the days to bleed into one another until his mom finally cajoled him into showering.

New Year's Eve was a different story, though—that was hands down his favorite holiday. His grandparents would come for dinner bearing belated Christmas gifts, and then stay for his parents' annual New Year's Eve bash, to which Deaf families from across the tri-state came to party. All week he had been contemplating whether or not he should invite Charlie—it was childish to celebrate New Year's with your family, and undoubtedly she'd have other, cooler plans. But at the same time, it was a night that always felt special, and he wanted to share it with her. Each morning he'd begin writing a text explaining the family tradition and inviting her to come. Then he'd save the message to his drafts, postponing the inevitable rejection for another day.

Then, the day before New Year's Eve, his finger slipped. As he watched the check marks beside the text materialize to confirm its delivery, his stomach knotted, a little from fear, but from excitement, too. So what if it was a boring grown-up party? Maybe they could siphon off some booze and slip into his bedroom unnoticed. He barely had time to dream up what might transpire between them when his phone vibrated with her response—she'd said yes. Austin couldn't help but do a little victory dance in the kitchen. His mother looked on, eyebrows raised, trying to stifle a laugh.

I invited them!

Who? said his mother.

The girl that made me turn red.

Invite her to dinner, too!

Austin frowned. Sometimes his parents could so effectively kill a buzz he wondered whether they'd taken a class in the skill. There was no way he was going to subject Charlie to being his grandparents' captive audience on their first date, if you could call it that.

Definitely not, he said.

All right, all right. Just a suggestion.

Austin texted his address and the best SORTA routes from all directions to Charlie, then retreated to his room, eager to see where the fantasy of their reunion might take him.

*M*erry Christmas! her father shouted as Charlie entered the kitchen.

You're cheery this morning, said Charlie, still rubbing the sleep from her eyes.

Sorry, E–b–e–n–e–z–e–r, said her father.

Merry Christmas, she said.

Coffee?

Charlie nodded, though she knew her father's brew would be strong for her. He handed her a mug and she added too much sugar and chugged the gritty mixture with displeasure. She wondered what Kayla's Christmas morning might look like, or Austin's. She had been hoping he'd ask her to do something for New Year's, had tried hinting at it during the last play practice before break, but so far he hadn't bitten.

You sure you're o–k?

I'm fine. Just not looking forward to the chaos.

Charlie recognized the lost look in her dad's eyes.

Mom and Grandma aren't exactly the most relaxing company, she said in English.

Welcome to adulthood.

He put his arm around her and turned her toward the living room, where a naked little pine tree wilted in the corner. Her mother had kept the ornaments.

Come on, he said. Let's open some presents.

That afternoon, Charlie did get a reprieve of sorts from her Christmas family dinner—when she and her father arrived at her mother's, Charlie exited the car and fainted dead out on the driveway.

She woke moments later, still splayed there, though now her mother was cradling Charlie's head in her lap, her face too close. Charlie took stock—she blinked, wiggled her fingers and toes—she felt fine. She tried to remember a time she had ever seen her mother sit on the ground before, but came up blank.

Sorry, she said. *I don't know
what happened.*

You o–k? said her father. *You
want me to call the doctor?*

Charlie shook her head, feeling her mother's hands cupping her ears.

No, I think I'm all right.

Her mother said something she couldn't lipread upside down. Her father held out a hand to help her up. What did she say? she saw her mother ask.

Slowly, Charlie took her father's hand to steady herself and stood. Her parents had begun to bicker about whether they should call someone, and she struggled to follow, but then the conversation stopped suddenly, Charlie's mother looking beyond her and her father. Charlie knew it meant that her grandmother had pulled in.

The four of them went inside and Charlie's mother suggested with uncharacteristic tenderness that Charlie rest on the couch while dinner was warming. From the corner of her eye, Charlie saw her father slip into the foyer and make a call. Wyatt, who was staring intently at a basketball game featuring two teams Charlie didn't recognize, scooched to the far end of the couch to make room for her. She fell asleep deep and quick, and when she woke, everyone was at the table, eating without her.

On the afternoon of the thirty-first, Austin's parents took Sky to the audiologist. His mother, annoyed that his father had scheduled an appointment for New Year's Eve day when they were about to have a bunch of people over to the house, was not shy about showing her displeasure, slamming the side door as they went out to the car. Austin tried his best to tidy up and follow his mother's list of preparatory to-dos—vacuuming, unfolding the card tables where they would set out snacks. Then his grandparents arrived, Grandma Lorna showering him with fuchsia-lipped kisses, Grandpa Willis clapping him too hard on the back. Austin got them drinks and turned on the Christmas tree lights. He tried not to look at the clock overhead—he didn't want to appear too eager and leave himself vulnerable to a line of his grandparents' questioning that would lead them to Charlie.

Where did your parents take the baby again? said Grandma Lorna after a while.

New earmolds, I think, he said, though as he did, he realized he wasn't actually sure what the appointment was for.

They should give her little ears a

break. It's almost a national holi-
day!

Grandma Lorna changed the subject, asked Austin about school, the play, girls. He was glad he had opted not to invite Charlie to dinner. Her sign had improved rapidly over the past few months, but when it came to his grandparents' old-fashioned signs and arthritic cadences, she would be underwater. Finally, his family returned, his grandma rushing to the door to retrieve Sky from her carrier, while Austin's parents gave them terse hugs and headed into the kitchen. Austin looked on while his grandparents played with the baby, Grandma Lorna with Sky on her lap facing Grandpa Willis, their grandpa beginning a version of Goldilocks and the Three Deaf Bears that Austin remembered from when he was small.

He went to the kitchen to lend a hand. His mother was at the stove, bent too close over a pot of bubbling oil. She looked pale, but when she saw Austin, she quickly began to emit a brightness he knew was fake, not from its quality—which was actually quite authentic, his mother had always been good at that—but from the speed at which her demeanor had changed.

Are you o-k?

Her face fell, then reset, so quick other people might not have noticed.

Can you check if I put utensils
out? I can't remember.

Sure.

She turned away again. His father appeared through the side door, carrying several bags of ice, and a Ziploc containing Sky's hearing aids with their newest earmolds, this set flecked with gold glitter.

Back in the living room, Austin watched his father remove the aids from the bag, gingerly inserting them back into her ears and adjusting the lanyard typically used on babies to prevent aids from getting lost if they ripped them out of their heads. Sky didn't seem to mind them, though—after a brief swipe at her ear to inspect the new device, she continued chewing on the end of the remote control as if nothing had happened. His father sighed.

I saw Skylar trying to sign! said
Grandpa Willis.
                    She's definitely babbling, said
                    Austin's father.
That's early, right?
                    She's just stretching her hands.
        Still.
                    She gets a lot of practice, his
                    mother said, appearing just in
                    time to glare at her husband.
                            Are you two o-k? said Grandma
                            Lorna.

Austin remembered his mother saying that she'd never seen her parents argue. Grandma Lorna believed in a strict closed-door policy with regard to children and marital strife, and Grandpa Willis followed her lead. It was unclear whether Austin's parents actively held an opposing belief or just couldn't be bothered to hide from him, but in either case, he'd seen them fight plenty and he could tell that wasn't about to change now, not for his or Sky's or even his grandparents' sakes.

Now Austin's mother nodded, but it was obvious that neither she nor his father was okay, or at least they weren't acting themselves. They were curt, stiff-shouldered, their signs clipped. He tried to recall whether he'd seen evidence of a rift earlier, or if something had happened on their outing. How had they been this morning? Two days ago? Christmas had been fine, right? His father had left them hanging more readily than usual during the family brawl, but, if they were being honest, neither Austin nor his mother had really wanted to join in that mess.

                    Should we do presents?
                        Let's eat first, said Austin's
                        mother.

Austin's father carried in a heaping plate of fried chicken, the crust still glistening with oil in spots. They took their seats, passed side dishes to one another. Sky smacked a light-up rattle against the side of her bouncer, then bit the handle with fervor.

          Cute hearing aids, said Grandpa
          Willis. *Not like when we were*
          in school.

His grandpa described the hearing aids Austin had seen in old photos: a big electronic microphone box strapped to the chest, two wires snaking up to his ears.

                         Not even like when we were
                         adults! said his grandma.

Neither of his parents responded.

    O-k, what's wrong? said Austin,
looking pointedly at his father.

               Nothing.
        You don't like the pink hearing
        aids?

               I like them fine. They just don't
               work.
    They're broken? I thought she just
    needed new earmolds. What'd the
    doctor say?

His father shook his head and took a bite of chicken, big enough that Austin knew he had been trying to buy himself some time. But that was the thing about ASL—you could talk with your mouth full.

          Threshold for her left ear has de-
          clined, said his mother. *She's no*
          longer benefiting from the aid on
          that side.
               Doctor thinks it's reasonable to
               expect the same in the other ear
               over time, said his father.

    S-o. She's deaf?
        Officially.
    Strong genes, his grandfather.

His grandma patted Grandpa Willis on the arm as if to shush him, but it was clear she took some pride in the news, too.

Well, maybe it's good, said Austin.

He thought of Charlie, the way she was always upset with her parents, how she had to take all remedial classes even though she was obviously smart. He felt relieved for Sky, who would be sure who she was from the onset.

*Better to be full deaf than stuck
in the middle.*

Austin's grandparents nodded with approval, but he noticed right away that his parents were both staring hard at their plates.

Things are different now, said
his father, nodding at Austin
across the table. *Even from
when you were little.*

And it can be different for girls,
said his mother.

What's different? said his
grandma. *What happened?*

*Nothing happened. I just mean
people can take advantage.*

What are you talking about? said
Austin.

The community is shrinking, said
his father. *There are budget cuts
in the district—*

*Hey, wait a minute! We're not
that old!* said Grandpa Willis,
still in his easy, joking way.
Don't rush the funeral over here.

*She's a good candidate for a co-
chlear implant,* his father
blurted.

Austin dropped his fork, the mashed potatoes in his mouth now gluey and hard to swallow.

What? I don't understand.

We think it's what's best, said his father. *She's heard speech naturally for a few months, she has a good foundation. The less gap in sound input, the better.*

His father paused to take another bite of chicken, as if they were having a completely normal conversation. Austin couldn't think straight; he was suddenly overcome by the thick smell of the grease. Grandma Lorna looked right past his father and turned her attention to her daughter.

How could you allow this?

Austin's mother, who'd eaten nothing, straightened the cutlery on the table beside her plate.

Safety concerns? School budgets? Deaf people have been under attack for centuries. Who are you trying to fool? said Grandma Lorna.

I want to give her as many opportunities as I can.

I knew this would happen, said Grandpa Willis, now scowling openly at Austin's father. *We raised you better than this.*

Better than trying to get the best for my child?

Better than letting some hearing man step on your neck!

Austin's mind, which had gone blank after the mention of the implant, was now full of thoughts, only they were moving much too fast.

You're going against everything
you taught me, he said. *What*
about Deaf pride? Deaf gain?
You're just giving up?

His mother looked hurt, but did she expect him to be diplomatic? Pragmatic? She'd made him this way.

Skylar will still be Deaf, said his
father. *She'll still sign. And im-*
plants have changed so much
since you were a kid. They're
really powerful tools.

Why don't you love her the way
she is? Why do you have to drill a
fucking hole in her head?

Of course we love her, said his
mother. *We want to give her the*
best life we can. The best educa-
tion.

What are you TALKING about?
River Valley is a great school.

Austin burst up from his chair, his body apparently planning to flee this conversation. But at the mention of River Valley, his parents exchanged a look that froze him in place. Clearly they had not meant for the conversation to go there. His father tried to look away, but his mother held his gaze, her eyes slicing through the room's stillness.

What? said Austin.

Again, his mother's stare.

I can't! said his father in close,
restrained sign. *It violates the*
code of ethics.

What, said Austin with his mouth, is going on?

His father, who'd been in the midst of offering up another excuse, was halted by the sound of Austin's voice. He dropped his hands into his lap and looked to Austin's mother.

Your father was interpreting an
administrative meeting. They're
closing River Valley.

What?

He looked to his father, who only gave a small nod. Grandpa Willis had also pushed himself back from the table and was now rooting around the kitchen junk drawer, for a lighter, Austin guessed.

Closing down? Permanently?

This is not public information.
You CAN'T TELL ANYONE.

We don't want to create a panic.

You really think the community
will keep it a secret? said
Grandma Lorna.

No one else knows yet. Only Feb-
ruary and Phil were at the meet-
ing.

Austin felt his dinner churning inside him and thought he might throw up, so he ran down the hall into the bathroom and stood with his face over the toilet. Nothing happened, and his parents didn't come after him. He fled to his room but only felt caged. Were they even planning to tell him, or just leave it as a surprise for next school year? What would happen to his classmates? And why the hell did he always lose his goddamn sneakers? He finally found them beneath his desk and pulled them on, thought of running into the dining room, grabbing Sky, and making a break for it, but even in his mind's eye he knew that was ridiculous. Instead he slunk back down the hall—a slow and ragged route avoiding the loose floorboards. But his father was there anyway, blocking the front door.

Where are you going?

Out.

Austin had never missed a New Year's party and was expecting to meet with more of a fight, or at least to have to put forth an explanation of where, exactly, he was going, but his father didn't press further.

> *I'm serious about the River Valley*
> *stuff. It can't get out.*

What do you care?

> *This isn't about me, or you, or*
> *Sky. Let Headmistress bring it to*
> *the community in due time. Not*
> *ours to tell.*

Whatever.

Austin tried to reach around his father for the doorknob, but his dad wouldn't budge.

O-k. FINE, he said.

His father moved, and Austin opened the door. There on his door-step, face cast blue in the light of her phone screen, was Charlie.

> *Hey,* she said. *Was just texting*
> *you.*

Austin only shook his head and took her hand, leading her away from the house.

Outside, the crisp air and Charlie's presence quelled his upset stom-ach a little. He'd forgotten his coat, but the wind had died down and anyway it was too late now. He pointed to the SORTA stop on the far side of the interstate, and they waited for a long gap in the head-lights, then bolted across.

> *Are you o-k? What's going on?*

Yeah, I'm just . . . I just need a
few minutes to process. Is that
o-k?

> *Of course,* Charlie said.

An inbound bus appeared, and they boarded. Austin could tell the SORTA driver was seething, the way employees who have to work on the eves of national holidays were prone to (not that he blamed them), so he tried to pay quickly and move out of the way. Instead he somehow inserted his bills upside down, and then the driver was full-on shouting, giving instructions that Austin would've struggled to lipread even if he hadn't been flustered. Austin turned to Charlie, but she'd been digging in her wallet for fare and had missed the start of whatever the driver had said; she was just as lost as Austin.

Hearing people turned aggressive so quickly, at even a momentary failure to respond, so sometimes Austin gave them the kind of answer they wanted, albeit loud and slurred. "Deaf" was a mercifully easy word to say, and he pointed to his ear and said it now. The driver reddened, handed Austin back the five, and motioned for him and Charlie to sit.

It was hard to imagine what the world might be like if deaf people had as short a fuse about hearing people's inability to sign, their neglect or refusal to caption TV, or, hell, the announcements on this bus. Of course, that was their privilege—to conflate majority with superiority. He had grown up seeing other people's anger embedded in a thousand little chores: the disdain with which the man at the deli counter looked at them when he was forced to read his mother's written note, exasperation at the Popeyes drive-thru when they bypassed the intercom and pulled directly to the window, his mother being skipped at the DMV when she'd missed her number called out, the bank hanging up on her over and over when she tried to call via videophone.

Sometimes the hostility remained, but usually it dropped away when they realized his mother, or he, was deaf. It was never replaced with contrition, though—it was always pity, which was worse. Now that most everyone in their corner of Colson recognized the family, they often skipped the anger phase, but the pity never faded.

Would Skylar's implant give her the opportunity to be free of strangers' rage? If so, maybe it wasn't a bad thing. He managed to convince himself of this for a minute, until he remembered that in a few hours it would be next year, and next year RVSD would be gone, and there was nothing he, or his parents, or Headmistress Waters could do to stop it.

You sure you're o-k? said Charlie after a while. *You're scaring me a little.*

He nodded again and let his head drop to her shoulder.

Where are we going?

Austin didn't want to tell her that he had no idea.

*a*s she watched Mel lean in close to the mirror to apply her mascara, a small part of February wished she had her own cosmetics routine. Makeup would come in handy now, the ability to dampen her expression behind foundation or a thick ring of eyeliner. Chemical armor.

Other than the tube of mauve lipstick she applied religiously before meetings at which she needed to intimidate someone, her last true foray into makeup had been a dense coat of frosty blue eye shadow, which she and her best friend at the time had brushed on one another's lids surreptitiously in the back of the car. And that had been in eighth grade; today she wouldn't even know where to start. She considered asking Mel to make her up, but that would come with its own problems. Why, Mel would wonder, was February suddenly interested? Was it because of Wanda? Others at the party were bound to notice if she were gussied up, too, and that'd be counterproductive to her desire to fade into the background. She settled for lotion and lip balm, then sat on the end of their bed and waited for Mel to finish.

In these idle moments, a new worry sprouted. February trusted sober Wanda and Phil not to say anything about River Valley, but alcohol was always a wild card. And they would certainly assume

Mel already knew—what if they tried to commiserate? February could feel her armpits getting sticky.

We can still skip out, you know, she said.

Glad to get you out of the house, said Mel.

I know Deaf parties aren't exactly your scene.

If they have alcohol, they're my scene.

Mel clacked over to the bathroom doorway, jutted out a hip.

You may now compliment me, she said.

February smiled, rose from the bed.

Babe, she said, running her hand down the curve of Mel's waist, emphasized by a black dress with a hint of cling. You're smokin'.

Mm-hmm.

I think you're getting even sexier with time, said February.

Like a fine wine, Mel said.

Exactly. You know we could stay in tonight.

Speaking of—

Mel snapped straight and crossed out of the bedroom, leaving February alone in the wake of her perfume, that amber and warm orange scent she knew so well.

—we should bring some wine to this thing.

February could hear Mel opening the liquor cabinet and followed helplessly after her.

They arrived late even by Deaf standards, for which February was thankful. She hadn't done any socializing since her mother's funeral, and the brash celebratory air was an affront to her cloistered senses, with a slight undercurrent of betrayal. The betrayal part was nonsense—her mother would have loved a Deaf New Year's party, so she tried to push through her discomfort. It was clear they had some catching up to do on the alcohol front. Fortunately, before they could make it out of the foyer, Beth Workman appeared with a pair of her signature cosmo shots, an offer both February and Mel downed with gusto.

Welcome to the land of the living,
said Wanda when they got to
the kitchen.

She says she's happy to see us out, February said to Mel.
Mel pulled her phone from the small purse she hung on her wrist
whenever she wore a dress.

That makes 2 of us, she typed. Only so much outlander a gal can
watch w/out going crosseyed.
Wanda's eyes widened.

You guys like O–u–t–l–a–n–d–e–r?

Not me, said February. *I don't do
time travel.*

Wanda's gaze shifted to Mel's screen, where she had written:

not Feb. time travel offends her rational sensibilities.
The two of them laughed knowingly, and Wanda reached for Mel's
phone, typed something back. At first, February tried to look over
their shoulders, but she didn't have her reading glasses, so she could
only watch as they huddled closer over the screen.

Beneath the kitchen island, February tapped Wanda on the thigh.

Quiet, she said when Wanda
looked up.

Either Wanda didn't register what February was talking about, or
didn't care. She gave February a polite smile and returned to the
conversation on the screen.

Well that's rich, February thought. She'd been *telling* Mel she
would like Wanda if she'd just give her a chance. She cast her eye
about the room, examining the rest of the party. Deaf couples, many
of them her teachers, swapping resolutions and pouring one another
drinks and laughing. Too much damn smiling. She waved to Willis
and Lorna Workman, who were both looking a little down, but
waved back and smiled when they saw her. They were sweet, but she
hoped she could avoid talking to them so she didn't have to rehash
her mother's death. She felt adrift until she peered across the room
and caught the only conversation in which participants did not seem

oppressively cheery, Beth Workman and River Valley's drama teacher, Deb Fickman, signing rapidly with their brows furrowed.

So is it K-r-a-m-e-r *versus* K-r-a-m-e-r *or what?* Fickman said.

No, I mean, part of me actually agrees with him, Beth said. *Does that make me a horrible person?*

Of course not. Have you told Austin?

February watched as Beth hefted a handle of Tito's from her side table and poured a few fingers into each of their glasses. They clinked and drank.

How's it going? February interjected as the two were mid-swallow. It was unlike her to insert herself into a conversation like this, but she couldn't bear to make small talk with anyone who looked like they were enjoying themselves, and she wasn't yet drunk enough to take up residence in the corner alone. Beth and Deb looked at February grimly. Deb pursed her lips and began to dab at a spot on her blouse.

Sorry. Didn't meant to intrude.

No, no it's fine. We were just talking about Sky.

Yes, congratulations! And bravo to you for throwing a party with an infant.

After a few months of sleep deprivation it's all the same, Beth said, smiling weakly.

Deb was still blotting away performatively at her blouse. February was beginning to think she'd put her foot in something she shouldn't have. Was something wrong with Sky? With Henry?

Are you o-k? Do you need any-thing?

I'm fine. Just a little family
drama. Henry's pushing hard for
an implant, and it all kind of
came out at dinner—

Beth gestured to the love seat where her parents were sitting; Willis was now snoring violently, paper hors d'oeuvres plate slipping from his slackening grip. February was thrown.

An implant? For Austin?
Both Beth and Deb laughed.

For Sky! Deb said. *Austin! That*
would be the day.

Sky? But Austin said— I thought
she was hearing.

So did we, said Beth.

How are you feeling about it?

I'm not sure.
At the end of the day, either way
will be fine. Lots of kids up at
River Valley have implants,
right, Feb? It's not even a big
deal anymore.

True.

Actually, Ben and I were just
talking about turning that utility
closet in the greenroom into some
kind of "listening room." A place
where they could go and play in-
struments, experiment with those
iPad music editing apps—that'd
be cool, right?

Yeah, said February tepidly.

February looked to Beth, who took a gulp from her cup. The longer February held her gaze, the more Beth drank. She knew about the closure. Of course she did. What kind of person wouldn't share such information with their spouse?

Again filled with fear that Wanda might let slip the news to Mel, February excused herself and returned to the kitchen, where Mel was grinning and beckoning her from across the island. The smile eased February's worries; she held up an index finger to buy herself a moment and went to the drink cart instead. She made a poor replica of whatever concoction Beth had been serving, and joined Mel and Wanda, who herself had now been joined by her husband.

Someone had switched on the television, and though they were not at the right angle to see the ball drop, they chanted the countdown and kissed alongside the rest of the guests. Then Mel went to find the bathroom, and February stood alone in a vodka haze, feeling a split second's solace that her mother was gone. At least she wouldn't be around to see what happened next.

*C*ome on, said Charlie. *Talk to me.*

She'd tried to be patient, let Austin rest his head on her shoulder as the bus hurtled through the dark to who knows where. She tried not to be annoyed that she'd agonized over choosing an outfit that was both alluring and acceptable for meeting someone's parents, only to be cut off on the stoop and dragged back onto the bus.

Maybe I can help.

She could see him weighing something; he was choosing his words carefully. He sighed.

My sister.

The baby? Is she o-k?

She's deaf.

At this Charlie couldn't help but laugh, and Austin looked taken aback.

Sorry, she said, drawing her hand across her mouth to hide her smirk. *But. Isn't your family, like, famous for that?*

She was born hearing but she's losing it. My parents—my dad—want to implant her.

What! Why?

Austin pursed his lips.

> *They're worried about her future,*
> *because—*

He stopped himself. Looked down at his feet.

> *I don't know.*

What about your mom?

> *She agrees with him! She had*
> *some bullshit line about implants*
> *being better for a girl's safety.*

It was Charlie's turn to avert her gaze.

That's not—it doesn't really work
that way.

She looked back up at Austin, let him see in her eyes the things she couldn't say. Her palms got clammy and she wiped them on her jeans.

Anyway.

> *I think she's gonna let him do it.*

That's so stupid.

> *It's ridiculous. I don't understand*
> *why they'd want to put her*
> *through surgery just to make her*
> *more hearing. If it even works at*
> *all!*

He gestured at Charlie like she was proof of his argument. Now it was her turn to measure her words—even though she agreed with him, she was well versed in the other side of this coin. Maybe seeing the counterargument would bring him some comfort. Given how upset he was, it probably wouldn't hurt.

It's not the end of the world,
right? I mean, most people's im-
plants aren't as shitty as mine.

> *Yeah, I know.*

She can always take it off.

> *I guess.*

And she'll still sign.

           I guess.

And she'll still come to River Valley.

Austin lifted his hands as if to say something, stopped.

           I don't know, he said after a while.

Definitely!

She pulled the magnet from her head, slid into silence.

    See? Super deaf now!

He smiled, but his smile didn't meet his eyes.

    She's gonna be o-k. You too.

           I could use a drink.

I heard Kevin's having a party.

           They'll probably just play video-games all night.

My dad's out. You could come back to the apartment. I'm sure he has something in the cabinet.

           Yeah, o-k.

She pulled her phone from her pocket and opened Google Maps.

    First we have to figure out where the hell we are.

They had already passed through downtown Colson and were heading into the No Fly. They'd have to get out and double back to get to her dad's. Or—

    Actually, I do know another party. On the East Side.

           Deaf?

Hearing.

           People from Jefferson?

Sort of . . . They're kind of weird. But they'll definitely have alcohol.

Let's go.

You sure?

Austin nodded, reanimated now, and Charlie pressed the yellow rubber strip to request a stop, waiting for the driver to release them into the night.

*a*ustin could feel the music long before they got where they were going. Though he didn't want to admit it, he'd found their desolate trek from the bus stop a bit frightening and was glad of the signs of life the noise represented, even if it was a hearing party. At the end of the row of warehouses one of the grilles was up halfway, and he followed Charlie as she pushed open a set of thick metal doors and let them in.

Inside, Charlie said something to a daunting woman with a bar through her nose; the woman pointed to the far-left corner, then handed them both tiny plastic cups, like the kind Austin's dentist used. The liquid inside smelled about the same as Listerine, but he knocked it back anyway. Charlie was already making her way into the crowd, and he reached for her hand. She looked at him over her shoulder, eye whites and teeth glowing purple in the black light. There in the dark, thumping heat, he felt the night crack wide open with possibility. He was thankful that he hadn't told her about the school closure, even if the only thing stopping him had been cowardice.

They were nearly at the front of the room, standing before a person-size speaker that made his joints feel wobbly, when she paused. She let go of his hand, hugged a boy with jagged jet-black hair, fist-bumped another with a purple mohawk, and offered a wary nod of acknowledgment to the girl between them.

S–l–u–s–h, L–e–m, S–i–d, she
said after a while, pointing to
the three.

Austin waved. The one called Slash stuck out his hand and they
shook. Austin made his sign name, looking to Charlie to relay.

A, Slash said, and copied his sign name. Right on.

There was something between Slash and Charlie he couldn't put his
finger on, as if the air changed viscosity when they got close, which,
on the dance floor, was happening with increasing frequency. His
immediate riposte had been to take two spite shots and a hit of
whatever had been in the mohawk guy's vape pen, but still their dy-
namic needled at him.

Casual, he thought. Be cool for once. He ran his fingers down the
length of Charlie's neck with as light a touch as he could, until he felt
her shiver.

How do you know these guys
again?

Long story, said Charlie.

From hearing school?

They're older than us.

Church?

Charlie frowned, but it wasn't clear whether that was at the thought
of church or at the continued line of questioning.

Juvie?

She sighed.

They're in a b–a–n–d, she said finally.

Like, a music group?

I knew the one guy from Jeff.
Did you know punk bands used
to rent out Deaf clubs as concert
venues?

I've heard of that, he said.

> *Of course you have.*

She rolled her eyes like she was teasing, but he could see there was a grain of hurt there. His mother liked to brag about having seen the Clash at a Deaf Club in Kalamazoo, but he decided it was best to leave that bit out for the moment.

> *I'm so far behind on everything.*
> *Even the Deafest kid in school*
> *knows more about music than*
> *me.*

I don't.

> *Sure.*

I don't know what it sounds like.
She paused at this.
Well?

> *You're asking the wrong girl.*

No, really—you hear stuff, right?

> *Not like hearing people.*

Still. What does listening feel
like?

Charlie looked up at the ceiling, as if maybe the answer was scrawled above her head. Around them, the music was running taut through the room.

> *Frustrating. Like, information is*
> *flowing in and I work really hard*
> *to sort through it but it still doesn't*
> *make sense. And it's slippery—*
> *it moves, changes, so when I—*
> *pah!—understand one thing, three*
> *more fly by. Plus when people see*
> *the CI they expect me to hear like*
> *a normal person, so they talk fast,*
> *they cover their mouths . . .*

That sounds . . . bad.

> *Yeah.*

> *But trying to follow a conversa-*
> *tion is different than this, right?*

He gestured at the speakers. To him, it felt a bit relentless, but he could see how someone might find solace in the steadiness, too.

> *This—*

She copied the sweep of his arm.

> *Amazing. But I turn my implant*
> *off here.*

> *You never listen?*

> *Why ruin a good thing?*

There were more shots, more vapor from Sid's pen. Following Charlie's lead, Austin downed a small white pill passed his way by one of the crew. The more he drank, the more he could see the bandmates' allure—they were confident, moved with the assurance that they were doing exactly what they should be at any moment, even when much of what they were doing on the dance floor was objectively awkward-looking.

Seeing Slash glom on to a girl from the crowd—one to whom they hadn't been introduced—helped his mood considerably. Austin held tight to Charlie as they danced, tried not to mind that the ferocity of her grinding intensified each time Slash inserted his tongue into the girl's mouth. Austin let her exorcise the dregs of whatever had happened between her and Slash against him. The room spun, time stretched out languid before him, he closed his eyes and allowed his senses to contract to two: scent and touch, salt and heat.

Only when he began to sweat off the drugs did the jealousy crop up again. Slash tapped Charlie on the shoulder and asked her something Austin couldn't track.

> *He says they've got a surprise.*
> *You want to go?* Charlie asked.

> *O-k,* he said, trying not to look
> too interested.

Right on, said Slash, and handed them both another shot.

. . .

Though he had been glad to be jacketless in the warehouse, outside it was freezing, and Austin pulled his hat down over his ears.

Where we going?

Their house.

He watched Slash and Lem slide behind a piece of plywood and into one in a row of boarded houses, to which Charlie had no reaction. The bandmates each returned with a brown paper grocery bag, a third boy now beside them.

G-r-e-g, said Charlie.

Slash tucked his bag under one arm, mimed a pair of little explosions with his free hand. Greg and Sid took off running, Sid waving for them to follow. Charlie said something aloud, Slash countered, then turned to catch up with his mates, who had already made it to the end of the street.

Maybe we should skip.

The glow of Charlie's high had faded; she looked rattled.

You feel o-k?

Yeah, she said. *It's just that S-l-a-s-h and them can be . . . wild.*

New Year's fireworks?

Sure, she said. *Right.*

She didn't look convinced, but Austin was still quite high and wanted to prove to Charlie that he could roll with a little mischief. He began to jog, pulling her along after her friends.

He and Charlie caught up with them at what looked like the on-ramp to an overpass, where the group had stalled and seemed to be arguing. He eyed the No Pedestrians sign at its mouth.

Do you know what they're say-ing?

Not really. They're looking for something.

Sid stomped his foot and the others rolled their eyes at him, but apparently his display of obstinence had decided something. Slash beckoned Austin and Charlie over.

R-e-a-d-y?

For what? Charlie said.

But Slash just bolted up the concrete incline. Charlie looked at Austin, then followed.

The highway was the emptiest Austin had ever seen it. It must've been nearly midnight, the whole county inside, staring at a tiny glass ball on television. Greg and Sid had run fifty feet down the road, where an abandoned car sat, a dirty undershirt tied to its sideview mirror. Greg smashed the passenger's side window with a chunk of tar, and then, with Sid, began to push at the car, rocking it side to side.

What are they doing?

No idea.

Austin saw Slash sigh and hand his brown bag to Lem, then run to help. The three boys got a little more leverage, but it wasn't enough. They turned to Austin.

You don't have to, Charlie said.

I know, he said, but he was already walking toward them.

The four of them had the car on its side quickly so that it fell into the road, blocking the right lane. Lem and Charlie trotted over with the bags, and Austin surveyed the contents—as far as he could tell, they were filled with Roman candles and other fireworks. A single car whizzed by.

Slash thrust his arm deep into his bag and pulled a pair of small red cylinders from the bottom. He held them up to Austin, waiting for him to be impressed.

M-8-0-s! he said, when Austin didn't respond.

Oh, he said, nodding, though
he knew nothing about them.
Cool.

Greg dumped the rest of the bag into the car through the broken
window, and Lem did the same with hers. Then Slash flicked his
lighter, flame undulating in the night wind, and pried open the fuel
tank.

Now! he shouted as he tucked the firecracker into the tank and lit
the fuse. The group sprinted back down to the lip of the ramp. Austin
felt the explosion before he had time to fully turn and watch the
show—crackle of red, white, and green cutting through the night. It
was easy to be in awe of the colorful clusters breaking against the
darkness of road and sky, conditioned as humans are to marvel at
pyrotechnic displays. Then the fireworks gave way to fire. A plume of
smoke rose, just a shade lighter than the cast of the sky itself, and
Slash and his friends took off down the street, past their house, and
deeper into the city.

Austin and Charlie followed them to a block that showed some
signs of life. The group ducked into a bar, where inside, the New
Year's crowd looked less than celebratory. They pushed into a back
room and took up residence in a corner booth.

They were all still heaving to catch their breath when a waitress
slammed a tray of sweaty beers on their table and shook her head at
them.

Hell yeah, said Lem, when the woman left.

I told you! said Sid.

The friends clinked bottles and Austin sat watching them revel for a
while, without trying to understand what they were saying, or even
what exactly had happened. The bartender brought a round of whis-
key shots. They drank.

Why? Austin said, looking to
Slash.

Huh? said Slash.

Austin cleared his throat:

Why did you do that?

He was grateful that the group seemed unfazed by the thickness of his accent. It made him wonder what Charlie's voice sounded like.

Two reasons, Slash said, holding up his fingers, but Austin lost him after that, and looked to Charlie.

He says it's a protest, she said.

Protesting what?

Well, more like general display of dissatisfaction.

But wasn't that someone's car?

Charlie relayed.

He says, S–i–d watched and it sat there a long time. He says if the city has to spend money for cleanup, they get the message.

What message?

Anger, she said.

Austin was thirsty, took a few big gulps of beer. He hoped someone might offer him the weed again. Prone to paranoia and expecting to be nervous around so many hearing people, he'd been careful not to smoke too much. But the anxiety hadn't come—these guys weren't so bad, they kind of made sense, actually. He could get behind some rage right about now—and he was quite drunk and wanted another toke.

What's the second reason? he said.

Why not? Slash said, grinning.

Austin shrugged and said *weed,* which he knew to be a universal sign, and Greg laughed and handed him the vape.

*C*harlie arrived home in the early hours of New Year's Day, still drunk, and crawled into bed. When she woke later, head pounding, she was impressed and a little regretful that she hadn't vomited.

Some party, her father said when she descended the stairs that afternoon.

Charlie could only groan.

Want some bacon?

Not hungry.

It'll help.

Fine, she said.

She sat while her father fried her bacon and eggs and stared at the sizzling grease until her eyes fell out of focus.

Anything you want to talk about? he said, sliding the plate across the counter.

Like what?

I don't know, the party? What'd you guys do? Any boys?

Ew, Dad, no.

No boys?

No talking to you about boys.

H–a! So there is one!

Charlie rubbed her temples.

Your mother said you were out
with a boy over Thanksgiving.

Who are you two, the Happiness
Police?

I'm just making sure you're—

Charlie could see him trying to figure out how to sign the rest of the sentence.

r-e-s-p-o-n-s-i-b-l-e.

OH MY GOD, Dad stop.

Fathers are supposed to w-o-r-
r-y about daughters and boy-
friends.

I don't have a boyfriend, she
said.

But she felt her cheeks warm at the thought that maybe she could. Austin had surprised her last night. He had hung in with the drugs and the partying, but more important, he had been vulnerable with her, which was something neither Kyle nor Slash had ever done.

I have homework.

Good luck with that, he said.

Charlie was glad when break came to an end, but was disappointed to find the first day back at school also felt like a slog. Things improved after play practice, once she was alone with Austin, holding hands as they crossed the quad. Then she saw her mother's car parked in front of her dorm and wished she could slip back into math class after all.

Austin, who'd given her the sign for "hangover" and was now deftly describing the pulse of his head as he and his family faced the fallout of their implant argument and the detritus of the party his parents had thrown, did not notice her go white. She pulled him behind a column.

I have to go. My mom.

Oh, can I meet your mom?

You don't wanna meet my mom.

For one minute!

She doesn't sign.

S-o? I'll wave.

Charlie considered. Her mother was always finding creative ways to mortify her, but there was also potential pleasure to be derived from rubbing a very Deaf boy in her mother's face. Eventually she nodded and led Austin to the car, where her mom got out and thrust her hand in his face. They shook.

Hello, she said. You must be—

My friend Austin, Charlie said

and signed at once.

Nice meeting you.

He says nice to meet you, said Charlie.

Congratulations on the play, her mother said.

She said congrats on Peter Pan.

Thanks.

Her mother fidgeted with her keys.

All right, we better go. In case there's traffic, said her mother.

Gotta go get poked in the head,

said Charlie.

Austin laughed, which startled her mother, which made Charlie laugh.

See you later, he said.

For a second Charlie was afraid he'd try to kiss her, but instead he just launched the sign for "kiss" toward her and winked.

What'd he say? asked her mother.

"See you later."

Her mother looked as if she wanted to press the issue, but instead just opened and closed her mouth. Charlie had a vision of her mother-as-goldfish, and laughed again as they drove toward the gate.

.   .   .

At Colson Children's, the interpreter was waiting for them in a chair
near the receptionist's window, flipping through a copy of *Time*. Her
mother checked in while Charlie chatted with him about Christmas
break and school.

> *RVSD? My son goes there*, the
> interpreter said. *Maybe you
> know him. Austin?*

Charlie's cheeks burned.

> *I know Austin*, she said. *We're
> in the play together. Well—*

The receptionist swung the door open, and Charlie was grateful for
the interruption, until she remembered what awaited her at the end
of the corridor.

Austin's father's smile congealed. Charlie tried not to think about
the debate going on in his house, the way their opinions might be at
odds. In this room, she needed him. The doctor appeared, shook her
mother's hand.

> *I hear you gave the family a scare
> over the holidays*, the
> interpreter-as-doctor said.

> *I got a little dizzy.*

> *She passed out cold!* said
> interpreter-mother.

> *Was there pain like with your
> previous headaches?*

> *I don't remember*, Charlie said.
> *It happened too fast.*

The doctor pulled on gloves, took her processor off, and ran his finger
along the curve of her scar. Charlie winced.

> *Any pain when I press?*

> *Some.*

> *And no discrimination im-
> provement with the new
> processor?*

Charlie shook her head. The interpreter stroked his chin. The doctor keyed something into the computer in the corner of the room.

> *All right, let's get you down to imaging.*

Where?

> *X-ray and CT, and we'll go from there.*

So Charlie spent an hour in the bowels of the hospital, shivering in her socks and a pair of mint hospital gowns—one backward, one forward to keep from flashing anyone was the trick she'd learned over the years—Austin's father relaying the techs' instructions to her through the window. Now that he was there, she had no idea how she'd ever gone through this process without him.

> *Unfortunately, I think this narrows our options,* said the doctor, when they returned upstairs.

He toggled between the on-screen images of Charlie's head, drawing a circle in the air around her cochlea.

> *Given that Charlie's version of implant has been recalled—*

Hold on, said her mother. *The thing inside her head was re-called?*

A nod.

> *Why didn't anyone tell us?*

> *It's a recent development—a voluntary recall. You should be receiving a letter—*

A letter?

> *The company's working first with self-reported malfunctions, to avoid unnecessary panic.*

You mean bad press, Charlie
said into her lap.
She gave Austin's father a look and he didn't translate.

                    I don't understand, said her
                    mother.

                                        Users themselves provide the
                                        most reliable information on effi-
                                        cacy. Case in point. He pointed
                                        to Charlie. *You experienced*
                                        problems, you came in. No dan-
                                        gerous outcomes have been re-
                                        ported or expected.

                    A letter.
What about babies? said Charlie.

                    What? one, or maybe both, of
                    them said.
Babies can't report themselves.
                    What is the recall for, exactly?
The doctor shifted on his stool.

                                        Some users have experienced
                                        moisture leakage.

What?

                    A moisture leak sounds danger-
                    ous! said her mother.
What about my headaches?
Austin's father gestured some mumbling on the doctor's behalf.

                    S-o what do we do?

                                        We'll remove internal components,
                                        clear out any damaged tissue.

Surgery again? Nope.

                                        As you can see—more circling—
                                        she does have some scar tissue.

Totally normal. Depending on the severity, we may or may not be able to insert a new electrode array and receiver. But we won't know until we're inside.

Not happening.

And what if you can't replace it?

We can explore candidacy on the other side.

MOM, NO WAY, Charlie shouted.

Charlie, don't get worked up.

Shouting was the least of what she wanted to do—that full-body, molten Quiet Room anger surged as she watched them discuss her in the third person.

She'd need a couple days for recovery. Three to six weeks until reactivation. We could schedule for spring break.

The thing in her head was trash, and it was *their* fault. They knew, and nobody said anything. All the headaches, the struggles in school, they'd been somebody else's failings. Someone who was too chicken-shit to even admit it.

The doctor shifted seamlessly into sales mode, and they endured a short presentation on the advances that had been made since she'd been implanted over a decade ago: more channels on the array, Bluetooth connectivity, and rechargeable batteries for the external processor. There was even a chance that with smaller components and more precise surgical methods a new implant wouldn't destroy her residual hearing. He handed her mother a pamphlet on the latest Edge Bionics models, and then another from a rival company when her mother questioned the safety of the first.

Out at the reception desk, her mother got the contact information for a surgical consult while Charlie said goodbye to the interpreter, who seemed to have forgotten any mention of his son. Had the appointment changed his mind about what he wanted for his daughter? Charlie and her mother left the hospital and headed straight for the Starbucks.

I can't believe no one told us any of this. I should sue that damn company. Grande skinny vanilla latte, please. Charlie, what do you want?

Hot chocolate.

Whipped cream? said the barista, pointing to a photo.

Charlie nodded. Her mother looked relieved by the ease of the interaction.

I'm not doing it, Charlie said once they'd claimed a table.

Charlie, don't start.

I don't want another surgery.

Well you're not leaving a chunk of rusting metal in your head.

Fair enough, but she wasn't about to give her mother the satisfaction of agreeing. She took a long draw from her drink.

Then I'm not getting a new implant, she said. Especially on the other side.

I don't think you understand what being a minor means.

You're lucky I understand anything! Charlie said, too loud.

She slammed her cup on the table, felt the insides slosh. Other patrons were looking at them; her mother turned pink, and Charlie sat back in her chair, took a breath.

Sorry, she said. But it's my head, not an oil field. You can't just drill around in there until you hit eureka.

Her mother's facial cues for horrified were subtle from decades of practiced repression, but the fact that she didn't admonish Charlie for being melodramatic was evidence that she, too, had been shaken.

We'll talk about it later, she said. With your father.

They drank in silence, both chewing on the lips of their plastic lids when they were done, eyeing one another with alarm when they noticed their shared habit. Muddled noises rattled through Charlie with every step back to the parking garage.

nonmanual markers and facial grammar

ASL doesn't only exist on the hands—it requires a complex use of the upper body, including shoulders, head tilt, and eyebrows, nose, and mouth to provide supplemental information. These movements, called "nonmanual markers," are <u>in addition</u> to the ways that speakers of any language (signed languages included) use their facial expressions as part of a conversation. They are standardized as part of the grammar itself.

- Shoulder raise to denote size or time since an event occurred, with close to cheek being small or recent
- Position shift to denote speaker or character shift

- Eyebrow raise to denote yes/no question
- Lower for wh- (who/what/when/where/why) questions
- Eyebrow and nose scrunch to denote size

TYPES OF MOUTH MORPHEMES:

1. sounds paired with a sign, unrelated to spoken English (ex: "cha" with sign "big" meaning *giant;* "pah" with sign "success" meaning *finally*)
2. use of mouth shape and teeth to emphasize speed, size, frequency

*t*he morning of the play, Charlie woke again with double vision. Kayla had already left to shower, and not knowing what else to do, Charlie FaceTimed her father.

It really hurts, she said, and knew from the look on his face he was thinking of calling her mother. He told her to drink a glass of water and lie down, then called back after what Charlie knew must have been just a few minutes, though it had felt like much longer.

> *School says you can rest and you're good to do the play if you're in class by lunch. Your mom's calling the doctor.*

I don't want another implant, she said. *Can they just remove the dead one and leave me alone?*

Her father rubbed his temple like she had transferred her headache to him. His sign language was maxing out.

> *We got lucky this summer. That j-u-d-g-e, Deaf school,* he said after a while. *I'm not sure we'd win a C-I fight.*

I'm just gonna get it taken out when I'm eighteen, she said. It's a waste of money.

Maybe the new one will be better.

Not you, too.

Try to sleep. I'll call you back at 11:30.

Charlie staggered to the bathroom and wet a washcloth, then returned to bed and laid it across her forehead. She wished for her father's frozen spinach.

She woke later to the flash of his phone call.

How you feeling?

Charlie sat up. Her vision was still blurry but not doubled, and she did feel a little better.

O-k, she said.

Good enough to go to class?

She nodded. They hung up, and she returned to the bathroom to wet her hair in the sink and pull it up into a ponytail. Then she put on her all-black stagehand ensemble and ventured out onto the quad, blinking hard against the sun.

She managed to navigate the afternoon unscathed; teachers seemed to notice she wasn't feeling well and didn't bother her much. At the final dress rehearsal, they ran lighting cues and curtain call and polished off a dozen pizzas, and too soon, it was time for costumes, places. Fickman strobed hard on the light switch, which, for Charlie, sent the room swirling, a top in its final wobbly spins.

In the dressing room, the girls-as-Lost-Boys streaked brown eye shadow as faux dirt on each other's faces, while across the table, Gabriella was wrangling herself into a push-up bra to achieve maximum nightgown cleavage. Not a chance, girl, Charlie thought, and went backstage to look for Austin.

She found him beside the ghost light, fussing with the feather in his hat.

You look hot in tights.

> *Shut up,* he said, a little too
>
> harshly.

But he pulled her by her belt loop close against him.

> *Where you been?*

> *Sick,* she said, and gestured to
>
> her head.

Fickman rounded the corner, now wearing her headlamp and waving frantically.

> *Ready? Ready!*

> *You gonna be o-k?*

> *Go!* said Charlie.

She gestured to the video monitor they'd rigged, where she could see they'd already dimmed the houselights. Austin kissed her cheek and ran behind the cyc to stage left. Charlie waited until the Darling children were frozen onstage, then opened the curtain.

The show was running smoothly, but somewhere toward the back end of the first act the pain in Charlie's head returned full force. During intermission, she poked her head out and spotted her parents, plus Wyatt and her grandmother, in the fourth row, looking bewildered. Charlie was rocked with surprise, not only that her mom had shown up, but that she'd invited her own mother. Could it be that she was actually proud? The thought softened Charlie, and she pulled her implant from her pocket, reattached it for appeasement purposes, and hopped down from the stage to say hello.

Thanks for coming, she said.

Nice hat, her father said, motioning to the headlamp.

Here's our little heartthrob of the theater, said Charlie's grand-mother. I hear it's Peter Pan himself you've ensnared?

Are you kidding me? she said, shooting a look at her parents. Her father stuffed his hands in his pockets.

Your father and I are just looking out for you, said her mother.

Right, Charlie said. Can we do this literally any other time?

But her mother could not be stopped midperformance.

Emotions run high at your age, she said. God knows I always felt like the world was ending. Makes it hard to think.

We're just friends, Charlie said, directing the comment at her grandmother because that was easier than looking at her parents.

Oh what the hell, go have some fun, her grandmother said. Charlie's mother looked at her own mother in horror, then put her hand on Charlie's shoulder.

Well, that'd be for the best, staying friends, she said. Charlie knew she should bite her tongue and let that be the end of it. And she tried, she really did. But it came out anyway.

And why is that? she said. Is it beyond you to consider I'm not totally unlovable?

Don't be a drama queen—I was thinking of *him*.

How kind.

You think you belong in this bubble? It won't last forever, you know.

That's what this is about? I'm dating a Deaf guy?

Oh, now you're dating him?

What's it to you?—Charlie snapped the headlamp band against her head, for emphasis—You only care about stuffing my head with enough metal to pretend with your shitty friends I'm normal! Her mother was saying some other things now, but Charlie didn't know what they were, because she left them all standing there and slipped back behind the curtain.

By the time they got to "I Won't Grow Up," Charlie could feel her whole body shaking—not a rhythm but an open run of voltage from her head and down her neck. She yanked the processor from her head, but it didn't seem to matter. Her mouth felt cottony thick, her jaw tight. Charlie imagined herself going pale, or green, or maybe very red, but whichever it was, the cast members were eyeing her funny as they ran on- and offstage. Her body was a hummingbird's thrum.

And then Tinker Bell came through the wing, her glow stick tutu bouncing past. The neon pinks and yellows and greens blurred together, a plait of light trailing behind her as she returned to the stage. Charlie grasped at the braid, tried to follow it hand over hand— surely the life buoy at the other end of that phosphorescent rope contained the antidote for her pain. But the light was slick; it slid and refracted in her grip until she could no longer see it at all, everything was too bright. She inspected her hands and looked up, realizing she was onstage beneath a spotlight. The pirates scattered and Gabriella-Wendy's face scrunched into a knot of horror at her approach, but Austin stayed fixed to his mark. She held out her empty hands to him, and he looked from her palms to her face utterly derailed, but smiling.

It was getting harder to see now, but out in the house a figure that must've been Fickman was storming down the center aisle. Charlie, though, was fixated on row four, or at least where she remembered it to be. Even her mother would know there was something wrong— everyone's eyes on this lost child—and there was power in her chest right before she hit the floor.

IN CASE OF EMERGENCY

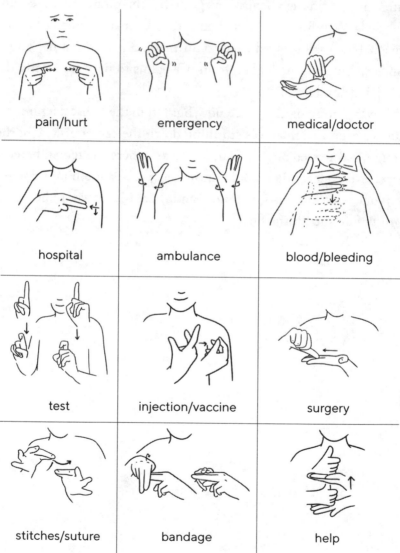

pain/hurt	emergency	medical/doctor
hospital	ambulance	blood/bleeding
test	injection/vaccine	surgery
stitches/suture	bandage	help

*l*ook, I'm not a monster. I only tried to do what was best for her. To give her every opportunity. To balance an injustice. To fix my mistakes.

When she was born, I studied her tiny hands, her fingers curled in so tight and thought, Perfect, she's so perfect, how could someone like me have made something so lovely? I was exhausted and yet full of love and wonder and fear. That first night I was afraid to put her down, held her against my chest until dawn. And I knew right away I would do anything to protect her.

When she still wasn't talking at two, I panicked. We began the circuit—early interventionists, autism screenings. Finally audiology, otolaryngology, speech pathology. The results were clear: I had failed her. Victor had failed her. Especially him.

The doctors spoke of miraculous new technology, proselytized really, and their enthusiasm was contagious. It was all very expensive—the surgery, the device, the therapy that was to come, but what price tag can you put on hope? Charlie had already lost so much time. I knew we had to make it up to her. I liquidated my grandfather's inheritance. Victor picked up some extra gigs. We would make it work. We would open doors for her.

It was the doctors who told me not to sign, not to let her sign, did you know that? It would confuse her, they said, cause further delays. Your people—medical experts. I trusted you.

When I was very young, my mother entered me in beauty pageants. I hated them—the early morning wake-ups and long drives, afternoons in strange hotel ballrooms, the hot and terrible assaults on my hair—but I was too young to know this wasn't how all girls spent their weekends. They were good for me, my mother said. I was developing confidence. Maybe I'd even get a scholarship somewhere.

I never won, but once I came in second. I was pleased with myself. Finally, I was one of the last girls left standing on the stage. I was given a bouquet and crowned with a tiara just like the one Miss Tennessee wore in the autographed picture that hung above my bed. But when I met my mother by the stage door afterward, I could see right away she wasn't happy.

So close, she said as we walked to the car. And nothing else. So please, don't judge me. There is no one more disappointing to me than myself.

Ma'am, I really need you to step away from the desk, said the nurse as she waved the next person forward. They're moving her down from ICU now, and you'll be allowed to see her in just a moment.

february had been at it long enough to know that she could not blame herself for her students' every hurt—pain wrought by their families, by one another. And yet. Whenever a student was in crisis, she found it impossible to disengage, and the night of the play was no exception. She had even jumped in her car and sped behind the ambulance, though she realized as soon as she got to the hospital there was nothing she could do beyond crowd the waiting room.

She'd lost only one student in residence during her time as headmistress, Benjamin, a third grader, more than a decade ago. He'd had a seizure in his sleep—massive cerebral hemorrhage, nothing anyone could have done, but it had been her second year in charge and his death had marked her, a line dividing the Before and After. February, like everyone, had a few major delineations in her life, bad and good—the loss of each of her parents, but also the day she'd come out to them, the night she met Mel. She imagined these moments as force fields, once one was raised it was difficult to return to the place that sat behind it, obliging a person to remain changed and hurtling ever forward. Though it had been After Ben for a long time, time didn't lessen his power.

So February offered to bring Charlie's parents something from the cafeteria and then returned home to pace the upstairs hall, thinking Not your hall much longer with every turn. Mel had tried to get her to sleep, or at least sit down, coaxing her into the living room for a few minutes with a cup of tea, but it didn't last long. After tossing and turning for a while, she caught up on emails, then dishes. More pacing. At 5:30 A.M. she got in the shower.

It was still dark when she left the house, but the first sunlight was peeking out behind Clerc by the time she got to campus. She startled a groggy Walt in the guard's box at the gate, and he jumped up and saluted her, at which she couldn't help but laugh. She looked at the upper dorms, pictured the students dreaming in their beds. That was the thing she loved most about River Valley—even without seeing another soul on the quad, she knew she wasn't alone. The feeling sustained her, at least enough to get her into her office with a cup of coffee and her laptop, blank Word document open and a cursor blinking like a tapping foot, waiting for her to find the words she knew she had to say at the faculty summit in just three days.

*C*harlie woke twice that night: once on the gurney on the way to the OR, snapping her eyes shut when the ceiling lights drilled right through her, then again in a calmer room, dim, her father asleep in a chair beside her, bent forward with his head on her leg. Was her mother here? She wanted to ask, or at least tell her father that she was awake, but nothing would move, not her tongue, not her fingers. Two languages, both useless, she thought before she sank back into the dark.

She came round again in the morning. By then her father, mother, and grandmother had all set up camp around her bed. Her mother noticed first, sprang from her chair and said a run of things Charlie couldn't follow, kissed her forehead. Her father was next, tried using some signs with whatever he was saying, though Charlie was so overwhelmed it didn't help. Her grandmother settled for a pat on the hand and said nothing at all.

Her mother raised the bed and adjusted Charlie's pillows, held a Styrofoam cup before her so she could sip through a bendy straw. The water razed her throat and stung her empty stomach.

The three of them were staring at Charlie with such anticipation, she found herself thinking—what, do you want me to do a trick? But she could not wrangle her snark with the speed she was used to, and after some frustration, settled instead for,

What happened?

Well, said her mother.

But Charlie's eyes felt jumpy, and she couldn't convert her mother's lips into meaning. Perhaps the implant had helped more than she'd given it credit for. She looked to her father, hoping he might be able to sign, but he was out of his depth with anything medical. So she gestured at a pen; her mother took a stack of napkins from her purse and began to write.

I'll go look for the interpreter,
said her father.

Charlie watched him out the door. She wished he wouldn't go. Her mother handed her the napkin.

Remember the implant moisture problem?

Charlie nodded. Next napkin:

There was a bit of a short circuit.

I got electrocuted?

Her mother's eyes widened.

My implant electrocuted me. In the head.

Her mother was still frozen. Charlie looked to her grandmother.

In so many words, said her grandmother.

But they took it out? Am I gonna be okay?

Another napkin: Yes, wrote her mother. It's out.

Her father returned, but much to Charlie's horror, instead of an interpreter it was Austin behind him. She reached up to smooth her hair, but her hand met a clot of packed gauze and she yelped. Her mother, grandmother, and father all jumped, and Austin sucked in his cheek when he saw the wound, but she forced a smile and he returned it.

I was really worried about you,
he said.

What are you doing here?
I was really worried about you.
Have you been here this whole
time?

A nurse in lavender scrubs appeared, leaning in too close and speaking with exaggerated lip movements at Charlie; she and Austin both cringed.

WELL LOOK WHO'S AWAKE, she said

Not long today. I came by yesterday.

Yesterday?

The nurse slid her stethoscope beneath Charlie's shirt and the chill of the metal on her chest made her gasp. She closed her eyes—she couldn't look at Austin with this woman's hands up her shirt. Then the nurse stood and gave Charlie a thumbs-up, and began to futz with the bag of fluids on the pole above her, making notations on a whiteboard.

You've been out for two days.

Well shit.

HUNGRY? the nurse said, miming a spoon dramatically.

A little, she said, trying not to laugh at the woman's clownish expression.

How do you feel?

O-k now. I think there's some
drugs in here.

She tapped the IV tether running down into her hand.

Fun.

I'LL BRING A MENU, said the nurse.

Does everyone at school hate me?

Hate you? No! Why?

I ruined the play.

That was the most interesting
ending to Peter Pan *ever.*

Charlie smiled.

Was Gabriella mad?

Oh, she was furious. That was a
bonus.

Austin tapped out a quick message on his phone, shoved it back in his pocket. Charlie laughed, then winced. Austin's phone flashed and he looked at it with disappointment.

My mom's out front. I gotta go.

Go, she said, shooing him
toward the door.

*Text me when you charge your
phone?*

She looked around, wondering where all her stuff was, and spotted a plastic bag with the hospital's logo hanging on the far wall, one leg of her black jeans protruding out the top.

I will.

Then Austin leaned down and kissed her on the lips, right there in front of everyone, waved to her family, and left. Her mother began to tidy the room in an aggressive manner designed to attract attention. Finally, Charlie returned her gaze.

What was that? her mother said.

What?

Her mother tilted her head toward the door.

Mom, you've met him.

Yes, but—

But what? Me dating a Deaf guy makes it harder for you to live in your fantasy world?

Her mother reddened, and Charlie held up a hand to halt any response she was preparing.

No. No more of this until I get to talk to the doctor about exactly how fried my brain is.

Did we find an interpreter? she
asked her father, who had re-
entered the room.

Her mother dropped back into her chair as if she'd been shoved.

I think your brain's fine, said her
father.

No thanks to you, Charlie thought, though she realized he was probably right: things were clearer to her now than they ever had been. The old battles were still raging and her father couldn't protect her. No one could.

*f*ebruary was in the shower when her cover was blown. She'd been standing under the pulsing water tweaking the speech she would give at the summit when Mel stuck her head into the steaming bathroom, delivering the news almost sweetly:

A Realtor is here to take photos to list our house. He says the school district sent him. Care to comment?

February wrenched the water off and stepped out of the shower, wide-eyed. Unsurprisingly, Mel's saccharine tone was not mirrored in her facial expression.

I—

February strained to reach her towel from its hook on the back of the door. She still had soap on her arm and swiped it away.

What the fuck is going on?

February hung her head.

Mel, I'm so sorry.

Fuck sorry. What is happening?

River Valley's closing. I didn't know how to tell you.

You didn't know *how*?

I tried! I just couldn't deal.

How you "deal" is by talking to your wife about a life-altering event.

I know, you're right.

Or at least have the common courtesy to let me know I'm being evicted from my own damn house!

You're right.

How long have you known? Mel said.

February shuddered.

Since the district meeting, she said, though it had been even longer.

Jesus Christ. December?

I'm so sorry, babe. Really.

Who else knows?

No one. Phil. And Henry. He was the terp at the meeting.

Your teachers?

February shook her head.

Swall and I have to tell them at the faculty meeting tomorrow.

Wanda?

Though she was looking down at her feet, she could feel the weight of Mel's eyes.

I—

Oh for fuck's sake, said Mel.

She slammed the bathroom door on her way out. February hurried to pull on her robe and go after her, but when she got down the stairs, there was only a bewildered-looking man in a sport coat, holding a tape measure and a digital camera.

Ma'am? If this is a bad time I can come back later.

No, please, said February with ire in her voice and a sweeping grand gesture toward the living room. Now's just perfect.

After the Realtor left, February wrote a long, convoluted text to Mel, saying she was sorry, and that she was going to stay in Old Quarters so they had space until Mel was ready to talk, and sorry one more time. It was hard to say whether Mel would see this as a courtesy or just another selfish move on February's part, but she didn't know what else to do. She had to deal with her teachers on Monday, and couldn't be fighting this war on two fronts. She packed a suitcase and wheeled it down the street toward campus.

deaf president now

Most of you have probably seen the phrase, but what do you know about the "Deaf President Now" movement? Despite being the first Deaf university in the world, Gallaudet had never had a Deaf president before, and in March 1988 that was finally about to change. The Board of Trustees was slated to choose the next president from a list of three finalist candidates, two Deaf, one hearing.

In the lead-up to the board meeting, students and faculty had been campaigning and rallying in support of a Deaf president.

THE CANDIDATES

DR. ELIZABETH ZINSER, hearing, Vice-Chancellor of Academic Affairs at University of North Carolina

DR. HARVEY CORSON, Deaf, Superintendent of the Louisiana School for the Deaf

DR. I. KING JORDAN, Deaf, Dean of College of Arts and Sciences at Gallaudet

On March 6th, the board selected Zinser. No announcement was made. Students found out only after visiting the school's PR office to extract the information.

Students marched to the Mayflower hotel to confront the Board. Chair Jane Spilman defended the selection to the crowd, reportedly saying, "deaf people can't function in the hearing world."

WHAT HAPPENED NEXT?

MARCH 7TH: Students hot-wire buses to barricade campus gates, only allowing certain people on campus. Students meet with Board, no concessions made. Protesters march to the Capitol.

MARCH 8TH: Students burn effigies, form a 16-member council of students, faculty, and staff to organize the movement.

THE FOUR DEMANDS:

1. Zinser's resignation and the selection of a Deaf president
2. Resignation of Jane Spilman
3. A 51% Deaf majority on the Board of Trustees
4. No reprisals against protesters

WHAT HAPPENED NEXT?

MARCH 9TH: Movement grows, gains widespread national support. Protest is featured on ABC's *Nightline.*

MARCH 10TH: Jordan, who'd previously conceded to Zinser's appointment, joins the protests, saying "the four demands are justified." Protests receive endorsements from national unions and politicians.

DEAF PRESIDENT NOW!

MARCH 10TH: Zinser resigns.

MARCH 11TH: 2,500 march on Capitol Hill, bearing a banner that says "We still have a dream."

MARCH 13: Spilman resigns, Jordan is announced president. Protesters receive no punishments, DPN is hailed as a success and one of the precursors to the passing of the Americans with Disabilities Act (ADA).

*C*harlie spent a few days at home recuperating after she was re-leased from the hospital, her teachers emailing her well wishes and assignments so she wouldn't fall behind. Headmistress even set up a special video chat to walk her through the latest lesson, about the protests at Gallaudet. Charlie marveled at the students' ability to organize so quickly and managed to pull out of Headmistress Waters a lengthy explanation of a thing called "hot-wiring." She bet this was something Slash knew how to do, but it hadn't occurred to her that there could be Deaf Slashes.

She missed being on campus, but mostly she was glad about the arrangement; she had a bald chunk of head complete with Franken-stein stitches that she wasn't in a hurry to show off. And she was so tired all the time. Simple things like helping load the dishwasher or finishing a math worksheet had her crawling back to the couch, blanket pulled up to her chin. It could take days for the effects of the anesthesia to wear off, the doctor had cautioned her. Then there was the body's own healing to attend to.

After a week, though, she felt more herself, even had the presence of mind to try for civility with her mother on the drive to Colson Children's. The doctor checked her wound, said it was healing nicely, made an asinine joke about how it was very chic to shave a piece of one's head these days. It seemed as if they might all escape the outing

unscathed. But as the doctor was wrapping up his additional guidance on aftercare—prescribing more ointment to use until the
stitches were removed—Charlie noticed her mother turning vaguely
purple in her periphery, as if she was holding her breath.

Mom? You o-k? Charlie said,
interrupting the doctor.

Just had a question, said
interpreter-as-mom.

The doctor nodded for her to go ahead, but Charlie's stomach pitted;
she knew what it was already. She closed her eyes for a few seconds,
hoping that either she was wrong or the interpreter might press on
without her having to look, but when she returned to the conversation the doctor was saying,

*—too much tissue damage to re-
implant. But we can certainly
explore candidacy on the right
side.*

Are you fucking kidding me?
Charlie said, and left.

She arrived on Slash's doorstep without quite knowing how she
found it—she had never sought it out in daylight (not to mention
sober), but the house had somehow burrowed a place in her memory
and she slid her hand beneath the plywood and knocked on the door.

Someone opened it a sliver so that only a single, shifty eye was
visible, but soon the person was fiddling with the chain, and Lem, as
it turned out to be, pulled open the door and sighed.

Jailbait, hey. You scared the shit outta me.
She pulled Charlie inside by the elbow, locked the door. Behind her
the house smelled faintly of burnt plastic. Charlie could feel Lem's
eyes run over the bald part of her head, revving up for some com-
mentary, then catch on the stitches and leave it alone.

Everyone's downstairs, she said.

Charlie followed her to the cellar door, where Lem yelled down into a fluorescent haze. Charlie watched for any sign that Slash had responded, but Lem was stolid.

You can go down if you want, she said.

Lem returned to the living room, peered out through a small hole drilled in one of the window boards, then dropped down on the couch, eyes still trained on the door. Charlie felt uneasy. She could tell something weird was going on. She knew, too, that even her mother would have managed to find her way back to the car by now, and would panic in the hyperbolic manner of Proper Southern Ladies upon not finding Charlie there. In the end, though, her curiosity got the better of her and she descended the stairs.

The cellar was dim with low ceilings, and smelled of mold and cat litter. Charlie could feel the thrum of loud music running through the concrete floor. In the back corner, she saw movement and started toward it, but Slash materialized from the shadows and intercepted her.

C, hey! What are you doing here?

Charlie watched him try to shove a tattered book into his back pocket, but it was too big and eventually he gave up.

What's that? she said.

He looked down at it with an almost hangdog expression but handed it to her.

Recipes? Charlie repeated as she read the cover.

Of sorts.

More fireworks?

Something like that. Vintage copy, though. The new editions are useless. All "community organizing" or some shit.

Charlie could see the light returning to his eyes.

I mean, this shit's all over the internet. The trick is being able to look it up without getting tracked. We used to have an in for burner library cards, but our guy is . . . well, anyway . . .

Slash trailed off and Charlie peered over his shoulder to the far side of the basement, where Greg and Sid were bent over something she couldn't see. Beside them, flattened pressure cooker boxes were neatly piled and tied together with twine. Greg wore a pair of glasses with big, built-in magnifiers, like Charlie's orthodontist used. Sid was tinkering with a run of wire inside the base of what, Charlie realized now, was one of the pots.

I better go, she said. My mom's in town. I just wanted to say hi.

Yeah, said Slash. We're kind of in the thick of it. Hey, what happened to your head?

I got electrocuted.

Slash cracked a grin, but stopped short, leaving his chapped lip caught crooked on his bicuspid.

Jesus, he said.

You're serious.

Charlie nodded.

I'm fine now.

Electrocuted how? By what?

Big Pharma, Charlie said.

Fuck, are you okay?

The question felt more leaden that she'd expected it to. She thought for a moment.

I don't know yet, she said.

Slash told her to come back if she needed anything and hugged her goodbye. Upstairs she nodded to Lem and let herself out.

She returned to Colson Children's to find her mom outside the garage throwing a fit into her phone. Charlie waved once she got close enough and watched her mother's face shift from worry to anger. She jabbed at the end call button with her ridiculous acrylic nail and crossed the street without even looking for traffic.

Charlie, what in the ever-loving hell! Where were you! You think you can just take off in the middle of the city!

Charlie understood that these weren't really questions, though she briefly reveled in imagining her mother's reaction if Charlie were to tell the truth, that she was in the basement with a bunch of drug-addled anarchists and their bomb cookbook.

What is wrong with you?

YOU'RE what's wrong with me! Charlie shouted. You're trying to kill me with these fucking—she pointed to her scar—things!

I was just asking about our options.

No more options. Not for you.

Have some respect, Charlie, Jesus.

No more surgery. I will—

Charlie paused. She had learned a word, exactly the right one, recently in Headmistress's class—but she had no idea how to say it aloud. She took out her phone and typed:

i will filibuster you until im 18.

She held the screen up to her, and her mother paused, taken aback, though by what—her defiance? the typing workaround? the fact that Charlie knew a four-syllable word?—it was hard to say.

Get in the car, her mother said.

So Charlie had gotten in the car, but her mind stayed in the city, turning over what she'd seen. It scared her a little, sure, but it hadn't repelled her like the night at Holden's, or even on New Year's. Maybe she was just getting used to it, or maybe she was finally mad enough to see its use.

Her mother dropped her back at her father's, but Charlie was no less angry with him. He wouldn't stop her mother when it came down to it—he was either still harboring some romantic allegiance, or totally spineless, or secretly agreed with her, but whatever it was, it all added up to another hole in Charlie's head.

I wanna go back to school, she said.

O-k, he said. *I'll drive you in the*
morning.

No, tonight.

Charlie, let's not fight about this. Go do your homework and get your stuff packed up, and we'll go first thing tomorrow.

Fine, she said.

Do you want dinner?

I ate, she lied.

All right, well, I'm gonna—he gestured over his shoulder to his office—I have some stuff to wrap up.

Whatever.

Love you.

She went upstairs and shoved what she could in her backpack, pulled on a hat, then stole back down and out the door, hoping the click shut wasn't loud enough to rouse her father from his blue screen trance.

*t*uesday evening, February returned to Old Quarters, exhausted. It had been twenty-four hours since the summit where she and Swall delivered the news that River Valley would be shuttered. In return, she had received mostly icy stares it was hard not to read as resentment. She knew sadness and shock were the more likely realities—her teachers were bright, generous people, savvy about the ways in which the system so relentlessly failed them. They wouldn't scapegoat her, even as she blamed herself.

Now it was only a matter of time before the news spread to the students. She scheduled a schoolwide assembly for Friday, but she wasn't sure they'd make it that long. It would be difficult to keep the kids from seeing a conversation in the hall not meant for them. She had drawn up a list of action items for what might come after: walk-in hours for Phil, her, and the guidance counselor, literature to send to the families about working with home districts in the fall. It all looked laughably inadequate on a single sheet of paper like that, and of course it was.

It had been three days since she'd spoken to Mel. She was a little frightened by the number. Usually when they were fighting, Mel couldn't help but message February after a few hours, even if it was just to issue a fresh batch of insults to pierce the silence. Then again, this wasn't your average spat. And February was so squarely in the wrong; part of her knew she would have to be the first to make a move. She just had no idea how to explain her own deceit.

It had been five hours since she'd last seen Charlie Serrano, a number she was not keeping track of in the moment but would return to calculate later. She had video-chatted with her and gone over the latest slides from her course, a series on the Deaf President Now! protests. Charlie had looked significantly less ill, had spoken of her desire to return to campus soon, and was completely enraptured by the story of the student takeover of their university. This had warmed February—it was an iconic event, a centerpiece in Deaf mythology, and a master class in direct action. When Charlie had asked a string of questions—*What does "hot-wiring" mean? How did the students know how to hot-wire? What's a r-e-p-r-i-s-a-l?*—February had even allowed herself a few moments of pride—the girl had come such a long way. The thought of Charlie having to return to Jeff in a few months depressed her.

The front-facing wall of Old Quarters had been left exposed, without plaster, and February turned to it now to feel the familiar freestone, cold and furrowed. She let her finger fall into a gulley of mortar between the stones, followed its path. The grit accumulated beneath her nail and she felt bad, and then foolish—as if deteriorating grout was the source of River Valley's peril. She wondered what would become of these buildings, vessels that had carried her people through so much. She imagined the city demolishing them and building a strip mall, or turning the dorms into lofts, and couldn't decide which was worse. She hoped they might be allowed to decay in peace, at least for a while, for the roofs to cave in and the walls to be overrun by thick, woody vines—for the artifacts and stories to be swallowed back into the earth the way it was for all lost civilizations. She patted the wall tenderly, as if to thank it for a job well done, and watched the sun set over the quad.

role shift: become one with your story

Role shift is a grammatical component of ASL in which a signer uses body, head tilt, and eye gaze, along with other affective traits, to assume the role of another person or object in a narrative. For example:

Shoulder shift: in basic role shift, a signer shifts their shoulders and body to the left to establish one character or speaker, then to the right to establish another.

Head tilt and eye gaze: these can be used to illustrate physical height or authority. For example, tilting the head up as if to look at someone taller, and back down to address someone smaller, could indicate a conversation between a teacher and a student.

A skilled storyteller can use role shift, along with facial expression, signing speed, size, space, dialectic word choice, and other mannerisms to fully transform into an array of characters.

♀ **DID YOU KNOW?** Role shift isn't just for people. Deaf storytellers frequently embody nontraditional perspectives like animals, plants, buildings, and all kinds of inanimate objects to tell a three-dimensional story.

*a*ustin was staring at the blinking cursor in his still-blank lab report, thinking that perhaps if he flunked all his classes he could drop out and be spared a transfer to Jeff, when he noticed a sharp beam of light outside his window.

Do you see that?

Eliot, who was closer to the window, looked up.

Yeah, it's your girlfriend, he said nonchalantly.

Austin jumped from the bed and went to open the window, where he was pleasantly surprised to find Charlie standing in the hedge, shining her phone's flashlight in his face.

What are you doing? he said, squinting into the light.

Sorry, she said, lowering the phone. *You busy?*

She leaned in and kissed him. He offered his arms to steady her as she climbed into the room.

When did you get back?

Right now.

Are you, like . . . o–k to be back?

You're not happy to see me?

Of course I am.

He closed the window and shade, led her to his bed. They kissed again, and she let him run his hand the length of her thigh before stopping him. Across the room, Eliot had returned to his laptop glaze. Austin waved a hand to catch his attention.

Mind if we have a minute?

Sure, Eliot said.

He scooped up his computer and ambled out into the common room, and Austin and Charlie picked up where they'd left off, Austin sliding his hand beneath her shirt, slowly, as if counting vertebrae, until he reached her bra.

O-k?

She nodded. He unhooked the clasp and Charlie climbed on top of him and pulled off her shirt.

Afterward, they lay atop the comforter for a precious few minutes, Charlie in the crook of his arm. It was an irresponsible thing to do with bed checks looming, but that made it all the more pleasurable. He would never tell anyone, but this was actually the thing he liked most about sex, the bright high afterward that bleached the outside world from sight. It was difficult to sign lying this way, but that was another part of it—their bodies still so close together, they didn't need to.

It was too short a moment for his liking. Their sweat cooled, Charlie shivered. He could feel her fingerspelling something into his chest:

S-o-r-r-y.

He shifted a little so they could see one another.

What's wrong?

I think I need to leave.

She pulled her bra and T-shirt back on.

Did I do something?

No, like, leave Colson.

What are you talking about?

>*My parents, they want to im-*
>*plant me again.*

What? After . . .

Austin gestured to her stitches and she nodded.

>*That's what I'm saying. They*
>*won't stop and there's nothing I*
>*can do to stop them.*

A sliver of Eliot appeared in the doorway. He looked relieved that he had not interrupted.

>*Hey. Sam says they're doing*
>*checks on east side.*

Shit, thanks.

Eliot nodded and sat back down on his bed. They finished dressing and Austin opened the door to his wardrobe and swiped his clothes to one side. Charlie just looked at him.

You have a better idea?

She climbed in and he repositioned his row of hanging shirts neatly in front of her, then closed the door. They never checked closets but his heart was still pounding, so hard that he was afraid the dorm-keeper might see it through his shirt. He held his history book up against his chest as armor.

>*Smooth,* said Eliot when they'd
>gone.

What?

Eliot laughed.

>*Nothing. You just looked squir-*
>*relly is all.*

Whatever, they left, didn't they?

Austin opened the closet. Charlie climbed out and returned to his bed.

You o-k?

>*Fine. I mean, besides not know-*
>*ing what to do with my life.*

Austin wanted to tell her not to leave, that he would find a way to protect her, but he knew it wasn't true. Worse than that, in a few months, none of them would be safe.

Where would you go?

I don't know, maybe stay with Slash and them until I figure things out.

I'll go with you.

What? No way. I'm gonna have to drop out.

S-o?

S-o? You can't leave.

He dug at the carpet with his toe.

I have to tell you something.

It was difficult to get his hands to move now, but he was propelled by the expression on Charlie's face. She looked terrified, almost like she worried he was about to turn her in.

What is it?

River Valley is closing.

What? said Eliot, jumping up from his bed.

Austin had forgotten Eliot was there, but it didn't matter anymore.

What? When?

End of the school year. My dad was interpreting a district meeting and they announced it. It's why they want to implant Sky.

And you've known this since—

Since break.

Jesus.

Fuck.

Charlie ran a hand through her hair, her usual nervous habit, but it caught on her wound and she recoiled.

What are we gonna do?

What can we do? They don't lis-
ten. No one listens.

We could make them listen.

Here Charlie paused. It was almost dramatic, the way she froze mid-sign, her hand beside her eye the way he'd taught her, not by her ear like hearing people signed it. In retrospect, he realized this had been *the* moment for her, that for years people in power had overrun her body, and this was the shutdown, the hard reset. At the time, though, he worried something bad was happening, a complication from the surgery, a seizure maybe. He ran to her and took her hand in an attempt to guide her back to the bed.

You o-k?

I'm fine, she said.

And then he saw the smile, a grin so wide he could see a fleck of silver filling in a back tooth. So much strength behind it, it crinkled her nose.

You're beautiful, he couldn't
help saying.

I have an idea. Let's go into Col-
son.

O-k . . . right now?

She nodded.

We're gonna stage a protest. Deaf
President Now–style.

But it's dark out. No one will
even see us.

That's the point.

I don't get it. DPN was a huge
march. It only worked because it
was all over the news.

She shook her head.

It wasn't the marching, she said.
It was the takeover.

Austin's cheeks were tingling, which sometimes happened when he was very nervous. Still, he already knew whatever it was, he was in.

Besides, if we do it right, we will make the news.

Should I check the bus schedule?

Forget it. I have a car.

Charlie and Austin both looked at Eliot, startled.

All right if I join?

If you want, but—

Eliot wrenched his own phone from his pocket, held out his hand for theirs.

I'm leaving them in the common room.

Charlie and Austin each switched their phones off, handed them to Eliot.

Wait, said Charlie, grabbing Eliot's arm. *Why are you helping us?*

I'll tell you on the way, he said.

*t*hese are the things that had happened to Eliot Quinn:

The summer before his junior year, on the side of I-64 east, Eliot first met death. Colson was in full scorch, and he and his parents had taken a day trip down to the national forest to escape the heat. It had been idyllic—he'd been in a good mood, free-floating between school years, far enough from either end to distance himself from the teen angst that sometimes overtook him, the fretting over SAT scores and football practice, and that most neuroses-addled subject of all: girls. He didn't even have a thing for one girl in particular, but that was worse somehow—he couldn't stop thinking about them, all of them, eleventh-grade girls on a conveyor belt in his head on repeat, making him crazy. But that day, all three of them had been happy. They'd picked up a giant tub of buffalo wings, drowned them in bleu cheese, and ate them on Pendleton beach. It was humid, but the breeze off the lake was mollifying, and Eliot had been content to sit and let the sun eat away at his farmer's tan. Later, he and his father had thrown the ball around at water's edge and joked about celebrity crushes—some real picturesque 1950s shit.

Even when it started to rain, their spirits were high. They returned to their car in the tepid drizzle, cooled and satisfied by the day.

By the time they made it back to the highway, the rain was a torrent. And this was the part where, in retrospect, Eliot knew it was all his fault. His father had kept the map lights on in front so Eliot could see, so they could all sign. It was slippery, there was a glare, his father should have been concentrating on the road.

Did someone cut them off? Had there been an animal, an orange construction cone? Eliot wasn't sure. He hadn't been paying attention—none of them were paying attention—probably because he was absorbed in saying something inane and his parents were busy being such good fucking parents. Whatever it had been, his father pounded the brakes but the car didn't stop. They skidded through a puddle, hydroplaned across a lane. Then they flipped.

None of that "it happened so fast" bullshit. It happened in real time. Nothing but the excruciating awareness of the moment and its inescapability. Dulled only when Eliot smacked his face against the window as they corkscrewed over the shoulder and deep into a ditch.

The adrenaline when he came to upside down, seatbelt cutting into his windpipe. He unstrapped himself and climbed up and out the opposite window, came round to his mother in the passenger seat. She was screaming, he saw when he got there, but the sight of Eliot snapped her out of it, and he peeled back the misshapen metal of what had been her door and steadied her while she pushed free.

With his mother out, Eliot stuck his head back into the car, but his father wasn't inside. His mother said something with her mouth he couldn't see, then took off running back up to the road. Eliot pulled his phone from his pocket and tried to make it dial.

Car accident car accident, he yelled into the receiver, and left the call running, like they'd learned in school.

He ran in the direction his mother had gone until he caught sight of them, huddled in streaks of headlight: his mother on the ground, stroking his father's hair. His father's face cut up, already swollen. His father, who was so sturdy he never wore his seatbelt.

Eliot knelt in the wet beside them. A thick vane of glass protruded from his father's neck, blood everywhere, blood multiplied by rain.

Dad! he said, and his father's eyelids fluttered open.
When he saw Eliot, he raised a shaky hand and tried to sign.

It's okay, Eliot said, but his father's fingers continued to spasm
with a desire to say something. You can talk to me. What is it?

Don't you see? The angels?

What? said Eliot's mother.

The angels from heaven. They're so beautiful. Lighting up that
tree.

Eliot looked over his shoulder at the tree line, but he didn't see anything bright until the ambulance showed up—by then his father was
gone—and he didn't see anything beautiful for a long time after that.

After the funeral, Eliot and his mother spent three weeks in a tun-
dral living room, lights dim and AC blasting, and his mother asked
him if he believed in heaven.

> *Like angels and stuff? Like what*
> *Dad said?*

> > > > *Yeah.*

> *I don't know. You?*

> > > > *I think maybe we should go to*
> > > > *church,* she said.

They were not churchgoing people, a minority in Ohio. Eliot had
been inside a church only a handful of times for Cub Scout meetings
when he was small. But his father hadn't been religious, not ever, and
still in the end he'd seemed so convinced. Eliot didn't know what to
make of it, but the idea of church seemed to perk his mom up a little,
so they googled places, found one with an imposing steeple and a
flashy website: NEWBIRTH EVANGELICAL. MAKE YOUR FRESH START
TODAY.

The website said COME AS YOU ARE, and inside the atrium didn't
look like a church at all. It was round and bright, with floor-to-
ceiling windows and high-top café tables and chairs scattered around
the perimeter. In the center was a Pepsi machine and a huge banner

that said, FREE COFFEE! FREE POP! FREE WI-FI! PASSWORD: JESUS1. Ahead, two sets of thick wooden doors opened into the sanctuary.

Here, things looked a bit more familiar—pews, a stage with a terrifying life-size crucifix. But soon it was clear more modern elements had infiltrated the sanctuary itself, too: diffuse concert lighting in a purple hue, a giant LED screen suspended from the ceiling, and, now assembling on the raised platform in front of the altar, a rock band with electric guitars and a drum kit, big amps on the floor and three giant speakers on stands aimed out at the congregation. Everyone was on their feet smiling and singing and clapping, and Eliot had thought, All right, they are unreasonably happy, but I can handle this.

He and his mother slid into a pew. The music stopped rippling, and everyone else sat, too. The man Eliot assumed was the priest leapt to the stage with his hands raised in victory. On the screen, a slow zoom into a close-up of priest guy's face as he began his sermon. Eliot had tried to follow along, but lipreading was a slippery business, and he was soon lost somewhere in the desert with a guy named Jacob, who had been wrestling (resting? festering?) an angel.

That's when he'd seen her, across the aisle, and a few rows ahead: wild auburn hair hanging long down her back, white T-shirt revealing freckled arms. He had never been so taken by a person's profile, and willed her to turn, just a little. Then his mother was nudging him—time to go, how long had he been staring? As the girl stepped into the aisle, he caught a glimpse of her face, fair and freckled and hazel-eyed, and even better than he'd imagined. Eliot felt a cog turn inside his chest, his grief for the moment dammed off. His brain, once racked by the idea of girls, would hereafter be consumed by only this girl—a nameless dappled mystery.

And so they had gone on that way for months, memories of his father receding in one direction, his mother headed another way, transforming into someone else entirely. She bought a Bible, and prayed, kneeling beside her bed each night. She spoke of miracles, of Halloween and rap music as portals to Satan, of the importance of modest dress for women. Most of all, she was relentlessly compliant in the face of the reverend, as if, in his presence, her personality evacuated to make room for his. Each week Eliot returned to the church out of concern for his mother, for another glimpse of the girl, all the while holding his tongue on the things he was coming to learn from the Bible: that deafness was sickness, a punishment for sins, and he was a child of indiscretion, an Eliot among the Johns and Peters and Noahs. Jesus had cured a deaf man in front of a crowd, with two wet willies and a dab of saliva on the man's tongue. The night he'd learned that, Eliot dreamt of what another man's spit might taste like.

Then one Sunday after services, Pastor Sherman cornered Eliot's mother at the far end of the chapel. Eliot had tried to get close enough to see what they were saying, but he could only see his mother nodding along saying, Absolutely, absolutely. When Eliot tore her away, it was only to find that she wanted to return to church that night for a special service—a "revival," she'd called it. They'd spent the rest of the afternoon running around doing Reverend Sherman's errands, searching for items that sounded like the components to some mythological shopping list. They retrieved an assortment of essential oils from the pharmacy; they bought things from the food store that did not sound edible: rose hips and tukmaria and frankincense. It all filled up two bags, and Eliot lugged them out to the trunk.

By the time they'd returned to the church, the second service had already started, REVIVAL! written in bright purple 3-D WordArt on the screen. He and his mother slid into what had become their customary pew, but after just a few minutes, Eliot saw the girl getting up from hers. She locked eyes with him as she passed.

He waited until she left the sanctuary to follow her. In the mouth of the atrium, there was no trace of her, but then he felt a hand—her hand—on his arm. She pulled him into a storage room.

The girl tugged at a string overhead and a naked bulb illuminated the closet. The room was crammed with metal shelves, which were in turn stuffed with big Tupperware canisters of communion wafers.

He'd almost laughed when he saw them lined up like that, imagined Reverend Sherman going to Costco to buy a case of Jesus crackers. But the girl had come close, put her finger to her lips in a gesture of secrecy.

Eliot, she'd said, I'm happy you came.

He was so nervous right before he kissed her that he actually felt nauseous, but once they started his body relaxed into it, moving like it had always known what to do. She was soft and smelled like baby powder, and he ran his fingers along her neck and down the curve of her waist, then back up her stomach beneath her shirt. The girl exhaled sharply but didn't pull away.

When he freed up the top button on her jeans, though, she quickly shoved him backward. Eliot smacked his elbow on one of the wafer shelves and bit his lip to keep from making noise. He reached for her hand to show her he was sorry, but her eyes had changed, were wide with something beyond the unbuttoning of pants.

They're calling you, she said.

Eliot raised a whatareyoutalkingabout eyebrow.

You'll do great, he could have sworn she said, though that didn't make sense, at least not yet. She pushed him from the closet through the lobby and back into the sanctuary, where everyone was on their feet, hands raised, guitar guys amped up and power-chording, three sets of the reverend's giant projected lips saying,

Come and you will be healed!

Onstage they were smashing their hands on an old man's head, and Eliot stood mid-aisle wondering for a second before it all clicked, how anyone could've possibly known he'd hurt his funny bone. The people onstage returned the old man to his feet.

Healed! said Sherman. Healed and saved! And then the Lord said, "Be strong, do not fear; your God will come to save you! Then will the eyes of the blind be opened and the ears of the deaf unstopped!"

The bile began gnawing the walls of Eliot's stomach as soon as Sherman said *that* word, and he started to move away, but quickly there were hands on his back and all around him, and it wasn't like with the girl, they were much stronger. He tried to find his mother in the crowd, but up onstage, the lights were blazing, blazing like the light his father'd seen. So bright he couldn't see anything at all

They laid him on the floor. Reverend Sherman loomed over him yelling who knows what, his knee pinning Eliot's shoulder, and when they turned his head to the side he tried to fight back, but there were so many of them now, people pressing on his arms and legs and chest. They poured something in his ear and it was scalding, slick, and razed through him. Eliot thought he saw the outline of his mother, or maybe it was the girl, but either way he'd busted one hand free and said:

Help! Make them stop! until the people got control of his arms again.

Beneath the white-hot glow of the spotlights, the oil searing its way down his ear canal and deep into his head, Eliot felt himself scream.

*a*t some point, Eliot's story is so harrowing Charlie can no longer multitask, and finds herself struck frozen in the middle of the quad. Austin takes her gently by the elbow and guides her back into the shadows, where they continue to learn the details of his betrayal. When he is finished, she wants to hug him, but he doesn't look like he wants to be hugged. He looks like he is ready to fight.

I'm so sorry, she can't help but say.

Austin runs his hands over his face, as if to clear away the visual of his roommate's melting flesh. Eliot doesn't say anything, leads them across the unlit parking lot.

They climb into Eliot's truck, Charlie pressed between the two boys in the cab, all three of them pitched a bit forward, too close and too tense to lean back in their seats. Austin turns on the map light and Eliot flinches, but nods to show that he should leave it. Charlie gives him directions to Slash's place, and tells them her plan.

Wait here, she says.

She runs up the steps, bangs on the plywood. No answer. If this is going to work, they need to avoid being seen. She returns to the curb and says through the window:

One other place. But leave the truck.

Eliot parks in the alley and she takes them to the Gas Can—no streetlamps, no signs of life along the way.

The Robespierres have just finished a set. Charlie can tell from how sweaty they are, and the way Slash shrugs and gives Greg back his dime bag. She holds a hand up to catch Slash's eye. He is about to do a shot, does a double take instead.

C! he says. Didn't know you were coming tonight.

Change of plans, she says.

Charlie takes the shot glass from his hand, downs whatever brown liquor it contains. Slash smiles.

Hey man, he says to Austin.

Austin nods.

Charlie points to Eliot: *E-l-i-o-t.*

S-l-a-s-h, he says back.

He and Eliot fist-bump.

You wanna party? says Greg. What are we celebrating?

But Charlie just ignores him, and the boys don't understand what he's said.

Look, I figured it out, she says. But we need your help.

Slash looks at her blankly.

It! she says.

What are you talking about?

The guillotine thing. The thing we'd be better off without.

When they get to the bar, Eliot wonders whether he's made a mistake. Charlie's plan is dangerous enough as is without dragging more people into it. Then again, they don't have the equipment to pull it off themselves. He tracks Charlie's sight line to a group holed up in a booth in the far corner. He can't remember the last time he's even been to this side of Colson. The place is filthy, and he wonders how sophomores came to hang out in a dive like this. He knows Charlie went to Jeff, but these guys don't look like they've seen the inside of a classroom in a while.

Charlie introduces them. One of them knows how to fingerspell, but booze has always been better than small talk as far as Eliot's concerned. With each shot, he feels more assured that they can pull this off.

They return to the house and Slash checks to make sure they don't have their phones—another good sign, it means they're careful, too—then peels back the plywood to let them in. They follow him to the basement.

Well fuck, Eliot says when they
descend the stairs.

Even though he agrees with Charlie's idea in theory, it feels different when he sees the pressure cookers splayed out on the table like that. He tries to follow a conversation between Charlie and Slash, then

Slash and his crew. He can see they are debating whether to delay their plans for whatever they were originally going to blow up in order to reallocate their equipment. He is brimming with a nervous energy that makes him want to shout, or just run away from the place, but what good has that done him so far?

You o-k? says Charlie.

If she is at all worried about standing in a room full of homespun explosives, she doesn't show it. He looks to Austin, who also seems unfazed.

> *Yeah,* Eliot says, and on his
> hands it feels true. *Just think-*
> *ing.*

We're not hurting anyone.

You can go back if you want, says
Austin. We trust you not to say
anything.

Charlie gives him a nod of encouragement, traces her gaze down his neck.

> *No,* he says after a while.

She smiles, the real one again. Austin does, too.

> *And you trust these guys?*
>> *Yes.*

Yes.

Slash breaks from the huddle with his friends and approaches.

> You didn't take the bus, did you?

Austin looks to Charlie to translate. Eliot and Charlie shake their heads.

His car.

> Where is it?

Eliot points to the back of the basement, describes the skinny alley behind their house.

> Okay, lemme think.

Lem looks up from her work and hands Eliot a roll of blue electrical tape, which he takes without knowing why.

Go fix your plate numbers, she says.

What? Eliot says.

It's the first time he's spoken aloud in a while and he's not even sure he's made a sound at first.

Your license plate. You know, like make a 3 into an 8, or a D to a B or something?

She mimes ripping and then pressing small strips of tape out in front of her.

D . . . make B? Slash tries.

Okay, Eliot says.

Greg is upstairs, Slash says, points to the ceiling. He'll let you back in when you're done.

Outside, Eliot's eyes are assaulted by the morning sun. He feels foolish doing this in broad daylight, but there is no indication that the neighborhood is any busier than it had been when they arrived. Last chance, he thinks. You can still leave. But he doesn't know if this is true.

When he returns, Greg offers him a cigarette and a warm Natty Ice, and the nicotine reminds him all is well, that it is only logical, long overdue, really, to fight fire with fire. He finishes the beer and Greg points to the corner of the room, where the rest of the case sits. Eliot carries it downstairs.

Breakfast of champions, says Lem. She pulls a beer from the box and downs the can in five great slugs.

*a*ustin, they quickly work out, has the steadiest hands of the group. He leans against the wall nursing beer after beer, but the alcohol has no effect on this skill, and Slash increasingly motions him to the table to help make the most intricate connections.

Slash waves, Austin goes to him. Slash, leaning back over an old travel alarm clock, says something he can't see.

What?

Austin looks for Charlie. Slash calls her name, then facepalms himself, and the sequence makes Austin laugh. The joke being that Charlie has long been the deafest one of them all—the electrode array of her CI razored whatever hearing she'd had left. The joke being that hearing people, in their fear, tried to create cures that only made deafness more absolute. Now that the device is gone, Charlie won't hear the sound her parents wished upon her, not voices, or music, not even the strange, ghostly echoes of extremely loud things he himself sometimes hears. It's not a bad thing, he thinks, that kind of quiet. Except for the part where she nearly died to get it. Except for her scars. He couldn't protect Charlie, but he will never let that happen to Sky. He goes to Charlie, taps her on the shoulder.

    Help, he says. *Don't want to*
    mess this up.

She smiles and follows him to the table, relays Slash's instructions.

    Austin nods. He feels proud that his hands have given him this. He holds the two wires close while Slash turns up the flame.

*a*fter she pukes onto their tire, February knocks on the door of the police camper, and tells them to amend the Amber Alert to include a third student, Charlie Serrano. Back outside, she tries to bring Mr. Serrano up to speed, but eventually he gets so frustrated with her non-answers he makes a wide arc around her and bangs on the door of the camper himself. They can't help him either, she knows, but she understands—in his shoes, she'd probably do the same.

Then, for the rest of the morning, she ping-pongs between phone calls with journalists, parents, district administrators, and the sheriff's tech people. They've cracked the kids' phones, but besides a lot of flirting between Charlie and Austin, they don't reveal much. Apart from River Valley, there are only three locations where Charlie and Austin have been at the same time. One is quickly identified as the Workmans' house, and the other two—one on State Street, and the third in East Colson—are handed off to patrol units for follow-up. Still, February leans close over the desk in the police camper and snaps a photo of the coordinate list as surreptitiously as she can, just in case.

Her teachers have an in-service day now that classes are canceled. Some are catching up on paperwork, some lending a hand in the dorms for the students on lockdown, others milling about on campus trying to help but not being of much use. It's the kind of adrift behavior that February normally finds annoying but can't really admonish today—she also doesn't know what the hell she is doing. Henry appears in her doorway.

Any news? she says.

No, but . . .

He stops himself.

What is it?

I think this is my fault, him running away. We told him we wanted to implant Sky, and he ran out of the house, and, well, we never really recovered.

Implant her? February says, feigning surprise.

It's clear Beth hasn't relayed their New Year's conversation to Henry, and February isn't about to third-wheel her way into that argument.

It's complicated, says Henry.

Of course, says February. I'd never presume . . .

She lets herself trail off. Of course she *would* presume; she's presuming all kinds of things right now, none of them helpful.

There's something else, Henry says. He knows the school is closing.

Jesus. Shit. Okay.

I'm really sorry. I didn't mean to tell him.

February isn't sure what to say. She can't very well scold Henry when she's the one who has lost his son, however large a breach of ethics he might have committed.

This is helpful, she says finally. Thanks for letting me know.

Henry nods and lingers in the doorway. She can see he doesn't want to go—maybe he just doesn't want to be alone—but eventually he leaves, and she jogs down the hall to Wanda's lab, flashes the lights to get her attention.

They know the school is closing,
the kids. Austin at least. I'm as-
suming he told Charlie and
Eliot.

Everyone will know soon enough.

But do you think that could have something to do with them running away?

Maybe. Did he just find out?

She shakes her head. That is a sticking point—if Austin had learned about River Valley's closure over a month ago, why now? Could the three of them really have been planning to disappear for so long without a teacher or parent noticing? She spoke to Charlie just the day before for history tutoring, and she seemed fine, given the circumstances. Obviously February has missed something. The key will be in finding what tethered these three students together beyond simple proximity. She can feel the silvery thread of an idea forming, but it is still slick and new, and she cannot yet grasp it.

Henry said he's known since December.

Did he say anything else? How did Austin take it?

Badly, obviously, February says. She sweeps her arm across the room as if the empty lab somehow proves her point.

And he didn't like the idea of them implanting the baby, either.

What? Sky? I thought she was hearing.

So did I.

Well, that could be something.

What could be what?

Austin and the new girl were pretty flirty outside my classroom the other day.

Yeah, the sheriff's tech team cracked their texts. Seems like they were an item.

Wanda leaves the perch of her swivel stool and begins to pace the length of the room.

> *But what does that have to do*
> *with it? They never said any-*
> *thing about taking off.*

Wanda sighs, impatient, as if February's inability to see the connection is willful.

> *Austin has the hots for a girl who*
> *just got zapped by her implant*
> *onstage, in front of everyone. You*
> *think he's feeling fine about his*
> *baby sister getting one?*

February nods, grabs her chin the way she does when she is thinking. Okay, so Austin and Charlie are a unit, and pissed.

> *But where would they go,*
> *though? And why bring Eliot*
> *with?*

But when she feels his name on her hands, she is drawn back in time: it was almost exactly a year ago that Eliot turned up at the front gate at dawn, delirious with pain, begging her to let him stay in the dorms. She'd held his hand as the nurse debrided his wounds, let him stay in Old Quarters until the paperwork came through. With the school closing, Eliot will have to risk going back to his mother or face the foster system, homelessness.

> *He's got a lot to lose.*

> *Or nothing to lose.*

February takes her phone from her pocket, pulls up the picture of the GPS coordinates she snapped that morning. It's blurry and she has to zoom in, which makes it blurrier.

> *Google this,* she says, and reads
> off the first string of numbers.

> *Downtown,* Wanda says.
> *T–i–j–e–s–t–o–'s.*

*The pizza place? O-k, try this
one.*

She feeds Wanda the second string.

East Colson, Wanda says, looking at the map. *If it is about implants, could be the clinic. Colson
Children's?*

But what would they do there?

*I don't know. Protest? Sit-in?
Didn't you just teach your kids
DPN?*

Zoom in.

Wanda does. At first the map still looks blank, but when she double-
clicks, the small orange icon that signifies a destination appears.
When she hovers over it, the pop-up says, "The Gas Can. Hours:
Permanently Closed." There's no other information about the place—
what is it and when did it shut down?—but the name is enough to
make February nervous.

*Do you think we should update
the cops?*

Wanda shakes her head, picks up her purse.

We should get to them first.

VLOG 87: SERIAL KILLER IN COLSON?!
#SAVECOLSONSKIDS

HTTP://YOUTUBE.COM/GABBYSDEAFWORLD/WATCHV_87

Hey, guys, how you doing out there, and welcome back to Gabby's Deaf World.

This morning I've got some breaking news and I'll be honest with you, I am pretty terrified right now: last night, three of my very best friends were kidnapped right from their beds here at River Valley School for the Deaf.

Obviously, I'm really shaken up and scared. What if there's, like, a serial killer wandering around campus? It could have easily been me, or any one of us. You know, I just love my friends so much.

[Gabriella dabs at her eyes with a tissue.]

I can't bear to think of what kind of perv might have taken them.

Thanks to all of you who've been reaching out in the DMs to check on me. We all know how bad Austin broke my heart, but I've decided to be the bigger person and put it behind me, because now's the time for us to really band together.

If you have any information about my friends' disappearances you can call the Colson County Sheriff's Office, or message me and I will pass it along for you.

O-k, I think that's it for today. Don't forget to like, comment, and subscribe to my channel, or check out my Insta stories for live case updates. Stay safe out there!

S lash says they'll only need a couple hours to finish up, though they'll have to wait until it's dark again to move. Lem and Slash fight about whether they can use some kind of private internet browser to look at a map, but Slash is adamant that they don't.

If it were just us, maybe, he says, but—

He gestures at Charlie.

Instead, he commands Charlie to draw a map outlining the route from the house to the plant as best she can. They all memorize it so there's no confusion later and they don't have to risk signing in public.

Afterward, she sits in front of a small pile of plastic baggies. Each contains an assortment of screws and nails that will be useful, Slash has told her, though the cooker will be its own best shrapnel. The job—opening them and sorting them into equal sets—allows her eyes, and her mind, to wander.

In her mother's version of things, love was always singular—if not everlasting then at least in turn, with one love growing up from the place where another before it had died. Now Charlie sees that love can be plural, even concurrent. She watches Slash and Austin, each handsome in his way, as they solder new connections. She marvels at the way life has brought her exactly what she needs.

When it's time to go, they climb the basement stairs solemnly, each carrying a cooker in a wraparound embrace. Before the front door, Charlie gingerly sets hers down to double-knot her sneakers. Slash lifts the plywood and ushers them outside.

february drives them into Colson, Wanda directing via Google Maps. The long shadows intensify the grim cast of the streets' disrepair.

Turn here! Wanda says, unexpectedly.

She motions to a one-way street off Vine and February cuts the wheel just in time.

Sorry. I was just—this drive brings back memories.

I get it, February says, though she doesn't.

She knows Wanda is not from here, though it's likely East Colson has a host of doppelgängers across the Rust Belt, the country. It dawns on her that she and Wanda have not spoken much about their childhoods. February finds Wanda's presence so all-consuming that whenever she is with her, it's difficult to think beyond that present moment. This is what she loves about Wanda, just as her intricate knowledge of Mel's every childhood triumph and mishap is why she loves Mel. She cannot decide whether the heart's craving for opposites—not only from itself, but from the others it loves—is its greatest strength or biggest failing.

She parks the car and they continue down the block on foot, until

Wanda points across the street at an all-black building, THE GAS CAN hand-painted directly onto its parapet. When they enter and find a bar, February feels a moment's hope that the children's disappearance is some run-of-the-mill beery mishap, albeit against a dismal backdrop.

We don't serve minors, the bartender says with tight-lipped courtesy when February inquires.

Or talk to the pigs! someone shouts from the galley.

We're not pi— We're not cops, says February. We're actually from the Deaf school.

Then I'll tell you the same thing I told the cops, says the bartender. I would have noticed if there were a crew of deaf kids in here.

See, that's not really an answer though, is it, says February.

Guess not, he says.

February relays the conversation as she and Wanda return to the car, though Wanda has gotten the gist. They drive to the children's hospital and loop around the campus and parking garage, but there's no sign of the kids. In fact, they don't see much of anybody at all. Wanda slumps in her seat.

I really thought they'd be here.

She is a woman of formulas, of calculations. She hates being wrong. February reaches over and rubs her shoulder in consolation.

It's dead out here. Not exactly
ripe for a protest.

Unless they want it that way.

Why stage a protest no one will
see?

Wanda's smile is small, but there's a little mischief along its edges. February is overcome with the urge to touch her, and brushes a finger along her cheek. When she does, she sees her own wedding band, and drops her hand back into her lap.

Why would they want it to be
empty?

I don't know. Maybe if they were
going a different route. Like
graffiti, or flaming bags of shit or
something.

Vandalism?

February tries to keep her face calm, though inside she finds this idea frightening. She does not want her students and the cops to meet. Even for a bag of shit, the potential for deadly interaction is there, so long as the police are free to list "failure to respond to verbal commands" as a justification.

Don't look so scandalized. They're
teenagers. And anyway I was
wrong.

Wanda gestures to the empty campus.

Maybe they really are just out
getting drunk in the woods some-
where.

Maybe, February says.

She doesn't believe it, though. Wanda's theory has resonated. At first, she can't put her finger on why, but now she runs over her last conversation with Charlie again and again in her mind, notices the sparkle in her eye when February explained what "hot-wire" meant.

Let's go check the district admin
building, just in case.

S-w-a-l-l deserves a flaming
shit bag as far as I'm concerned,
says Wanda.

February nods, then pulls out of the parking lot and aims them back toward the interstate. As they hurtle toward Colson's edges, it's difficult to say who sees it first.

Wait!

You don't think— says February.

But *she* thinks it, apparently, because she passes the highway on-ramp and continues toward the sprawling brick building, the crisp blue block letters a beacon across the factory's face: EDGE BIONICS.

They circle the building twice, stash the car on a side street, get out, and round the plant by foot once more in a wide arc. But there is no one—no overnight workers, no sign of her students. One big eighties surveillance camera above the front door and another hanging over the loading dock, but they look so archaic she is willing to bet they're Goodyear holdovers. Out ahead of them by the front gates, a motion sensor flicks on a light at the movement of a tabby cat. February and Wanda cross the street to avoid triggering it again.

They stay huddled in the shadows of a shuttered travel agency, blowing into their hands for warmth. February is nervous and nearly jumps out of her skin when a police cruiser appears, but he doesn't even bother to slow as he passes, and she tries her best to lower the frantic beat of blood in her temples.

Finally, when the last of the blues have folded back into the horizon, and she and Wanda are about to abandon their post, she sees them. They're a block north and have black bandannas tied over their faces, but she knows it's them: Charlie in her Army surplus jacket hugging something shiny and cylindrical to her chest, flanked by a trio of boys. February's stomach knots—who is the fourth?

She wants to catch them before they trip the floodlight, so she jogs until she's near enough to cross the street and cut them off. She steps directly into their path, though as she's in motion it occurs to her that her own broad silhouette is a formidable one, and it may not be a good idea to startle this crew.

Too late. Charlie lurches backward into Austin, who February can see is carrying a matching cylinder, which, upon closer inspection, looks a bit like Mel's Instant Pot. Eliot stands frozen, his arms around a container of his own, while the unknown boy turns to run, encountering a fresh fright when he finds Wanda in his path. February motions to the vacant lot across the street, and the group crosses, buttressed by her and Wanda.

What the hell are these? February gestures to their cargo.

You know them, oh thank god, says the third boy, his voice unfamiliar and without a trace of deaf accent, at which February breathes her own sigh of relief. Don't tell them anything! he says, looking to Charlie, but it's dark and his face is covered, and no one has heard him but February.

You stay put, she says to him.

She tries to inject an adult sternness into her voice, but she's unpracticed at authoritarian English. She sees not fear but challenge in his eyes. She turns to her students. Austin steps in front of Charlie as if to shield her from February's wrath, hoisting his pot onto his hip to free up one arm.

What is going on?

True biz? he says.

When Austin has finished, February doesn't know what to say. She glances at Wanda, who looks more impressed than angry. Finally, she settles on pragmatism.

They have an Amber Alert out on
you, she says. *They'll catch you so*
fast your head will spin round.
Where the hell did you get an
idea like this?

The boys don't say anything, but they are both looking sidelong at Charlie, who's in turn looking straight back at February. And February realizes, she is the thread that has bound them together. She had hoped they might influence one another. She designed it this way.

Deaf people need direct action,
like you said, says Charlie.

But this is— What if you hurt
someone? You'll go to jail!

They don't seem as perturbed by the idea as she'd like them to be. But reason is for people who still have something to fear. The hearing boy shrugs.

It's purely a profit-busting mission, he says. There's no one in there at night.

Where the fuck did you come from? February mutters.

She doesn't really want an answer, and he doesn't try to give her one. She looks at her children, their scars glowing beneath the street's single lamp, the knotted blue flesh on Charlie's head; the slick, shiny rivulets of Eliot's cheek disappearing beneath his bandanna. And Austin, unmarred, and emitting perhaps the most rage of all.

February motions to Austin's device, and he hands it over. Then she looks to Wanda.

Take them to the car?

Carefully, Eliot and Charlie leave their pots on the sidewalk at February's feet and follow Wanda, heads low. The hearing boy hesitates, staring at the explosives and jiggling his leg. She knows he is about to make a break for it, that he is trying to calculate how much he can carry.

Wait, she feels herself say.

To her surprise the boy actually looks up, his eyes even with hers. He is tall; now that he's not hunching, she can see that he's probably older than her students, though not by much. He, too, has a wound that gleams, a slice that bisects his forehead. The boy reaches for the pot in February's arms and she hands it to him. She looks down at the others and he shakes his head to ward off further inquiry. Behind him, movement catches her eye—someone lanky with a mask pulled up over their nose and mouth is crouching in the shadows.

Not today, she says.

The boy nods, and February crosses the street to return to the car. She does not look back on the boy and his friend, doesn't see them gathering the pressure cookers beneath their arms like parents collecting their children. She doesn't know in which direction they recede back into the night.

Gloves and masks, she says with
a hand outstretched to the
backseat.

The children surrender their bandannas and February stuffs them in
her purse.

Where—

I trashed everything, February
says.

Is that safe . . . to throw away?
says Wanda.

*It's all disconnected. Scrap metal
now.*

February looks in the rearview mirror when she says this, but whatever they're thinking, her students' faces do not betray them. Neither
does hers.

Let's go home, she says.

*e*ight days later, Austin rises for cafeteria duty a little after dawn and sees the news as he scrolls through his phone: there's been an explosion in East Colson, with extensive damage to the Edge Bionics plant. He nudges Eliot awake and they stagger bleary-eyed over to Austin's desk and pull up the Channel 10 site. A helicopter is at the scene, but not much is visible through whorls of ash as the city block smolders. The captain of Company 14 tells reporters that the fire has been neutralized with no casualties, and thanks colleagues at Companies 3 and 5 for their assistance. The smoke will linger for a while, depending on the weather. The cause of the fire, he says, is under active investigation.

Austin and Eliot know it's a risk to write anything down, but it's a difficult thing to keep to themselves, and after some discussion they decide on the right text to send to Charlie. They want something that is both a mark of their achievement and a warning, so they choose the same words that are scrawled as graffiti across each face of the campus—in bathroom stalls and locker rooms, etched into desks and cafeteria benches. It gives them plausible deniability, a toothless, campuswide joke. Austin types it out and pauses for a final nod from Eliot before he presses send:

silence is golden

.   .   .

Up in Old Quarters, February is perched by the window, and catches bits of the morning news via bunny-eared TV. She returns her coffee cup to her lips to divert her smile, then descends the spiral stairs and walks back toward her house. Not wanting to scare Mel, she rings the doorbell first. Mel appears in her pajamas, holding a mug of her own.

Can we talk? says February.

Mel opens the door wider to let her in.

Across the quad, sunlight vaults off the pavement and steals into Charlie's room through the space between window shade and sill. A text message arrives, vibrates her phone and bedside table. The boys are anxious for her to wake, but Charlie sleeps soundly. Around her swirl the echoes of 150 years' worth of pranks played and loves lost, of scraped knees and stomach viruses, breakfasts served and cigarettes smoked. Of experiments warmed over laboratory flames or carried out in darkness, breath quickened beneath blankets. Of silent conversations stirring air into motion, stories receding back into stone. If these walls could talk, would it matter? Who would hear the secrets we bear?

author's note

To be a member of the Deaf community has been a great source of joy in my life—it has made me a better writer, thinker, parent, and friend. Though River Valley School for the Deaf is an imagined place, the essential nature of Deaf schools as community hubs—the safe-keepers of our language, our history, and our dreams for the future—is very real.

So is the threat of their closure, and with those shutterings, the slow destruction of a rich culture and tradition. Today's prevailing educational philosophy centers on a mainstream approach, but at what cost? For many deaf and hard-of-hearing students, the result has been a veneer of "inclusion," without true equity. While society praises hearing children for being unique, deaf children are taught that they are a broken version of their peers, and should invest all their energy in trying to fit in. Kept apart from one another, deaf children frequently receive not only substandard education without full access to language, but a suppressed understanding of the self that can only be righted by representation and a sense of larger community belonging.

It's my hope that we will find allies in the hearing world willing to stand with us and fight for our self-governance, dignity, and the value of human diversity before the effects of educational isolation and genetic manipulation are irreversible.

Alabama School for the Negro Deaf-Blind, 1891–1968
Austine School for the Deaf, 1904–2014

Braidwood Institute for the Deaf and Dumb (Cobbs School), 1812–1821

Central North Carolina School for the Deaf, 1975–2000

Colored Department for the Arkansas & Madison School for the Deaf, 1887–1965

Crotched Mountain School for the Deaf, 1955–1979

Detroit Day School for the Deaf, 1893–2012

Florida Institute for the Blind, Deaf, and Dumb Colored Department, 1882–1967

Georgia School for the Negro Deaf, 1882–1975

Kentucky School for the Negro Deaf, 1884–1963

Maryland School for the Colored Blind and Deaf, 1872–1956

National Deaf Academy, 2000–2016

Nebraska School for the Deaf, 1869–1998

North Carolina School for Colored Deaf and Blind, 1869–1967

Oklahoma Industrial Institution for the Deaf, Blind, and Orphans of the Colored Race, 1909–?

South Carolina Institution for the Education of the Deaf and Dumb and the Blind, Colored Department, 1883–1967

South Dakota School for the Deaf, 1880–2011

Southern School for the Colored Deaf and Blind, 1938–1978

Tennessee School for the Colored Deaf and Dumb, 1881–1965

Texas Blind, Deaf and Orphan School, 1887–1965

West Virginia School for the Colored Deaf and Blind, 1919–1955

Wyoming School for the Deaf, 1961–2000

acknowledgments

I am greatly indebted to so many in the wake of this project. Thank you:

To the Deaf community, which has given me ASL and the confidence to be myself—without you I could not have written this, or any, book.

To the brilliant Caitlin McKenna—this book is smarter, cleaner, and all-around better because of you. Thank you for your passion and your patience.

To Wylie wonder team Jin, Alex, Alba, and Elizabeth, and to genius/confidante, Kristina—the best agents and advocates in the game.

To Emma and all those at Random House who kept the wheels turning on this project through strange and terrible times. To the thoughtful people in design and production who helped make the 3-D language of ASL a little more alive on the page. And to the publicity and marketing teams who are already working hard to hurl this weird little book out into the world.

To Brittany, for your beautiful illustrations and linguistic expertise. This book would not be complete without your work.

To Teraca Florence, for your astute feedback toward an authentic representation of intersectional identity in our community.

To the students at Deaf schools around the country who shared their stories, and meals, and dreams with me. To the Deaf adults who opened up to me about their educational experiences as part of my research, in particular Rosa Lee Timm, Joseph Tien, and Alexander and Dru Balsley.

To Kathleen Brockaway, for her breadth of historical knowledge, and her willingness to share it. To Ted Evans for his short "The End," which made a lasting impact on me, and informs some of my characters' worldviews as a result.

To the residencies who housed and fed me and filled me with joy at various stages of this project—The Anderson Center, Hedgebrook, and Civitella. I learned so much from my fellow artists in these spaces.

To my friends, for cheering me on and talking me down, especially Sam, Eliza, Lauren, and Jami.

To my parents and sister for always enthusiastically being on my side, even when my side was subject to change several times a day. (Where's the beef?)

To Zach, for anchoring me, for your calming presence, for always being willing to read that chapter again. I love you.

To Sully, for teaching me to see the world afresh each morning. For your laughter.

And to the girls at St. Rita who snuck out of the dorm that night to chat—thank you for your inspiration. I hope you made it to New York.

ABOUT THE AUTHOR

SARA NOVIĆ is the author of *Girl at War* and *America Is Immigrants*. She studied fiction and literary translation at Columbia University, and teaches creative writing and Deaf studies at Emerson College and Stockton University. She lives with her family in Philadelphia.

sara-novic.com
Twitter: @novicsara
Instagram: @photonovic

ABOUT THE ILLUSTRATOR

BRITTANY CASTLE is a Deaf graphic artist and owner of the American Sign Language art business 58 Creativity. Her art is inspired by her Deaf culture, and uses sign language to create a visual emotional connection in her work.

58creativity.com